ONE RIGHT
TRICKY BASTARD

ONE RIGHT TRICKY BASTARD

A Mystic Noir Adventure

TENTH(ISH) ANNIVERSARY EDITION

C. M. Sottolano

Ordering Information:

For orders and inquiries, please contact:
1-888-404-1388
www.goldtouchpress.com
book.orders@goldtouchpress.com

Printed in the United States of America

PART 1

Chapter One

"**G**ET UP, FAT ASS!"

I heard this as I regained consciousness. I was lying face down on the pavement. It's the kind of thing I've yet to get used to. I tried to stand. My brain reeled putting together the last few moments. There was the smell of alcohol. The gleam of a neon bar sign reflected in the rain-soaked asphalt.

Perhaps I had been out drinking and merely stumbled. I liked that idea. Perhaps I had been forcibly ejected for being too high-spirited. This was also a nice possibility. Better than some others. That didn't explain the person shouting at me.

There was a kick to my ribs. The pain sharpened my recall. I had been drinking but I wasn't drunk. I hadn't even been disorderly. I was simply ambushed on the way back to my car.

I got up to one knee. I could see my attacker. It was just some guy in his late teens, early twenties. His expression was grim. He was tall and gangly, almost my opposite. This wasn't his first dance in the asphalt ballroom. Still, there was nothing to be worried about, yet.

In the dark, I didn't see any gang colors. Gangs aren't my area of expertise, however. Purely human threats are not my department.

Perhaps this was a simple mugging. I reached into my coat's inner pocket and tossed him a wallet. My attacker caught it then he kicked me in the face. I rolled with the kick onto my back.

If this were a normal mugging, he would take the wallet and walk away.

"I saw you dropping some mad cash back at the bar. All that's in here is a bunch of ones."

There were thirteen dollars in the wallet, twelve pieces of paper, and one silver. The silver dollar might have fetched a good price from a collector if it weren't scratched, scarred, and tarnished.

Trying to sound cowed I said, "I was running out of money. That's why I was leaving . . ."

This was true. I went to the bar to buy information. I had been quite free with the cash. I hoped it would draw attention. Obviously, it had, but was it the kind I wanted? The young man swore and walked off.

I dusted myself off. I hoped that the young man was really what he seemed to be, a greedy kid with a violent temper.

As I watched him go, I shifted my focus. Whether we call ourselves, wizards, witches, magicians, or magi, we all see the world in ways that most people don't. It's a way of seeing the spiritual side of things

I call mine "The Wheel of Sight." Whenever I open up to "The Sight," I am spinning a roulette wheel. Usually, it comes up with vision or hearing; occasionally it gets really strange. That night I got "visual." It's my favorite, the one I understand best.

Now I could *see* that this young man wasn't my quarry. I looked away quickly. In the soul sight, even the worst people can be heartbreakingly beautiful. Despite veins of greed and arrogance, the star-burst glow of his humanity was breathtaking.

I can't explain how I see beauty in a "thug" who just thrashed me. Either you understand that or you don't. There simply are no words to convey it. It's something we all have to learn for ourselves, like walking or breathing.

I looked away from my assailant. I kept the Sight up and gave a quick go round the area. The bar had been here longer than I thought. I could see the old outlines before the most recent renovations. I could see two distinct glows from the parking lot. One, I expected to see, my own unusual car.

The other was coming from inside a vintage, luxury car. A streetlight lit up most of the parking lot. The car was parked just where the light failed to quite cover.

The glow had a human tint. They were watching for something. Very possibly, they were watching for me.

Perhaps a bit of an introduction is in order. Hello, I'm Milo Gives (hard "G", rhymes with "strives") and I'm a Disreputable Urban Magus. I think magus is an ugly word that simply means magician. It's the singular of Magi. You might recognize that word from Christmas stories, yes there's a connection. As to "urban," the city I live in may be small but it is a city nonetheless. "Disreputable" that's the embarrassing one. I'm not as disreputable as I could be. Okay, I do (almost) support myself by selling correspondence courses for wannabe mystics.[1] I suppose that's a little sketchy.

It's my demeanor that got me invited into the Association. I go about in a long, black duster. Often, it's over my favorite t-shirt, the black one with white letters. It reads, "I survived my three wishes." All my pants are black as well, jeans or otherwise. Even my Khakis are black.

Why so much black? It's slimming and it's kind of expected. Also, it makes my wardrobe choices simple. I have untamed, shoulder-length, black hair and a scraggly beard forming a leonine corona about my face.

I'm five foot seven and look like 250 of my 350 pounds (I accidentally altered my bone structure a few years ago) while I make adults uneasy, I'm a hit with the neighborhood kids. They call me Hagrid Jr.

The Disreputable Urban Magician and Sorcerers Association (D.U.M. Ass. for short) is not an official organization. It's just a few of us who don't fit well more formal mystical traditions. Come to think of it, we don't always fit in well with each other. How disreputable am I, really? Judge for yourself.

With my senses opened up to a higher level, I studied the person watching me. I couldn't tell much about them yet. Details like age and gender were lost. Distance and the body of the car blocked them. If the person inside weren't "projecting" attention I wouldn't have picked up anything. All I could get was "human,"

Whoever it wasn't using anything like The Sight. Someone using The Sight would have glowed like a beacon. Still, this person might be related to my case. My car was parked where I would walk past this watcher to get to it.

I walked past the other car slowly, looking at the glow from the corner of my eye. I steeled myself against its growing beauty.

As I approached, I could discern more information with The Sight. The watcher was anxious, middle-aged, and female. As I drew up even with the driver's side door, it flung open, blocking my path. The woman stepped out of the car and into my Sight directly. Her aura shone brightly once unobstructed. I had to take a deep breath in order to keep focused.

Some people who read auras say that certain colors mean certain things. Nonsense. We see what we see and the mind scrambles to make sense of it.

---

[1] (Soon to be on the *World Wide Web*. Look for them)

people assign colors to help them sort it out. I knew one woman who didn't see aura but smelled them.

How do I tell you what I saw? That she wore the color of regretted decisions, the hue of painful burdens?

Does it matter?

I couldn't see anything beyond normal human in her so I turned down my Sight. The sight is a great gift but it renders the physical less memorable. I wanted to have a full physical description.

It was barely worth it. I wouldn't have much of a description to give. She was of medium height and wearing a ridiculous "disguise" she bought at Clichés 'R' Us. She wore a full-length, tan trench coat. Her hair was hidden under a wide-brimmed hat that shadowed her face. She hid her eyes behind dark glasses.

"Are you kidding," I said.

"Mr. Gives?" she asked. Her voice was flat with enforced calm

I nodded. She didn't say anything. She handed me an envelope, got back in her car, and drove away. My first thought was "is she really driving at night with dark glasses on?"

Her car passed under the street light. What I had mistaken for tinting was actually a coat of matte black paint.

I wondered how she was driving. Either she had fooled my Sight (difficult but possible) and had supernatural abilities or she had some technological gizmo. Hell, the car could be remote controlled via satellite. I wouldn't know. I'm a mystic. Even if I knew how to open my Sight to radio waves, I'd need an engineering degree to understand them.

I looked at the envelope. It was ordinary enough. If it wasn't, I would have noticed it when I looked at the woman with the Sight? I opened it up.

It was a piece of ordinary 8 ½ by 11 printer papers. It read:

Mr. Gives;

It has come to my attention that you are seeking my so-called better half. I have endeavored for quite some time to prevent my actions from coming to the attentions of the authorities but more importantly, from my "Jekyll."

It would be extremely inconvenient for my other self to discover what I am doing. It could well be disastrous, perhaps even fatal, for myself and others in my organization.

Before I let this come to pass, I will take every conceivable step to prevent you from finding her. If this kindly remonstration should fail, I will avail myself of other, more strident, measures.

So, take care of yourself Mr. Gives, so that I needn't,
Gretchen Koenig

It was the most politely threatening letter I had ever received. I must be moving up in the world.

Chapter Two

I GOT BACK TO MY apartment an hour and a half before sunrise. I rarely get to sleep before sunrise. That was fine by me. I've always been a night owl.

Of course, if you had my apartment, you'd spend most of your time elsewhere. The apartment should have been comfortable and roomy. It wasn't. I kept it because of the nominal rent. Nobody else wanted it because it was stuffy, cramped, and haunted.

The ghost has given up trying to scare me. It just annoys me by rearranging things. It does more than rearrange things. I often find the belongings of previous tenants mixed in with mine. While finding things when I want them is quite a chore, it's not that bad a haunting, all things considered. I've had worse roommates. Probably so have you.

I rummaged through the kitchen to find a clean glass. There were plenty of dirty ones in my sink including some, I had never seen before.

Eventually, I found a child's sippy cup that was clean enough. I ran cold tap water into it. I wanted something harder but my poltergeist had been busy. I didn't have the verve to track down my liquor cabinet. There was another source of alcohol. I wasn't about to crack that open. A half bottle of Southern Comfort sat on my desk. The ghost never moved it; I suspect out of professional courtesy. One spirit to another, as it were. Sounds like a bad pun. If only.

No, the spirit I refer to is a djinn trapped inside the bottle. Yep, I have a wish-granting Djinn trapped in a half-empty bottle of Southern Comfort. Why? The flippant answer would be, "because the Jack Daniels was too full."

About six months before, I was sent this bottle as a gift. It was anonymous. I'm normally suspicious of that sort of thing, I opened the bottle anyway. When I opened the bottle, a djinn came out.

"I am Sarathan!" he told me. "You may have up to three wishes. No more!" Before me stood a man of Arabic descent in a dark blue, three-piece suit. He was lean, handsome, and had only a hint of translucence. He smiled broadly. The smile seemed genuine.

I was lucky. In my studies, I had come across tales of Sarathan. That wasn't his true name, of course. True-Name magic can be very powerful. If the book had told me his true name, I would have had the upper hand. Without his name, he was the one in charge, no matter how obsequiously he may present himself.

"Nothing doing," I told him. "You're one of those malicious wish granters. If I ask for million dollars, I'll get it in confederate currency. And that's if you're in a good mood."

"Nonsense," Sarathan said, "you have but to ask and it is yours."

"Like the guy who asked for long life and ended up a sequoia?"

"It was a vaguely worded wish. I can see by your manner that you are a magus. Certainly, you would be wiser than that."

"I am. No wishes."

"But you must, otherwise . . ." He let his words trail off.

He was hoping I'd fill in my own threat. I didn't.

"Otherwise, you can't collect your little reward and go."

The worst part of getting wishes from Sarathan was that after he granted your wishes, he could depart taking with him a small, personal item. It could be any little thing of yours that catches his fancy. If he hasn't caused you enough suffering through the wishes, this is where he gets you.

"It is only a small item, a mere token," Sarathan's voice was warm, avuncular.

"Stuff it," I said, "I know about the violinist."

"I granted each wish exactly as the old man wished, first, a Stradivarius, second, the skill to play it masterfully. Thirdly, he asked for, and I quote, 'another ten years of life that I might enjoy my first two wishes.' I gave him all this then left with my token,"

"'Might' being the operative word. All you took from him was a matched set of eardrums."

"You must be a great master to know of that little snip of trivia. Do you know this other trivial, little point?

If you refuse your wishes, I am allowed to smite you terribly." He said this in the same tone a high-class waiter recommends avoiding the red wine with the fish.

I wondered just who the hell made the rules concerning djinn. The gleam in his eyes robbed me of my desire to gamble on this point. I took him at his word.

"So, what happens if I ask for a wish you can't or won't grant?"

"Simple enough, gracious one, I return to the bottle and remain until you make another, more reasonable request. Mind you, kind and benevolent Master, that I am a very powerful djinn."

I made my first wish. I wish for a t-shirt that read, "I survived my three wishes." He produced it. It was even the right size.

My second wish, "I wish that bottle of southern comfort would never be empty." He promptly sealed the top of the bottle so thoroughly it'll outlast the cockroaches and Keith Richards.

Sarathan looked at me and gave me an "oops-did-I-do-that" shrug.

"Sorry, I should have been clearer," I said.

My third wish, "I wish you would tell me your true name."

Sarathan glowered at me and went back to the permanently sealed bottle. I'm sure he can leave if he wanted. He's just biding time until I'm desperate enough to make a different third wish. Meanwhile, I get on with my life and I have this nifty T-shirt. Someday I'll find out who sent the bottle.

Back to the case. I shouldn't really call it a case. I'm not a detective, private or otherwise. The skills of one would come in pretty handy though. I was, after all, looking for a missing person. In fact, I was looking for a person and a half.

That sounds grisly. I'm trying to find a "Dr. Jekyll" and a friend. Yeah, I know how it sounds. Don't think I can't hear the laughter. I'm not actually trying to find Dr. Jekyll. It's just the easiest reference.

Imagine a split personality that has gone too far. Sorry, that's misleading. Dissociative Identity Disorder is one person with multiple personalities housed in one body, often as the result of horrific abuse.

Like Stevenson's *The Strange Case of Dr. Jekyll and Mr. Hyde,* I'm seeking someone who undergoes a complete bodily transformation. Talk about psychosomatic. I didn't know what caused it. It was unlikely caused by drinking a scientific potion.

The politely threatening letter showed I knew half of this equation. I knew who our Ms. Hyde was, Gretchen Koenig, a would-be crime boss. Her gang was small-time but on the rise.

If Koenig's Jekyll really didn't suspect, that's quite an advantage. It's one hell of a way to hide in plain sight.

How can her Jekyll not know? I didn't know and that wasn't all. I went over the case in mind.

"Start at the beginning," I told myself. I mulled over the events of the previous few days. It had started with a phone call, a wrong number. The caller intended it for someone else. In my line of work, odd meetings are par for the course. I was sitting at the local community activities center. It's like the YMCA without the nifty, gay anthem. It's where I try to walk off my extra weight. I was waiting for a new ID card. A rather large, nasty "dog" ate my last one. That's another story.

The ancient pay phone near the game room started ringing. I looked around. No one seemed to be waiting for a call. Everyone else was ignoring it.

"What the hell? Why not?" I thought and got up to answer it.

"Hello?" said a voice on the other end. The caller was almost whispering. "Hello? Hello? I got your number from Castillo. He said you could help me. Hello?

The voice sounded like a young woman. I thought it was a prank but there was something in her voice that made me wonder. I fell back on my favorite trick and opened my senses. This time my sense of hearing expanded. Not really a surprise, the "wheel" seldom lets me down, even when it's being difficult. Not only could I hear the ring of truth in her words, but I also got a bit of an echo. Actually, more like the reverb you get when two people speak simultaneously.

"Slow down, now what's the problem?"

"It's my brother. He's missing and I need to find him." I could hear the truth in that easily enough. Suddenly the "echo" clicked. It was coming from the back of the game room. I turned and looked into it. There was a young woman, the girl really, facing into the corner between the ancient Ms. Pac-Man machine and the ironically newer pinball machine.

My view of her was partially obstructed by a couple of middle-schoolers. From what little I could see of her she was dressed all in black. Her hair was long, straight, and pitch black. While she spoke, she reached up and adjusted her hair, revealing it to be a wig.

She stepped further into the corner. She huddled in the corner by the games. Her eyes darted around the room "Look, can we meet somewhere?" she said, "I can't really talk here."

"Sure," I said, "where do you want to meet?"

She thought for a moment "How about that coffee place on the Square."

The square was the effective center of downtown. This was convenient enough. My apartment is in a building on the other side of "the Square." In fact, if I were to lean suicidally out my bedroom window, I could see the coffee shop.

"Sounds great. When?"

She shuffled around a bit and looked down at something. "Give me an hour," she said. "I've . . . I've got something to do." With my ordinary hearing, that statement sounded as flat and unimportant as anyone might say, "I have to run to the bank." With The Sight working as Hearing, there was a world of heartbreak in her words. So much heartbreak it nearly staggered me. I knew this was one of those "cases" Providence throws my way. I had to take a deep breath before I continued.

"9:30 at the coffee shop. I'll be waiting. I'm pretty easy to spot." I mentioned my neighborhood nickname thinking it might lighten her mood.

She didn't laugh, "Yea. Hagrid junior. I'll be the one in white." then she hung up. She ducked out of the game room into the women's room. There was too much of a crowd to get a good look. I watched for her to leave.

Then one of the center workers called my name. He needed more information to renew my card. I hurried over to the desk. There went my chance to get a better look at my client before the meeting. Going to the desk put my back to the front doors of the center and the women's room. I would have to crane my neck around to watch for her. It would make it obvious that I was watching the women's restroom. I didn't think that was a good idea. I make strangers nervous enough as it is.

Chapter Three

HAVING MISSED HER EXIT completely, I decided to go home and change. Once there I put on my one suit. It's charcoal gray. It goes well with the duster. I wanted to look as professional as I could. I don't know whom she intended to call but Providence had sent her to me so I wanted her to feel comfortable when I broke the news of the "wrong number."

"I'll get a P.I. license someday," I swore to myself. I wanted to use words like "case" and "client" legitimately.

We met that hour later at the coffee shop. I was already inside sitting at a table when the very young woman came inside. I was drinking an Italian soda. She walked up to my table. She had gotten herself a tall Coffee and a handful of the flavored liquid creamers the coffee shop provided. She sat down and poured half of a single-serve creamer cup into her coffee. She pocketed the rest. She folded the torn paper lid back over to secure the remaining liquid. I think she had intended to take it home with the rest of the creamers she had grabbed.

"You were right," she said. "You are easy to spot." She introduced herself as Pandora. She had changed her look drastically. Gone were the black clothes, wig, and lace.

She was a petite, young woman, about 5'2" and slender. Her hair was bleached to ash platinum and styled in a pixie cut. Her skin was so pale it was almost ethereal. Her simple dress, though whiter, was less luminous. She had a pretty face, a bright smile, and eyes of painted lead. Everything else about her gave the impression of such light frivolity that I almost expected her to float away. Her eyes carried all the weight of her despair. She may have been seventeen.

Pandora began her story. Her leaden eyes stared me firmly in the chest. She spoke in short quiet bursts. Her voice was saved from monotone by an occasional quaver in her pitch. Whenever this happened, she'd gulp her coffee. "My brother and I ran away from our . . .," she paused for a moment then her eyes flickered up to mine then back down, "foster home." She waited a second. When I didn't interject, she continued.

"It was pretty bad there. Stephan and I were pretty much on our own anyway. We headed south. We made it as far as Richmond. We were doing okay there for over a month then we ran into money troubles.

That's when Koenig came along to 'save' us.

"She found a nice place for Stephan and me to stay. She didn't ask anything of us. At least, not right away." She looked down at the table. She deflated a little, and then took a deep breath, soldiering on.

"I thought I could keep Stephan out of it." She didn't tell me what "it" was and I didn't ask. Her eyes flickered up to me again. This time she searched my face for something, repulsion perhaps. Maybe she feared to find judgment and commendation or possibly, even worse, excitement.

I said nothing. I just nodded, encouraging her to continue. I made a strong effort to conceal my anger at this Koenig. I didn't want Pandora to feel my anger was directed at her.

"After she had me working for a while, she dragged Stephan in. I didn't even know at first. She'd send someone for him when I was already out on a call." She spoke this last part as if it were personal self-recrimination. "I wanted to get us out, of course, but her goons always had a way of showing up unexpectedly. I knew we were good and caught when one of them showed up in uniform."

"In uniform? What kind?"

Pandora grimaced, "Local PD. I thought it was fake but then I had a little ride in his squad card." She didn't elaborate. I didn't push.

"That all happened about a year and a half ago. Something changed maybe three weeks ago. I don't know what. But suddenly Koenig took a much greater interest in Stephan. I thought it was, you know, personal. But then she had all these doctors and weird experts looking him over. He told me about that. I got worried.

I started making get-away plans again. I acted like I didn't notice anything or that it didn't matter to me. Before I could come up with any way out, Stephan was just gone. That was just a week ago."

She sat quietly, staring down at the table. She started drinking her coffee in earnest instead of just taking little sips as she talked. She would look up at me occasionally then back down into her coffee I had listened to her story with the Sight on. My "Sight" was still in my ears, so to speak. Most of what she had said was true except about the foster home. Perhaps she was afraid if I found out who she really was I would send her away. I wasn't there to pass those judgments. She needed my help and she was going to get it.

I had only one small reservation, as tragic as her story was, I still didn't see why her call had been "forwarded" to me. Pandora's problem seemed best dealt with by the normal authorities. If that seems callous, what can I say? It sounded like she needed someone with real detective skills or more appropriately the police.

As one of the Magi (I've never really liked the term Magus, sounds too close to maggot for me) I have a certain expertise that is fairly specialized and hard to come by.[2] To put it bluntly I help those with supernatural problems; hauntings, possessions, and monsters of various shades and ilk. Koenig sounded like a monster by metaphor only. I decided to listen some more before making that judgment. "Tell me more about Koenig," I said.

Next, she told me how she had done some investigative work on her own. There wasn't much she could do. Pandora had tailed Koenig from a meeting in a bar. Koenig had driven out of the city north to one of the "park and ride" commuter parking lots. It's meant for people to form car pools for the two-and-a-half-hour commute to Washington, DC.

I could hear a mixture of pride, confusion, and frustration as Pandora continued her story. "So, I had this 'borrowed' car and was doing a pretty good job keeping her car in sight on the highway. It was about a quarter to eight and there weren't that many cars on the road. That just made it harder to stay under her radar. So, she pulls into the Park and Ride. I cruise by slowly. I see a woman get out of the car. Only it's not Gretchen. Gretchen is a tall woman, and big . . . not fat but robust. She must be about 6'3, long, dark hair and it's not a wig. You know, the kind of woman who looks really good in a dominatrix outfit. Well, the woman who got out of that car was not Gretchen. I pulled off to the side of the road and crept back to the park and ride. I swear to you I saw Gretchen get in and her car never left my sight after that. The woman who got out of that car would have only come up to Gretchen's shoulder. Plus, she had a pageboy haircut, do you know what a pageboy never mind that. She was also as skinny as a rail.

---

2   *Will-Weaving for Beginners*. Correspondence Course #101 not withstanding

"Gretchen always walks as if she owned the world, this girl, well . . . she did a timid little scamper from one car to another. I couldn't get the second car's plate but it was a Hyundai, I think. She drove out the other entrance. I ran up to Koenig's car and looked in. I thought maybe Koenig was still hiding inside. She wasn't. It's like she turned into that other woman. While I was looking into Koenig's car there was this weird blue light from behind me. I looked back over to the other car. I should have been able to still see it on the road. But it was gone, totally gone." She punctuated the end of her account by draining the last of her coffee and smacking the empty cup on the table. It made a hollow thwak

That was the reason I got mixed up in this. From the description, I had an idea of what we were dealing with. It's a lot more common than one might think. I explained to Pandora that Gretchen was, for lack of a more accurate term, a "Hyde" as in Dr. Jekyll and Hyde. Luckily, she was literate enough to know what I meant.

"So, I'm not crazy? I mean I was really beginning to think I was cracking up."

I tried giving her my most reassuring smile. Her eyes remained dead. I couldn't tell if it had worked. "Certain supernatural creatures have that effect."

"Supernatural? That's hard to believe"

I chuckled, "You have a better name for it?" "Mutant? Maybe?"

"Look, those are actually the tough questions. Let's focus on finding your brother. If we can track her movements in both forms, that should lead us to him. She probably covers up her actions by shifting forms. It helps obscure connections. Some Hydes are so good at it that their Jekyll's don't know even know there is a Hyde.

"Huh, so that's what she meant. I overheard her tell one of her goons that she had Stephan with her "better half." I thought she meant a lover or something."

"So presumably Koenig has stashed your brother away with her other-self. This leaves us with questions of who and where" I asked Pandora to go over in detail the description of Koenig's other-self. I also had her tell me where I might pick up Koenig's trail for some shadowing of my own. Though I'm not a trained investigator, I do have a few tricks up my sleeve.

With the best descriptions that I could get from Pandora, I had only one more task before I got down to business.

"Pandora, I'm not the person your friend intended you to call."

"But I asked Castillo for someone professional, someone who could handle it."

"Well, I am a professional who can handle your problem. Just not the one Castillo intended.

"I doubt whoever that was could handle this. Even an inexperienced Jekyll/Hyde could prove frustrating to a mundane detective. Their assumptions would lead them away from, not towards, a solution.

I actually saw something stir in Pandora's eyes. Sadly, it was mistrust. "So, who are you then?"

"Have you ever heard of the Magi?"

"You mean, 'We Three Kings of Orient Are,' those guys?"

"Hey, I'm impressed. Yes, those guys."

"Right. I remember reading that Magi is part of the root word for magician. So, you can do magic then?"

I nodded slightly, "for lack of a better word. I like to think I deal more in signs and wonders."

"What's the difference."

"Magic's more under the magician's control. And I can do that but that control has a price. It puts a cap on what you can get. Wonders do require a leap of faith but there's no limiting them."

"I'm a little short of faith," she said.

"That's what "signs" are for. They're a little nudge to help faith along."

This time Pandora smirked and drained the last little dregs of her coffee. "I think I'd like to see one of your little signs. I mean I've seen some weird shit in my life. I think Stephan's seen even more." She looked like she had another question to ask then suddenly she changed gears.

"Okay bottom line this for me. You can help me find Stephan, right?"

"Where few else could."

"Why should I trust you? How do I know you aren't just another liar?"

I took her now empty coffee cup and the half-empty single-serve liquid creamer. I poured the creamer into her empty tall coffee cup until it overflowed onto the table

Pandora held her breath for a long moment looking for the trick up my sleeve. The hardness in her eyes softens for a moment while she let her breath out slowly.

"Okay then, you're hired."

Chapter Four

AFTER HIRING ME, PANDORA extracted a set of "promises" from me. One was not to protect her from the truth. If things looked bad or I had bad news I was to tell her directly. Another was to work the case no matter what. Even if she couldn't untangle herself from Koenig, she wanted to make sure that her brother was. The last "promise" was to not make promises.

"I've been set up too often by people promising me things," she said. "When you get stabbed in the back, the knife's handle is usually a promise."

When our little meeting was over, I retired back to my apartment. It's really the only office I have. I do a lot of my work right there. It's not glamorous but then I can't complain about the overhead. I can easily grab the few tools I do use, if the ghost hasn't hidden them. For a change, I didn't have to hunt for my tools.

Theoretically, this case could have been simple. A J/H split is something that is clearly visible with the Sight. I should have been able to tail Koenig. Even if she tried losing herself in the crowd, with the sight I would still see the fracture in the soul. It's hard to miss and harder to hide.

Of course, it didn't work that way.

The first thing I tried was my most subtle way of tracking someone. Some call it remote viewing, others scrying. I like to think of it as daydreaming with a G.P.S zoom function.

I'd like to say I went into my inner sanctum, lit some candles, and called forth a vision from the flame. I mean it sounds cool or rather it would look cool in the movie of my life.[3] The truth is I just dimmed the lights in my kitchen and put on some music.

Music often helps mystics muster their will. Some use chants or classical music. I work best to the music of Weird Al Yankovic. This does nothing to improve my standing with other, more respectable Magi. I sat down at the table. I have a small bowl that I fill with water that I use for viewing. I hear Nostradamus used one like it.

I looked into the water. The gentle strains of *The Saga Begins* floated around me. It wasn't long before an image formed "behind" my eyes. I saw Gretchen Koenig smoking a cigarette. I drew my focus outward. It's a bit like pulling back from a zoomed-in camera shot. I pulled back so I could see she was driving. As I pulled back a little farther, I could see the car and the road she traveled.

It looked to be the same road that Pandora had told me about. "What a stroke of luck." I thought. I had tuned in at just the right time to see exactly what I needed to see. As Koenig pulled into the park and ride, a cloud covered my vision. Now scrying like this isn't like using normal sight. Atmospheric conditions aren't going to stop it. I tried to pierce the "cloud." All I got was more static. I pulled back up and out. Now I could see the edges of the cloud. It covered the whole of the *Park and Ride* but no further.

So, I waited. When Koenig's Jekyll pulled out in the other car, I should be able to spot her again. I waited five minutes nothing, ten minutes, nothing. Half hour, full hour, two hours finally passed. Still, nothing happened. No one came out.

I brought myself out of the vision and back into the world. I went down to my car and drove out to the location physically. When I got there, there was only Koenig's car. No sign of any other. Koenig may have simply driven out while I was busy driving out here. That didn't set right with my gut but it was the simplest explanation. Simple explanations are usually good. In my line, however, you can't take anything for granted. Once again, I withheld judgment.

"I've got to get an assistant," I thought to myself. They could have come out here and I could have been home scrying and caught her leaving.

I got out of my car and spun that "wheel of vision". This time everything came up roses. Almost literally. I had landed on olfactory for the Sight this

---

[3]   Hollywood producers feel free to contact me at the address on the order form.

time. For some reason having a heightened sense of smell always makes me want to howl at the moon. I didn't. I could catch the scent of two different people both female. It seemed like the women might be related. That's what I got from the simple sharpening of my ordinary sense of smell. The mystic side could only tell me "Roses" the whole place stank of roses. For me, that's one of the scents of Goodness, wholesomeness.

Someone had laid a serious blessing on this place. It was strong enough to block out my scrying and anything else my Sight might pick up. For once I was glad not to get sight or even sound. I might have been blinded or deafened temporarily by the blessing's strength.

I needed to come back there with a little more prep and see about the nature of this blessing. Was it old and Koenig was just taking advantage of it? I hoped not. If it was new, perhaps I could find the Priest/Priestess/ Pastor/Rabbi/Shaman/ Imam that laid it down. That could be a usable lead.

I wondered who was advising her. Most Jekyll/Hydes don't know much more esoterica than the rest of the population. It would take a bit of know-how to make use of a blessing like this to hide your activities, whether it was an old blessing or a new one.

I looked at Koenig's car from a distance. It was the only car here. I did my best not to approach it too closely. It may have had enough security features to tip-off Koenig that someone was here. I was doubly glad I was nowhere near it a few minutes later when a dark sedan pulled into the stop.

A guy who had the word 'thug' written all over his face, jacket and walking gait got out of the passenger side. He looked around and spotted my car. The driver of the sedan had already driven off. He looked as if he was taking mental notes on my car. Then he swept his gaze around the little parking area again. I don't know if he saw me.

After his little look around, he just shrugged, got into Koenig's car, and drove off with it. I hoped that he didn't see me. I didn't want word to get back that someone was snooping. I wanted her to feel safe using this place again. I had another plan.

I was going to need some sleep before implementing it. I was also going to need a raven or at the very least a trustworthy crow.

Chapter Five

I AWOKE WITH THE DAWN. I'd like to make a snappy little joke about waking up with Dawn. But the truth, by contrast, would just depress me. My apartment is on the west side of the building so I don't get the early morning light coming in. So how do I know I awoke with the dawn? Because I've got an alarm clock and an almanac.

Regardless, I made my way up to the roof of the building. The super hates anyone coming up here. Except for Bob and Sandra in 5g. The super's got a soft spot for fresh veggies and lets them keep a rooftop garden.

Needless to say, Bob and Sandra are a bit proprietary about the roof. Still, some of my rituals work better with sky access. I try to be discrete as possible.

Once there I did a simple energy gathering technique. I was told it had a Native American root.

Unfortunately, I can't be more specific. I didn't learn it from my magi mentor but from one of my drama prof's in college. I wasn't really paying that close of attention then. It wasn't until later that I found it actually helped in mystical matters.

After gathering new energy from, then releasing old energy to, the four directions, the sky and earth and so on. (Sorry no more details without a signed check . . . I mean waiver) I turned my focus to finding a friend.

I was looking for a raven. Ravens have weight, I mean more than just being big. I mean mystic weight. They pop up all over folklore and legend. Odin had ravens. The Morrigan of Irish legends took raven form. Noah sent out a raven from the Ark before the dove. God commanded ravens to feed the prophet, Elijah, when he would have otherwise starved.

This surprises some because ravens are called "unclean" by Kosher laws. Personally, I think "unclean" meant bad to eat and wasn't a reflection on their character.

I also have a fondness for ravens because my late wife was from Baltimore. So we supported their NFL team over the closer Washington team. They won the super bowl the year we got married.

In any event, ravens have always been good to me. So I sent out a call. And waited. And waited. I remained perfectly still, letting my call go out from my mind and will. I stood there, my arms outstretched like the Jesus statue that looks over Rio de Janeiro from the hill. Okay a short, chubby Jesus in a tattered robe and "sleeping" boxers

The roof access door opened up. I could see it out of the corner of my eye. I didn't turn. My concentration was taxed enough. Someone stepped through the door out onto the roof. It was Bob from 5g. Apparently, Bob is a farmer at heart and up with the sun.

"What the hell you doing, Gives?"

At that moment a raven did finally respond to my call. He swooped past Bob making him duck slightly. The raven then alighted on my head. I would have appreciated the gracefulness of his landing more if he hadn't dug talons into my scalp.

"Oh, you're bird training. That's nice. Just don't let it eat my plants"

"Ravens are carrion eaters, Bob."

"Then don't let it shit on my roof. Oh and Gives . . ."

"Yea?"

"Get out of my damn garden."

The raven and I hurried downs the stairs.

Koenig had gone to a lot of trouble to cover her tracks. I was torn. One way I could use the raven was to spot out the *park and ride*. I could wait to see who dropped off the car Koenig's Jekyll drives away at night.

Another was to try to keep tabs on Koenig and follow her to her switching point. I decided to go with the second option in case she varied her routine.

First things first. I set the raven down to perch on the kitchen windowsill. He sat there watching me. I gave him a piece of hamburger to reward him for his patience.

I made myself a couple of sandwiches and a thermos of mint tea. Afterward, I showered and dressed. Only then did I clear a space in my living room. On the floor, I arranged a few cushions and made myself comfortable. The raven found a perch on the edge of my coffee table. He stood on the edge and regarded me silently. His head occasionally flipping so he could look at me from one eye then the other.

For my part, I unfocused my eyes and refocused my will. This is a difficult process for me. I find merging senses a bit disconcerting. I always think that the next time will be easier but it never is. It's a bit hard for me to explain. I'm not sure that I understand the process all that well. I understand well enough to do it, but not to do well or easily.

The first part *is* easy. I let my own consciousness become diffuse. It starts very much like daydreaming. In fact, I have to say that it lies somewhere between dreaming and outright astral projection.[4] Next comes the paradoxical expansion/contraction stage. I should say that my awareness expands but my sense of self diminishes. So there's at once expansion and contraction. It would be just as true to say that my sense of self enlarges so much that it encompasses my surroundings and I begin to become one with them. I see what's around me as aspects of myself.

I'm aware of everything around me but the details lose their meanings as the big picture forms. Sort of the way that you really aren't paying attention to the white spaces on the page but you'd be screwed trying to read this without them. I float in a room like this for only a short period of time. (Objectively that is, subjectively it can seem like days) It's pleasant and relaxing. I love that first part. Floating there in my living room calm, carefree, and in a state of subdued euphoria.

I reached out for the raven. It's a gentle sort of motion. Imagine stretching out your arms while you float in sun-drenched waters off a white sand beach somewhere in the Caribbean.

Next comes the hard part. The hard part is when you stop being generally one with everything to specifically one with another. I want you to imagine that as you stretch your arms out in that lovely Caribbean scene you are suddenly drowning. You're being pulled beneath by a slow but unyielding undertow. You instinctively gasp for air but you only swallow more water. Now add someone taking a pick-ax to your temples.

---

[4] For those of you who wonder, yes I could astrally project and then enter the bird. (I won't because that's possession and generally considered a no-no.) I needed to interact "locally" so to speak. Next I put my brain into a "data download" mode. When I'm merged I perceive as *the other*. For example, ravens don't read. I would have to "record" its' visual impressions and "read" anything I saw later in my memory.

The water forces you down and crams you through a hole in a coral reef. The jagged edges scraping and ripping at you until you emerge on the other side like a fish.

I said it was hard to explain but that's what it's like for me to reshape myself to something else's form. I'm sure there's a shaman or magus or witch out there who could do this in their sleep. Just not me.

Eventually, I could "see" through the raven's eyes (and hear through its ears, etc) and it through mine. To avoid too much confusion, I shut down most of my own senses. I left just enough to keep me alert just in case.

I stood up and made my way carefully to the door. I needed to go outside because something about my apartment blocks my links once either I or the other move outside of it. I suspect the apartment ghost is responsible. I don't know if it's intentional or just a by-product of its presence.

Moving my own body during a sense merge is a bit like controlling a third-person video game character.

You see yourself from the outside and it takes some adjustment. Many Magi just go into a trance and keep still. In fact, it's so common that many non-magi think it's mandatory. I try to use that to my advantage.

Once we made it outside my building I let the raven take to the air. Through its eyes, I watched my body's movements. It took a little extra time to walk down to the little park bench out in front of the old municipal building in the middle of the square.

Soon enough I was set up on the park bench, sitting there with my thermos and sandwiches. I pulled a little notebook from my pocket and began to "write" in it. Most of my neighbors already believed that I was a writer or artist or something, so this behavior wasn't out of character for me. I've done some of my best surveillance sitting on this bench.

I sent the raven off to the first place on Pandora's list. Koenig spends most of her earlier mornings running her legitimate business enterprise. She does make-up. She's an independent Sales Director for *Katy May Cosmetics* (No, that's not really the name, but I don't want to be sued, do I?)

She's built up quite a client list for that makeup. She has a number of sales associates who handle the actual face-to-face selling. She just coordinates them. According to Pandora she keeps this absolutely divorced from her other businesses. So much so that once she had one of her criminal lackeys charged with harassment when he broke protocol and contacted her during her "Katy May Hours"

Koenig liked to conduct her morning business out of coffee shops and restaurants. Not unlike her evening business that was conducted out of bars and clubs. Hmm, Koenig is a very social Hyde.

It was about three in the afternoon by the time I managed to be at the right place at the right time. The raven caught a glimpse of her heading into the Hillcrest Tavern. It wasn't the kind of dive where people drank to forget trouble. It was the kind where people drank to find it. The raven let me know that it was hungry, tired, and felt that it had put in more than an honest day's work. I had to agree. I brought the raven back to me. I gave it my now stale sandwiches as partial payment. I let the raven go, owing it a favor.

Now if only Koenig would still be at the Hillcrest by the time I could get there. I packed my things up and made my way quickly to my car.

Chapter Six

I WAS OVER TO THE Hillcrest Tavern in record time. I pulled into its meager, gravel parking area. I was heading inside the building when I hesitated. The tavern looked like an old dilapidated house with peeling paint. A tiny, old, wooden sign hung over the door. The fading paint on it read simply "The Hillcrest." Other than the parking lot and the sign itself, there were no obvious signs that this was a place of business. This place had its customers and wasn't looking for more.

That's one of the reasons I was hesitant to go in. It may not say "for members only" on the door but, trust me, it was.

Recalling how confident Koenig looked strutting in here. I had the feeling she arranged a fair amount of her business here. If I showed my face inside, it was likely to draw attention. I wasn't ready to do that then. I can divert attention away from myself but it's not foolproof.

The other reason I hesitated is that the sedan I saw the night before pulled into the gravel lot just before I got out of my car. The same two thugs were in the sedan. After they got out of their car, they gave a quick look around. They gave no indication that they had seen me or my car. Still, they moved inside very quickly. I decided it would be better to stake out the "Park and Ride".

To do that, I wanted a different car. I love my car, don't get me wrong, but it does stand out. I called the discount rental place in town. My taxed credit limit had just barely enough to get their cheapest car "in town" for one day. At least they delivered.

The rental car turned out to be a blue-gray Kia Rio. On my way out to the park and ride, I hit a drive-through. Normally fast food is as bad for mystic workings as it is for digestion and general health. Which is, ironically, why I got it. Koenig was savvy enough to use a place mystically protected to make her change-overs.

I could go in there and cloak myself to normal senses but that would possibly set off a few of the more unusual senses. As a Magus, I normally have a bit of an extra "glow" even if I'm not up to something. A couple of quarter-pound burgers should dampen my inner-light a bit.

Most detective work is tedious. This was no exception. Surveillance is a bore, whether you're waiting for an adulterous spouse or a denizen of the nether-dark.

There was nothing unusual until about eight o'clock. By seven forty-five all the other cars had been picked up by their car pooling owners. At just a little after eight, I felt something. I wasn't using my "sight." That might have drawn attention to me. Luckily this registered on that extra sense we all have; the one that makes the small hairs on the back of the neck rise.

Suddenly there was a small whirl-wind, not even a true dust devil, whipping through the parking lot. When it reached my car, it dissipated. Five minutes later it happened again. I played a hunch and drove out of the lot and parked by the side of the road. A quick run back and I was on the edge of the lot in time to see the wind sweep through again. This time there were no cars to interrupt its journey.

I hid among the trees that lined the edge of the lot. Suddenly I felt the air go very chilly. Next, there was a swirl of blue light in the air. At first, nothing seemed to have happened. Then it slowly dawned on me that there was a car in the parking lot that wasn't there before the blue light weirdness special. I wonder how long it had been there. Someday I'm going to learn how to be a real detective and observe properly. I depend way too much on my otherworldly senses.

For instance, if I had been using my Sight, I would have noticed the new car right away. If I'm not using the Sight I'm pathetically easy to sneak up on. Which is exactly what one of Koenig's thugs did.

I think it was the one who noticed me the other night. I didn't get another look at his face. He had put me in a quick half nelson with one of his arms and pinned my arms with his other. Next, he walk-dragged me all the way back to my rental car. He never said a word that whole time.

When we got to the car he pinned me up against the car. He pulled my wallet out of my jacket, The real one with my actual ID in it. Still, he didn't say anything. He just grunted as he read it. He put my wallet back and took out my car keys.

He still had me pinned so I couldn't look around at him. He opened up the driver's side door and his partner got into the car. The thug kept my head pushed down the whole while. I didn't see a face for either one of them.

"Now wise up and stop snooping. Just to show you we're nice guys we'll take your car back into town for you, " he finally said.

He pushed my head very hard into the side of the car. Hard enough that I saw stars for a second or two. I was still shaking off the blow when my rental car drove away. When I looked around both cars were driving away. I thought they might take more drastic measures. I still didn't want to peek around with my Sight. I was afraid that might tip my hand more than it had been already. The walk back to town got me home well after midnight. I found the rental car parked in my reserved parking spot. It wasn't comforting to know that my quarry now knew so much about me.

I returned the rental then spent the rest of the night researching. It only took an hour to find my bookcase. The appearing (and possibly disappearing) car trick had added another wrinkle. This was getting complicated real quick. Most "Hydes" just aren't this creative. Either she wasn't the real force behind all this or she had one hell of an adviser.

Either way, the "Park and Ride" lead was now dead. This is what led me to attempt the little information-gathering jaunt at another bar on Pandora's list.

The Cayo Hueso is a Key West-themed bar. I went there the next evening. That's the little excursion that ended so nicely with a beating and a threatening letter.

At least I knew I was making progress. After all, why threaten me if I was going wrong. I just hoped I hadn't met a dead end. Still, I didn't have much to tell Pandora when we met the following day in the relative anonymity of the coffee shop.

She came in just after noon. There's a little booth in there towards the back where one can watch the doors easily enough without being too noticeable. She took her place in line and cast a casual glance over toward my booth. It was still early enough that Koenig should still be dealing with her legitimate business.

I was running my Sight trying to spot anyone taking too much notice of either of us. When I was confident that we weren't being watched I nodded her over. She sat down across from me.

Without preamble, she asked, "Have you been able to find out anything?" For the too short time it took me to say "not much" there was something else in those eyes. A something else that was too afraid to call itself hope. It was almost more heartbreaking than the lead her eyes usually carried.

"I must be on to something. She had someone drop off a threatening letter. It opens up some leads maybe."

"Do you know who gave you the letter?"

"No, not yet."

"Could she be this Jekyll you've been looking for?"

"No. I used the sight on her. It would have shown if she was the one."

Pandora flinched when I mentioned the Sight. I don't think she was comfortable with the idea of anyone being able to look that deeply into her.

"I should know something by tonight. Well, very early tomorrow morning. So, same bat time?

"What?"

"Sorry, that's from a TV show. Before your time."

The smile she gave looked so genuine that it would have fooled me if I hadn't known better.

"What should I do?"

"Lay low, read a book, watch TV, whatever you do normally when Koenig doesn't have you working."

At the mention of working . . . well I couldn't call it to flinch, it was more like she turned off the person she was and became a thing. It felt wrong to let her keep working but Pandora insisted. She didn't want Koenig to suspect that her brother's disappearance had even registered. I found it hard to be that mercenary.

"Can you call in sick?"

"No, she has pills for every occasion."

At that moment I wanted to tell Pandora everything would be all right. That we'd get her brother back and both of them free from Koenig. But I couldn't.

Don't get me wrong, I firmly believed that all that would come to pass. But I knew how hollow my words would sound to her. I'd be just one more adult making empty promises. It was hard enough for her to trust. It would be better to give her results later than vague reassurances now.

"You should go now. In case someone is watching you." I told her.

"Sure. Thanks. Tomorrow." she said. Pandora got up and left the coffee shop.

Now I wasn't worried about someone was tailing her. I was hoping. I followed Pandora out of the shop as quickly as I dared. I turned on my sight and looked about. Half a block up the street I could see the bright aura of somebody watching. From this distance I could only tell a few things. One, the watcher was male, two he was extremely physically fit, and three, he was as predatory as a shark.

This was going to be fun.

Chapter Seven

THE MAN WAS STALKING prey. Even I could see that. He moved down the sidewalk in a quiet, determined way. He arrogantly pushed aside an obnoxious real estate agent coming out nearby store. No, my Sight doesn't tell me occupations. So how did I know he was a real estate agent? His face was plastered on park bench advertising.

What my Sight could tell me at this distance is that both men considered themselves at the center of the universe. Sure most people do to a certain extent, I mean, after all, it's hard to ignore yourself in your own viewpoint. It *is* your perspective after all.

Both these guys took it to the extreme. The real estate agent didn't even register the people around him as people but as objects. Pandora's pursuer was only really aware of her and how he would feel when he caught up with her. The rest of us may have popped up on his radar but as obstacles only.

That put me into serious danger mode. I had thought he was just a flunky sent to keep tabs on her for Koenig. Now that I had a gotten a closer read on him I could see that predatory vibe was more than general thuggery. He was very possibly someone whom the media would call a monster.

"You've got the Sight," you say, "can't you tell?"

Well, no. The sight is great for the here and now. While that includes current guilt or remorse for past actions, I can't actually see what they have done. I can also tell who's got predatory inclinations but not who has acted on it or how. I could see into a true psychopath all day and not know if he or she had committed a particular crime from the sight alone. It really doesn't do much more than an F.B.I. profiler could. It can just do it much faster and sometimes with greater accuracy.

I certainly wasn't going to let some predator catch up to my "client." It may be that Pandora is quite capable of handling herself. I wasn't going to take that chance. People think that night is the most dangerous time on the street. Maybe for muggings, it is, but people can go missing at any time. The presence of light only deters the amateurs.

If this were a movie, now would come one of the cool bits. This is where I work a wonder, do some magic, cast a spell, achieve an effect, whatever you want to call it.

This is the part where I turn invisible. Okay, not actually invisible but close. Part of it is certainly in the ordinary, everyday, explainable realm. I adjust my body language so that I give off the nonverbal cues of "ignore me please, I'm nobody."

That's over half the job right there. Most people screw this up when they sneak about and actually draw attention to themselves.

Next, I drew on the energy that we all swim through each day, ambient heat, radio waves, the gravity we all take for granted, Etc. I altered it subtly, funneling it through my will. Exactly how is a trade secret.[5]

After I drew in the energy, I broadcasted it back out. Not as so much on a physical wavelength but a mental one. A simple transmission that said, "Hey, look at that over there." This helped in two ways. One was drawing attention away from me. The other was that I was bringing the predator more notice than he would like.

Most people just let a determined person slide by, shrug off the rudeness, and get on with their lives. Not today. Today everyone he brushed past on the sidewalk looked at him, really looked at him. Everyone he jostled would turn and remember his face. I wanted him to feel the eyes of the world upon him.

"That should be enough to dissuade his hunting," I thought.

We walked on following behind Pandora. She was setting a pretty good pace. Sooner than one would think we had passed out of the nicer downtown business district. We were passing into the rougher neighborhoods where territory was a way of life not just an idea. It wouldn't be very long until . . .

"Look, you cretin, watch where you are going."

The predator had jostled through a small knot of people at a crosswalk. A young man and his little following of cronies had risen to the implied challenge. There were four of them all told. The leader was an African-American man of medium height and build. Though dressed casually his clothing was immaculate. He also wore a pair of sunglasses that

---

[5]   See the last page order form for my very reasonably priced correspondence courses

complimented his face admirably. Two of the other men looked Hispanic. One of them was tall and quite athletic. The other was short, slight, and bookish. The fourth youth looked like he had mixed heritage, of Asian and European extraction. He, too, was of average size. What really set him apart was his impish smile and all too clever look in his eyes.

All of them were dressed casually. They didn't look especially dangerous but looks can be deceiving. Even with the Sight, more than anything else, I saw a sense of commitment to each other and fierce protectiveness.

Normally those are good things. Sometimes that can be twisted toward harmful purposes, like in crime families or street gangs. I didn't know if they were actually street gang members or not. Again that's not really my area of expertise. At the very least though they had the territorial inclination needed to resent this predator's intrusion.

The stalker tried to brush the young man away. He mumbled, "Fuck off."

The young man grabbed the predator by the shoulder and spun him around. His little band of cronies took up positions around the predator. It was four on one. This was going to get more violent than I had anticipated.

"It appears as if you are following that girl," said the leader, "Perhaps you should wait behind a moment lest someone think you have some dire purpose."

"I. Said. Fuck. Off!" There was no more conversation after that.

The tall, athletic, Latino youth pulled back to take a swing at Pandora's stalker. The stalker guy must have had some kind of fierce training. Because when the blow should have landed, the stalker guy just wasn't there. No magic, mind you, just a fluid balance shift and duck around. With my Sight, I could tell that stalker boys' emotions and vitals didn't spike a bit.

With four evenly placed blows, he struck each one of the youths. Two went down with broken jaws. The third was concussed straight into unconsciousness. The last one lost an eye.

Stalker boy barely looked down at then and started to move on. He was already in the middle of the crosswalk when he realized that he had lost track of Pandora. He swore, quietly, to himself. Then he simply turned back around and headed back past me. I rushed to where the four young men lay on the pavement.

I wanted to follow stalker boy. He was dangerous. Deprived of one quarry he may just go find another. I had to help the four young men, however. They had been unwitting tools of my intention. Some would say they made their own choices. Maybe, but they were still lying there injured because I had wanted something to slow the stalker guy down.

They were in pretty bad shape. Damn, Stalker boy was way too good at causing pain. I definitely needed to find out more about him.

Usually, I try to work subtly. It's less of a strain on my system. I didn't have the option here. If I was going to undo my indirect harm, I needed to work fast and dirty.

I took the risk of opening up all the way. Full sight, full energy access. It's real easy to burn out or lose yourself doing that.

Suddenly I was at one with the world, the universe. I was an aspect of the sun, the city, the sky. I dreamed of a light that dreamed of me. When I reached that kind of loopy thinking, I knew I was ready.

Sorrow and Hope flooded into me from the surrounding neighborhood. I was the newly immigrated grocer, I was the native-born citizen whose family had been here 450 years and still treated as second-class newcomers.

I was the four, young men. I was myself seeing that I was the four, young men. I was also my body tortured by sudden pain. I was the light, sparkling rain that would fall in ten minutes' time.

We were the life of the world renewing itself like an instant spring. I took hold of all that life, all that energy, and drew it into me. Then, quickly so it wouldn't burn me too deeply, I started radiating that life out. I channeled it into the young men. I began to knit together broken bones, to stitch sinews. The flowing energy bolstered and amplified their own natural healing processes.

"What the fuck happened?" We asked ourselves as we rose from the ground bewildered by fading images of half-remembered pain.

"That guy hit us..." okay, time to pull out.

I broke contact. Fortunately, none of the four, young men were able to maintain contact with me on their own. Even with my sight turned off I could see the work had been successful.

Hector and Ramón had their jaws back in their normal places. James was able to see from both eyes. Ty was going to be able to continue feeding and dressing himself.

"Ah man, I got names," I thought. I had gone deeper than I needed. That meant the withdrawal was going to hit me hard.

Fortunately, these four friends, along with fiercely protecting their home and each other, were basically good guys. Ty was already calling 911 on his cell phone as I slumped to the pavement, conscious only of a distant light in a great void.

Chapter Eight

WHEN I WAS FINALLY aware of myself again, I was in a hospital bed. A curtain was drawn around my bed. From the noise beyond it, I guessed I was still in the ER.

I was still dressed in my regular clothes. Only my hat and duster had been removed. They sat on a chair beside my bed.

I started to move. Sudden pain in my shoulder told me this should be done in an unhurried manner. I must have wrenched it when I hit the pavement. It was a little too soon to go all "one with the Life Force" again to heal myself. I was just going to have to bear with it. I wasn't too worried. I heal fast normally.

I had just managed to get one sleeve of my duster on when "my" doctor came in to check on me. Her name is Dr. Sandra McBride. You'll have noticed the quotes around the "my" in "My Doctor". She's not my primary care physician. I'm not officially a patient of hers. Even this time I was certain I would be listed as a John Doe.

As you know, I keep my real wallet in a hidden pocket. Sure a thorough search would turn it up. That hadn't been done on any of my previous trips in here. I don't live in a large city like Chicago or New York but it still has a fair amount of traffic in the local hospital's ER.

It's clean. it's efficient and I can rely on it. Actually, I can rely on it for three things;

One: No one steals my stuff while I'm unconscious.

Two: I'm always allowed to leave "Against Medical Advice."

Three: Sandra McBride is always going to be the doctor on my case.

I honestly haven't figured that last one out myself. I just chalk it up to the strange luck I enjoy as part of my "gift." So I wasn't surprised when she came in before I had gotten my coat all the way on. She pulled the curtain back in place, shutting us off from the rest of the room. She came over to stand dead set in front of me, crossed her arms, and glared at me.

"Oh no, this is the third time this year you've come into my ER. It's the second time you've been unconscious for no apparent reason. I'm not just going to let you go that easily."

What she said was true. Every now and then, I end up pushing myself too hard. Hard enough that I backlash into a trance-like state. If it happens in public, like it did today, I usually wake up here.

"You are staying overnight for observation."

"Don't I have the right to refuse medical treatment?" I asked

Dr. McBride smiled at me. "You don't want me to push the 'danger to yourself' angle, Do you?" Something told me that if I pushed her on this I'd end up in the psych unit and by the time it got sorted out, I'd have spent the night there anyway. Still, I have to try "Can't I just pay my ER fees and go?"

"No, Mr. Gives, you may not."

Ah shit, she knew my name. She even pronounced right so it rhymed with strives. She answered my unspoken question of how she knew my name

"The four young men who brought you in were able to find your wallet. They seem quite concerned about you. They seemed to think that they owed you something."

No good deed goes unpunished I thought.

"They brought you in with your wallet this time, finally you are getting properly admitted to the ER. We were even able to contact your wife. She's out there now filling in the insurance forms and giving us the proper releases."

"My wife . . ." I'm sure I went ashen at this point. I know I felt wobbly. I started to sit back down on the bed.

"See, Mr. Gives, this is exactly what I was worried about. Just lay back a moment we should be able to get you upstairs very quickly."

"Sheila," I said.

"Just a moment, I'll go send her in. She can wait with you until we send you up."

Sheila! I didn't think I would ever see her again. We had parted under the worst of circumstances. She was brutally murdered. Then she tried to kill me.

Damn my procrastination. My wallet had come with an emergency info card. My then-new wife generously filled it out for me. I never updated the "person to contact in case of emergency" portion. There was no one really. She must still have the same cell phone number.

The curtain drew back. And there she was, but not quite as I remembered her. Her dark, curly hair still cascaded down to her shoulders. Golden eyes still shone from beneath perfectly arched eyebrows. Her face and body had once had a bit more rounding. Now she was more angular and lithe. It was still appealing in its own way, just not as cuddly.

Her choice of clothing had also changed. She'd gone from flowing silk dresses that she had dyed herself to some designer's idea of the perfect corporate vixen. She was wearing a business suit. The skirt was of respectable length. The charcoal gray and navy color scheme were what you'd expect to find to find on any banker; solid, dependable, conservative. The suit as a whole was perfectly tailored to show off her figure without advertising it blatantly. She was also wearing the kind of high spiked heal that one seldom sees outside a certain kind of fantasy video. Despite the changes, there was no mistaking Sheila.

Ladies and gentlemen, may I present Sheila Thompson-Gives, my late wife.

Chapter Nine

SOME DAY I'LL TELL you about how I ended with this "Job" and the group I only half-jokingly call the Disreputable Urban Magi Association. If I do you'll have to listen closely to make out what I'm saying because of the alcohol-induced slurring and the head injury incoherence.

It's not that we are so much a secret group as a group with secrets. How many we are, who we are, why it's safer for us to work in very small groups most of the time. Those are all things I'd rather not talk about.

It should tell you something that I'm going on about that rather than continue telling you about my late wife.

At the time what ran most through my mind was "Damn it! I've got to get back on Pandora's case." It was a most pragmatic avoidance technique.

Sheila looked at me. I braced myself, drawing in energy to bolster my will in case I needed it. I couldn't imagine not needing it. The last time I saw her, she wanted to carve out my heart. I'm fairly sure she was planning to eat it.

"Stop looking at me like that," she said. "You can relax I'm not going to hurt you. I'm just going to make sure you get any medical treatment you need."

Needless to say, I was a bit leery here. I didn't bother with my sight. There are a few things I don't want to see through the Sight again. My wife as undead is number one on that list. Been there, done that, got the emotional scarring

"There's no way I trust you," I said

"I know." She smiled so prettily I actually felt a twinge for those good old days when we first married and were both alive.

"I've managed to get control of my hunger," she said. "I think it might be because I didn't actually get to eat your heart. Once I got a handle on that, my new life came easier. Don't snort like that it's unattractive. I tried to re-assume as much of my old life as possible"

"So you're still in teaching? Night school I presume"

"Don't be an ass, Milo. I'm not a vampire. I don't have a problem with daylight. Well, not much of one.

Mostly it's just unflattering and only a tad bit uncomfortable."

From my studies and limited experience with the undead, she sounded like a ghoul. Except that all the ghouls I have ever heard of descended into gibbering mindlessness. All of them do, without exception. It's what makes them less of a threat than other undead, vampires for example.

Ghouls have a few advantages over vampires. They can walk around in the daylight and don't develop the same weaknesses that vampires do.[6] Sadly for them, they have only a smidgen more ability to think than a zombie from the Romero "living dead" movies. Which, by the way, don't exist (those kinds of zombies, not the movies).

Your average ghoul can keep it together enough to hide and hunt but not much more. They aren't going to be passing for humans under any circumstance. They have a special mesmerizing voice they can use to lure in prey. They are not good at mimicking life. Especially not as effectively as Shelia was doing right in front of me.

"Daylight's unflattering . . . odd that, Eh?" I was trying to keep up a good banter and failing horribly. I suspect it was the rampaging fear of having my heart torn out. I have faced worse monsters before and since.

Some even could use sex as a weapon. Others could induce obsessions that seemed like love.

What scared me was this, this monster didn't have to fake it, Shelia already had my love. She didn't have to counterfeit it.

"Look, I'm not here to hurt you. If I have my way, you won't be in any danger at all. But my new life is complicated. I live in a world cobwebbed by favors owed and traded.

Shelia continued, "I know the doctor told you they reached me by your emergency contact numbers. She didn't. I've actually been keeping tabs on you. I just edited the proper memories to make her life easier.

---

6 CC# 314 *Ghouls and Ghosts: knowing your undead.* Not to be confused with *Ghosts and Vamps: Knowing you're undead* by another author.

"Don't think you are the only one who can investigate," she said, "Koenig did a little checking on you, found out about me, and called in a favor."

"A favor from you?"

"A favor from someone I owed. Look, I just need to keep you out of the way for the next little while. How is up to me. I can make sure you spend the next week here in the hospital, maybe in the psych unit. I'd hate to think about you needing the ICU."

She looked me straight in the eye as she delivered that last remark. Abruptly her demeanor changed. She looked down a little. Then back up at me, cocked her head to the side, and smiled. Her eyelids fluttered artfully. She reached out and ran a finger down my cheek then under my chin.

"Or we could make it fun . . ."

Chapter Ten

I GAVE IN. I DECIDED it was safer staying where I was. In a few moments, an orderly returned to take me to my room. I'm not sure how my late wife swung it, but I had a private room. I was certain that she was keeping a watch on my room. After all, she was able to follow me without my knowing it. I was determined to figure that out. More pressingly, I was trying to figure out how to help Pandora from the hospital room. I had a plan but not a great one. If I was discovered I might never get out of the hospital.

I would try astral projection. Upside, it's hard to detect. I would simply look asleep. I could "slumber" peacefully while actually getting something done. Downside: If the nurses gave me more than a cursory glance they might see I was not in normal sleep. This could lead to tests and questions and a much longer stay, which is exactly what Shelia wanted. I hoped she couldn't tell what I was doing. If she could I'm certain she'd make sure the nursing staff noticed.

I relaxed back into my hospital bed. I closed my eyes, made the necessary adjustments within myself, then left my body.[7]

Once outside my body, my perceptions changed. I now saw the world as if I hit the jackpot on the Wheel of Sight. Instead of one sense having the "Sight" all of them did. As I drifted up out of my body I could smell the dedication in the nurse making her rounds down the hall. I could see the health (and disease) of the man as I passed through the room directly above

---

[7]   CC# 202A Your Astral Self and You

me. I could hear the boredom of the charge nurse blaring as she sat at the nurses' station. I took a sharp right and left the hospital.

Projecting not only changes your perceptions but sometimes your priorities. For example, a lot of my fear for my physical person melted away. Not surprising considering I was leaving my physical self behind.

It was an amazingly stress-free moment. No distracting concerns like the rent, making ends meet, or even "was the new tenet in 3B really making eyes at me when we cross in the hall." Now if something is truly important, trying to save the lives of two young people, for example, that stays crystal clear.

I floated outside the hospital for an instant or an hour. Then I thought myself across the city, buoyed by an imaginary wind.

There was only one real psychic in town. By that I mean only one of the mediums (should that be media?) that put out the fortune-telling sign had any real talent.

Marguerite was about 45. She wasn't really Romani but she had the dark hair and complexion to be convincing to people who didn't know any better. She never claims to be of Romani stock, mind you, but her style of dress doesn't exactly say banker either. She, unlike myself, will talk to the dead for you. She only charges a small fee, relatively speaking.

I don't speak to the dead, my late wife notwithstanding. I won't do it. Don't ask. I also won't tell you your future beyond things like, "You know that smoking is going to hurt you." Or "If you keeping treating your wife/ husband/ kid/ employee like that they are just going to walk out on you."

Again, It's not that I couldn't, it's just a bad plan. At least I've always found it to be so, especially that talking with the dead. I really don't like that. Even if sometimes it seems necessary. Fortunately for me, Marguerite doesn't feel the same way.

When I found Marguerite, she was dressed for bed in a silky negligee. Presumably because of the way wearing it made her feel. She clearly wasn't entertaining. She was dozing lightly in a chair. A book lay across her chest. I had chosen Marguerite because it was easier for me to talk to someone who could sense a spirit form on their own.

With the Sight automatically running I could tell she was about to slip into a dream state. I didn't want that. Sure I could still talk to her, I could talk to just about anybody in a dream state. That's not the problem. It's whether or not they remember when they wake up. I needed her to remember my plan to work.

I needed something to jog her back to wakefulness, something to physically wake her up. I couldn't just shout. My voice wasn't physical and would just work its way into her dream.

It takes a considerable act of will to interact with the physical world when projecting. At least it does for me.

"Actually this should be simple enough," I thought. "I 'll just move her book and the motion should wake her up." So I concentrated and I pushed my hand forward to jostle the book. I needn't have bothered. It may have been my presence or just the moment when she would awaken anyway. Marguerite sat upright then. My hand missed her book. Instead, I reached out and just a little bit into her left breast.

Sadly in my astral form, it didn't even occur to me to enjoy this moment of serendipity. Marguerite is the kind of woman who makes forty-five look like the new twenty. Normally when I've met with her I've never failed to notice her beauty and vitality. I wasn't unaware of it then. I just didn't have my normal hormonal reaction to make me feel like a gawky teenager again.

"You projected over here to feel me up? You really are an odd duck aren't you.?"

"Sorry, I was trying to make sure you didn't fall fully asleep, I just wanted to jostle the book."

She looked at me closely; She could tell I wasn't lying. That's another advantage for those who develop the Sight.

"Still seems a little Freudian to me. What do you need?

"Well, I'm in the hospital . . ." immediately her expression changed. The playful banter drained out of her voice. It was replaced with a more solemn, serious tone.

"Is this a near-death? The last visitation?" The concern in her voice was quite touching. I was quick to reassure her.

"No, no, a bad element caught up with me. I ended up getting admitted overnight for observation. I need your help to make sure that I can get out in the morning. My current adversary could pull the right strings and get me admitted for a serious psych Eval."

"So you want me to bust you out of a locked, psychiatric ward."

"Either that or go to the DMV for me."

"So what's your break-out plan?" she asked. The playful tone in her voice had returned.

I had to admit at the moment I didn't have one. I didn't really have all the facts. So I quickly explained as much of the case as I could without feeling like I was betraying the confidences of my client. Stressing more the sudden reappearance of my late wife and that I wasn't in a locked ward yet."

In short, Marguerite agreed to help me. We worked out a tentative plan. As I was drifting out to return to my body she asked me a question.

"By the way have you ever really looked at your astral form?"

I stopped and looked down. It was as I thought of myself, only naked. Oops.

"Don't be embarrassed. I'm impressed."

I found this odd given the state of my physique and that it was faithfully represented in my astral form. "What?" I said

"Let's just leave it as a testament to your honesty."

I could feel something begin to tug on my silver cord. I hoped it wasn't what I feared.

Jetting back to my body I found my ex-wife in a nurse's uniform standing over me with a grin that had gone way past mischievous. There was a time that would have been a good thing

"Naughty, naughty, " she said, then pressed her mouth down upon mine. Once again the lights went out.

Chapter Eleven

THE LIGHTS MAY HAVE gone out but this was far from done. Shelia was vomiting a cold, acrid emptiness into me. It felt like all the air in my lungs disappeared. I felt them shrivel like leaky balloons. I struggled for breath but all I found was a nothingness so thick you could chew it.

I tried to chant but the darkness rushed further down my throat. An icy burn ripped through my lungs and gut.

Sheila had made the most of her undeath it seems. I had never encountered an attack like this. Not in my own experience, not in the lessons my mentor taught, nor in the books he left me after his sudden death. I was in new territory here. All I had was my gut instinct. Even if that gut was filling with shards of the void.

Sheila may have learned a great deal in the last few years but then so had I. The energy I had been squirreling away earlier was still there, hidden within my will. I unleashed that energy. At first, it was like lighting a candle in an unlit room. It was small and flickering and it didn't seem like much at all. But like an actual candle, mere darkness could not extinguish it.

That inner light steadied, then began to push outward. Every second I gained a small but crucial advantage. First, the light was the size of a candle then a flashlight next to a lantern and still growing. I was able to gain enough strength to split my focus. With one part of my will, I pushed harder against Sheila's darkness. With another, I tried to gird myself for her second assault. She had always been clever and never one to give up easily. If one tactic failed she'd try anything and everything else to succeed. I didn't imagine undeath would dampen her tenacity.

Sheila merely tried to flood that darkness deeper into me. I was surprised, I had expected more than just this one trick. As swiftly as her attack had begun, the battle shifted to my favor. The light in my belly was now more than just pushing back the darkness. It was eating the dark. Now she was trying to douse a flame with oil.

The flame within me fed on that darkness. Soon it rushed up through me. I sat up in my hospital bed. To an observer, it must look as though I was now vigorously returning Sheila's kiss. The light erupted from within me. It spilled out of my mouth and eyes. Sheila stopped her dreadful "kiss" but not before the light had burned its way out of me and into her. I could sense it spreading into her, filling her throat, her lungs, all of her chest.

For a second it seemed as though that her heart might begin to beat, that her lungs might start to draw breath. Then she actually looked at me. She really looked at me and *saw* me. She looked at me, not as hunter and prey or even adversaries in a game but looked at me person to person

Her eyes glittered with an internal, golden light. I think she might have been crying. She turned away from me. Shadows flew from the edges of the room to cloak her.

Suddenly she was gone

If some of this imagery has seemed sexual to you. That isn't accidental. Beyond the primal forces we were thrusting into one another (really, doesn't it just sound like that should be fun) there was something else. I mentioned earlier that I still loved her. Her method of attack could not have been better chosen if she wanted to try to use that against me. If she had let the "kiss" be a kiss for even a moment before her attack I may have been unable to defend against it.

I don't know why she didn't. It seemed unlike her not to use every resource she could. Either her new "life" had dulled her thinking or she had set herself up to fail.

Why would she do that? Two reasons occurred to me. One was that she was setting me up, that she was trying to lure me into a false sense of security. I didn't know how to think about the other possible reason. Could she still have had real feelings for me?

I was fairly certain that either case could get me killed. Particularly since our contact, our "kiss", brief and frightening as it was, was hanging around my neck like an albatros

Chapter Twelve

As SOON AS VISITING hours began, Marguerite was there. She was dressed much more conventionally than when she gave readings. She could have passed for a lawyer.

"I didn't know your wardrobe had muted colors," I said.

"I keep a few serious outfits, just in case," she said with a wry smile.

I felt it prudent not to pry into the "just in case" scenarios considering that right then, I was one of them. "Here's the stuff you asked for," Marguerite said.

She set a paper shopping bag down on the bed. It had a number of items that I thought I would need to effect my escape. It contained a pale blue t-shirt, nearly worn-out jeans, and a trucker hat. It also contained an electric beard trimmer. Between the change of clothes, hiding my hair under a hat and a serious trim to my beard, my physical appearance should be sufficiently altered.

I didn't know how long I would have that morning. I didn't know how shaken Shelia might be by our confrontation. I had to assume that even if she weren't right there, She might still tracking me somehow.

Besides altering my appearance. I needed a decoy. That's where I needed Marguerite's help specifically. Marguerite and I implemented our little plan quickly. It involved something I really dislike doing. Some might consider it a roundabout form of necromancy.[8] Something I didn't even come within spitting distance of normally. But first the easy part.

---

[8] Necromancy isn't just raising Zombies you know. It's any calling up or exploiting of the dead. I don't even like Ouija Boards.

Marguerite pulled the curtain around my bed. I began a quick low chant. I pulled in the energies again. This time I used them to fabricate a physical form. Actually, it wasn't that dissimilar from a ghostly manifestation. Ghosts can tap the same energies to give themselves rudimentary, temporary bodies. Here, I was the one creating a short-term shell. I pieced together just enough of a form to sit up in the bed, perhaps talk. Of course, that would be after Marguerite's contribution. At that moment it looked like a plastic mannequin. Even when I was done with the early phase, it would never pass a close examination by a doctor, however. It would lack a heartbeat. Heck, it would only be room temperature.

There was one ingredient that I couldn't give it. perhaps I should say that I refused to give it. There are certain Magi (or wizards, witches, what have you) who would have simply bound a spirit of one sort or another into it. This is something I'm unwilling to do. I'd either have to coerce it or convince it to do the job of animating the shell. I won't coerce. I oppose slavery. Be it person, god, or woodland sprite. So that would leave convincing something, most likely a Fairy or a ghost. I'm kind of out of luck convincing either of them for various reasons.

As for your basic faerie types, it's a trust issue really. I don't trust them to do it and they aren't likely to do it without making some kind of deal. Deals that I'm not willing to risk. I won't go into it here.[9] As for ghosts, Ghosts don't seem to like me much. I honestly don't know why. So they're unlikely to help me even if I would ask.

One of the signs of a good medium is that they make the dead feel at ease. This is why I desperately needed Marguerite's help to make this work.

I finished crafting my doppelganger. I stood over the vague form and used the beard trimmer to take off most of my beard. The whiskers fell onto the doppelganger like black snow. The form absorbed the hair and as more hair fell into it the doppelganger began to live up to its name. Soon it looked enough like me to pass all but the closest inspection.

I looked over at Marguerite and saw that she was not alone. Standing next to the bed was the spirit of a young man dressed in jeans patched with red and green fabrics, cowboy boots, a Stetson hat, and a shirt that may have just as well had "1969" written on it in bold, underlined print.

---

[9]   Correspondence Course 313f *Perils and Pitfalls of Fay Negotiations*

I don't know what killed our hippie cowboy friend, unless it was his wardrobe.

Marguerite smiled as she made the introductions "Milo, this is Ted. Ted has agreed to animate your friend there for a while."

"Ted, hello, " I waved a hand in greeting.

"What's the matter?" Ted said, "Can't shake my hand? I tell you if I didn't like Miss Margie here . . ."

"Enough Ted. He's my friend and we both appreciate your help."

I mentioned that good mediums seem to have a knack for putting the dead at ease. Marguerite does that very well. Whereas I seem to piss them off just as easily.

So with a little bit of griping, Ted climbed inside the shell bringing it to "life." I put on the change of clothes Marguerite brought me. Then I pulled out the final item for my disguise, a bacon double cheese breakfast burrito.

My life is dangerous enough so I like to play it safe when I can. Safer, at any rate, there is a lot of fat and cholesterol in one of those things after all. Remember what I said about fast food dampening things down. If I was going to sneak out of here I was going to have to stay as low on the radar as possible.

The "don't mind me" effect wasn't likely to work on Shelia. In fact, it might draw her attention. Any significant use of power would. I assumed that she picked up on the energy used to construct my double. I didn't think she'd know exactly what I was up to. Her uncertainty might buy us some time. I hoped that would open a window of opportunity for my escape.

Shelia should be looking for me to use that energy in my escape somehow. She'd be looking for me (or anyone else) carting around a boatload of extra "mojo." With a breakfast burrito lump sitting in my stomach I should look like almost everybody else astrally. If I tried to walk out as I normally am, she'd spot me trying to leave the hospital and drag me back to my room one way or another.

As far as the law was concerned my late wife and I are still married, so she still has certain rights as my next of kin. Such as getting me committed if she could convince a doctor I was a danger to myself. Dr. McBride was already more than half sold on that idea. I doubted Shelia would even need to resort to whatever mind magics she slings around.

I pulled the trucker cap low over my eyes and left my room with a determined slouch. Sheila didn't immediately pounce on me. I didn't even see her waiting around. That was good. I made it into the elevator. I was confident that if I could sneak out I could sneak back inside in time for whatever tests Dr. McBride had dreamed up.

If this worked, I'd have Dr. McBride off my case. Dr. McBride just wants to do her job and make sure her patient is well as much as she'd like to satisfy her curiosity.

Between Shelia and Dr. McBride, I could be in a lot of trouble. Sure it would get sorted out eventually but I was already running behind. I needed to get a clean bill of health from McBride as quickly as possible.

Ted and Marguerite running interference should buy me enough time for me to get out and back before I was missed.

I exited the hospital by a back service entrance. I knew my way around a bit from the times I had to temp to make ends meet. I crossed the employee parking lot into the visitor parking deck. I did a quick sweep around the first two levels just to make sure, but I was fairly certain I would find my car parked on the third level, the top.

I emerged onto the top deck. And there it was, my car, sunning itself. It is an old Butterscotch yellow 1983 Volvo 244 DL. I have named it Azgard, an intentional misspelling of the Home of the Gods in Norse mythology. It seemed fitting. Volvos have Nordic origins and prodigious appetites after all. I was glad to see it.

"Just how did the car get there?" you may ask or "He was on foot when he collapsed."

True enough. I had left my car back at my apartment when I had ventured out to meet Pandora. I was going to go back for it but the man following her presented an immediate opportunity. But then you know all this.

"Perhaps Marguerite brought it for him," some might say.

"Must be magic, after all, he is a Magician," chime in others

Truthfully, I don't really know how it gets around without me. I have my theories. It may be magic, most likely it is. Just not mine. All I know is that about ninety percent of the time that I really need my car, if I look around hard enough, it's there nearby. My car is full of surprises and, according to some, sharp edges.

The parking deck itself is built into a hillside so the top level is also an entrance. This made getting on with my journey easy enough. I know this town fairly well. Having once worked in pizza delivery and as seasonal help for the local water dept. I've been all over this burg at all times of the day.

Fortunately, my little burg is only about 60, 000 people when the universities are in session. Congestion isn't as bad as in many other cities except at certain times of the day. Even that is only on the main streets through town. A knowledgeable driver could drive from one end of the town to other quickly if needs be. And my needs have been.

I slipped easily from the main roads to side streets and alleyways then back again. Cutting my travel time to the DMV by half or more.

Investigators in fiction always seem to have contacts either with the police or in the DMV to run plates for them. Either that or they are, or know, someone who can hack the computer files to get the information.

Not me. I have to do this the hard way. I was far enough from the hospital that I felt I could use my "don't mind me" effect without drawing Shelia's attention.

It was simple enough to walk into DMV and back to where I could find a computer. Now I just had to wait. It shouldn't be too long.

I stood leaning against a wall my hat pulled down and turned away from the security cameras as much as possible. I didn't want trouble later if I could avoid it.

I dread the day when security systems become completely automated. My invisibility works even through video cameras, so long as each time, a human mind is looking I'm maintaining the effect. When computers become sophisticated enough to replace human observers completely, this isn't going to work anymore.

So while I'm there, anyone looking at me on a screen isn't going to notice anything. Later, if they have a need to review the footage I'll be clearly visible. That's when it'd be good to be unrecognizable. So I stood there playing Mr. Unnoticeable, waiting for someone to get bored.

I didn't have to wait as long as a feared. About half an hour later I sensed the necessary distraction. One of the long-time employees of the DMV was having a problem with a customer. Ms. Leshandra White was explaining to a young, wealthy, and entitled, James Michael Carlson all the information he should have filled in on his form. She did this a hundred times a day. She could do it in her sleep. In fact, she nearly was.

This left her open to a suggestion from me. I gave the subtle suggestion that she should run a particular license plate. It was the plate from the car just outside the Cayo Hueso where I met Koenig's Delivery Woman.

Even I could tell the plate belonged to a rental company. But which one did it belong to? Was it local? Leshandra didn't even break her stride. She never even looked over at the screen. Literally, her left hand did not know what her right hand was doing. She finished explaining the form so even a kid like Jimmy could understand it. By the time she pulled up the proper screen for her next customer. I was on my way outside.

I was less than happy. The plate was registered to a rental company. While it was here in the Shenandoah Valley, it wasn't in this town. It was in Winchester, about a forty-minute drive north. I was going to check back at the hospital. Hopefully, I would be able to talk my way out once the tests were done.

I needn't have worried. My plan had made sure I wouldn't have to worry about McBride keeping me another night or my late wife convincing her I needed an extended psychiatric evaluation. It also made sure I wouldn't have to file my taxes again, or access my bank account, or hold property.

I was slipping back up to my hospital room when I met Marguerite at the elevators downstairs. She is one of the few people in town that I know can pierce my "cloak." She is also the only one I trust.

"Don't bother" She said when I continued toward the elevator. She took my arm and steered me back the way we came.

Before I could ask she continued, "Look, I'm hungry, I tell it to you over lunch." She didn't even slow down as she said this. She was certainly making a beeline out of the hospital.

"What's up?" My cloak dropped as soon as we're back outside the building.

"Well," she began, still not breaking her stride. She must be really upset. I've never seen Marguerite rush for anything. She always said haste makes one seem unprepared and that just wouldn't do for a "psychic."

We got to her car. An old 70s tan Le Baron she had inherited from her grandmother. Once she was inside she relaxed. I sat in the passenger seat next to her

"So do you want the quick and dirty or the slow sexy build-up?" Her humor was returning, a good sign I thought. I had assumed by then that my little ploy had failed. I just hoped the fallout wouldn't be too severe.

"Quick and dirty, baby," I said trying to match her humor.

"Okay. You're dead."

Chapter Thirteen

"Y**OU'RE DEAD." I'VE HEARD** those words before, usually in one of two ways. The first way was in some hypothetical sense. My mentor had been fond of punctuating his instructions with them. Such as "If you fail to follow step three precisely, well then, you're dead."

I had found that my path wasn't as exacting as he made it out to be. But then Magi have a tendency to get caught up in the rush of power. I think it was his hedge against overconfidence. Of course, right now I was wishing I had listened a little more closely.

The other way I have heard "you're dead." has been in the overly optimistic, threatening manner. Of course, I can only say "overly" because they've all been wrong so far.

Enough bragging. I was in serious trouble. Marguerite continued the story of my demise.

"Your plan was working great. Ted was animating the shell perfectly. He gave it a pulse, remembered to breathe, everything. The nurse who came in to take your vitals didn't find anything odd. He had a conversation with your doctor. The old boy even came this close to convincing her it was a blood sugar problem and was in the process of scheduling a Glucose tolerance test for next week. Then your dead wife showed up.

"Man does she have some whammy. Once she walked in, she hit McBride right between the eyes, metaphysically speaking. She started talking in some sort of sing-song voice and the next thing I knew Dr. Macbride was carting Ted off for a complete MRI work-up"

It was one of the things I was worried about. I didn't think my shell could stand up to a serious scan like an MRI. An X-ray might not reveal the truth. A blood sample would most likely evaporate soon after being drawn, that is if I even got the blood right. A test that could really map out the internal structure was likely to find some anomaly. Any anomaly would have kept me here longer. Though Marguerite had already told me the punch line. So I was momentarily more concerned with my late wife's mesmerizing abilities.

"She got the test set up fast. I thought that took a lot more time than that."

"So did I," Marguerite said, "but that's what happened. Whatever her whammy is, it's good."

"So what was Sheila using, some kind of hypnotism?"

"Can't tell you. All I know is that she didn't even have to make eye contact. It seemed to be all about the voice."

"Were you affected?" I was worried and curious.

"No, I think she may need to be aware of her targets. I had slipped into the bathroom earlier so Ted could talk to McBride Privately"

"So what happened? How exactly did I 'die'?"

"Ted got taken to the imaging room., strapped in, and slid into the chamber. Except poor Ted is claustrophobic. He tried, bless his soul. but it was too much for him and he split."

I held up my hand. I knew the rest. Without Ted to counterfeit life for the shell, it would shut back down. To a person who was only looking at the physical, it would appear as though I died. At least until someone cut it open. Then the true nature of the shell would be apparent. An autopsy would find all the mistakes I must have made in constructing the form. I'm no doctor of medicine; it's unlikely that I'd recall every detail. Plus I'd be lucky if the blood wasn't blue marshmallow fluff.

Still, that was the least of my concerns. "How long ago did all this happen? Have they started the autopsy?"

"About an hour ago. And no. Why?"

I breathed a sigh of relief. "Well if we can stall the autopsy long enough the shell will dissipate on its own." I wasn't sure exactly how that would help things but a disappearing body would add some confusion that I may be able to take advantage of later.

Marguerite started laughing. Her face lit up like a ray of sunlight from behind a cloud. Her eyes positively shone. Ah . . . sorry got distracted for a moment.

"What's so funny?"

"Your late wife..." Marguerite finally got out, "She's using that whammy of hers to prevent the autopsy. She must think that this is some trick of yours and that she can wait you out. I think she's actually sitting vigil with the body."

"Okay, Ironic," I thought, "but not that funny," and said so to Marguerite.

"Don't you remember how I said your greatest asset was your 'fool's luck'?"

Ah yes, that's me, the mind of magi, soul of a jester with the "lucky" karma to match. That was kind of a sore spot with me. "Magus", "Magi" these words basically carry the idea of wisdom and knowledge and all that Jazz. Yet I'm a "Fool" So being a wise fool just seems so . . . sophomoric.

Back to my death. All in all, it was short-term good news. I was free from the hospital. At least until the next time I got stupid and ended up here. Plus, it would keep Sheila occupied watching my "corpse" waiting for it to wake up. Feigning death is a fairly standard trick. That kind of bodily control is an early curriculum in a number of paths. I'm sure it's the idea that would occur to her first. If I'm right, she won't let my body out of her sight until it dissipates. Faking my death to escape may not be a bad plan. After all, if a body goes missing from the morgue nobody expects *that* much of an inside job.

Let her wait for me to wake up. It just means I can get back to Pandora's case.

Chapter Fourteen

I GAVE MARGUERITE A RIDE back to her place and asked for a rain check on lunch. I didn't really want to see her go. I think she may have wanted to come along as well. She said she only had few readings that day. She seemed perfectly willing to rearrange them. I'd like to think she was enjoying my company. I fear that's just wishful thinking on my part. I've always enjoyed her company.

I imagine she was just enjoying a break from her routine. Perhaps it was the excitement of playing detective. I didn't want to disillusion her with the actual tedium of investigation. I liked that she thought I had an exciting career.

I made the effort to switch gears mentally. I had more immediate concerns than the nature of my friendship with Marguerite. I had already missed my appointment with Pandora. I swung by the coffee shop anyway. I hoped she took my absence as a sign of being on the case rather than neglecting it. I didn't want her to feel this was another case of broken promises.

I thought about calling her but figured it was too risky. She might be with a client or even Koenig herself. I decided to press on to Winchester. Then maybe I'd have something substantial to report when we could speak again.

It only took me about forty-five minutes to get to my destination. Just a short jump up I-81 and I was pulling into the Maximilian Rental Agency.

It was a local business, not part of the chain. They were a specialty rental agency. They rented cars primarily for occasions rather than mere transportation. They had limos for proms and weddings, Luxury town cars, and classic sports cars for any occasion where you might wish to make an impression.

I parked in the lot used for agency cars. My dented, early '80s Volvo looked considerably out of place next to a Jag and an Aston Martin. There was a mechanic who came out. For a second he looked like he was going to give me hard time about parking there.

Now I've given a brief description of myself earlier. I'm on the shorter side of average but stocky with very broad shoulders, a corona of long, dark hair, and a bushy yet somehow still straggly beard. The fact that my beard had just recently been trimmed only gave my face a harder, leaner look.

To that description, I should add that I have an unsettling combination of a fierce gaze and a whimsically mysterious grin. Throw all that in an outback duster and I generally get as much latitude as I need.

Of course, it doesn't hurt that when I need to, I can push my "aura." When I do that it's like my presence is tapping you on the nose from across the room. For a guy who dislikes bullies, I am not above throwing my weight around.

After smiling down the service tech. I made my way into the office. There are times when the seemingly random coincidences that haunt me seem beneficent, other times merely ironic. Of course, there are times when they're just plain cruel.

I wasn't sure how to take what I found. Pandora was standing at the rental counter talking to the woman behind it. A quick peek with the wheel O' Sight told me that the woman behind the counter was the same woman who was the messenger from two nights before.

I may as well have just followed Pandora. I hadn't because I was trying to minimize the danger of the two of us being linked. I thought other leads might be more beneficial. Koenig may know I was trying to find her Jekyll but she might not know why.

If she did, she'd have disappeared Pandora as well as her brother. I was sure of that. Having a rep as a meddling magus was helpful for once. Koenig probably thought I was just do-gooding in general.

At least this must be the right track. I just hoped this intersection didn't lead to a deadly collision.

The woman behind the counter looked up as I came in. She recognized me. She gave a quick glance at Pandora. That look must have conveyed reams of information. Pandora immediately excused herself and started to head back outside. I made sure to watch her only in my peripheral vision. I didn't want anyone to realize that there could be a connection between us.

Pandora, to her credit, did the same. I doubt she even glanced back as she closed the door behind her.

I smiled at the woman behind the counter. Her name tag said she was Roberta Driscoll. She was about 38. Although she was only of medium height, without her disguise seemed taller. She had a slender build. If she were a taller woman, she would have been called willowy. Everything about her said slender, graceful curves. Her dark brown hair waved as it tumbled about her face to her shoulders. The curve of her nose, the arch of her eyebrows . . .

You may have guessed by now that I'm a bit on the lonely side. These moments when I seem to go off into a daydream, that really only happens as I relate these moments. At the time, my attention was much more occupied with the small caliber weapon she had pointed in my face.

"Look," she said, "I'm just the messenger. It's not going to do you any good to hurt me. So don't you so much as mumble or wave a pinky. I've heard about you."

She looked really nervous. I wondered as to what kind of monster Koenig had painted me. As an up-and-comer wannabe crime boss, she was used to playing different factions against each other. I could easily believe she would tell her messenger that I was a lot more fearsome than I was. Of course, Roberta had also seen me letting a young thug kick my ass only a few nights ago, so how tough could she think I was?

"Look, I'm harmless," I said. "I'm just looking for some information, just like the other night."

At this point, she cocked the gun and pointed right at my forehead.

"Yea and I also saw that little fight outside. What were you doing? Toying with that kid? I saw enough to recognize him on the news the next evening. I'm not going to let you cut out my heart. "

I've got to start watching newscasts. I can't get all my info from the cartoon network. I had to assume the young man's murder wasn't a coincidence, not with his heart removed. That was Shelia's specialty.

I took a deep breath. This woman was very frightened, apparently not without cause. I didn't think that protestations of innocence would help much. She was convinced I was a killer.

Unfortunately, help was about to arrive. The door behind me opened. Roberta looked at the person entering. She seemed very surprised.

"Jackie?" She said.

I turned my head slightly to look at whoever was entering. I kept an eye on Roberta's gun. As soon as I saw who it was I turned completely, not caring about Roberta's gun. It was Sheila.

"Don't worry Roberta. He won't hurt you." Sheila glided across the space from the door to right next to me. Roberta seemed to relax marginally.

I tensed up. Sheila was uncomfortably close. An unwelcome reminder of how she once was more than welcome in my personal space.

Sheila kept speaking in a soothing tone. "Obviously he's made the connection between the rental service and our employer." Sheila had said she had only recently started working for Koenig, had she been lying?

"But there's nothing here in writing or on the computers that will take that link any farther. Except you and me. Now I'm not going to tell him anything . . ."

I had a bad feeling about where this conversation was going. I think Roberta did as well. Her gun started to swing over toward Sheila.

"So do something about him," Roberta said, "Koenig won't mind. I'm sure." The gun pointed directly at Sheila for a moment then right back at me.

"She wouldn't. I would," Sheila said. Her hand blurred into near invisibility. I heard the nauseating crack of bone, almost felt the tearing of flesh. What I saw next was one of the few non-Sight images that I will never be able to forget. The visceral clash of responses it evoked in me still makes me shudder.

Sheila had turned to look back at me. She was sitting up on the counter. Half reclined in that quasi-subtle, provocative position that magazine models use to sell cars. Her hair was only mildly mussed by the exertion, adding to its powerful allure. The tailoring of her business suit accentuated the inviting curve of her pose. The very top button of her blouse had come undone. Not exposing much actual flesh but giving a tantalizing suggestion.

Her golden eyes held a gleam of mischief, not malice. Her whole posture was one sweeping curve of invitation that guided my eyes into horror.

Her little tableau seemed calculated to direct my attention over her whole body towards her left hand. In it, she was holding Roberta's heart, casually, negligently. Blood ran down her hand, clinging to it for a moment before dripping onto the counter, the floor, and the rest of Roberta.

Roberta didn't even have time to get the shot off. I doubt it would have mattered.

Sheila looked down at the heart in her hand, then directly at me. "There are things we need to discuss but perhaps not now. Since you probably don't want to join me in my snack or even stay to watch, you should tottle off.

"Don't worry. I'll find you again. Whatever little trick you played at the hospital won't work a second time, but feel free to try."

She appeared to mull something over in her mind. Going over a mental to-do list maybe. I had seen her do just that hundreds of times in our marriage, another thing that hadn't changed.

"So, I'll see you about seven. Pick a nice spot. Somewhere private but where you'll feel safe."

She turned her attention back to the heart in her hand. I was out that door before I could see her take a bite.

Chapter Fifteen

I WAS BARRELING DOWN I-81 before I could get my breathing under control. I raced past a state police cruiser who ignored me. That was a function of the car I believe. I'm certain I was breaking the speed limit if not the sound barrier.

It suddenly occurred to me to be worried about Pandora. I didn't have a way to get in contact with her. We only met at our daily rendezvous to discuss the case. Sometimes I really hate the cloak and dagger stuff. Give me a simple haunting any day.

I took a deep breath and released it slowly. I would just have to have faith that Pandora had gotten herself out before Sheila had shown up. I prayed that Sheila would have no reason to pursue the girl.

Looking at the dashboard clock, I saw that I was going to have a few hours before Sheila came looking for me again. I decided I might as well stop by my apartment first. When I got there, I found that the super had let himself in and had started to take inventory.

"Mr. Johanson?" I said. He dropped the tablet he was writing on. He turned toward me with a look of real surprise on his face. His expression changed quickly to one of unmitigated relief.

"Oh thank God. I had heard you were dead. "After a quiet moment where he gathered his breath, he was back to his usual mile-a-minute talking. "So what happened? Why'd someone think you were dead? Was that really your ex-wife? She was kinda cute. How'd you ever snag her? Oh, I was just making a list for your next of kin when they came. Damn, boy, but you got a lot of useless stuff."

He paused at this point as if I should suddenly comment. So I tried, "Yea, my wife actually made me get a useless items box and I'd . . ."

"Glad to see you're not dead. I'd miss a good tenant like you." He gave my arm a little punch, more of a closed fist pat than a strike. "Never get this pace rented again. You know no one ever kept this place longer than three months before you. Did you know that?"

Not only did I know that, I knew why. But Johanson isn't a believer in anything too unusual so I kept that knowledge to myself.

Once Mr. Johanson had satisfied himself that everything was okay, he left. I was almost alone in my apartment. Actually, for once, I didn't feel the presence of my spirit roommate. It was almostdisconcerting.

I would puzzle it out later. Right now I was going to shower. After seeing what I had just seen, I needed a cleansing. A good shower could do that physically and spiritually.

Although I didn't rush through my shower I also didn't dawdle. Soon I was wrapping a towel around my shoulders as I went into my bedroom.

I was startled by what I saw. Someone had laid out a fresh set of clothes for me. Although I'm used to my friendly neighborhood poltergeist moving my stuff, it's never played valet before.

Sure, sometimes it moves my stuff in a useful way. For example, when I'm about to be descended upon by my upstairs neighbor, Mrs. Beaumont. She's a kind, elderly woman with way too much time on her hands. She also has an obsessive need to fix me up with her granddaughter, or her grandniece, or her bridge partner's nephew's co-worker's cousin's daughter. Whenever she goes into fix-up mode she usually drops by with some little knick-knack or souvenir, an excuse to try to talk up her candidate.

For reasons of its own, my poltergeist will put out every little knickknack she's given me over the last three years. This is handy in two ways. First I get about a five-minute warning if I'm alert enough. The second is she never has to ask, "Oh, where is the palm springs snow globe? didn't you like it?"

Once she's gone away the knick-knacks go away. Sometimes I think the ghost likes to redecorate. Not that the poltergeist redecorates well, mind you. But I never get bored with it. I don't have time.

My ghost mostly seems to be involved in a long-term, ongoing prank of some kind. Occasionally it seems to anticipate things that could actually benefit me. I find that odd mostly because that might mean it doesn't hate me the way every other ghost I've met does.

So that's why I was alarmed that along with the clothes, my charcoal gray business suit, my duster, and my hat. It had laid out a fairly serious handgun and a couple of clips of extra ammunition. I didn't even know I owed a gun

I dressed quickly. I wasn't sure what to do about the gun. Presumably, it belonged to a previous tenant of the apartment. It looked powerful, but I don't know how to use one. I didn't have a permit to carry one. My understanding of gun safety is "If you don't know what you're doing, you have no business carrying a gun." And that described me.

I looked up into the air around me generally.

"Thanks, but I don't use guns," I said

I left the gun there and turned to go. At this point, I tripped over the gun safe.

"Ah, now this may be useful." I thought. I could lock the gun up while I carried it. This seemed a good enough compromise. Perhaps I'd figure out why the ghost wanted me to have it along the way.

I lugged the damn safe out to my car. Even a portable gun safe is still pretty hefty. I was sure I didn't know the proper way to transport the weapon entirely legally. In my defense, I had just found out I was a gun owner.

I don't like guns. Perhaps I should say I'm uncomfortable with them. Not really for moral or political reasons. There are a number of reasons. The first is simple unfamiliarity. I never had a need for one. I didn't hunt and once I started on my current path I certainly didn't need one for protection. This leads me to the second reason. The things can be quite lethal even in untrained hands; unfortunately, all too often they are lethal to those untrained hands.

Compare that to what I can do. Sure I can whip of an effect that has deadly consequences. That ability didn't spring up overnight. My control over it has to be almost absolute in order for it to work at all.

Consequently, there are damn few who could take my magic and use it against me. The same simply isn't true of a physical weapon. When I carry a gun, I get the feeling I'm doing favors for my enemy.

Even though the coffee shop is just across the square from my building, I took my car. The square is in The middle of town, where routes 11 and 33 meet. Azgard was now parked on the street near the coffee shop's door. I strolled by trying to "causally" glance in. I was trying to see if Pandora was there. It was the last place we met. She might try to find me there again.

I didn't see her in there. I took the risk of looping around the square again and then went inside. It's times like these I wish I drank coffee. Instead, I went up to the counter and ordered an Italian soda. A bit pretentious maybe but man they're good. Torani mint and some cream mixed in a carbonated water base, I only wished I could make an elixir as reviving

I sat down at a table to wait for it. I was pondering my next move when Pandora walked in. I didn't need the sight to see she was shaken to the core.

She ordered at the counter then sat down at the table just behind mine. We were now sitting with our backs to each other but we could hear each other quite easily. Certainly, a trained eye wouldn't have been fooled by this ruse. I doubt that someone who was even merely suspicious would have dismissed it as coincidence. Hopefully, we weren't being watched at all.

She spoke quietly but clearly, "Did you really do it?"

"No, I haven't found your brother yet, I didn't get to question Ms. Driscoll"

There was a gasp and then a pause. "No, I meant about Roberta." Her voice was tightened by fear. It only came out as a strained whisper, not clear like before. "Did you... were you the one . . .?"

I sighed I tried to sound calm. But to be honest thinking about what happened to Roberta still made my flesh crawl.

"I didn't hurt her. I wouldn't. I don't kill people. In a very real way, I can't."

"Really?" Pandora didn't sound at all reassured, more suspicious with a tiny bit of surprise thrown in.

"I thought that you defended people against the dark forces of the world."

"I try to." Was she saying that Roberta was one of the dark forces?

"Who else would have killed her, then?" Pandora asked

I wasn't sure how to say what had really happened. So I lied.

"Koenig has hired herself a monster, an honest to God supernatural entity. It wanted to make sure I couldn't track my leads any further than I had."

I lied. I lied by omission. Granted everything said was absolutely true. Somehow I couldn't tell her the monster in question was my late wife.

Pandora is a bright girl. She knew the implications.

"So it must not know about you trying to find my brother for me or I'd be dead already . . . Still, it's only a matter of time, I guess," suddenly she paused, a suspicious edge crept into her voice. "So why kill her and not you?"

"Honestly, I'm not sure," I said. That was true enough. "It may just be I'm harder kill." Still true. "Perhaps it enjoys toying with me as an adversary." That was was possible even plausible.

"Maybe she won't kill me for old times sake," I think quietly, at the back of my mind, trying not to hear myself.

Pandora spoke up, forcing me to focus on the now again. "So what kind of monster is it?"

"It looks like a very pretty woman with dark, curly hair and golden eyes."

Pandora gasped, I think. Perhaps she just exhaled. Pandora stayed pretty cool most of the time.

"I've seen her," she said. "About two days ago, she came in with Koenig to see Roberta at the rental service."

That reminded me. "What can you tell me about that. I didn't see anything that showed that Koenig owned it. Maybe it's an alias I could track."

"Unlikely, Roberta's Aunt owns the place and Roberta ran it for her. Koenig made some kind of deal to use the place. It's pretty simple. Koenig gives a client that phone number. Koenig's client calls and rents a car giving a code word. Then Roberta calls one of us in the stable and we get delivered with the car."

She said this so matter-of-factly it was heart-breaking. It was like a highly sharpened knife cutting deeply before you even felt it. I changed the subject to matters more immediate. I could see the two of us reflected in the front window of the coffee shop. We were sitting back to back at adjacent tables.

"You're right. It's only a matter of time before someone makes the connection. I think we need to get you someplace safe. I know a place where we can go that we won't be disturbed."

In the front window reflection, I saw her stiffen up for an instant and then sag again. Then she just sat there for a moment and watched the steam rise from her coffee.

"Okay," she said her voice came back small and almost child-like, as ifshe were afraid of something about to happen . . . No, it was more like she was afraid that something had just happened.

It troubled me, but I also knew that I had to get her someplace safe (or safer anyway) and away from me well before seven o'clock. I couldn't risk Sheila seeing us in the same place again

I never had to worry about Shelia catching me with a girl half my age when she was alive. At the moment, however, that irony was lost on me

I was at a loss for what to do. The only thing I could think to do was call on Pastor Geoff. I wondered if I could make it to Pastor Geoff's church and be gone far enough that Sheila wouldn't make the connection.

It was getting later and something told me it wouldn't be easy to convince Pandora to go to a church for help.

"I know someone who could give you some sanctuary." It seemed as though her ears had perked up. That whatever fear had struck her may be passing. "He's at a church over on . . ."

I didn't finish the statement. Pandora's deep freeze had returned. I was starting to get the picture.

"You've had a bad experience with a priest or a minister haven't you? Someone who took you where you 'wouldn't be disturbed.'"

Pandora snorted out a laugh. "Let's just say The Right Reverends Carl and Janet Pinkerton ran a very cozy Sunday School. You may have heard about it a few years ago. It was one of the few times our parents climbed out of the bottle to take notice. Anyway, Pastor Carl got 30 years. Poor pastor Janet was left to pick up the pieces. And carry on the 'Work', I'm sure."

There was bitterness in the way she said "work" that you could almost taste.

"You mean . . ."

"Yeah, it seems people have trouble spotting a predator behind a pretty face and a pair of breasts."

"So a church is not going to make you feel safe."

There was a long pause then simply "ah, . . . no."

I needed her to feel safe not just to be hidden. Some monsters could home in on fear. Was Sheila one of those monsters? Was she even going to be looking for Pandora? There were too many questions, too many unnecessary chances. I didn't really know what to do. I prayed for an idea, for an inkling of an idea, for the echo of an inkling of an idea.

Then it came to me. Or should I say they came to me? And a real Godsend they were.

Chapter Sixteen

FOUR YOUNG MEN ENTERED the coffee shop. They were the four youths who had unknowingly protected Pandora the day before. Their names were Hector, Ty, Ramón and James. They each wore an expression of mild distress. For a second they stood just inside the door and looked about the coffee shop. Each one's gaze took in a different portion of the shop.

Ramón caught sight of me. Without any visible signal between them, they all turned and looked at me. They headed over to my table and sat down. Hector had to grab a chair from neighboring table. The other three moved in sync to open up a space for him so smoothly I felt I was watching some odd, absurdist ballet.

I looked around the table and regarded each of them for a moment. Because of yesterday's incident I already knew a little bit about each of them.

Ramon, tall and muscular, sat to my left. His family had emigrated from El Salvador in the early Nineteen-Eighties, when the death squads were going strong. His family still sent money to relatives in the city of San Salvador. Ramon had always been athletic and excelled at the more solitary sports like track and field.

He had straight black hair that fell to chin length. He was clean-shaven. This added to his very youthful appearance. If it weren't for his height he would easily be mistaken for a much younger person. He wore dark blue jeans and a plain, red T-shirt.

Next to him was Tyrell, Ty for short. Ty was still grieving the death of his father a few years ago. Ty expected that in a few years he would take on the role his father had enjoyed in the community. Though still active in advocating for social justice, particularly around race issues, Ty felt that his youth prevented him from having the gravitas that had allowed his father to be a leader.

This didn't dampen his social impulse though. He was always gregarious and had a knack for putting people at ease. He was of medium height and lean build. Ty kept his scalp clean-shaven and wore a very neatly trimmed Van Dyke. He wore a red dress-shirt with navy blue trousers. He was also the only one of the guys to wear a tie.

"Man, are we glad to see you . . .," said Hector. He was seated next to Ty. Hector's family had been in the Americas since the founding of St. Augustine, Florida in 1565. Unlike Ty, he was rabidly apolitical. Unless you made the mistake of calling him Mexican, that is. The other sure way to get his goat is to try to imply that your family has been here longer than his. So take that you mayflower descendants.

Hector was the most bookish of the four. He was widely read and had a gift for manipulating numbers. He was slight of build and a few inches under average height. His hair was the fairest of the guys. This meant it was dark brown. He wore it short and business like. He was also the only one of the guys to wear corrective lenses.

He was wearing black jeans and red polo pullover.

". . . We heard you were dead," James continued Hector statement, "That scary chick said she was your wife." James was almost a mystery. He was of mixed ancestry, Scottish and Chinese. Or more accurately he was Scottish and Chinese-American. James's Chinese ancestors had come into the united state in the 1800's as part of the coolie work force. James's father had been born and raised in Edinburgh.

If anyone acted as the sense of humor for the group it was James. He was arguably the smartest but worst student of the group. He was a fan of the clever solution and the "bad plan." His gift for getting out of trouble had developed to match his gift for finding it.

James had unruly black hair, grown long on the top and shaved on the sides. He wore a black tracksuit with blue piping and a black t-shirt. The T-shirt read, "I sold my soul and all I got was this lousy t-shirt" in red letters.

All four young men had shuddered at the mention of Sheila. Interesting, her "mojo" must have limited effect on them She can be quite appealing when she wishes to be. I certainly felt a tug when we were together, despite our recent history.

Ty spoke up. He had the air of the born diplomat about him, "Mr. Gives, while we are extremely glad to find that you are well, we have come to you for reasons that are less than altruistic." He paused to make sure that he had my attention. He took off his sunglasses then looked directly into my eyes. He lowered his voice to just above a whisper. His manner conveyed both an impression of earnestness and conspiratorial discretion.

"The reason we have been looking for you is simply this. We seek answers to explain our new found 'condition', " He paused again. When I didn't immediately jump in he continued. "Ever since the altercation yesterday afternoon we have been experiencing something that is, well, frighteningly unusual."

Now I started to say something. I'm not really sure what. I didn't get a chance to say much of anything past "Um, Ah" before Hector interrupted me.

"We know you did something to help us after that guy handed us our asses. We just want to know what."

Ty took back the reins of the conversation. "Certainly we are grateful. I believe that you somehow saved us from being greatly, possibly permanently, incapacitated by our assailant. We would be even more grateful if you could offer us some explanation. We feel certain that you are aware of what is going on with us."

They all nodded in unison. Ty was right. I knew what was going on with them. I felt guilty about it. If I was right it wasn't something I could undo. If I were at all lucky they wouldn't want me to, once they got used to the idea.

Now here is where I do something truly shitty.

"Yes, gentlemen, I think I can help you and I will as soon as I can. However, (they cringed at the however) literally at this moment, I need assistance to help a young woman who is in immediate danger. I think you are just the help I was looking for. "

As you can guess, this got suspicious looks from the young men and an alarmed response from Pandora.

"The young woman behind me is in desperate need of sanctuary."

I could feel Pandora tense up, getting ready to bolt. Handing her off to strangers must have pushed every button she had. Again I feel shitty about pushing this next part. My only comfort is that I was telling the truth when I did it.

"Pandora," I said still looking at the guys clustered around my table, "If you can trust me enough to go with these young gentlemen, I can continue looking for you brother without worrying that Koenig will find you. These men may have saved my life last night, I am certain that they are worthy of your trust."

"Promise?" she said.

I almost said "yes." Fortunately I remembered.

"I won't promise you anything. However I would trust these guys with my life, in fact, I did. They are the ones who got me to the hospital last night and then made sure I was treated besides I have answers they need. You heard that. They only get what they want by making sure you're safe."

Obviously that was for the guys' benefit as well as Pandora's.

I could see from the guys' reactions that they didn't need the promise of an answer to help out Pandora. Just as I saw the day before, they were four, decent, young men just waiting for an occasion to which they can rise.

"Okay, Ty, I want you and Hector to escort Pandora to Bethany United Church of Christ. She won't feel safe in the church so I want you to stay with her at all times. Talk to Geoff (I intentionally left off the "pastor" part. it just seemed prudent) he's my contact there. Make sure he knows to get her to another safe place. I want you and Hector to stay with her until I contact you again in the morning.

"Ramón and James, I want you to shadow the three of them. Keep an eye out for anyone else following them, in case there is trouble. That new 'oddness' you've mentioned, I believe can actually help you, if you allow it. It can be quite an asset if you just trust it."

It took a bit more explaining and encouraging to get the whole thing on the move but in the end the five of them left, hopefully out of danger.

So why do I feel dirty? Well on one day I led the four young men into a fight. While I hadn't intended that to happened, I still bear the responsibility. What's more, that fight almost killed them. It would have crippled them.

Then I accidentally, irrevocably altered the paths of their lives. I altered them without their knowledge or consent and presumably against their will. Even if they eventually come to value the change, that doesn't abate my culpability. Now this is the really lowdown part. The very next day, when they come looking for help, I further exploit the situation for my own purposes

Yeah, I'm a good guy. Really. But for how much longer if I keep playing it like that?

Chapter Seventeen

SEVEN O'CLOCK CAME AND went. I was still sitting in the coffee shop. My patronage had long since lapsed into loitering. The staff didn't seem to mind. It's one of the things I liked about that place.

If Sheila were going to show up, she would have done so by then. Perhaps she was delayed or changed her mind I thought. I hoped she wasn't off pursuing Pandora and The Guys.

Perhaps she was lurking just outside, waiting for me to end up somewhere more private like she had wanted.

I wasn't sure how worried I should be. She could have killed me a couple of times by now. Why hadn't she? Perhaps it was just a case of toying with her food. Ironically she was now my best lead on finding Koenig's Jekyll.

"Damn." I thought, "I'm just spinning my wheels here."

I got up. I was sick of waiting around. If she finds me, she finds me. I was going to go to my favorite meditation spot. Well, one of my favorites. Certainly it was the closest. I walked out the door of the coffee shop then down the square about half a block

O'Bryan's, despite it's Irish sounding name, was a semi-generic upscale nightspot that was trying to cash in on the micro-brew trend. O'Bryan's was fairly bland and rather tame as bars go. I suppose you're asking:

A. Since when do Magi go to bars to meditate?
B. Why go to one with such a lack of character?
C. The answers are simple:

A. I'm a Disreputable Urban Magi for a reason.
B. I'm not going for the bar. The bar, itself, is crap, in my humblest opinion.

I went for the roof top terrace. The terrace overlooks the square. The square was the intersection of two roads, interstates actually, Routes 11 and 33. Until I-81 was put in RT. 11 was the major thoroughfare north and south around here for quite some time. Rt. 11 was built on the old valley turnpike, which was itself founded on a trail the Delaware and Catawba tribes used to go from Canada to Georgia. It is an *old* road. Old roads carry power.

Rt. 33 meanders it way east and west. It goes from lowlands through mountains and back into plains again. It travels from Virginia through West Virginia, Kentucky into Indiana. It crosses through as many small towns and mountain villages as it can. Unlike a limited access hi-way that bypasses the life of a community, roads like 33 and 11 carry a bit of the life and pulse of those communities up and down their entire length

Altogether that makes for a fairly potent crossroad.

In the middle of the square there is the old municipal building. On the southwest corner of the grounds a natural spring wells up. It has it own quaint little housing and a sign that says the water is not safe for drinking. The terrace gives a great view of all of this.

That's why I went there. It's an ancient crossroads with a natural spring right in the middle. There's a lot of energy floating about that I could tap into. Not only that but on the O'Bryan's terrace I could get someone to bring me a drink while I did it.

I sat down at my "usual" table and ordered my drink. I know there are some people whose paths don't mix well with alcohol. Margaritas have always worked for me. I was sipping on my second Margarita when Sheila showed her lovely, haunting, menacing face.

"Didn't I say to find someplace private?"

I smiled slowly, looking straight into her golden eyes. I had been gathering power as I had sipped my drinks. I was feeling pretty charged by then. Indeed anyone with the Sight could have seen me from a mile away.

Being this juiced up gives one an enormous sense of confidence. That's dangerous in its own way, especially considering the crash that is sure to follow.

Still, I could gauge how juiced I was by comparing my reaction then to when I first saw Sheila at the hospital. The night before, I had been scared shitless. The deep-core fear I had felt in the hospital seemed almost inconceivable to me on the terrace. That suggested it was going to be a very hard crash later.

She looked at me hungrily. And it wasn't in the good, sexually euphemistic way. All undead feed off life energy. No matter what form the physical act takes, blood drinking, flesh eating, sexual acts or even simple brutalization, they eat someone's very life. An undead feeding off of you can kill you even if the physical wounds shouldn't.

"I've been watching you for a while now. I had wanted to wait until you left so I could talk to you absolutely privately. But you smell just so yummy right now."

Obviously not all forms of the Sight are vision based. My own shifting senses are evidence of that. It made sense Shelia's paranormal perception would be scent based. A predator like her would sniff out her food. And I had just made myself smell like double chocolate mocha fudge ice cream to her.[*]

I'm man enough to admit that may have been a flawed plan.

Sheila sat down across the table from me. My view of the square was blocked. I think it was safe to assume my meditation time was over anyway.

"I never met anyone so full of life . . . at least not anyone who hasn't stolen it from someone else." I was acutely uncomfortable with the comparison.

"Look, I really, really, really want you to stop whatever do-gooding mission you're on. If you keep this up Koenig is going to want me to kill you. That is something I'm not prepared to do."

"You seemed pretty prepared that night right after . . ." I had meant to sound flippant and perhaps nonchalant. My voice cracking and the abrupt stop before I could say, "you died" blunted the impact.

"After I died, I was driven only by instinct and hunger. Actually I'm grateful to you. Discovering your abilities helped prevent me from becoming a slave to those hungers."

This was news. I had a small inkling where she might be going. I stayed silent, hoping she'd say more. I hoped that I might find away to turn this encounter to my advantage.

"If I had succeeded in killing you, I wouldn't have the restraint I have today."

I found this odd, in light of her brutal murder of Roberta only a few hours before.

"You know I'm glad that you're all buffed up. It will allow me make a point."

---

[*] Her favorite flavor when alive.

Even in my heightened state her hand was blur. She struck my chest in three very specific spots. I felt my heart seize up. I couldn't move or breathe. If I hadn't been saturated with energy I would have been dead.

"I learned that fighting others of my kind. Ravenous monsters, the lot of them. Really there's no reasoning with them. That little combo paralyzes both autonomic and voluntary muscles. An inconvenience for my kind, it's a tad worse for you. Isn't it lucky you got your funky mojo rising? Your current charge should last twice that.

She inhaled deeply and thought for a moment. She looked as though she were savoring the bouquet of a wine, "You should even have enough left over to hide yourself while I have a little chat with Koenig."

Obviously I couldn't respond. I was busy using the energy I had drawn in to replace my breathing and blood circulation. It doesn't take that much energy but it does take focus.

All she did was force me to go into a form of suspended animation. This was a little trickier than normal since I was also trying to stay conscious.

Sheila's cell phone chirped out a phone number as she dialed. Under normal conditions I might have been able to catch it. Not tonight.

"Come on up," Shelia said into the phone. "I sent your message. But I think we need to talk before your next client." Sheila put away her cell phone. Without looking at me, she simply said, "Conceal yourself."

I did as I was told. Normally a cloak doesn't take that much out of me. Tonight? Well, I knew that if I survived this, I was going to hurt like hell in the morning.

It wasn't long before Gretchen Koenig made her appearance. She must have been waiting for this signal. She came over to the table and sat down. She completely ignored me even as she chose the less convenient chair so she didn't sit on me. Nice to know I got something right that night.

"So is he going to stop looking for her?" Koenig asked.

"It's only a matter of time before I've convinced him to stop hunting your alter ego."

"I still say it would be better to kill him. He's gotten too close. Nosing around the bars where I do business, finding the rental agency. That was way too close."

"And your own fault. If you hadn't sent Roberta you wouldn't have had to loose her."

"How did he find her?" Don't tell me, 'He's a magus.' I'm sick of that response." It was interesting to see Koenig so frustrated.

"Then listen to it. Look, just because he looks alone doesn't mean he is alone."

"Right the Magi council, if they're so high and mighty why haven't they jumped on me already."

Sheila let out an exasperated gasp. It must have been for effect. After all, she only breathes when she remembers to.

"You are still small potatoes in the mystic world. You're a simple Hyde. Your mark has been in the mundane criminal underworld. You're still beneath their radar. Take him out and that'll change. You need to get Stephan under your control before you can start making head way in mystic circles."

"I'm not used to this. Normally my servants don't instruct me."

"Then consider me an adviser." With that Shelia closed the book on that part of the conversation. She finished off the last of my drink and stood up to walk away. It was an afterthought when she said "Oh. You may have to do something about Stephan's sister."

"I have already made arraignments for her to come to the attention of a particularly vile individual, someone from my black list "

"Black list?" Sheila sounded amused.

"Customers who have proved dangerous to my investments." (Sheesh, how detached can you get?) "Still it's just a precaution, she hasn't even noticed her brother's absence yet. I doubt she'd go about business as usual if she had. Why? Has there been trouble?"

This is when Sheila really surprised me. "I think Gives tracked her down. I saw her leaving the Rental agency as I got there. Then just a little while ago he was sitting near her in the coffee shop just down the block. He might have approached her. But she left with a couple of guys. Clients I assume."

How long had she been watching? If she saw anything but the very last moments of the conversation she would know that I had the connection to the young men not Pandora. Had she really been fooled? Was she playing some kind of game?

"Hmm," Koenig said, "it shouldn't be a problem much longer whatever the case."

Sheila stood up "I'm just going for a bite to eat. I saw something tasty at the coffee shop. I'm going to see if I can't run it to ground. I'll talk you at the office."

Suddenly she cloaked herself. I knew she was taking advantage of my condition to hunt right in front of me, so to speak. There was no way I could stop her. I still needed to counter the deadly effects of her nerve strike. I couldn't do that, track her, and intervene all at the same time. I just didn't have it in me.

It was one of my most demoralizing moments in my life. I was sitting across from my quarry, or at least my best lead, she couldn't even see me. She just went about her business brokering despicable deals on her cell phone. There was nothing I could do.

Nothing. I couldn't move past an eye blink while my late wife taunted me about murders she was going to commit. If I ever wanted a guardian angel, I wanted one now.

Well, my angel must have heard me. I caught another good break "coincidence."

Someone who knew Koenig came up to her and started chatting. It was a woman who knew her from her front operation of cosmetics sales.

Koenig laid her cell phone down right next to my "invisible" hand. It was just within range for me to extend my cloak over it. It wouldn't be easy but I could do it.

When the brief conversation was over poor Gretchen just left without her cell phone. Thank heaven for small victories! I was sure there was all sorts of information to be gained from it.

It's ironic that I had my late wife to thank for it. I had a sudden fear this was all part of Shelia's game again. I was going to drive myself crazier with all this second-guessing. I needed to focus.

I needed to stop her hunt. I was just about out of the energy. Fortunately I could feel the paralysis easing. My heart was beating on its own again. I still couldn't breathe normally but at least I could force myself to breathe. Now I could use a little bit of mystic energy elsewhere.

I had a basic plan. Unfortunately, like all my moves of late, it was a desperation play.

Chapter Eighteen

I WAS ABLE TO MOVE my hand a little now. I pulled the phone around so I could use it. I prayed that I'd be able to figure this phone out. I don't own one myself but I had borrowed them on occasion. I've used them enough to know that they are all different. Koenig's phone looked pretty high end to me. I hoped that meant that it would have an intuitive design. I would have hated for my desperate plan to fail because I couldn't find the "Send" button.

I flipped the phone open easily enough. Koenig hadn't engaged a key guard, Thank God. Right now I was betting several lives on this stunt.

My plan was simple. Incredibly hard to mange but the ideas are simple enough. First I had to navigate Koenig's phone menu. I found the Caller ID list. Shelia's had been a fairly recent call. It should still be on the list. I looked through the list until I found one that matched the time Sheila made her call. It was there sure enough. I would have hated trying to figure out which number might be Sheila's from a contact list alone.

Once I saw the label Koenig gave Sheila's incoming number, I might have guessed it. It simply read "Hired Help."

Having found the number I pushed send. Pushing buttons was close to the limit of what I could do physically. With an effort I pulled the phone up to my ear. I could hear it ringing. A terrible thought occurred to me. What if she had turned off her phone while she hunted or just let it go to voice mail? My plan would have been screwed. Still while it rang I was drawing up more energy around me. What I was about to do would take it out of me for days, literally.

There were a lot a gambles with this plan. One of which was playing on Sheila's apparent unwillingness to kill me. If I was wrong about that it would be game over.

I was going to exploit sympathetic connections to lock onto Sheila. Sympathetic magic is basic magic theory. Put simply "Like calls to like." You take part of something and get it to resonate with the whole. It's the idea behind having someone's hair for a voodoo doll.

I was trying something a little trickier. Instead of physical objects I was going to try to use emotions. I was going to go for whatever personal resonance that Shelia and I might still share. We were once married. A little of that connection might still exist, I reasoned.

Once I had established a connection I could attempt to use my will to work an effect on her. Just as I was convinced that Shelia's phone must be about to go to voice mail, Sheila picked up. My plan was still alive.

"What is it now, Gretchen. Can't I even have one hunt in peace."

I started to speak, "Hennno, Sheaaa."

"What? Hello?"

I spoke again. It was only barely intelligible as "Hello, Sheila" this time

"Milo?" As soon as she said my name there was a tag of connection. It was still too little to use. I needed to make a deeper connection, something more emotional. (did she even still have emotions?)

I didn't have time to build slowly with a conversation. I need something that would shock open the doors and let me in, if only for a split second. In times of desperation sometimes I get very, very lucky. I had an intuitive flash.

"Hi, Sheila, this is Milo, from your *folklore as literature* class. Um. My *Modern Drama* class is going up to DC for 'Into the Woods.'" There's extra room I was wondering if . . ." I left it hanging just like I had the first time I had made that call.

On the other end of that line I heard a sharp inhalation, a gasp, maybe even a sob.

Her voice cracked as she responded. "Sure sounds like fun . . ."

Blammo! I was in. The psychic connection between us surged. I was able to use the last of my drawn in energy to lock that connection in place.

Now all I would have to do is deplete all my own personal resources to execute this plan. There are times when, loathe, as I am to do it, I will violate space-time. I really hate to do it. Not just because it holds potential danger but, well, it *hurts*.

The only other time I felt forced to do this I needed three hours to recover and that was just for "porting" the length of a small room.

"Great, it's a date then," I said. I shifted Sheila and myself through space. For me it wasn't that far comparatively, only back up to my apartment.

Sheila, it seems, was coming from further than that. She had made about a mile and half. I guess she was hunting on foot.

I was taking her to my apartment for two reasons. One it's easier to teleport to familiar places. The other reason is that I wasn't going to arrive awake. At least I wouldn't be for very long. I was hoping that Sheila's reluctance to kill me would hold true. I was also gambling that if I arrive out cold with a guest, the ghost would make sure no one left. My plan was all a big bunch of risky gambles. But how could I live with myself if I hadn't tried.

When you slide through space-time like that, it messes with your brain. I saw all sorts of strange images in the split-second in-between. I saw rainbows, hellscapes, and rainbow hellscapes, angels that melted into demons and back again. I saw a cathedral made of prismatic glass shatter when it reflected my face. Most disturbingly, I saw Bob Barker chiding me for not spaying a cat I didn't know I owned.

The thousand shards of the broken glass cathedral coalesced into my apartment. I saw Marguerite standing in front of me in my living room holding an aluminum baseball bat.

"But I don't even have a cat," I told her then passed out

When I awoke, I was in my own bed wearing a set of red, velvet pajamas. I swear that they weren't mine, that I had never seen before, and I wouldn't have worn them on a bet. Either Marguerite or the apartment ghost had an odd sense of humor.

I tried to get out of bed. Given how quickly I met with failure I hadn't been out for too long.

"Milo?" It was Marguerite. The look of concern on her face was touching.

"How long . . . how . . .," damn, I ran out breath asking the question.

"It's been about sixteen hours. She moved over to the bed. She placed her hand on my forehead. I hadn't even realized how hot I was until her touch brought a welcome coolness.

"You're burning up," she told me unnecessarily.

"Sh-Sh- Sheila," I stammered

"She's in the other room. Don't worry she's restrained." I wasn't surprised to hear it. I had hoped the Ghost could mange it. I wonder how it had it had prevented Sheila from killing Marguerite. Most likely Sheila had some reason not to.

Once again I tried to get out of bed. Marguerite stopped me.

"Go back to sleep. Whatever little stunt you pulled seems to have put the game on hold."

"How do you know?" Another thought suddenly occurred to me "How did you know to be here?"

"I am a psychic. It's good for some things after all. Now sleep. I'll fill you in when you can actually do something with the information." She pushed my head back down on the pillow. I became pleasantly unaware of anything.

Chapter Nineteen

THE NEXT TIME I awoke, it was to the smell of sage and lilacs. Marguerite sat beside my bed. She had changed her clothes. I could hear a voice in the other room. It sounded like Ty. He was having a quiet, though heated, discussion with . . . It took me another second to place the other voices. They were Pandora and Sheila. Oh God what had they done? I jumped out bed. I noticed but didn't take time to comment on my new pajamas, blue silk with yellow polka dots.

I rushed out of the bedroom and down the short hall to what passed as my living room. I had been concerned that Sheila was just biding her time. Now that Pandora's connection to my activities had been exposed, Sheila could dispose of her. She'd then let Koenig know what I was really after and all hope of getting Stephan back would be gone.

The sight that greeted me when I got there shocked and astounded me. Ty and Pandora were giving a very restrained Sheila the third degree.

"I told you." Marguerite said.

She had. I just hadn't guessed how restrained she meant. Sheila wasn't merely trussed up, or bound, or even shackled. For lack of a better word, she was crucified. No, no actual crosses were used. But she had been, ahem, thoroughly nailed.

No make that screwed and, as I looked closer in a few places, bolted. Foot long screws had been drilled through her palms, wrists, elbows and shoulders into a steel frame. Her knees and ankles had been bolted together. Her feet were pierced and screwed into the frame as well. A length of barbed wire had been used to secure her head on to the frame.

I believe all the hardware and the frame came down to us from the industrial artist who had lived here in the sixties. I really wish I knew where the ghost was stashing all this stuff.

Marguerite turned to Ty and Pandora, "Remember, I said Mr. Gives was going to need some privacy? Well now's the time."

"Certainly, dinner has been too long delayed as it is," Ty said.

"Let's just get something at the Quick Lunch down stairs. I don't want to go too far," Pandora said.

"Fair enough, the others guys are already down there, surveillng the street."

I envied them as they left. Even though I was still queasy, I'd much rather go for food than face Shelia again. Marguerite filled me in. I think she tried to gloss over some of the more gruesome details.

Marguerite had gotten a "feeling." She felt unequivocally that I was in danger. She rushed over to my apartment. She had armed herself with the aluminum baseball bat she had found upon entering the apartment.

A moment later Sheila and I appeared. Fortunately Sheila had been disoriented by the teleportation even if she wasn't knocked unconscious. Shelia's disorientation allowed Marguerite to land a telling blow.

Marguerite shattered Sheila's spine just below the base of the skull with one smooth shot. A living person would have been dead almost instantly. I made a mental note not to piss off Marguerite.

What would have killed a human only temporarily subdued Shelia. It doesn't take her undead form long to regenerate. Unlife, like life, was not without its ironies. Sheila would have been back up and swinging in about twenty minutes. That was long enough for Marguerite to call in back up. She called Pastor Geoff. Pastor Geoff sent the Guys right over.

Marguerite took advantage of that time to look for a way to binding up Sheila. Looking for the hall closet, she discovered the old artist's studio instead. Even before the guys arrived, she was at work creating the grotesque work that now decorated my living room.

I made an underline to my mental note to never piss off Marguerite.

I confronted Sheila. Or at least I tried. Before I could speak she looked right into my eyes and said, "You know if anyone sees me like this you'll loose all credibility with your feminist friends."

"Perhaps," I said, "but then the Goth chicks will love it." I wondered if my flippancy covered how appalled I felt.

"Do you really think so?" Her tone was even, calm and dismissive

"How the hell should I know? The last woman I slept with just got herself bolted to a metal sculpture by my best friend."

"Really? No one since . . . I'm flattered." Her voice had a quality of genuineness as she spoke. Not so much as if she cared but more as if it had surprised her. Whatever the reason, the honesty tugged at me. I turned away. I couldn't bear to look at her mutilated like that.

Marguerite caught my eye. She came up to me. She put her arm around my shoulder.

"I know it's hard but you need to question her. We haven't gotten anything out her in the past two days."

Two days! Jesus H. for "help me" Christ. Two days with no progress. If Koenig suspected that we were trying to find Stephan she could disappear him thoroughly in those two days.

On the other hand, Koenig must really be getting desperate. We had her biggest gun and her cell phone, which might be the equivalent to having her little black book.

"Margie . . . I know she doesn't still love me but to see at her in such pain . . ."

"Milo," Marguerite looked me dead in the eyes and held me by my shoulders. "I promise you your wife doesn't feel any pain."

"Are you . . .?"

"Sure? Yes, mostly because that isn't your wife. It's the monster that decided to live in her skin."

Again, Sheila surprised me. Her next words were an obvious ploy. Ploy or not they still had an impact.

"Last I checked, he's still my husband not yours. He needs a real woman."

Marguerite just sighed and walked over to Sheila. "Maybe," she said, "but just so we are clear 'real women' breathe."

The next three hours were some of the most frustrating I had ever spent with my wife. And that's including the time we got lost going to a Baltimore Ravens game.

I wish I could say we were able get something out of her. We didn't. I wish I could relate an interrogation full of drama and witty retorts. Essentially the interrogation went like this

"Tell us where Koenig has Stephan."

"Why don't you still love me?"

"Who is Koenig's Jekyll?"

"We could still have something"

Round and round, Brick walls and roadblocks. For a split second I entertained the idea of torture. But not only did my ethics disallow it, my more pragmatic side pointed out that she was restrained by steel screws and bolts through her flesh. I wasn't sure what we could top that. Unless . . .

I had been on to an idea but, at that moment, Ty and Pandora came running back in. Ty ran up to me. Pandora disappeared into the kitchen

"We've got trouble downstairs at the Quick Lunch." He barely paused to tell us that when he picked up Marguerite's bat and headed out my front door. Pandora followed after him. I could see she was brandishing a long, wicked looking knife. They disappeared out the door before I could start on my views concerning violence.[10]

I started to follow when Margie stopped me. "You're still not recovered enough. Stay here."

With that she too had fled the apartment. This left me alone with Sheila (and, of course, the Apartment Ghost). As soon as they had cleared out, I heard the wrenching of twisting metal behind me.

I turned to see Sheila struggling against her restraints and winning. I don't know if it was as painful as it looked. I don't see how it couldn't be.

She flexed her arms tearing the screws through her palms and wrists. A bit more wrenching around and she had freed her elbows. Why didn't I stop her? Make no mistake I wanted to. I just didn't have the strength. Perhaps even rested I wouldn't have. Despite how slow it seemed to happen at the time, all too quickly she was free and standing in front of me. The wounds in her torso already closing visibly through her torn clothing

Then she smiled at me, her golden eyes glinting. The barbwire wreathed around her head looked like a sick hybrid between a tiara and crown of thorns.

She crossed the tiny distance between us. She looked deeply into my eyes. Sheila adjusted her "barbed crown" using my eyes as a mirror.

"Interesting look. I think I'll keep it"

When she kissed me, she bit my lower lip, drawing blood. After that she ran the length of my apartment until she could dive head first out my kitchen window. By the time I reached it and looked down I could see no trace of her in the alley, three stories below. What I could see were the four guys, Pandora and Marguerite standing off against one man and barely holding their own.

That one man was Pandora's stalker from just a few days before.

---

[10]   Less is better. I may not be a total pacifist but I believe violence should be reserved for those who either can't, of already have, died.

Chapter Twenty

THIS WAS THE KIND of thing I had worried about when I learned how long I had been out. Koenig must have sent him over to find me when Shelia didn't report back in.

Like the last time this man fought The Guys, I was only able to watch. Visions of the earlier carnage this man had inflicted replayed in my head. It seemed a mixed blessing that I had such a great view of the fight.

I shuddered imagining what he might do again, this time to Pandora and Marguerite as well. Ty swung at him with the aluminum bat. The stalker caught it, tore from Ty's grasp and flung it away. Hector moved in trying to take advantage of the Stalker's focus on Ty. The stalker caught him as well. But instead of having time to do something lethal and vicious to Hector, he had to counter James and Ramón driving their fists into his kidneys.

The guys were certainly doing better than last time. They didn't seem to be gaining ground however. The stalker moved with such effortless strength that I thought it must be something supernatural.

I invoked my Sight and actually got visuals. I couldn't see anything boosting the stalker, no evidence of drugs or magic. All I could see was the amazing level of physical health this man had. It seemed inversely proportional to his mental health.

Pandora was standing on the sidewalk, neither running nor fighting. Marguerite was with her trying to tug her along.

The fight brought the stalker quite close to her. He spoke loud enough for me to hear him three stories up.

"Our play time's next, little girl."

Pandora still didn't move.

With my sight on I noticed something I had over looked. Azgard was parked, blocking one end of the alley.

"Marguerite!" I called out. She looked up to me. I tossed her my car keys. "In the trunk. In the safe. "

If you are wondering why I'd supply a gun to someone when I'm against violence, it's simple. As hard as it would be for me to live with Marguerite, the guys or Pandora doing violence to this man, I'd find it harder to live with myself if he did lasting harm to them. Marguerite should play sports professionally. She caught the keys out the air and streaked over to my car.

She was reaching into the trunk just as a sickening cracking reached my ears. It was Hector's arm breaking. With the sight I could tell it was a spiral fracture of the ulna.

The other three dived and wove about the stalker. They were no longer trying offensive moves but defensive ones. They were drawing him away from Hector.

Marguerite had found the gun my ghost had provided. Marguerite came back around the car and tossed the hand cannon to James. He was closest to her at the time. He threw the gun, not to Ty or Ramón, who were closer to him, but past them and the stalker. The gun sailed toward Hector in a wide arc intended to keep it from the stalker's view. Hector caught the gun with his good arm. Ty, James and Ramón kept circling.

Soon Ty and Ramón were between Hector and the stalker. Hector threw the gun at Ty's back. Ramón however caught it without ever glancing at it or at Hector. He tossed it past the head of the stalker. The stalker turned to make a grab for the gun. Instead of catching it, James who had gotten behind the stalker deflected the gun with Marguerite's bat back over to Ty.

The stalker made a swipe at James. However Ramón had blitzed around the stalker, pushing James out of the way.

At this point, Ty cocked the Desert Eagle and pushed it into the base of the stalker's skull

The man froze. There was no fear about him, only caution. Slowly he lifted his hands. Even with a gun to his head, he still looked overwhelmingly dangerous. He looked even stronger than the whole assortment that faced him.

I could tell he was only biding his time. In a moment, he would disarm Ty and most likely finish whatever it was he had started. I had to do something.

I could only think of one thing right then, something I hate to do. I could probe the stalker's mind. I didn't like doing that it. It's a violation, not a physical violation but a mental one.

Let's call it what it is, a psychic rape, I suppose it's better than having your head shot off. At least this would serve a purpose. I wouldn't have to go in that far. Damn it, it all sounds like thin rationalizations now. God forgive me but it seemed like the best thing to do at the time.

I gathered what little energy I could and penetrated his mind. I didn't need to go deep. Ty had just asked him "Who the hell" he was. Though he didn't reply verbally, a name floated there in his thoughts. I seized on it and yelled from my apartment window

"That's enough Jason Edgars. Your games are over."

I was still inside his mind when the first wave of fear washed over him. It was the first time he had felt fear since entering military service. He was physically well trained and he knew it.

I suddenly caught another name. He had adopted an alias. Unlike some, he had never really thought of himself by that name. So "Tony Moss," his current alias, popped into his mind second.

But enough background, there was action happening. At the sound of his name, he jumped. I don't mean Edgars was startled, I mean he actually leaped forward and rolled on landing. Ty, who had little experience with guns, shot at him but missed.

Edgars put all of his physical prowess into escaping. There was little we could do but watch him run away. Since I was already violating his mind, I did a quick filter, a sort of a psychic smash and grab. Looking into his mind, there was a nearly overwhelming sense of violation, both from his actions in the past and mine right then. I had to fight down the nausea I felt. I got some important details. We may have to deal with him later.

There were other fish to fry, arguably bigger. At least Edgars was going to be too busy hiding himself to hurt anyone in the immediate future. Now we had to lick our wounds and make our next plan.

In a few short minutes the team, as it were, had gathered in my kitchen.

"We can't stay here." I said. We need a new place to go."

Marguerite's place was far too small. It was essentially two rooms. She lived in one and used the other for her readings. In any event, they all had family that could be put in danger. None of the guys had any extra room. Hector and James Both still lived with their respective parents. Ramón was renting a room with a family. Ty, who had inherited a small house on the passing of his father, had his grandmother and a young cousin living with him.

"I'm not about to expose them to this crowd," Ty said. "Besides the danger, I'd hate to hear what my grandmother would say. She already thinks Ramón, Hector and James are trouble. I don't want to hear what she'd say about you Mr. Gives."

"I know a place," said Pandora, "I doubt anyone would look for us there." Pandora had a pained expression.

"That's great! Where?"

Pandora took a deep breath. Then she gritted her teeth and actually closed her eyes.

"My parent's house," said Pandora.

Chapter Twenty-One

WE WERE ON THE road by midnight. It might have been earlier but Pandora insisted we all wear suits. Fortunately, the Guys all had their own suits. The best I could come up with was a Tuxedo the ghost "found." My charcoal gray suit had been shredded in the teleport the other night

In the end, I settled for a dress shirt, black Khakis and a tie. Even Hector with his arm in a make-shift sling looked more dignified than I did. As soon as I was strong enough, I would help Hector with his arm.

I took the tux just in case. I didn't know why. I just had a feeling.

Ramón drove Azgard. Pandora rode in the passenger seat next to him. I lay down in the back to recover more of my strength. The other three of "The Guys", as we had taken to calling them, followed behind us with Marguerite in her car. She had gotten herself a late model Lexus since that morning at the hospital.

I teased her about that when I first saw it.

"Lying to your clients again, I see."

"What makes you say that?"

"Who makes money telling the truth?"

She had called me a cynic and slapped me lightly on the forehead. "Seriously, can you afford this?"

"Sure, It may be small but I own my place, so I have fairly low overhead. I also have some profitably insecure, repeat clients."

I felt a pang of envy that her clients can actually pay her as a rule. I changed the subject slightly.

"What happened to the Le Baron?" I asked.

She shrugged. "I just felt like a change after what happened in the hospital. The death of a friend can do that to you." She stood there deadpanning the line, waiting for me to say something. I had no snappy rejoinder.

For a change that actually stopped me.

When I didn't make a smart-assed comment she said. "I had a feeling that a nice, black car could be useful."

I had long since learned to trust Marguerite's instincts.

We headed north on I-81 to catch the interchange for I-66. From there we headed east towards Washington DC. It seems Pandora and her brother ran away from the Northern Virginia area. Known to many as NoVa, it is basically suburban Washington, DC. It stretches far enough that the far western edges are not nearly as congested as the city itself or its immediate environs.

Pandora and Stephan had hitchhiked down Interstate-95 toward Florida. Why Florida? She didn't tell me. They had been robbed in Richmond. With no money, they fell into desperate times. Soon enough, they had ended up in Koenig's "stable."

We had just turned off I-81 to catch the eastbound 66 when Ramón suddenly spoke up.

"Hector's got an idea. We've got her phone. She has a lot contact information in it. She used code words in the entries so she must be hiding something, right?"

"Go on" I said.

"Hector thinks we can use a reverse directory to look up the numbers and find out who they belong to.

Even if it doesn't help find Stephan directly it, Ty thinks that could give us leverage."

"Ty? I thought this was Hector's Idea."

"It was, but Ty just chimed in."

Pandora looked over at Ramón, "You know that trick you guys do is kinda of creepy."

"Sorry." Ramon said, "The really funny part is how natural it seems to us. Even as kids, we always knew what the others were thinking. Since the other day . . . ," Ramón paused. He seemed at a loss for words. Then his face brightened. He continued, "Hector describes it like being computers connected by a network. We can all share information but we each run our own programs."

"Well, that sounds less creepy," Pandora said. I'd say there was slight note of disappointment in her voice. Ramón picked up on it too.

"Um, it was still brought about by someone messing around with unnatural forces beyond the ken of man." Ramón sounded just like James. He had affected a thick Scottish brogue. I suspect Ramón was quoting James though the link.

"Hey." I objected from the back seat.

Ramón used the rear-view mirror to look me in the eyes.

"Marguerite says that you are a magician. A real one, not somebody doing stage tricks."

It was one of those statements that worked like a question. I certainly felt he was owed more of an explanation.

"That's pretty close. I can give a more detailed explanation, if you want." At first he just shrugged, then midway through the shrug, a small, annoyed look crossed his face.

"Hector and Ty say start at the beginning."

So I did. It still sums up to what I told Pandora. Except this time I took the long way round. "I'm a Magus of the same tradition that came to be know as the Magi, or Wise Men, of the Biblical Nativity Story. Our path encompasses many streams of mystical thought, Zoroastrian, Jewish, and, of course, Christian. The Nativity, or more accurately, The Epiphany, that's when the Magi showed up. The Epiphany was a defining event for us . . ."

I went on to describe how the Magi written of in the bible forged into new territory afterwards. I also described Will-Working and how I understood it.

As I described it, Ramón stopped me.

"You ever play Dungeons and Dragons?" He asked

"No. When I was a kid I wasn't allowed, later I just didn't see a reason, why?"

"Cause you sound more like a cleric than a wizard. Excuse me, James says you're more of Mystic Theurge"

"Excuse me." I said. Now I was the one who need explanation.

This took a while. Essentially they described someone who worked magic with a particularly spiritual bent.

"That sounds about right," I said. It describes most of the will workers I ever encountered. We all seem to worship something. Even if all they worshiped was the power of their Gift.

There was silence for a short time after we clarified who and what I was.

"So what did you do to us?" He asked. His eyes met mine in the rear-view mirror again. I could see that Ramón was more interested in this than my background.

"You know we're only helping you out because we need answers."

"Is that the only reason?" I asked. I tried to keep my tone innocuous. I wanted to hear his response but hopped not to make him defensive.

Ramon's eyes slid over to look at Pandora for an instant before he responded.

"Mostly that's why. But um . . . well, it looks like you could use some help . . . It seems like a good cause. Still, we'd to know, " He paused briefly, as if he were trying to find a polite way of rephrasing, "What the hell did you do to us." In the end he failed.

"So what the hell did you do to us? And why?"

"Good questions,"I said, "I'll start with the why, it's easier to explain. What happened to you is my fault in two ways. The first is that I put you in harms way unintentionally. That was when I laid an effect on the man stalking Pandora." I got perplexed looks from both Ramón and Pandora. "I wanted to make sure people noticed him."

"We sure as hell noticed him," Ramón said. "Did you mean for him to tear us up like that?"

"No," I said. "I just wanted him to feel conspicuous and go home. I didn't realize you guys would take it so far as to challenge him."

"We couldn't let something happen to Pandora. Not that we knew who she was. It was the principle of the thing."

"I can see that. I suspect what you really want to know is what I did that made this change."

Ramónsimply nodded.

"You know that you guys were hurt bad. Really, really bad. I think a couple of you might have been maimed for life. I had to do something. Even if it hadn't been my fault, I couldn't just ignore it."

I set about trying to explain what I had done. "Imagine your life as a tapestry," I told the Guys. "The various threads of your being are woven together, physical mental, spiritual. What that guy did was rip great big holes in your physical being. These weren't small tears. They were big enough to affect your whole being. I couldn't just patch you with a small application of life energy. You guys were "unraveling." I needed to do something big. I had to do a basic reweave of your patterns and do it quickly. I went with the most powerful healing I know. I found the Unity Point."

"The unity point?" Ramón and Pandora said together. I had a feeling that I could have heard at lest three other voices as well if I had listened in the right way.

"The Unity Point. You may have heard some people say 'We're all one.'"

"From hippies and crazy preachers," Ramón said.

"Say 'Thank you' the next time you see one," I told him. "By going into the Unity Point. I brought us together so that I could use the energy we all share to rebuild your being. I just went a little too far and united your minds. Permanently."

"Well that was sloppy," Ramón said. "I guess were lucky you aren't in here too." Ramón was quiet for a few moments then asked, "So is there a name for what we are now?"

"I'd have to say you are most like a hive mind. But not quite"

"What? like a bee hive?"

"Sort of. Hive minds tend to be one mind that is spread out over a number of bodies. Sometimes bees are like that. You guys seem to be more like four minds joined at the roots. I think the networked computer analogy is actually pretty apt. "

Ramón didn't say anything. He just waited until I continued my explanation. "You all still have your own thoughts and responses to things but what one of you knows, you all know."

"Sort of like telepathy but just between us four," Ramón said.

Close enough. "Yeah," I said. I suspected it might be more than that. They might be capable of much more than just sharing thoughts. I didn't want to make a bunch of guesses to Ramón though. I had done enough damage without meaning to. I thought it best to let things develop as naturally as possible.

After a short silence Ramón broached a new subject. He asked Pandora what her parents were like.

"Alcoholics," she said. The story that followed was one of neglect and emotional control rather than physical or sexual abuse from inside the family. Her dad had to have the perfect little family. Which of course meant having the perfect wife. His control of Pandora's mom seemed absolute. He didn't control her through threats or physical abuse. According to Pandora, he controlled her by cleaning up after her alcoholism then shaming her with it.

"Not that he didn't down gallons more than she did." Pandora was quick to add, "He just hid it from the world better.

"Mom, in turn, strove to make us into the perfect Stepford kids. It's part of why it took a while for my parents to do something about the good Reverends Pinkerton. The damage was getting to be a bit too obvious. After that dad took more interest in our lives. That was a bit of a mixed blessing."

Pandora went on to say that to the rest of the world her father always acted like she was his little princess. Really, she was just a trophy child. She was a smart, pretty girl to be trotted out to impress the neighbors or the partners at work.

It was a different story for her brother. One might say Pandora was lucky. She was pretty, smart, and athletic in a graceful sort of way. She had the gifts that "good girls" are supposed to have. Unfortunately for Stephan, so had he. Being graceful and pretty with a naturally poetic nature served Pandora much better than Stephan.

Things had really gotten rough for Stephan around his 11th birthday. He disappeared for a whole 24-hour period. When he returned he couldn't or wouldn't say where he had been, not even to Stacie, (Pandora's given name) his normal confidant. Not only had he worried his parents, they had to "bear the shame" of calling the police.

On top of this, he came back with a number of valuable items. They were tiny, exquisitely worked handicrafts. Each painstakingly carved or formed from expensive and rare materials. There was a golden pocket watch studded with diamonds. The clock face only told "daytime" and "nighttime." There was a carving of a small doe and faun that no appraiser could identify exactly. The carving was made by an unparalleled artisan.

This was nothing new in itself. These little gifts had been showing up for years. Mrs. Vanderhorn always made sure these things disappeared again. She also made it clear that they were not to be talked about again.

Mr. Vanderhorn had always considered it petty larceny and would instruct Mrs. Vanderhorn to discipline the boy.

Mrs. Vanderhorn had noticed the oohing and awing over her son's elfin looks. She had assumed that they were payments for things she could not bear to think about, let alone mention. To name these things would have brought the whole little "dream world" of their perfect family crashing down for all to see.

"You know," Pandora observed, "working for Koenig wasn't that much of a change. We were just the objects of a different kind of fantasy."

I must have fallen asleep again after that. I awoke as we pulled up to a long semi-circular driveway. The name on the mailbox was Vanderhorn. The large house was almost hidden from view by a substantial copse of trees. It wasn't the only house in the neighborhood trying to hide that way.

The downstairs lights were still on, even though it was quite late. Pandora motioned for us to stop just before we came to the top of the driveway's curve.

Pandora got out of the car quickly, then seemed to freeze as she faced the house. Marguerite's Lexus came to a stop behind us. Pandora took a series of deep breaths. She inhaled deeply through her nose then exhaled slowly out her mouth several times. She threw back her shoulders and held her head high.

'Let's go meet my folks." she said

Chapter Twenty-Two

Deciding who looks the most official is kind of difficult at 2 am. In The end, we chose Marguerite and Ty. The rest of the guys stayed with the cars. I hung back just close enough to observe. Marguerite and Ty, with Pandora, went to the front door and rang the bell. A small green light appeared on the doorway intercom. A man's voice followed.

"Who is it? " The voice didn't sound like someone awoken or even annoyed at such a late night intrusion. Pandora hesitated only for a second before saying "It's me, daddy."

I swear there was an audible thump on the front door an instant later. There was the sound of locks being undone. The door opened so forcefully I doubt a battering ram could have done better.

A fiftyish, balding, portly man of average height stood at the door. For a moment he just stared at Pandora. Even in the half-light of the open door he was visibly overcome with emotion.

"Stacie, My God . . ."

He started forward to embrace her and then stopped as Pandora took a step back. Mr. Vanderhorn flinched like she had slapped him. He also took a step back. He breathed deeply trying to compose himself. It didn't help much. He wept openly.

"Will you come inside?" he asked. His voice trembled even more than his hand as he gestured toward the door.

"Ah, Dad," Pandora began, her own voice tentative, "can I bring my friends inside?"

Her dad didn't say a word. He just motioned in Pandora, Ty and Marguerite. Then he caught sight of the rest of us standing further back by the cars. We, too, were waved inside. In very short order we were sitting around the very nice, formal living room.

That is to say Ty, Pandora's dad and Marguerite were sitting in the living room. The rest of us stood around hoping to look official. Pandora was standing over by the corner of the room. She was staring at a large, glass cabinet. It looked sort of like a trophy case. There were a lot of pictures of Pandora and her Brother in it. Pandora stayed focused on the cabinet.

Marguerite caught my eye. I nodded to her. She began talking to Pandora's father.

"Mr. Vanderhorn, I'm sure you have a lot of questions, but your daughter really needs your help right now."

"She can have it," he said.

"Actually both your children need your help."

Mr. Vanderhorn swallowed hard and his voice cracked, "Both?"

"Yes, both, you see after they ran way . . ."

"They can have whatever they need."

"I'm afraid that this doesn't necessarily mean that they are going to come back to stay."

"It doesn't matter. They can have anything I can give." Vanderhorn had the air of man who was deeply afraid. It was a kind of fear I haven't seen very often. It was not a fear of injury, nor a fear of loss. It was the fear of something being too wonderful, too good to be true, of waking up too soon.

Pandora came over and joined the conversation, "Aren't you mad?"

"No. I can't imagine anything making me angry again." It was simple statement. I didn't need the Sight to feel it resonate as Truth through the room. He really couldn't imagine anything making him angry again. He was wrong, of course, but the feeling told me a lot.

"You don't know what I've been doing since I've been gone. You'll be so ashamed"

"I have my own shame to worry about. How do I help you and Stephan?"

For a second Pandora's leaden eyes began to soften. Suddenly, they hardened again.

"Are you doing this out of guilt, because you want to feel like a 'good dad' again? Are you just trying to ease your own pain?"

"It's been almost two years since you ran away. My pain isn't about the running away."

"But . . ." Pandora began. Her father cut her off.

"You don't understand. I'm sorry you felt you had to run away and certainly I want to make up for it. I'll make amends any way I can, if I can. But I'm not offering my help out of guilt. It's out of joy." He got up and walked quickly from the living room. The rest of us looked at Pandora questioningly.

She shrugged, "Sounds like he's getting something from his den. It's his little sanctum Sanctorum. Stephan and I were never supposed to go inside. Hell, he didn't even like it when mom went in there."

A moment later, Mr. Vanderhorn returned. He had a small sheaf of papers. He handed them first to Pandora. She stared at them for a moment then shook her head in an uncomprehending manner. She handed them back to her father.

Mr. Vanderhorn next gave the papers to Marguerite. "I presume that these didn't come out of your office."

"No, sir, I can safely say they didn't. Mr. Wingate, Mr. Gives please take a look at this"

Ty and I stepped up. I doubt I was convincing as an official anybody, even at this late hour. I was glad Ty was there.

When I read the paper, I could understand Mr. Vanderhorn's distraction. The Papers were two official documents from the Office of the Chief Medical Examiner of Richmond, Virginia

They were detailed Coroner reports. They were complete with photographs. The names of the deceased were Stacie and Stephan Vanderhorn.

"So you see," Mr. Vanderhorn said to Pandora, "I don't care where you've been. I don't care what you done. You aren't coming back from running away; you're coming back from the dead.

I don't want to help because I feel guilty. I'm not trying to buy back your love, I want to help because you standing here is some kind of sign."

Pandora sat down on the couch. Her father sat next to her. For a moment she just stared at her father. Anger burned in her eyes. It must have been a particularly fierce heat because it melted the lead from her eyes.

Those eyes flashed as she asked her next question

"A sign? A sign of what?"

Mr. Vanderhorn was calm but still crying. "That forgiveness can be real."

"You think my coming back means I forgive you?"

"No. That I have the chance to ask."

Chapter Twenty-Three

A WHOLE NEW WORLD OF understanding opened before Stacie and her father. At the same time a lead opened up in the case. Ty was going over the documents; Hector noticed one of the phone numbers in the Coroner's report was also in Koenig's phone list.

While Pandora and Mr. Vanderhorn were bonding, perhaps for the first time, we used his home office. He had turned his den into a resource station for the parents of runaway children.

When the Vanderhorns were told that their runway children were dead, a miracle happened. They hit rock bottom. They hit it hard. Within a month they were both in recovery following the Twelve Steps. Their way of making amends to their children was to help other families. Pandora's mom now volunteered regularly at a shelter for runaway teens. Mr. Vanderhorn now helped track down missing teens. Mr. Vanderhorn used his "spare time." By this I mean he retired and began to pursue a new vocation.

As a small part of his arsenal, Mr. Vanderhorn had a wonderful hi-speed Internet connection plus a subscription to an online research company. It included a background check service and a reverse phone directory.

If you've never used one, it's simple. You enter the phone number and it gives you a name rather than the other way around. Using it, we tracked down a fistful of the numbers in the phone.

Many of Koenig's clients were Richmond based. It made a kind of sense. Our tiny city was about an hour and half to two hours drive from Richmond. Traveling from there out to middle of the Shenandoah Valley gave Koenig's clients greater anonymity. The greater anonymity meant a lower risk involvement.

We had about a dozen names and address to follow up with. Eight of which were in or around Richmond. The other four were back home. We decided to split the team. Hector, Marguerite and I would head south to Richmond. Ty, Ramón, and James would head back home. We would do this in the morning. By then I should be up to fixing Hector's arm good and proper.

Mr. Vanderhorn showed us places to sleep. He even offered up the master bedroom. Mrs. Vanderhorn was doing an overnight shift at the teen shelter.

"I only sleep in there when she's home too," he said, "otherwise I just sleep on the cot in my office."

Which is exactly what he did that night. Marguerite took the master bedroom. The guys crashed in a room just off the kitchen. Pandora called it the living-living room. It was the room her family had actually used as a living room rather than the formal living room near the front door. Pandora slept, not in her old room, but in Stephan's.

I did what I usually did when not sleeping in my own bed. I went back out to the cars and laid down in Azgard's back seat.

Morning came awfully early. Mrs. Carol Vanderhorn was at first distressed when she came home from the shelter. Strange cars in the driveway, one of them mine. I can understand her apprehension. It was lucky she didn't see me sleeping in the back or her first imprecisions might have been even worse.

It wasn't made any easier when she came inside. James, it seems, is an early riser. He was already fixing breakfast for the team.

James, besides being the best cook of the four guys, also has an odd sense of humor. In physical features he favors his mother's Chinese heritage. However he tends to sound more like his dad, a Scottish immigrant. When he wants to, he can really lay on the brogue.

Carol came in through the kitchen back door. Her long stressful night at the shelter got even longer. A strange, young, Asian man greeted her, in a rumpled suit and one her aprons. This odd "apparition" was cooking breakfast. When James saw her, he looked her dead in the eye, asking in his thickest brogue,

"Would you like some haggis, lassie?"

At this point Pandora bounced down the back stairs into the kitchen. Her return from death relieved Mrs.Vanderhorn of having to answer the haggis question, and for a few seconds, her ability to stand upright.

James scrambled to catch Mrs Vanderhorn.

"It's true. Nobody likes haggis, do they?" he asked Pandora.

James and Pandora helped Mrs. Vanderhorn into the living room. The reunion between Pandora and her mother was, if, possible even more tearful than with her father. I'm told that not a lot words were exchanged. I don't think there needed to be many. I also don't know exactly what they said. I wasn't there and I didn't think it was my place to ask.

All that happened about seven AM. James had perhaps about an hour of sleep but he seemed to be going strong. The rest of the guys were still sleeping, as was I. I was blissfully unaware of anything until about 10:30 when Marguerite finally awakened me.

"Why are you in the back seat of your car?" she asked.

"Familiarity," I said. I didn't add that that familiarity came from a staunch refusal to drink and drive.

"What's the news this morning?" I asked.

She filled me in. I was sorry to miss the mother and child reunion.

The Vanderhorns were exceedingly gracious to me, Marguerite and the guys. The fed us and more. They must have had a thousand questions about who we were but they refrained from asking. They seemed afraid to poke too hard lest they pop the magic bubble. We had promised to bring back both of their children and had already delivered one. I suppose that is one heck of a gift horse.

When I got out of the shower I discovered two things. The first was that all my clothes, except my duster, had been replaced. The other was that we had picked up more than moral support from the Vanderhorns

Charles had given me one of his suits. Though taller than I was, Charles was also narrower in the shoulder so over-all his suit fit me. Except that sleeves were far to long. The same principle held true for the pants. I looked like an exceptionally scruffy child in his father's clothes. Ty quickly hemmed up the sleeves and pants legs.

"The hems wont stay for long," he told me, "but this will keep them from dragging for today."

As soon as I was dressed, I headed downstairs. Charles had already ushered the rest of the gang out to the cars. Well, the guys anyway. They were in Marguerite's Lexus and pulling away.

I turned and was about to ask when Charles beat me to the punch.

"I sent them ahead to get us a table. It's an old superstition of mine. Back in my corporate raider days, I always ate at one specific restaurant before a big campaign.

"Last night, even though you let others do the talking, I got the feeling you were the one in charge," he told me. "So you, your people and I are going to sit down and have a war council."

"War council? We're just trying to get your son back."

His tone, which had been a bit terse, softened.

"I understand. That is my first priority. But you need to understand I was a shitty father. Stacie probably hasn't told you the half of it. By the time I realized how shitty a dad I was, some empty suit was telling me that my kids were dead.

"Now, I've found out that it was a lie. Not only did I miss the chance to find them, I wasn't even looking.

"All the while, they were enslaved. Enslaved by a woman who had them routinely raped and abused."

Vanderhorn's face hardened into a humorless mask. "I'm going to do what any rational and caring dad would do. First I'm going to make sure my kids are both home and safe."

"Good," I said.

"Then I'm going to kill Gretchen Koenig."

See, I told you he would get angry again.

Chapter Twenty-Four

"THIS IS GOING TO be long breakfast, isn't it?" I asked.

It wasn't. I was a little surprised that Charles had chosen a Denny's. Apparently, it was one of the better ones. By the time the rest of us arrived the guys had already procured a decent table. We also got service pretty quickly. So breakfast didn't last that long after all.

Though I'm not a breakfast person, this was a pretty good one. Everything seemed more possible than it did prior to eating. I had real confidence that we'd be able to track down Koenig before anything much worse could happen.

Breakfast even managed to ease Charles Vanderhorn's anger, a little.

"You know it would be wrong to kill Koenig," I said.

"You don't think she deserves it?" Charles asked.

"It's not my place to judge that. But it's not her fate that worries me. It's yours. She's pretty well connected. Killing her is just going to make sure you're not there for your family."

He contemplated this for a few moments silently.

"That's true," he grumbled. "I won't risk that again if I can help it. "

"Besides if we dismantle her organization like I hope too, she'll receive her justice one way or the other."

"You have that much faith in the legal system?"

"Not really, but the world is filled with natural consequence."

"Interesting. Perhaps I'll see how things play out before making specific plans." Having set the issue aside, Charles turned to more immediate matters.

"Okay so what kind of war chest are you working with?"

The tea I ordered came and I stared into for a second before responding.

"That's what I thought," Charles said before I answered.

"Well, Let's talk plans. This time your plan can depend on better funding."

Always pragmatic, Marguerite asked, "Just how much better?"

"You've heard of guys who made their first million by thirty? Those guys got my coffee."

"Really?" I spurted out. I don't know why that surprised me. I should have guessed it from the stories I heard.

"Well, perhaps I'm exaggerating but I do have considerable assets to contribute. I'd have paid anything to get back my kids and you already brought us Stacie. There is honestly no expense I'd spare to have my family whole again . . ., " He stopped mid-sentence. "Whole for the first time, I mean."

After that Charles and Marguerite hammered out a plan. It was more about operations funding than real strategy. Which is exactly what we needed. It would give us the flexibility to make the best use of our "improvisational" approach, as Marguerite put it.

"You mean you make it up as you go along." Charles commented. He held up his hand to cut off any rejoinder to that statement. "I'm pragmatist enough to know that I shouldn't fix what works. Your style has brought me back one of my kids, I'll bet that it can bring home Stephan.

While they worked out the finer details, I took Hector out to the car and looked at his arm.

"Holy shit!" was my first reaction. "How the hell . . ." was my second. Hector's arm was just a thin layer of skin away from being a serious compound fracture. I could see the bulge where his broken forearm threatened to penetrate the skin.

"How do you stand the pain?" I asked.

"I'm not really sure," he said, "Sometimes when it gets to be too much, it's like the others, they help me out. They share the pain somehow."

"Hmm that could be handy," I thought. It could also be trouble. "That's great. But don't let the sharing thing stop you from getting real help when you need it."

"Can you do something now?"

"Yea," I said, "this is going to hurt."

Once again I drew in energy from the ambient. I opened my senses and knowledge flooded into me. The new knowledge told me that I had to hold Hector's arm just so, apply pressure in this exact way.

I pushed the bone back into it's proper alignment. Then my intention into the wounded arm. My will carried the energy with it. I poured that "force" into the bones and the soft tissue. I urged them to grow, to knit themselves back together. As I did, I felt some of Hector's pain. I had flashes of his excruciating pain. The flashes were brief enough that they didn't break my concentration. It was always close. By the time I was finished I was drenched in sweat.

Hector gingerly flexed his arm. It was still sore but usable. His concern was more for me, "Man, you look almost as beat as you did that day on the street."

"Yeah, I'm not as fresh. I really need to rest longer. I don't see how we can afford the time. We need to get Stephan back as fast as we can.

"Sounds good to me," said Charles. The rest of the team stood with him. He and Marguerite had come to an agreement. James brought the breakfast leftovers over to Hector and me.

"Let's get moving to my bank. I want this operation on solid footing by lunch time."

If I said watching the money movers do their thing was fascinating, you know I would be lying. If it hadn't been for the stakes at hand, I'd have been bored out of my mind. I wanted to use the time it took to work out a more concrete plan. I was too beat. I had to settle for trying to rest as much as I could.

Marguerite and Ty handled the whole thing with Charles and his bankers. In less time than it felt like, we had a line of credit and some working capital. It was made somewhat easier because Marguerite already had a business license in this state. Voila, we all became her employees.

By one-thirty that afternoon we had split into our two teams. Marguerite, Hector, and I headed to Richmond in my car. Ramón, Ty, and James headed back to the 'Burg using Marguerite's Lexus. That was very gracious of her really.

"That's very nice of you to let them use you car." I told her.

"Thanks, they're pretty responsible for guys their age. She said. "I think it'll help. They'll look more imposing driving an black car. It'll be good for their confidence. Besides I can get the scratch repainted easy enough."

Psychics! What can you say?

Chapter Twenty-Five

THE VANDERHORNS WERE GOING to run operational headquarters out of their house. We had a group cell phone account. It wasn't strictly necessary but it helped keep the Vanderhorns informed. Field communications were handled through the guys. Hector was able to stay connected with the rest of the guys all the way to and from Richmond. I don't know if there is a geographical limit but we didn't find it that day

Each team had a list of people to check out based on our research of Koenig's cell phone. The first on our list was a Dr Wilson Kettleworth, an Assistant Chief Medical Examiner for Virginia's central district. Place of employment: 400 East Jackson street, Richmond, Virginia.

We had run into a dead end trying to find his home address. The building was a fairly typical office complex not far from the Richmond Coliseum

For all our clever planning, this first lead was looking like a bust. When we got to the offices, we tried getting the Doc on the phone. We were told he was out that day.

We felt we were on a roll so that barely slowed us down. Putting on my "cloak of unimportance" is even easier when I have someone running interference for me. The surprising part was that Hector did a great job of bluffing his way through. As a process server no less. Apparently his suit was coming in handy. He managed to get all the way to Kettleworth's office suite. Here he was finally rebuffed. Apparently because the "good" doctor really wasn't in.

It was enough. By the time Hector was leaving I was quietly, nonchalantly, unnoticeably going through Dr. Kettleworth's desk. Hector rejoined Marguerite down at the car. They waited with the engine running.

There wasn't anything in his physical files to give us more leads. I was about to call Hector and ask him to talk me through searching the computer when the room went frigid. There was a small, bluish light swirling in the air about chest height. I ducked around one of the filing cabinets. The cloak's great but a little physical obstruction wouldn't kill me I figured.

I spun the wheel of "Sight." and the lucky winner was "touch." Damn! Touch is a hard one to work with. It's the basis for things like psychometry. While picking up vibes from an object is great for detective work, it's almost worthless for taking immediate action. It's great for telling you that the person you're shaking hands with has supernatural strength or that they are violent by nature, or even that they bear you ill will. When you learn that information as their knuckles are vigorously massaging your face, the information is a tad redundant.

It wasn't completely useless at the moment. I could feel a chill in the air that had nothing to do with temperature.

The small, bluish light was growing. The light was like a rip in the air. It was an ugly, ragged thing. The opening was more like a wound than a simple tear. Soon, it was big enough for a large man to thrust his head and upper body through.

This is not a hypothetical measurement. A man, I'd put him about six foot three maybe four, was awkwardly trying to climb through the hole. The awkwardness seemed to stem from the fact that the hole in the air was about 2 ½ feet high and 1 ½ feet wide while being about five feet off the ground.

The man was swearing, I think, at least the English words I heard were defiantly swear words. My grasp of foreign languages it shoddy at best. I thought I recognized Spanish and French and some German. Though to be fair I think most German sounds like swearing.

The man poured himself through and hit the floor rather hard, landing on his hands. Sadly, that didn't slow him down. He turned this into a forward tumble and sprang back up quickly. It might have appeared comical if he hadn't had such an air of menace.

He was dressed much like a police officer that was expecting a riot. Save there was nothing on his uniform identifying him as "POLICE" or "FBI.." He was both heavily armed and armored. The rip closed behind him and the "chill" left the air. The room and the man now seemed utterly mundane.

Three ideas struck me in rapid succession.

First: This little trick may be how Koenig gave me the slip. It sure was quieter (mystically speaking) and less personally painful than my kind of teleport.

Second: Since this guy seemed utterly mundane maybe Koenig's "magic shop" only had a few tricks.

Third: If this guy finds me, he's going to pulp me.

He started looking around the room. His eyes swept over the place where I was concealing myself and kept going.

Suddenly he spoke, "No, I don't see anybody. It looks likes someone riffled the files but they're gone now." He was speaking into a headset mic. Oddly, this comforted me. The man had what looked like high-end, commercially available security gear. It was pricey, well made, and if I played this right, utterly useless.

"Fine, fine." he said and slipped a pair of goggles down over his eyes. I suddenly felt heat coming off of them. Damn. That heat was like the chill from the portal earlier, not related to temperature at all. It had a small but solid enchantment on it. I had thought they were low-light goggles made unnecessary by the late afternoon sunlight coming through the windows.

Armor boy was slowly sweeping his gaze around the room. He did this partly out thoroughness, partly out of disbelief that anything could have fooled his trained eyes. I'm not so much a mind reader here as I gathered it from his muttering while he looked about the room.

I prepared two effects. Once again I found myself trying to draw energy in much quicker than I liked. It's a lot more tiring doing things that way. I wasn't going to be able to fine-tune either of these effects.

When his gaze finally fell upon me "hiding" behind the filing cabinet he let go with an "oh, shit" and went for something holstered at his hip.

I let loose with a flash of raw magic. I was hoping that it would work like shining a light into someone's night vision goggles. The loud string of mismatched curses told me it had worked.

The second effect was simply flinging some kinetic energy at him. It wasn't much more that I could have thrown had I simply pushed him. The biggest difference was that I could do it from across the room. I could also hit him from two directions at once. One push sent his forehead back; the other push struck him in the back of the knees

I managed to get one leg out from under him. He was good enough that he didn't fall but rolled up into a shooting stance. Still blinded, he shot a few times towards the sound of movement.

The movement he heard was the pencil holder on the desk. I had sent it sprawling with a telekinetic push while he was rolling up to fire.

I flung myself through the office window. I still had a little bit of juice to throw. I converted my momentum so that instead of falling, I was flung upward. I had planned to swing myself up against the outside wall. There I could use a fairly simple clinging effect.[11]

Instead, I went through a window on the floor above me. I must have had more mojo than I thought because it managed to throw me all the way into the room and onto the long conference table in its center.

I was winded and tapped out. There were alarms blaring now. A mixed blessing. It cut off pursuit by Koenig's man. On the other hand I would likely spend the night in jail if I didn't come up with something really good to tell security.

---

[11] *Things Iktomi told me. Lessons from the Spider.* CC #423

Chapter Twenty-Six

SO JUST TO ADD to the dramatic tension, let's switch over to
what the other crew was doing. Ty, Ramón and James had driven back
home in Marguerite's Lexus. Their job was supposed to be surveillance.
Not having some of the gifts that Marguerite or I could make use of, it was
decided they needed tech support. This meant it took them a little longer
to prepare. Hector kept us updated via the link as our team hit the road.

Pandora got digital cameras for The Guys headed back to the 'Burg. She
still had one of her own at home. It was a few years old. Her name, "Stacie",
was written in pink magic marker. There was a small heart dotting the eye.

Ty took it and said. "I'll just keep my hand over that part. It a clashes
with the professionalism we are trying to project"

Ramón butted in, "If we do our job right, no one will see it but us."

"Is this more of that method acting crap you keep going on about?" This
was James. Those last two statements happened across the link. Hector gave
us the play by play of the conversations he found amusing.

James, according to Hector, had managed to lay on his thickest brogue.
How one conveys accent through telepathy is beyond me. I don't even want
to attempt it in print.

After the camcorder, Pandora managed to scrounge up another digital
camera from her mother. It was a simple thing. No clever features or lenses,
even the little viewing screen in the back was on the 'are you serious" side.

Before the guys left Charles inspected their gear. He was less than
impressed.

"I'll see what I can do for you in terms of equipment. But this'll have
to do for today."

According to Hector there was a fairly heated debate about who would
drive. None of the three of them actually wanted to drive the car. Let me

rephrase, none of the three of them felt comfortable driving it. Ramón had a bad track record with automotive collisions and was currently uninsured, possibly uninsurable. It would be bad for him to be in the driver's seat if anything happened. (Something he hadn't minded when driving my car, I noticed)

James complained that Ramón was a big back seat driver and didn't want to put up with it, particularly now because of their link.

Ty simply didn't like the idea of driving a borrowed Lexus and running the risk of a D.W.B. (A lot of things may have changed in Virginia as far as civil rights, but there are still places where "Driving While Black" is a *very* serious charge.)

In the end, Ramón agreed to keep his mouth shut and his thoughts to himself. James agreed to drive.

Fortunately their ride back to our fair city was uneventful.

The 'Burg Team only had to check out four addresses. The first location went fine. It was a home out in the Belmont area of town. Belmont is a classier subdivision. The residents are mostly professionals, doctors, lawyers, and some of the more successful local business owners.

The guys took pictures of the place. It was early afternoon. No one seemed to be home.

The second address was a small office. The office building was in an industrial park southeast of town. The building itself was tiny, as far as office complexes go. There were only three offices in the squat one level building. The name that went with the address was Unlimited Horizons Sales. Of the other two office spaces, one was vacant. The other housed a telemarketing firm.

James went in and discovered the address on the list was little more than a mail drop. The office itself was closed and had no posted hours. The office door had frosted glass. There was no light visible inside.

James knocked and received no answer. He tried to talk to someone at the telemarketing office but they were all too busy or too rude to be of any real help.

They decided that this place bore further investigation.

As the exuberance of youth drove them, they decided it would be a good idea to break in. At least they wanted to wait until after the telemarketers would be gone. So to kill time, they headed out to the third location.

It was at the third location that things began to go badly. The address was a private residence in a fairly middle class section of town. The guys set up an observation point near the house.

At first nothing extraordinary happened. A Fifty-year-old woman pulled out of the garage and drove away. Some teen-aged boys breezed through a few minutes later. Nothing untoward happened. The guys kept an eye on the house for about an hour. A man in his late fifties pulled up driving the latest commercial hummer. He parked in front of, not in, the garage.

As this older man climbed out of the Hummer, Ty recognized him.

"Holy Shit, that's Officer Merton."

None of the guys needed an explanation. Even without the link they all knew who Merton was in Ty's life.

About fifteen years ago a little shop near Ty's home got robbed. For reasons known only to him, Officer Merton decided that Ty's father must have committed the crime. Certainly racism played a part in it, but Ty's father, William, wasn't the only African-American man in the neighborhood, some of whom would have been easier targets.

William Wingate had always striven to be a man of decency and integrity. So much so, that he had become something of leader in the neighborhood. (Perhaps that was reason enough)

To make, a long, horrible story shorter, Merton began harassing Ty's father and family. Fortunately Ty's father was not just decent and honest, he was smart. Merton could never get him to say anything that could be misconstrued as incriminating. William always made sure he could account for his whereabouts. He crossed and recrossed his "T"s and double dotted his "I"s. He managed to fend off the most direct of Merton's machinations.

This went on for years. But Merton's one-man campaign did take its toll. William was always a big man and given to high blood pressure. He had always managed to keep his cool even in the face of extreme provocation. On that point I can say Merton never won.

Merton never provoked William into doing anything truly stupid, even when it was clear that William was furious. Over time it must have built up. One day after a particularly abusive encounter with Officer Merton that rage boiled over. William's rage erupted, not as violence, but as a fatal pulmonary aneurysm. Ty was fourteen when his father died.

"There's the fucker that killed my father," thought Ty. No one in the link disagreed with him. Even as Ty started to move to get out of the car, James smacked the auto-locks shut again.

"Man, what are you doing?"

"I'm not letting you go over there half-cocked. I don't want you to do something stupid."

"Man, you know me, especially now. You know I'm not going to do anything to hinder finding Pandora's brother."

"Actually, Hermano, all we're getting from you is 'red.' You know as in "seeing."

"Ramón's right," James added, "We can still feel you in the link but all we're getting is a boat load o'rage."

Ty forced himself to calm down. It took a bit of talking down from James and Ramón. If you were to simply watch this conversation it would have looked like about 30 seconds of staring at each other. Hector didn't bother mentioning it to us at the time. The situation had already resolved itself by the time he could have told us it was happening.

Besides by this point in the afternoon we were trying to find Dr. Kettleworth's office.

The guys managed to content themselves with watching Merton. A short while passed. Mrs. Merton came home and then left again. As far as the guys could tell they hadn't said a word to each other. Through a window they saw Merton pick up his cell phone. He didn't speak. He merely listened. After a moment he hung up the phone and hurried out of the house. The guys (or should I say Ty) decided to follow him. They managed to tail him to a local u-store-it place. It was one of the low rent kinds. It had Minimal security and little interest on what the renters may be storing.

The guys caught sight of Merton again as he approached the storage units. Merton opened up a large unit and then disappeared inside of it.

There are storage places with sophisticated computer coordinated security systems with lights, motion sensors and cameras. Not this place. This place looked as though the main item stored there might be rust. A few of the storage lockers looked as though the locks were there to keep the doors from falling off.

The Unit Merton had entered was fairly close to the back fence. James pulled the car up near the fence. Ramón and Ty slipped out of the car then made their way over the fence. Ty and Ramón crept up to the storage unit and observed from outside. They heard a bit of rustling around and then the sound of breaking glass. It was a small, sharp crack like a bottle dropping on cement. They thought they could see a faint blue light shine from underneath the door. Then it was silent. They waited for a moment but no more sound was to be heard. They decided to risk opening the door.

The storage unit was just a little larger than a one-car garage. It was empty. That is empty of Merton. The items in the unit had all been placed to allow a maximum of space in the middle of the floor. Along the walls were a series of workbenches and lockers. The lockers contained unmarked body armor and weapons similar to those that the police use.

Most of the workbenches had tools for repairing or modifying them. One workbench had a collection of vials, bottles, beakers and Bunsen burners. There was also a small, very old looking oven. Ty thought it looked like a miniature kiln. The table was covered with various papers with odd-looking diagrams.

"This shit looks like Harry Potter's potions class."

Of the three guys who were there, none of them could tell who had that idea first. Their assessment was fairly close. What it was was a half-assed alchemical lab. It should have been good for throwing together a few "tricks" but not much more. The disappearance of Merton belied that assumption however.

I shouldn't deride it too much, that lab did produce at least one impressive effect. In the cabinet next to the "lab" they found a number of small bottles. One of which was a small ampoule of a lightly glowing blue liquid. The bottle had a cork with a tag tied to it. The tag read, "Break in circle"

At this point the guys looked down and notice that in the middle of the unit was a fairly ornate and intricate magic circle. These guys had seen enough movies to know about the basic pentagram.

The one on the floor looked like it had been applied directly to the cement with gold and silver based paints, the really expensive kind with a lot of real metallic content.

"So," Ty said unnecessarily aloud, "let me sum up. Disappearing, asshole cop."

"Check," came the reply.

"Small armory of weapons and body armor."

"Check."

"Seriously fucked- up magic shit."

"Check"

"All in favor of letting Mr. gives handle this one say 'aye.'"

The "aye" came from the other two in unison with Ty's own.

"Let's go check on that office again."

"Sounds like a plan."

It's a shame that turned out to be the more dangerous plan.

Chapter Twenty-Seven

Back in richmond, building security had taken just
enough time getting up to the room. I was able to weave a minor cloak. I
lay on the conference table surrounded by broken glass.

The cloak was just enough for them to ignore me but not much else. As
they began to check out the scene, I rolled off the table and then under it.

While the security guards were checking out the broken window, I
crawled into the hall and made my way to the stairs.

I hurried down the stairs and rejoined Hector and Marguerite. We
wasted no time getting away from the M.E's Building. In our rush to get
out we drew attention to ourselves. It seems someone spotted us making
our mad dash. They gave security a description that would come back to
haunt us all too soon.

We, that should be I, made the mistake of trying to stake out our next
address. This address turned out to the home of one of the wealthier people
on the list. It was in a place called the fan district. Nice homes, ethnically
and culturally diverse. It had college students and young professionals and
even some Old Money. About the only thing that these neighbors had in
common was their affluence.

Since I can't run a cloak non-stop, Azgard stood out like a Vegas casino
on an Amish farm. It was just about as welcome. Unfortunately, someone
was alert enough to point out Azgard to the authorities. The witness back
at the ME's building had described Azgard well enough that it was easy to
recognize. Rather rapidly, I found myself trying to explain our presence to
some very suspicious officers of the law. They were suspicious enough that
the first officers had called for back up.

Other than that, it was going well. I got the nods and "uhuh"s of men who've already made up their mind. If there hadn't been the first incident, I think we would have just been asked to move on.

Instead we got, "Why don't you just come with us so we can sit down and chat this out, more comfortably." I doubted that the officer had my comfort truly at heart. I know his partner didn't. He kept shining his flashlight into our faces, even though there was still plenty of daylight left in the late afternoon sky.

I knew this wasn't going to go well. It was time for desperate measures. During the whole "who are you, why are you here" harangue. I was channeling energy. I poured that energy into the glow stick, I keep in one of my duster pockets.

Just as the barely polite questioning had reached its crescendo, I knew I would have to act. The officers began to herd us back toward the police cruisers

I've practiced this a bit so I'm glad it worked. With my hands in full view of both officers, I mentally reached into my duster's interior breast pocket and gave the glow stick a small telekinetic flip. I caught the glow stick in my hand and gave it the one-handed snap and shake. With the energy I had poured into the glows stick I magnified the light and sound from the snap to a blinding and deafening flash.

I felt a little sorry for the officers though. Though there wasn't going to be any harm to them physically, they would be stunned for perhaps ten seconds. That was the flashy part and, honestly, not all that hard. Subtler and harder was extending my "cloak" to Hector and Marguerite. I can't seem to get a group of us to just disappear like I can alone. The best I can do is make someone under the cloak unrecognizable.

That cloak was up and running well before those ten seconds had elapsed. So were we. We ran six blocks down and another three east before I let the cloak drop. We didn't cover nine blocks in ten seconds. We didn't need to. The officers would not be able to give an accurate description of us for at least the duration of the cloak.

We walked the streets of Richmond trying to appear innocuous. We could hear police sirens in the distance. Once, a criuser came past us, slowed for a moment, then sped up again. The flash and hide maneuver seemed to have worked. Hector brought up one small problem

"How are we going to get back home?" Hector asked.

"Why do you ask?" I said in lieu of an answer.

"I ask because your yellow beast is back by the cops. I doubt you want to try to reclaim it, after all that."

"I suppose you're right about not going back for Azgard. For the moment why don't we just take this car?"

I turned and unlocked the driver's side door of the butterscotch yellow car parked on the street. It was almost hidden between two SUVs.

It was the first time I saw Hector surprised. He looked down at my car, the yellow beast as he called it. "Damn," he said, "How'd you do that? It's even got the one windshield wiper held on with a band-aid, just like your car."

"It is my car."

"How'd you get it here from back there?"

We all climbed in, Marguerite in the passenger seat, Hector in the back, I drove. We pulled quietly away from the curve.

"Don't know. It's not me. It's the car"

"Now that's a good car," Hector responded, "No wonder you keep it."

I glared at him in the rear-view mirror. That only provoked laughter From him and Marguerite.

Chapter Twenty-Eight

THINGS WEREN'T GOING SO light-heartedly for the rest of the Guys. They were attempting surveillance on the office. Once they were back at the industrial park, The Guys sat in the car and watched the building for a while. Nothing happened that they could see.

"If we're going to do this kind of stuff, we need some real training," said Ty.

"And gear," added Ramón.

James stayed silent, only a vague suggestion of agreement trickled over the link. James was deep in thought. Something was bothering him. He had always gone quiet when contemplating a problem. According to Hector, when James went "deep" his part of the link was like listening to a conversation through a moderately thick wall. Thin enough to hear someone speaking yet too thick to make out words.

Suddenly James spoke up loud, clear, and directly to Hector. It was sudden enough that it startled Hector. He gave a small jump. That startled those of us who were riding with him.

"Hector, could you repeat what Gives said about the man in the office?" James asked over the link.

Hector recounted what I had told him.

"That's what I was afraid of." said James

James had noticed some crucial details from following Officer Merton. He had left mysteriously from a room that contained a bunch of unmarked police equipment. A man fitting Merton's description appeared mysteriously in Dr. Kettleworths's office. Officer Merton was the man had I tangled with in Kettleworth's office.

"We must have tipped off someone, somewhere." James said.

"Unless this M.E. guy told his office to secretly alert him if any one came asking for him." Ramón suggested playing devil's advocate.

"I doubt it. Someone on his staff would have to be in on it. He wouldn't just ask any employee to do it. It's kind of a shady thing to do and these guys would want as much unsaid as possible," said Ty.

"So either he's got an accomplice in his office . . ."

"Which we think is unlikely," continued Ramón.

"Or at least dangerous to assume," said James.

"So then we tipped somebody off up here. They had him check things out as a precaution."

"Which means . . .?"

"They may have somebody watching for us here as well."

"Time to get serious." Ty thought. Formulating a plan on the run, the Guys slid gracefully into action. There were four buildings in this little industrial park. Three were office buildings. One was a small warehouse.

All were closed by six in the evening, save one. Unfortunately this one housed the telemarketing office right next door to the target.

The three Guys quickly discovered the management of the industrial park had contracted a private security firm to do rounds of the buildings. The guys were smart though. Ramón watched for the security vehicles coming around. Ty watched the building itself. James stayed with the car and moved it as needed based on Ramón's observations.

The telemarketers emptied out of their office starting at ten. The last stragglers were gone by 10:20. The guys waited a full hour before going in.

The Azgard contingent had been busy laying low for a while. Once we did get on the road again we avoided the main highways for fear of being spotted by law enforcement. I was sure we had gotten their attention with my little glow stick trick. Consequently we were taking the long way home.

Hector gave us a play-by-play account. I was uneasy about the whole thing and said so.

"You're the boss," Ramón said via Hector. "But we gotta get on this. God only knows what this Koenig *puta* has planned."

"Okay, you're right . . . but get out of there at the first sign of trouble." At this Hector let out a hearty laugh. I asked how that was funny.

He replied, "Ty just pointed out that they were about to break and enter a property that they know to be connected to a ruthless, shape-shifting, wannabe crime-lord who has an undead superwoman as an enforcer. We passed that trouble sign 500 miles and 3 days back."

I conceded the point. "Then just dive for cover when the shit hits the fan."

They Guys first real concern was how to enter the building. Ty knew enough about electronics to have noticed the security system when they checked the place earlier. He had learned enough to rebuild a faulty stereo or TV. He didn't feel competent enough to beat the security system.

Suddenly James had the answer. "Guys, you remember how my dad is always saying turn liabilities into assets. Well, we're sitting here trying to figure out how to get in and search the place without being noticed. That just isn't going to happen. I think we need to draw attention. Let's make someone come out to check on whatever is important. They'll lead us right to what we need."

Hector relayed all that.

"That's a pretty dangerous plan," I said.

"Maybe," James continued, "but it'd be a way to get information we can act on."

Once again I had to concede the point.

Ty picked up the idea of turning liabilities into assets. "We do have something that is an incredible benefit. Our connection. We don't need phones or walkie-talkies or gear of any kind to know what's going on with any one of us. There must be dozens of ways to exploit that. After all, we did do pretty good against the freak in the alley."

"As I recall Hector got his arm broke," I said.

"Yeah, but the first time we tangled, he nearly killed us all in an embarrassingly short time."

Hector got quiet for a bit. The Guys were trying to figure out their plan. After about ten minutes Hector actually cried out "Eureka."

"Wow! That was intense. We just found another way to exploit the connection. Using four brains to process information, Ty was able to figure at a way to defeat the security system, if he only had the right tools."

"So does that mean bad guy baiting is off the table?" I hoped.

"No, he doesn't have the right tools but they have a plan on how to handle the situations that do arise."

I had a feeling that it was more abut the thrill of risk than the lack of tools. The connection may have increased a lot of things about the Guys, available brain power, greater range of perception, a truly impressive ability to work as a unit, but in no way did it diminish their love of adventure, their youthful sense of immortality, or their complete willingness to make a bad plan and go with it.

They stationed Ty watching outside the building. He was able to get himself up to the roof of the neighboring office building where he had a good view of the main entrance. James and Ramón entered the building by breaking through the glass of the main door. Ramón went straight for the office in question; James got himself into the janitor's closet. From there he could keep an eye on the rear entrance and the hall just in front of the office.

He could also see the front door of the empty office space. The only real blind spots were covered by Ty, albeit from outside.

There was no alarm when they broke the first window.

"Must send a silent alert," thought Ty. Nor was there any obvious signal when Ramón broke the frosted glass of the suspect office door and entered.

"Damn, I wish I had a flashlight," he thought.

There was a little light coming in through windows at the back of the office from the street lights in the parking lot. Beyond the initial reception area there was a maze of cubicle walls blocking most of the light.

In the back seat of my car, Hector leaned forward and put his head in his hands, closing his eyes tightly.

Then he told me to turn down the radio.

a moment later he smiled and said "Yes. It works"

It seems that Hector WAS letting Ramón use his brain. With the aid, Ramón was able to maximize the input he got from his senses.

"It's not as good as having night-vision goggles." he told us via the link, "but I swear I can almost hear the shape of the room." He did a quick rummage through the absentee receptionist's desk. It was, as expected, empty. Ramón doubted he could have read anything anyway. He was just grateful that he could see well enough not to walk into things.

Ramón progressed back into the "maze" and found out that it was indeed a maze. Past the pretense of the reception desk there was no fooling anyone that this was a real working office.

There were no computers or phones in the cubicles. Only a few had desks, all of which had empty drawers. Ramón suspected that they might have hidden compartments but his quick checks proved fruitless.

"I'm going deeper in." Ramón worked his way around the odd arrangement of prefab walls. What was most unusual about them is that they were a bit taller than most cubicle set-ups. Ramón was 6'2 and these walls topped out at his eye line. They were just high enough that most people wouldn't be able to see over them very well, if at all. Ramón proceeded cautiously. He soon found himself back at the start of the path again.

"Hector. I need a bit more of an assist here. I think something is wrong."

"Got it."

Ramón looped through again taking the same path. At Hector's request he went again this time choosing his turns differently.

Hector tapped me on the shoulder as I drove. "Hey you got a pen and paper?"

"Dig around back there I said I'm sure you'll find something."

Hector did. And after only moment he said, "Found something. it'll have to do." You sure got some weird shit in your car.[12]"

What he had found was a children's reusable sketchpad. You may recall them. They predate the magnetic doodle pads. They consist of a semi-clear sheet of plastic stapled to a piece of cardboard. You draw on the top sheet of plastic with a little plastic stylus. That top sheet over lays some funky, dark substance that sticks to the upper sheet showing where you've been drawing. When you're done, you just lift the upper sheet and everything disappears.

Hector began to sketch out the cubicle floor plan while Ramón walked it over and over again. Ramón was getting quicker with each loop.

Hector became totally engrossed in the project. We risked heading back to I-81. We stopped for gas just before getting on it. Ironically we were not to far from the Waffle House where I had used the raven to spy on Koenig.

He didn't even notice when Marguerite asked if he wanted anything from the little convenience store at the gas station. He just remained huddled over in the back seat, drawing in the near darkness. As I filled the tank, I could peek into the back seat and over his shoulder. Enough of the gas station light fell onto the pad to show me what he was doing. I was shocked.

It wasn't anything bad. In fact, it was quite good. Seeing his incredibly detailed floor plan drawn on the kid's toy was a bit like seeing the Mona Lisa reproduced faithfully on an etch-a-sketch.

Marguerite and I were just getting back into the car when Hector actually cried out "eureka" again.

Hector had found out that there were indeed several hidden sections in the sprawling maze of the cubicles. He directed Ramón to the first of

---

12   No, I don't have the same thing going on with my car as with my apartment; I just carry a lot of random items in it.

them. Ramón, who was rather athletic, grabbed the top of the cubicle wall, pulled himself up and swung his legs over to land rather gracefully in the tiny cubicle.

"Pretty sturdy for prefab walls," he said.

Inside the doorless cubical, there was a small table and an Internet server. There was nothing else on the table. The server only had a power cord coming out it and since the lights were blinking, presumably, it was on.

Hector said that it appeared the server had a wireless connection. "What's on it?" I asked.

"I don't know. There's no monitor associated with it. So Ramón can't just look at a screen."

I was about to ask what we needed to do to get a look when Ty broke in with bad news. "We got incoming. Tell the boss his wife coming in through the front door."

If that weren't bad enough, James then added, "We also got a blue light special going on almost directly outside my closet." Merton was coming through from another portal.

Well, the shit was hitting the fan. The good news was that we were only about 15 minutes away from the guys, a lot less if we pushed it. The bad news was that may be far too long.

I told Hector to have everyone stay where they were. "Do not engage," I told them. If the guys stayed quiet enough probably only Ramón was in danger. And Ramon was only in danger if they actually checked on the hiding places. I had a bit of a plan. I wasn't sure it would work.

Though I hated to loose any time I pulled off to the shoulder. I made Marguerite take the wheel while I got in back with Hector.

I was going to try extending my cloak through the guys spiritual link. The cloak again you say? I know, I know, I try to use it for everything. I've had so much success with it. Besides it's a very handy tool and the only one for which my mentor ever gave me a compliment.

I sat beside Hector. While he concentrated on Ramón through the link, I tried to glean an image from his mind, a connection. Marguerite continued to race down the highway. I was able to latch on to the image in Hector's mind quite easily. In fact it was the strongest connection I've ever made at a distance. I was sure I was going to be able to exploit the guys' connection for their own good. Sympathetic magic is often fairly strong. In this case I had the equivalent of a full-sized, living voodoo doll.

When I tried to extend my cloak through Hector to Ramón, I got a nasty shock. Hector "disappeared" under the cloak just fine but Ramón was barely affected. The only benefit was that I was able to use a bit of my Sight through the guy's senses.

Because I was essentially eavesdropping in on Hector's mind I could "hear" James chime in over the link.

"Nasties one and two have just met and are having a little chat.

James let us listen in.

"So, Lucretia, are they still here?" There was a smug tone in Merton's voice.

"Can it Merton, there's something wrong."

"Oh is the big bad huntress stumped? Can't you sniff them out with your preternatural sense of smell?"

"Do I look like a werewolf? Now shush." She moved about, taking a hesitant step toward the janitor'scloset where James was hiding.

"What about zooming in on their precious life's blood?"

"That's vampires, Merton. Be glad you aren't working with one of them."

"So just how do you track and what makes it better than my equipment?"

"Simple," she took a step away from the closet and toward the office where Ramón huddled down on himself fearing discovery. "I don't actually sniff out their bodies. I track by life force, by essence, by the stink of their souls. I've never had a confused trail before."

"So that's your excuse?"

"It's that damn mind swirl. Instead of having four blips on my radar, I'm trying to find a spot in a pattern.

There's traces of them coming in from all over. It disguises their physical location. It's like trying to find a person in a body temperature room with infrared cameras."

"She's wasting her money on you. If I had my infrared equipment I'd have found them by now even in the situation you described."

"Merton you're really getting to annoy me. Besides it's not my only trick."

"I'll bet."

"Clever retort, Merton."Sheila continued to move about the corridor slowly as if trying to feel something on the air. Merton leaned against the wall. He was the very portrait of overconfidence and unprofessionalism.

"So if these guys are as weak as your ex-husband, this should be cake."

Shelia laughed. "I suspect he went easy on you. He dislikes violence."

"Like I said. Weak. Anyway let's get this going. We should be done by now."

"And would be if you were running things?"

"Yeah, it would."

"Okay, prove it." Now it was Sheila's turn to lean against a wall. Much of the view was blocked to James.

He was trying to watch through the slats at the bottom of the janitor's closet door. There wasn't much detail he could pick up. To him it appeared that Sheila had just pulled a cigarette out of nowhere and lit all in one fluid movement.

"Put that out they'll smell it and that'd ruin the surprise."

Relax, officer, they already know we here. I can smell their fear."

"Just not enough to track them."

Sheila inhaled deeply and then exhaled hard. James could see the smoke cloud even in the very dim lighting. Instinctively he knew there was some bad mojo in it.

"Go ahead prove yourself, bad ass."

Merton just grunted and moved over to the office suite where Ramón was hiding. James was certain that instead of dissipating, Sheila's smoke cloud had sunk to the floor and was clinging to Merton's shoes.

It was about this time that Ty had an idea.

"Hey guys," he thought. The rest sent back silent assents. "When we pooled our brain power we were able to do some amazing things.

"Go on." came the group response.

"Well the body is basically run out of the brain. You know the Medulla Oblongata deals with coordination, et cetera, et cetera." The conversation was interrupted as Ramón pointed out that Merton was getting awfully close to his position.

James kicked in with "Some dinosaurs needed two brains, one for the front one for the back . . ."

"So," continued Hector, "Imagine what one of us could do if we all worked together from the inside . . ."

"Hey. I can smell cigarette smoke." thought Ramón remembering James's glimpse of Sheila's little parlor trick. "It's like she was trying to tip us off."

Ramón caught sight of a black-gloved hand as it grasped the top the cubicle.

"Now or never guys." he thought.

With that the other three focused their consciousness, their awareness, and their will all within Ramón. It was as if they had all moved into different parts of his body. James described it like an orchestra. Ramón was the band leader, but each of the guys had a different part of the score to play.

Suddenly Ramón was one seriously multitasking "machine." He leapt to his feet and kicked down the cubicle wall in front of Merton. This forced the "good" officer to take a step back. Merton brought his shotgun to bear.

With his right hand Ramón had scooped up the wireless server. His left hand helped him to balance into a one-footed hop that spiraled him around to catch Merton in the chest with his right foot before Merton even got a bead on Ramón.

Merton was rolling with kick but Ramón kept his fluid motion going. With the server in his right hand, Ramón (or the guys in Ramón's body) swung at Merton's head forcing him to alter his direction in mid-dodge.

This exposed the right side of Merton's body. Ramón's left hand managed to wrest the side arm Merton still had holstered on his hip. He tore it away from the "uniform", holster and all. During all this Ramón's feet had turned him toward the quickest exit. The quickest exit was a window from the office to the parking lot, so long as he didn't mind diving through the window.

Merton still had his shotgun, it wasn't even a debate.

Ramón crashed through that window like a pro. He did a forward tumble as he landed. His momentum brought him upright into a run without losing a step or damaging the server.

He turned his run toward the main entrance of the industrial park.

He got there just in time to meet Marguerite, Hector and I flying in. I could see he was moving fast. Had the situation been less tense I might have made a matrix joke about his speed. He ran up to the car before Marguerite had time to slow it down. He pulled open the back door next to me, threw me over one shoulder and dropped the server in my place next to Hector in one fluid operation. Then he was running back to make sure he could get James and Ty out alive.

I felt less than dignified. I could feel the strain this was putting on Ramón, made worse by my not inconsiderable weight. For a second Marguerite caught my eyes and I gave her a nod. A nod she interpreted correctly as "get that server out of here now"

I smiled to think how well we were working together. A smile I lost as recalled that Ramón was taking me to face a well-trained, armed combatant and a vicious (albeit stunning) undead fiend.

You know I've just got to find a better hobby.

Chapter Twenty-Nine

WHEN HOLLYWOOD GETS AROUND to making the movie, I'm sure this next part will have all sorts of whiz-bang special effects. With Industrial Light and Magic (as opposed to my kind of magic) it would be quite spectacular.

It'll have searing lights, bolts of crackling energy, intricate CGI modeling and slow motion, lots and lots of slow motion. That is if you want to see how cool things really were.

I know I sound like I'm bragging but it really was one of our better early efforts. Ironically it may be more exciting to watch on the screen than actually being there. Most of the forces I wield are invisible. As for Ramón, he was still moving at eye-blink speeds.

Ramón rounded back to where he had burst out of the window. Merton was just coming out of it. The overhead parking lot lights made his night-vision goggles unnecessary. Merton wasn't taken unaware by Ramón's return. He had his shotgun up and leveled at us. Ramón wove around him dodging Merton's aim. Merton was patient enough to wait for Ramón to come to him. He timed his blast to do the maximum damage. The Guys had anticipated this however and just as he reached that critical spot, Ramón threw himself into a roll. The roll took him under the blast then down and around Merton. I, on the other hand, had been thrown up into the air in an arc. I had enough momentum to clear the shotgun slug and still come down on top of Merton.

Merton was quick and adapted well. He saw me coming down on him and he twisted his grip on the shotgun so that he could club me out of the air.

It might have worked too, except for this one thing. Despite all the evidence he had seen, Merton didn't really believe in magic. Not in the "I doubt its existence" sort of way. He'd have to be a fool to do that, what with him commuting hundreds of miles magically just that day. No he didn't believe in it enough to trust it. It wasn't a real consideration in his strategy.

The more fool him. I let slip earlier that I had accidentally altered my bone density. I'm about a hundred pounds heavier than I look and I am a fat man. Merton knew, given his own stature and prodigious strength, that he could swat a short man of 250 pounds out of the air. With the right leverage, he'd make it look easy. Even at plus one hundred pounds in my favor he'd probably still come out on top. That's where my awesome, if simple (and non-photogenically invisible) mystic skills came in handy.

I still had a reserve of energy I had drawn in earlier. I took that energy and used it to strengthen my connection to the earth. Some mystics might refer to it as "rooting" (even though I was in mid-air.) Others might call it "increasing my affinity for the primal earth element." The more scientific may think of it as modifying the local gravitational "constant".

Whatever you call it I put on weight (if not mass.) When I came down on top of Merton, I wasn't a mere hundred pounds over his estimate but closer to a thousand.

When Merton hit my face with the butt of his shotgun he left a nasty bruise that ran from my cheek to my ear. It still didn't budge me. I landed on him. Merton crumbled like a house cards in a bowling tournament.

Come to think of it, I probably looked like a bowling ball. I'm round enough and I was dressed in black.

In a pleasant reversal of our earlier bout, Merton was down for the count.

Ramón had rounded the far side of the building. He came in the door closest to where James was hiding. James considered shifting his awareness back but they agreed it might be too dangerous to try and shift on the fly.

Sheila was right where they remembered her. She was still next to the janitor's closet where James was hiding.

She was leaning against the wall, smoking a cigarette. Ramón zoomed in and threw a punch like a speeding locomotive. Sheila batted it away like a fly

"You're going to burn up your body doing that. If you keep that up, you'll make yourself all gross and no fun to eat."

Whoever was in charge of the legs did a heroic job keeping Ramón balanced after his big punch was denied. He swung back around with some sort of spin kick. Sheila's one-armed deflection made her look like a Tai-Chi master. (If Tai Chi masters wore "hot business woman" outfits and chain-smoked)

Then she went offensive. Blurring into motion she grabbed a hold of Ramón and "stole" his momentum for her own throw. Ramón went flying down the hall. He was able to tuck and roll to avoid cracking his head open on the floor.

Sheila was right there on him, waiting for him to spring up. Ramón continued the roll another half go, rose up on his hands and did an inverted spin-kick that caught her off guard. There was a crunch of bone as Ramón "loosened" Sheila's lower jaw (and stamped out her cigarette.)

Sheila hit the hallway wall with her shoulder. She turned back to face Ramón, the quiet disdain of earlier replaced by fury.

"That actually hurt," she said. (Okay, what she really said was "Tha accshully huurrd . . .")

Now Sheila pulled out her "lighting strike to the heart" maneuver. The one she had used on poor Roberta.

Ramón somehow caught and held her fist. Next he pressed the hand cannon he had stolen from Merton against Sheila's wrist and pulled the trigger. The blast was enough not only to sever Sheila's hand from her arm; it also drove a small piece of bone shrapnel in Ramón shoulder (that'll be important later so remember it).

Before Sheila could react to that, Ramón placed the massive revolver against her forehead, chest, and each of her knees firing into each location. Then he spun her around and fired again into the base of her spine.

When Sheila stopped twitching, each of the guys zoomed backed to their bodies. TY and James made a beeline for Marguerite's Lexus. Ramón limped around to where I lay dazed on the ground next to a very unconscious Merton.

In my befuddlement, I kept wondering why Merton's shoes were smoking. It was odd, I thought, because they didn't have a cigarette. Ramón helped me up, it was excruciating. Even with my increased bone density I must have had a hundred hairline fractures from the impact. Merton was wearing body armor but I doubted he was uninjured.

"Hey boss, security's on their way, we've got to move." with that he dropped the revolver down on the ground next to Merton.

Training can be a wonderful thing. Instinctively I cloaked Ramón and myself while invoking a "sense." I wanted to see if Merton had any life threatening injuries. I got a visual variation thankfully. He had a few broken bones that would heal in time and a ruptured spleen that wouldn't.

The bones I could let go but I had to save his life. Luckily because of the cloak, the security folks were more concerned about the mutilated corpse in the "break-in" building. It gave me enough time to stabilize Merton. It was just enough for the EMTs to finish saving his life.

Once again the confusion worked in our favor. After we had taken a few steps away from Merton, the security guards were able to find him and call for the help that he needed.

Ramón and I continued to walk under the protection of my cloak. We were completely ignored by the guards. We made it to the main road that ran by the industrial park. Marguerite's Lexus pulled up beside us. James was driving. Ty jumped out of the passenger seat and opened the back door for us. Ramón and I climbed in the back. I dropped the cloak. James was already whisking us away. I turned my attention to Ramon's shoulder wound. The piece of bone was about the size of a thumbnail. I didn't have anything to pull it out. I used my mystic skill to start knitting the flesh beneath the wound back together. Slowly, and painfully this began to push the bone out and close the wound. It was harder than I expected.

What I didn't know was that Shelia was able to leach some of this energy through a sympathetic connection with her shard of bone. It wasn't much. It was just enough to get her moving again.

Some of you may be asking "doesn't life energy hurt the undead?" That's only true in role playing games. All undead eat up life force energy in one form or another. Why would it hurt them? Even as Ramón's healthy flesh pushed the bone fragment free, Shelia was back up and on the move.

Chapter Thirty

WE HAD ALMOST MADE it back to my apartment, when the three guys all sat up straight. They had been allowing themselves to decompress a little. Especially Ramón, he looked about to pass out. Now they were on full alert again.

"Hector's telling us that Ms. Winston sees something bad back at your apartment," It was odd to hear Marguerite referred to that way. It sounded both natural and oddly formal. Perhaps it was the suits the Guys were wearing. Even rumpled, they carried an air of authority. No, it was more like confidence with a capital C.

We met up with Hector and Marguerite in the downtown parking garage. It was only a few blocks from my apartment. This was one of those times that I didn't take advice. I told the gang that I was going to go back to my apartment. I wanted to check out the problem Marguerite had sensed.

Marguerite wanted to send at least one of the guys with me. I told them no. I said they should head back up to Vanderhorns' to rest. "After a few hours of shut-eye we can try to crack that server."

It had been a long day. We all needed to get some sleep. I wanted everyone to head back to the Vanderhorns' to get that rest. Everyone else thought that was too far to go.

I didn't think it was safe sticking around the 'Burg. It was possible that Marguerite's car had been I.D.ed,. Even though she wasn't getting any bad vibes about going back to her house, I didn't want to risk it.

Eventually they decided to drive north for a bit and get a couple of rooms in one of the low budget non- chain motels just off the interstate. "After all," Marguerite said," we are being bank-rolled."

So Marguerite took back her Lexus then she and the guys headed out. I turned, locked up my car and started walking back towards my apartment.

I was fairly certain that the bad thing waiting for me there would not be Shelia. I didn't know if that pleased or disappointed me.

I hadn't gone more than a few steps when it occurred to me that I was putting myself in danger pointlessly.

All of the threats Koenig had thrown at us so far were physical in nature. Even her biggest supernatural stick, Sheila, was primarily a physical powerhouse. I hoofed it back to my car, got in and lay down in the back seat.

I sent myself into a trance and liberated my soul from my body. As I floated up out of my self, I discovered something interesting about my car. I couldn't pass through it. Physical barriers don't impede the astral form. At least they're not supposed to. This told me I needed to find out more about my own car.

I went back into my body so I could roll down the window. Once this short but annoying chore was accomplished I continued a gentle waft back toward my apartment.

As I went, I looked down at myself. I wondered again why Marguerite had been impressed when she saw my astral form. It looked almost exactly like the real me. I have a physique that I won't describe in detail as a mercy to you, the reader. Suffice it to say my astral self looks like it carries as much extra weight as my physical body and as for other aspects, well, I'd blush but there's not enough to be ashamed of.

The only thing that's different is my astral self is a snow white "ghost". Perhaps it was too many *Doctor Strange* comics as a kid. This, by way, was about my only acquaintance with anything supernatural before my Magi training began.

When you're astral, your whole perspective on the world changes. As before, my outlooked altered when I left behind my physical body. Not so much that I'd neglect doing what needed to be done but a lot of the emotional baggage got muted. For instance, I was still angry at Koenig but my desire to see her roasted on an open fire had waned.

I decided I would experiment when I got back to my apartment. I had never tried to cause anyone to see me before. The only people I had "appeared" to astrally were those who, like Marguerite, could already see the spirit world. Now I was going to try to become visible to ordinary sight. First, though, I thought it prudent to not be "naked."

I pictured my self dressed in a three piece suit with my duster replacing the jacket of the suit. I saw it in full detail down to the buttons on the vest. I got everything except the color. I was still as white as bleached polar bears.

My hair, my clothes, and skin were all a fairly uniform shade of pale. I paused for a moment as I considered this.

Earlier I said Ramón looked like something out of *The Matrix*. I guess now it was my turn

"What the hell," I thought "I'll go with it." It did look cool and tonight was all about appearances anyway.

I floated down to the ground about a block from my building. I willed myself to appear. It took me a moment. If sometimes it seems like I don't really know what I'm doing, that's true enough. My formal Magi training was, for lack of a better word, interrupted. My mentor went into depth on many topics . . . others I just barely grabbed the basics. I muddle through the best I can.

I wondered if I was going to be able tell if I had made myself visible.

I needn't have worried. When I "manifested" the world changed around me. Normally when I'm astral I see the world as if I had hit the jackpot on my "Wheel of Sight." All senses tuned to the higher plane. Now all my senses were grounded back in physical reality.

I could even see my shadow on the sidewalk in front of me. I had thought I was going to merely impress myself on the minds of people. I guess not. I had enough "presence" to block light.

I walked toward my building. I was hoping to flush out whatever trouble was waiting for me there.

Certainly any one lying in wait couldn't miss me. I looked like a photo negative of my normal self. My swarthy, olive tone was washed out like a kid's unused coloring book. I figured that I would be hard to miss.

I stepped into the relative shadow of the entrance to my building. The lobby was dark. In the gloom I could see that my "skin" glowed very faintly. I was about to push open the door when I remembered.

"Oh right. I'm intangible." I considered for a second. Then I drew on my energy to give the door a little telekinetic shove. The door received a feeble push. Most of my energy was back with my body. It seemed to lose something in transition. I also noticed a small lag. It wasn't even a full second of lag, but it was worth noting.

On my second try I got the door to fly open enough to slip through without giving away my temporary ability to walk through walls. I normally take the building's ancient elevator. I took the stairs up to my floor instead. Sure taking the elevator would only be a few small TK taps on the buttons but I wanted to see if "trouble" was lurking for me on the stairs. Plus, astrally, I could climb them without getting winded by the third floor.

When I got to my door, it was slightly ajar. I always make sure my door is closed when I leave. I seldom lock it though. My ghostly friend is as good a deterrent as I can imagine. A little "shove" and my apartment door swung open.

I walked into my apartment. Whenever I enter my apartment, I look around to see to how the ghost has rearranged things. He had out done himself this time. Usually, it's only small things that get moved. This time the change was fairly big. And thorough. For example, I don't normally leave my living room just inside the front door.

I had another surprise coming. Sitting on the couch of my rearranged front room was Gretchen Koenig herself. Next to her, in a chair taken from the kitchen, was a young man who appeared to be about 20. He was dressed like an 18th century sailor. Hell, if he had an eye patch he'd be the stereotypical pirate.

He was bound and gagged. Behind him, with a knife to the young man's throat, stood a grim looking man in a dark suit. There was glint of silver on the grim man's chest. He wore a tie tack that looked like it had been fashioned from some old coin.

"Do come in, I hope we aren't calling on you at an inconvenient time," Koenig said.

I really had a clever retort and I tried to say it but for a moment I was speechless. I mean that literally. I tried to speak but there was no sound. I suspect that I looked like I may have been caught off guard and struggling for something to say. I wasn't. It just took a moment to focus properly to make audible sounds. It felt like I was shouting. However the sound produced was more of a whisper. By the time I was audible, the moment for clever retorts had passed. All I managed to say was, "Koenig."

"Have a seat, Mister Gives, or should I say 'Reverend'?"

I shrugged trying to play this as cool as I could. "It's only an Internet ordination. I don't talk about it much."

"That's not what really interests me anyway."

I asked what did interest her. I was just talking to stall. I didn't know who the guy playing dress up was or why she would use him as a hostage. He was clearly too old to be Stephan, besides he looked nothing like the pictures Stacie showed us. I heard something rattle in the kitchen, or perhaps it was the bedroom. Given how the apartment's floor plan had been altered I couldn't tell.

That was what was bothering me most. I had seriously underestimated someone. Either Koenig or my friendly neighborhood ghost had done something I didn't know they could do. I was hoping that the ghost had done it and had something in mind. He seemed to be helping more than hindering me lately. I still knew very little about "him." For example, I didn't even know that my ghost was a him. I just assumed. The most I have ever seen of "him" was one night he barged in to the bathroom and flashed a series of spooky eyes at me. That's it. Just a pair of disembodied eyes cycling through a series of late, late show eye effects: all white, piercing red dots, deep black chasms, the works

Koenig was saying something but I was still pondering the who the young man was and what the ghost might be doing.

When I didn't respond Koenig repeated herself, "I said,'I want my server and servant, Pandora, back, Mister Gives.'"

"I'm sorry, what did you say? I was thinking about important things."

This response apparently surprised her a little, "Are you telling me that you don't care that I have your 'Roommate' with a knife pressed against his neck?"

Now it was my turn to be surprised but an idea dawned also. "Roommate?"

"I was trying to be delicate. I'm sure he is more than just a roommate given that there's only one bed in your minuscule apartment. Honestly I'm a bit surprised. There's conflicting scuttlebutt about you. Some say you're a drunkard, others a powerful witch, still others say you are a kind of priest. Your ex-wife told me stories that you were, oh so heterosexual, if a bit inept."

"That's my late wife, I'm not gay, and you might as well turn over Stephan, you're done anyway."

"So, it is about the boy . . . and you're not gay? Made up like that? No? Well, perhaps it was Pandora who *sucked* you into this mess after all."

"Not important," I said, "release, Stephan."

Koenig continued ignoring my demand, "Here you are unarmed. Your live-in-what-have is bound, gagged and an eye blink away from death and you make demands without even the hint of negotiation." Koenig smiled brightly, "I've got to admire you. I really do. You've got balls. I think I'll have them bronzed."

I did my best not to picture that.

I was fairly certain who the man in the chair was by now. I had been trying not to look him in eye so Koenig might get the impression that I didn't care and he'd be in less danger. Now that I was fairly certain who he was, I didn't think he was in any danger. I wanted to try my "wheel of sight" to be certain but I didn't know if I would fade from physical view if I did.

As I looked him in the eye, the man in the chair stared back at me and his eyes flickered from shock white to red to black. Yeah, he was my ghost all right. Koenig didn't seem to know that. I really did hold all the cards and not her.

I smiled. I wish I could say that I was flip and witty and said things like "go ahead, he's dead to me any way" but I didn't. I only thought of that later.

I just sighed and said, "Look, Koenig you can either give him up now and I'll go easy on you or I'll turn you over to the Authorities . . ."

"Or you'll turn me over to the police? That's funny."

"No, not the small "a" authorities."

"Oh," she said mockingly and just who are these 'Authorities'?"

"You're a supernatural being, Gretchen. There are Powers who have jurisdiction over you whether you recognize them or not.."

"And what would these powers do? My crimes are no worse than many so called mortals. Would they execute me? It would seem odd, your ex-wife is truly a monster and she is allowed to go on. I'm merely a madam."

"You profit from the rape of children. Don't even try to minimize that crime. But no, they probably wouldn't execute you. They would just lock you up. Inside your Jekyll"

Her face went as white as mine. She stood up and yelled for her grim-faced man to kill the "hostage." Then she drew a pistol from her bag. It was another Desert Eagle. It was a twin to the one Ramón took off Merton.

She fired quickly and accurately. She shot three times. I felt three bullets go through my chest in a tight formation. The grim face man slashed the ghost across the neck.

Koenig was so focused on the lack of effect her shots had on me, she almost missed the show the ghost put on. A fountain of gore spurted out of his neck, enough to make the even most avid horror movie fan cheer.

Gallons of it washed across the room, drenching everything in front of him including myself. That ghost is really talented; his blood, obviously illusionary, (otherwise how could it hit me?) had a tactile element that even my astral form could feel. He let his head flop backward, held on only by a tiny scrap of skin.

Then next part actually frightened me. The ghost turned on his attacker. Breaking out of his bonds and standing up. Turning to face Koenig's lackey, my "friendly" ghost grabbed him, lifted him like a rag doll then jammed him down the gushing wound that was his open throat.

I strode up to Koenig and got right in her face. I was a gruesome figure in red and white. "Looks like you need back up," I said.

She didn't say a word but turned and threw a small vial, breaking it on the floor. Suddenly there was a swirl of blue light in the air. It's risky to follow someone through an unknown gate. (Not that I had a lot of experience but it just seems like common sense.) Especially since I was not going to be taking my body. I was about to do it anyway when I "awoke" back beside my car. I was on the floor of the parking garage. Someone knelt over me and seemed to checking my pulse.

"Oh, thank God you are alive," Dr McBride said. "Don't worry I've got the paramedics on their way.

Chapter Thirty-One

I WAS CONFUSED, DISORIENTED. I knew I was in danger but I couldn't tell why. At first I thought it must be McBride. But her touch held only gentleness and compassion. Something had to have gone wrong to jerk my astral form back to my body like that.

Through my fog I realized that all my "Sights" were still on. Every sense I had was ramped up and overwhelming me. That wasn't the cause of my distress. At the moment I couldn't tell what was. All I "knew" was that I was in danger and had to get away.

I tried to stand but seriously misjudged which direction up was. I only managed to roll onto my side. I must have been babbling. Dr McBride kept trying to calm me down.

The paramedics arrived far too soon and with them the sense of danger increased ten-fold.

Yet it wasn't them. A police car followed the ambulance. As it got closer I could feel the danger rising. It felt as though my head had to burst from the pressure. An officer got out of the driver's seat. He walked over to McBride and me.

The paramedics, directed by McBride, were trying to calm me then load me onto a stretcher. It wasn't going to go well for any of us. I was too disoriented to make an effective resistance.

The threat seemed to coming from the officer. By the time the paramedics got me onto the stretcher my mind had cleared a little. But now I was restrained. I could only look at the ceiling or my right or left. My "extra" senses were still working overtime. Looking up I could "See" just how old the parking structure was. It was distressing how degraded the materials were.

In addition, through some non-direct sense I could now sense two "Vectors" of danger, one coming at me from the officer and one toward every one else. The second one came from behind the officer back at his police cruiser. Much to McBride's consternation, the officer stopped the paramedics from loading me onto the ambulance. I lay there, restrained on the stretcher.

"Good evening, Dr. McBride," the officer said. "I know your work is to save lives but tonight you've captured a dangerous criminal."

I couldn't see the expression on her face but her voice dripped with disdain.

She said, "Really, Officer Mathews? He's always seemed so harmless, except to maybe himself." As they talked I heard a step-drag-scrape like some trying to walk with a useless leg.

The officer continued speaking to McBride "Well, just how well do you know . . . excuse me, Doctor.

Ma'am, Ms. Thompson (Thompson? oh God no . . .) please stay back in the car. You're really not . . ."

"My God, what happened to you?" exclaimed McBride. I feel fortunate that I couldn't see Shelia. Even with all my Senses going, I still couldn't tell how damaged she was physically. Both my senses of smell and hearing told me the same thing. There was a walking corpse nearby. Imagine listening to iron nails on a chalkboard while having rotted meat shoved under your nose. That's what I reading off Sheila.

There was a whiff of another scent among the slaughterhouse aromas. It was a familiar one. It was the smell of one of my workings. It was my first clue that Shelia had siphoned off some of my healing of Ramón. I realized that it must have been the bone fragment.

I chastised myself. I should have removed the bone first, no matter how painful it would have been to Ramón. The only reason Sheila was able to move was because she stole healing right from under my nose.

Sheila answered Dr. McBride's question, "What happened to me? I was shot... In the head, hand. . . .Other Places."

My late wife's words were slowed and slurred. It reminded me of the few times she had too much to drink. She was always so cute when she was a little tipsy. Drunk, she was heartbreaking. She got morose and slurred out her pain, real or imagined, until she wept. I felt such pity for her. Even now my heart went out to her, to who she used to be.

"Officer Mathews," she said. Her voice was getting clearer as I listened. I know you think that you'd be doing the boss a favor by eliminating Gives but I just can't allow it."

Mathews' voice turned stern. "Now listen here," was as far as he got. With my heightened hearing I knew that the grotesque squish-crunch I heard next was Shelia's exposed ulna and radius penetrating officer Mathews throat.

McBride and one of the paramedics screamed together. Sheila's sudden violence broke through their stunned disbelief. The other paramedic made a break for the ambulance. Even hindered by her wounds, Sheila made sure that none of them were screaming long. My senses allowed me to feel something I hadn't before. I felt the presence of the others in the parking deck. More accurately I felt their sudden absences. As each of the men died, I felt his presence wink out. Each life taken was like a flashbulb, bright for an instant then gone. Then only Dr. McBride was left

"You're lucky, Doctor," said Sheila, "Milo would never forgive me if I killed you. This should hold you nicely."

I felt a wave of magic ripple across me. It wasn't directed at me. Even so I could feel it tugging at the edges of my mind. The light that was McBride was abruptly veiled.

Shelia now turned her attention to me. She began to speak, half to me, half ramble to herself. It was something very familiar when we had a life together. I used to find it endearing.

"Time to get you out of here . . . can't take your car. It hates me. The cruiser doesn't have room for the stretcher. I'm not letting you off it, just yet . . ." she dragged me over to the ambulance and heaved me into the back with her good hand.

She then climbed in and I could hear her rummaging around. "Ah, this will work." she said. She leaned over me. Sheila was using a blood soaked police cap to try to cover the exit wound in the back of her head.

Perhaps she was only trying to keep her brains in.

There was a sting in my arm and that's all I remembered for a while.

Chapter Thirty-Two

WHEN I AWOKE, I was lying in a bed. I would find out later it that I was at the fourth address on the Guys' list. The one that was out Highway 33 towards West Virginia. I'm glad they never made it here to investigate.

Despite what Shelia had said, I was surprised to be still alive. I told myself that I must be missing something. This was at least the third time that she didn't kill me when she could have. It was the second time she had killed one of Koenig's flunkies instead of me.

The horror of what she did to Dr McBride and the ambulance crew suddenly hit me. I almost panicked.

My survival instinct pushed the raw fear back down. I was in the hands of a monster. A monster I didn't even begin to understand. She was a monster about whom I couldn't trust my feelings. It was time to take stock of my situation.

I sat up in the bed. It was an old, brass framed bed. The bed was soft and comfortable. The sheets were smooth and cool to the touch, yet warm enough to keep the bed cozy.

The room smelled musty despite the fresh breeze coming in through the open window. The mustiness was like that of old books. In its own odd way, that made the room more pleasant to me. I could hear birds singing in the pre-dawn stillness. I had a sense of being at the top of the house.

It was a long, narrow room. The only light came in through the windows. A gorgeous, nearly full moon hung low on the western horizon. The other windows showed a sky with the tiniest tinges of the coming sunrise.

It was one of those quiet moments that should have become a treasured memory. I only saw it as a dangerous trap. Even knowing that, I still wanted to lose myself in that moment. And that was terrifying.

I realized that I was undressed. My clothes were neatly folded on the ancient dresser. My duster hung from peg on the door to the hall. I started to get up to get my things together. The door swung open silently.

Shelia entered the room carrying an ornately decorated, glazed, ceramic tray. On it sat a bottle of water on a cloth napkin and a single candle in an old fashioned candle holder. The candle light seemed especially bright.

Shelia moved slowly as if her wounds might still be bothering her. There were no longer any obvious wounds though. She had almost finished regenerating herself.

She came over to the bed. I pulled back further into it, trying to cover myself with the sheets like a child.

She put the candle down on the small nightstand beside the bed.

"I thought you might be thirsty," she said. She held up the bottle of water. She was right, I was thirsty. I was loathe to accept anything from her. She knew well enough what my hesitation meant.

"Look, it's an ordinary bottle of water. Straight from the store. You can see that the lid is still sealed. It's Okay. Go ahead. Take a look at it with whatever extra senses you want."

"Not with you near it. You could be masking it's foul aura with your own."

"Oh that's the way to sweet talk a girl."

"Ha, ha."

"Fine," she said, "I'll put the water down right here on the floor." She did so and stepped back out to hang in the doorway. She had a servile demeanor, waiting there with the tray. She had even moved the napkin over to her one forearm.

The wheel of Sight came up Scent. The first thing that I noticed was the smell of perfume. It was coming from Shelia. Specifically from the leather thong choker she wore. The choker had a number of small ceramic charms hanging from it. They were white with blue glaze patterns on them like the tray. I didn't recognize any of the patterns. The enchantment was on the leather itself. It did a little to obscure her nature to the Sight.

If you'll forgive the expression, it was an honest hiding. The effect masked most of her unpleasant aura. It was not a way to remain undetected. Any mystic who encountered that mask would wonder what was underneath. It was like throwing a sheet over a large, ugly sculpture. The details were obscured but you didn't forget it was there.

I turned my attention to the bottle of water. It had a clean, almost sterile odor. It lacked most of the vibrancy that natural spring waters have. This must be one of those distilled, re-oxygenated bottled waters. That kind of water doesn't enchant well. In effect, they are almost magically neutral. In this circumstance that was good. It was easier to trust that the water was clean of enchantments.

I could also tell from the water's "aroma" that it was not poisoned or drugged. I started to get up to pick up the water. I remembered I wasn't dressed.

"Shelia, would you mind," I said, gesturing for her to turn her head. Instead, she walked into the room. She picked up the water bottle. She crossed over to the bed and set the water and the tray down on the night stand next to the bed.

I turned off the "Scent" I didn't want to catch a whiff of her in case the mask wasn't effective at close range.

I looked at her closely now. I couldn't see any evidence of Sheila's previous injuries. She was wearing an open robe of a shimmering white, nearly translucent fabric. Its long sleeves ending in loosely tied ribbons at the wrist. She stood artfully near the window so her robe would blow open teasingly. Under the robe, she wore a matching nightgown, cut to emphasize her figure but not reveal it. The leather thong choker accentuated the sensuous line of her neck.

Her long, curly hair flowed out from under a hand-dyed silk scarf, very much like the ones she used to make. The ends of her hair were caught by the breeze. She had the scarf tied across her forehead, keeping the hair out her face.

The delicate pattern of the scarf drew attention to her eyes. In the candlelight, her golden eyes glowed with warmth and invitation. Her lips were drawn up in the barest hint of a smile. She was a vision, beautiful and enticing, erotic and yet wholesome, a complete and utter lie.

My mind told me that this was all artifice. It was a ploy, an attack on my defenses. My heart was breaking under the strain of memory. She was the image of everything I had missed since that night a monster took her from me. I suddenly needed a drink. I settled for the water from the bedside table.

She sat down on the edge of the bed next to me. A slight chill ran through me. It was a mixture of fear and nostalgic desire.

"I know how much I've changed," she said, "but you have changed as much or more. We can't have what we had before. That doesn't mean we can't have anything"

She gazed deeply into my eyes. I had the kind of chill that causes one's body to warm in response. My next sip drained half the bottle. A little of it dribbled down my chin. Shelia reached out to dab it away with the napkin. I push her hand away. She dropped the napkin on the night-stand beside the tray.

Shelia took the bottle from my hand. She took a demure little sip. The mouth of the bottle rested against her pursed lips afterward. She continued looking intently into my eyes.

"This is a trick." I said, "You're trying to hypnotize me.

"You know I can't use my 'whammy' on you. I swear by my name this isn't a trick to harm you or your friends. I just want you to love me. "

Even without the Sight, I could hear the ring of truth in her words. She drank all but the last gulp of the water and then put her hand on my face. She brushed the hair out of my eyes then traced small circles against my cheek with the backs of her fingers. I had really missed that. She used to do that absentmindedly on those nights we sat up just talking in bed.

Sorrow and longing rose up from my heart and caught fire in my veins. I knew I was at the edge of something dangerous, unnatural, unholy. I tried to stay her hand as it moved from my face down my neck towards my chest. Instead, I merely held it.

I drained that last mouthful of the water from the bottle, hoping to clear my head. When I turned back to look at Shelia, all I knew was that she was my wife and I wanted her. It seemed the most natural thing in the world.

To my shame, not only couldn't I find the strength to bring my Will to bear against her, I couldn't even summon up my will to push her away. Nor could I turn my head when she leaned in to kiss me.

It wouldn't be until later that the horror of my situation would hit me again. In that moment everything seemed natural. More than that, it seemed like something that had gone wrong was being set right. I suspect that was as much my self-deception as it was her artistry in crafting the moment.

As fascinating as the train wreck of my life was at the time, there were important things going on with Marguerite and the Guys. So now seems to be a good time to tell you of those events

If you feel this is a dodge to avoid giving details of my time with Shelia, you're right. Not only don't I want to revisit the event, this is not that kind of book.

Chapter Thirty- Three

MARGUERITE AND THE GUYS had planned to get a couple of motel rooms so they could crash part of the way to the Vanderhorns. In fact, they had just gotten settled when Marguerite got another premonition of danger.

This time it was a feeling that the Vanderhorns were in danger. This was just after Koenig had made her exit from my apartment. I had confirmed for Koenig exactly what I was seeking. It didn't take her long to realize that if I was hunting after Stephan, I was probably working with Pandora. Sure as clockwork, Koenig targeted her actual family.

As unpredictable as Marguerite's gift can be, it sure came through that time. Still drained from the arduous experiences at the office, Marguerite and the Guys tumbled back into the car and made their way up to Northern Virginia.

Marguerite had phoned ahead to the Vanderhorns. Charles assured her everything was fine but agreed that they should get back there as soon as possible. He was overjoyed to hear of the liberation of one of Koenig's servers. He still knew a few of the tech guys from the IT department of his old company. He had paid them handsomely under the table to help him set up his missing child website. He was going to call one of them as soon as he got off the phone with Marguerite.

"This late? "Marguerite asked, "won't you wake them?"

"Not a chance, I bet those boys are still awake, killing each other online."

The ride down to Vanderhorns went smoothly (other than Ramón swerving to avoid a herd of avocado's playing dodge-ball in the road.)[13]

It was as they approached the house that Marguerite's premonition crystallized. They noticed a black SUV sitting down the road. Though it was not right across from the house, anyone in the SUV would have a good view of the Vanderhorns' house.

"Surveillance," The team agreed.

"They are probably waiting to see if we show up," James said.

"No," said Marguerite, "They are just biding their time. I think there here to lean on Pandora's family. I sense they are just waiting for the go ahead."

Ramon started to open his door even though Marguerite hadn't slowed down. The car was passing by the black SUV. "We'll get this." he said

"Wait. There's a better way." Marguerite picked up her cell phone and made an anonymous tip to the police about a suspicious vehicle. With that the team rode past the SUV and simply waited.

Very swiftly there was a police cruiser pulling up next to the SUV. An officer got out and approached the SUV. After a brief discussion the police cruiser and the black SUV both pulled away. Marguerite's senses of imminent danger eased. The team went to the Vanderhorn home.

True to his word, Vanderhorn had a small team of tech geeks eagerly awaiting the chance to use their powers for good. The guys quickly found crash space. Even Hector, who lived for that sort of thing, took a pass on the hack and crack session.

Charles was about to sit down with the his tech team when Marguerite pulled him aside

"Charles, we think that there may be more than just information on that server. It's more than just her little black book."

"What are you saying?"

"Bluntly, there could be pictures of Pandora . . . Stacie or even Stephan on there. Pictures of them 'working.'"

---

[13] It's not good to be the only one of the Guys awake for an extended time. To quote Ramón, "I drove while every one else tried to catch some Zs. I was fine until the rest of them hit R.E.M. Sleep, then *pow * disorientation city." Fortunately he realized quickly what was going on and Marguerite took over driving. Perhaps this effect explains James's odd behavior when he first met Mrs. Vanderhorn.

Charles face turned ashen. As the reality of what that server contained penetrated his denial. Marguerite later said that Charles seemed to deflate like a slow leaking balloon. The drive that seemed to be sustaining him since his daughter's return shriveled up. He more fell than sat down on the couch in his den, his head in his hands.

"Dear God, of course, no father should have to see that. I've been telling myself that I was going to fix everything now that Stacie was back. Get back Stephan, punish those responsible . . ." he paused forcing back a sob so he could continue speaking.

"But there isn't fixing everything is there? I can't ever make it all go away. Can I?"

Marguerite didn't answer him. She just put her arm around his shoulder and led him out of the room. If he heard one of the tech boys say "Oh my god" as they left, he showed no signs of it.

Four hours later, he knocked on the door of his own den. Same, the youngest of the tech guys, opened the door just a crack.

"Dude, you do not want to see . . . ah what's with the sledge hammer?"

"Do you have any leads?" Charles asked sounding very, very calm.

"Ah, Yeah. We've been able to trace some stuff. Most of it is just anonymous proxies to protect user identity.

But there is something that does stand out, if you look hard enough."

Jack, another of the tech guys, joined them at the door. "Um. It's okay to come in. we've closed everything up."

Vanderhorn went in and sat down staring at the computer screen.

"We got lucky," Jack said. "They were really good about covering their tracks where the photographs are concerned. Anonymously uploaded and administered etc but there were a number of hits that came in a couple of times a week. They would use a back door to check on one thing and one thing only . . . how much money the site had made."

"Well that sounds promising."

Sam continued, "We checked those addresses and they all belong to libraries. All of them are in the same part of Oregon. I'm afraid that's about all we've found.

"It's enough." Vanderhorn said, "It gives us a place to start looking for more leads." It wasn't much but it was about as we could hope for at the time.

Chapter Thirty-Four

I SUPPOSE I SHOULD GET back to what I was doing. I hadn't realized that I could feel that good and that bad at the same time. I had missed my wife so much since her death. I missed her smile, warmth and companionship. I had also missed the more carnal aspects as well. I was lonely for her and lonely in general. I felt "good" because what we did seemed to erase all that had happened, my Epiphany, her death, her trying to rip out my heart and eat it. It was all water under the bridge, a humbug of mere trivia.

As we kissed, all my dread melted away. Each caress pealed away a layer of angst. Lying next to her felt like returning home. So that was the "good".

The bad . . . . Well, let's face it, I was now technically guilty of necrophilia. (Unnecrophilia? Pseudo- necrophilia?) My God, she's a monster, and I think that it's quite clear that we aren't talking in metaphors here.

Not only that, she's the enemy. If she wanted to, she could have turned over and told me exactly where Stephan was and how to get to him. But she didn't.

I was, however, beginning to suspect that she really wasn't going to kill me. She's had plenty of opportunities and never taken one. This last time she actually prevented a Koenig crony from spiriting me away.

I looked at her as she lay sleeping. If sleep was what it was. I realized that she wasn't bothering to breathe. In the morning light she looked more corpse-like than ever before. I didn't find that moment's honesty at all refreshing.

All the dread that had been eased in the early dawn came rushing back in with a vengeance. I gathered up energy from the ambient and sent it coursing through my body, strengthening me for whatever may happen.

Suddenly Shelia eyes shot open. Perhaps she was awakened by the power surge next to her. Beyond opening her eyes, she didn't move.

"Please, let's not. I don't want to fight." Her voice was low and sleepy sounding. I didn't buy it. Still, every fight you don't have is one you haven't lost. I was tired of trying to figure out her game. So I went for the direct approach. Hell, if she wasn't going to kill me, the worst she could do is leave me in ignorance.

"If you're my enemy, why aren't killing me? If you're a friend, why won't you help me find the boy?" I was surprised to find her giving direct answers. Direct but obviously incomplete.

"I can't help you because I'm bound by obligation. I am to prevent you from working effectively against my 'principle' which means the boy stays hidden. I don't kill you because I need you to stay alive and with most of your power intact. Before you ask, this morning was because I still think of you fondly and crave that you think well of me."

"Perhaps cutting down on killing people would help." I suggested. my tone much more bitter than the surface flippancy of the words.

"Oh, but I am." She looked at me sincerity shining out of her golden eyes "I've only killed two people since meeting you again. The dreadful woman at the car rental. She was no innocent. Trust me. She knew what Koenig was up to. As did that officer last night."

"The paramedics? The sounds I heard . . . they way the disappeared from my Senses"

She took a deep breath before she answered, probably for effect. "Sure I put them at death's door, but they'll recover . . . eventually. That's why I only fogged Dr McBride's mind, as soon as we were gone she could begin helping" Shelia yawned and stretched, displaying her figure quite effectively.

"So what now?" I asked

She laughed. It was a girlish giggle really. "Silly, I'm still technically your wife. We can stay here and play until Koenig's need for the boy is completed. I'm sure I can find many fun ways to entertain you." She struck another pose on the bed that showed her figure to great advantage. "You always said our honeymoon was too short."

"That's not going to work," I told her (and myself.)

"Need a little more variety? That can be arranged, just think for whom I work."

"That's nauseating," I said.

"Oh, she has plenty of *women* working for her not just girls."

"No, it's the betrayal of trust that's nauseating. I feel bad enough being with you."

Again she laughed, this time a bit heartier. It was the laugh I remember her having in college.

"Only part of you feels bad. Don't tell me you haven't noticed how much I've helped your flow of Chi, your elemental connections, what ever you call it?"

She was right. My "chi" was flowing exceeding well. Or, as some would say, my charkas were all open.

However you define it, I was saturated with power.

She rose from the bed and came over to where I was standing. Once again she embraced me. This time I resisted. More accurately, I fought the urge to respond in kind. She started kissing me, lightly on the lips then around the side of my face, just below my ear onto my neck.

"Share some of that power with me and I'll show you how good a team we can be." She balanced on one leg wrapping the other around my hips and pulled me tighter to her.

I had to do something before I gave in completely. I let fly the power I had been building. I didn't direct it. I'm not sure I could have. So, in essence I "detonated." (Please keep you're comments to yourselves)

Shelia flew, Literally. She was blasted out the window. I didn't think that would stop her for long.

After all, she had gotten up from worse not so very long ago.

I took the opportunity to grab my duster (everything else was replaceable) and ran. I was downstairs and out to the driveway by the time I heard Shelia stir behind the house. She was cursing loudly and furiously.

From what I can tell I got a few extra seconds because she had leaped back up to the top floor bedroom before following me downstairs. The rest of the time I needed I got when she came out of the front of the house.

She was stunned to find me getting in my butterscotch yellow Volvo. I turned over the engine with the keys that were conveniently already in the ignition.

Have I mentioned that I love my car?

I drove away as fast as I could manage. Perhaps faster. Highway 33 winds quite a bit as it snakes it way back from West Virginia. It felt as though the steering wheel was actually helping me to keep on the road as we screamed around the turns. It was still early enough that there wasn't much traffic.

The first pay phone I found was outside a little old-time country store in Hinton. As I approached Hinton, I started to get more traffic.

There's a meat packing plant that takes up most of the town. Their shift change was still an hour off so the traffic wasn't as bad as it could be. I was thankful. There was little enough traffic to not hinder me, but enough to slow down anyone chasing me. I hoped.

I stopped to try to use the pay phone. I noticed that there had been no pursuit from Sheila, at least none that I could see. I made sure my duster was closed securely before I got out of the car. I didn't need to get picked up for indecency.

Once I was certain of my modesty, I got out and went to the phone. I was a little worried that Sheila had followed. What was she playing at? I decided to use my "sight" to help warn me of danger.

I whirled that wheel of sight as I dialed Marguerite's cell phone. I got auditory again.

"Hello?" Marguerite answered her phone. With the "Hearing" turned up I learned a lot more than I expected from that hello. First, that she was worried, really worried. Second, That she also felt a sense of triumph. It seemed to me that we must have had some sort of victory overnight. The third thing I picked up was that she was over a hundred miles from where I expected her to be.

My best guess was that she was already at Pandora's parents' place. Fortunately, I was right, as she was about to tell me. She quickly filled me in on last night's happenings and the good news of the Oregon lead. She also told me that she was worried about how Koenig may try to get the server back.

"I kept having this sense of Shelia endangering us all night. The guys told me how hard Ramón had put her down. I still couldn't shake the feeling that she posed a real threat."

"Yeah, but not to you. I just got away from her."

"My God, are you alright?"

I wasn't sure how to answer. I didn't think I should (or could) lie to Marguerite.

"No, but I'll recover."

"Did she torture you?" The concern in her voice was almost too much to bear with the "hearing" on. It touched me how much she cared.

"Worse," I said, "she reminded me of how just how good the good old days were." I didn't get to hear Marguerite's immediate response. A hand that seemed to come out of nowhere yanked the receiver out of my hand.

"Excuse me; I need to talk *my* husband," Sheila said and hung up the phone. Not forcefully or even particularly abruptly but as gently as an afterthought.

Shelia was dressed head-to-toe in an outfit that superficially matched my normal attire. She wore black high heeled boots, (normally I wore black Converse high tops) Her shirt and pants were both black leather as opposed to my usual black cotton t-shirt and black denim jeans. Her duster was leather and fell to her mid-calf, while mine is oilskin and the hem tends to drag (which was nice right now because it helped conceal that it was my entire wardrobe at the moment.)

She wore her hair loose so it fell around her shoulders. Over her designer sunglasses, I could see the not-so-faint scarring from last night's gunshot wound.

Other than looking like an action movie cliché, I couldn't sense any menace from her. There was none in her stance, nor any in her voice. Even with the "Hearing" on, there was no trace that she meant me harm. I had heard a little menace when she had spoke to Marguerite so I know it wasn't simply being masked. What surprised me was that in her next little spiel she was telling the truth.

"Look, I told you I don't want to hurt you. I still need something from you. A favor I owed got traded to Koenig. I have to help her but I don't want to. Oddly, that's another thing protecting you, if not your friends.

Nobody kills Magi lightly. Too much potential for serious repercussions. If you take down Koenig, my debt is finished and you and I can be friends again I hope. Maybe more.

"Still, I can't help you and I have to try to stop you in whatever way I think will be most effective. If any one thinks that I haven't lived up to an obligation my "peers" will turn on me. I really don't want that to happen. I'm on shaky ground as it is."

"So why were having this conversation? Why not just knock me out and be done with it?"

She took a deep, dramatic and unnecessary breath. "Because that could always be more damaging than expected. I need you alive and as well as can be." Again this truth left me more worried than simply trying to kill me would.

"Now, I've been playing nice with you." She said this with out any trace of a smirk, "and you've been playing nice with me even if your friends haven't."

"I'm supposed to play nice remember, '. . . for even the least of these, my brethern' and all that.

"Yes, you're supposed to play nice with *people*." She let that hang in the air until the stress on people sank in. Whatever I still felt for my wife, my late wife, had been clouding my judgment.

I was acting as if the rules about ordinary people applied to her. I had let deadly force by others against her slide since I knew she wasn't alive. Without realizing it, I had been going too easy on her, because I didn't want to kill her. Ha, ha, joke on me.

At that moment, I stopped caring what her game was. I simply summoned up a bit of energy. I formed the effect in my mind. I even gave it an incantation and a quick gesture to help focus it.

So with a "Kai Hey Doonimous" and a wave of my hand, I sent a bolt of invisible force into Shelia's forehead, reopening (and enlarging) the gunshot wounds in both the front and back of her head.

She slumped backward onto the ground, her brains oozing out into gravel of the unpaved parking lot. That should take her another few hours to heal up. I didn't envy whomever had to open the store that morning.

I walked over to my car and drove to directly to Vanderhorn's place. I didn't even bother to get dressed until I got there.

The next few days, though far from uneventful, were also tedious. Once I was at the Vanderhorns we began to plan our strategy in earnest. We only had a small lead to work with. We had a set of IP addresses traced to a relatively small area of Oregon. They were all from community access internet terminals in public or university libraries. They all seemed to fall during times that Koenig's presence in Virginia could not be accounted for. So Oregon here we come.

PART II

Chapter One

A BRIEF LIST OF THE tedious travel preperations:
Get tickets for transcontinental flight.
Arrange accommodations for the Guys, Marguerite and myself.
Loose argument with Pandora about staying behind.
Amend accommodations to include Pandora.
Deflect the police harassment that Koenig's contacts sicced on us.

I know that sounds like it should be interesting. It wasn't. Once Marguerite had frustrated Koenig's attempt to use her own thugs, Koenig called in a few favors she was owed.

Marguerite had used the police to send Koenig's thugs packing. The next day the police were back. This time they were not on our side.

With Marguerite's forewarnings, I had boosted my cloak with a ritual and hid the house. It was kind of fun to let them wander around trying to find it. It might have gone on interminably had James not suggested reshaping the cloak.

Instead of just hiding the house, he suggested I make the house appear long abandoned then we let the police find it. It was a great idea that worked, ahem, like a charm. They gave us a lot less trouble after that. I wish I had thought of it. I must have been tired.

Back to the list:
Reserve transportation for use in the Pacific Northwest.
Buy raincoats.
Deliver the server to Law Enforcement. Actually this was easy. While I was maintaining the elaborate and very draining "abandonment" cloak, Hector just slipped it into one of the police cruisers.

We had most of the trip details worked out. With Vanderhorn bankrolling the operation, we were able to arrange for transportation and our base of operations. It consisted of two modest rental cars and several rooms at a budget motel. We wanted to keep a low profile after all.

Our actual plan of attack was less worked out. Once again, I wish I had real investigative training. Still between my abilities as a Magus, Marguerite's clairvoyance, Pandora's insight into Koenig and the Guys doing real leg work, we figured we should turn up something.

It was right before we left that the shit hit the fan. It was late Thursday afternoon and Mrs. V. was trying not to worry that her "little girl" was going off into to danger again. She tuned into one of the 24-hour cable news networks. What she saw gave us all pause.

On the screen there was an old photograph of Sheila and myself. It was our wedding photo. The one Shelia had used for her cell phone wallpaper when she was still truly alive. The news anchor said that I was wanted for questioning on a host of charges.

There was a Bombing (The incident in Richmond), Fraud (for faking my death in the 'Burg), Murder (someone found Shelia's body and identified it), and tampering with evidence (her body went missing just before her autopsy)

Besides repeatedly showing the one photograph over and over, they also had footage of a police raid on my apartment. The police found my apartment empty all items except a vintage Lava Lamp and a very small, very old portrait of a young, colonial sailor.

Eventually they gave some vague descriptions of suspected accomplices. They were identified as young couple of middle eastern origin and 3 Latino youths driving a Black Lexus.

All in all, it was way bad news. As a wanted fugitive, I couldn't just waltz through airport security. Well actually, I could. Cloaking just myself I can do in my sleep. Airports just have too many eyes watching. I couldn't run a big enough cloak to cover all of us long enough to get us all through airport security. I didn't want to risk sending any of our team uncovered. The authorities might have known more about the team than they were telling the press.

I wondered why they didn't mention Hector or Marguerite by name or even come close with their descriptions. They had been with me in Richmond.

I had been way sloppier than I should have been and it had caught up with me. Not knowing why they weren't releasing info on anyone else had me waiting for the other shoe to drop.

In the end, we decided that we would drive across the country. Mrs. Vanderhorn and I sat down with an atlas and figured our best route across the country. She had a passion for geography and Americana. Mr. Vanderhorn didn't mind going out and getting a vehicle. In fact before we had the trip by car planned out, Charles was back. He had bought an older, dark green Suburban from an ad in the *Autotrader*.

"I figured it could carry everybody plus your gear. More importantly it won't stand out." This was true enough.

"I'll do something to get rid of your old cars once you're gone." Marguerite was heartbroken to hear that she was going to loose her Lexus after saving for it for so long. Charles pointed out that replacing it wasn't going to be a problem.

"Hell, I'll buy you two for each of day of the week, one for bringing back Stacie, another for Stephan." Put that way Marguerite felt a little better about it.

I, on the other hand, had a slightly different dilemma. Sure I was opposed to the idea of giving up my car. I would have lobbied for stashing it somewhere if I thought that would work.

"Charles," I said, "I don't think I can leave my car behind."

"That old thing? Look I'm as sentimental as the next guy but you heard what I said to Ms. Winston . . ."

"No, the problem is that I don't think my car will stay behind."

Vanderhorn stopped and pondered this for a moment. To his credit, he didn't try to argue. He was also fairly bright.

"Your car has special properties, doesn't it?" he asked eventually

I simply nodded.

"Well, there's an advantage to having a second car anyway, especially if it's more like one of the team than mere transportation." The Vanderhorns really were remarkable people. Not many people accept such challenges to their world view so readily. I told him as much.

"I think I can speak for my wife on this as well . . . We've had to throw away everything we thought we knew several times. The first was when our kids wound up as just another couple of dead runaways. Getting them back meant throwing away all our assumptions again. I'm glad to do that. Hell, I'm begging to be allowed."

In the end, we all left the house quietly around midnight. Ramón, Pandora, and I were in Azgard, as we had been on that first drive to the Vanderhorn residence. Marguerite and the rest of the guys took the suburban.

It was by assumption rather than discussion that we formed these two teams. We had one team of four, one of three (or a second of four, if you count Azgard)

Pandora and Charles did their best not become teary as we said our good-byes. Mrs. Vanderhorn's face was wet with tears but her eyes shone brightly. She was so filled with hope and fear that I wouldn't have risked looking at her with the sight for almost any reason. Passion like that could be an overwhelming force. I almost wished I could tap into that force. I had a feeling we were going to need it.

Chapter Two

WE WERE OFF TO the Pacific Northwest. So naturally we headed south. There was a northern route across the country but Marguerite had taken the southern route a time or two and preferred it. Plus she "had a bad feeling" about heading north right away.

Our route would take us through Virginia, Kentucky, Indiana and then on westward. We could have headed down Interstate 95 to get I-64 and then points west easily enough. Instead, we went back to I-81 and picked I- 64 at Stanton.

This route took us right past Harrisonburg again. It'd be one last glimpse of home before our journey really got underway.

It was very tempting to try and grab items from our various homes. Even Pandora had things she would have liked from her old apartment. That wasn't going to happen. I didn't want to split us up and I couldn't cloak so many people in motion.

"But you just cloaked an entire house," James said.

"True but not everything is about size," I told him. "I could do the house because, essentially, it is one thing. Anything inside the house just gets swept up in the effect."

"Why not cloak the cars then?" James asked

"Well, I could do the cars if they were standing still. Even if I could do the cars in motion, the people would be exposed every time we stopped for gas or food."

"Which will happen anyway if you aren't cloaking," James countered.

"Exactly. I'd be expending too much energy for too little benefit. I'd rather run a bit of risk and be juiced up than run a slightly smaller risk and be too worn out to help if the shit hits the fan.

So it was, in transit, I wasn't covering anything. We were depending on other things to keep us out of trouble. First, there was my car's natural talent for eluding observation. Next was the generic nature of the suburban. Finally, there is Marguerite's, admittedly sporadic, sense of foreboding. It helped keep us off police radar, figuratively and literally.

I suppose the next question is "why go back if you aren't stopping for anything?"

That's simple.

Power.

I wanted to tap into the energy that pooled at the Rt.11 and Rt. 33 crossroads one more time. Certainly there are other crossroads like it. My familiarity with this one was key. After living right on the crossroad for so long, I could draw energy much more efficiently there than anywhere else. After all, there is no place like home.

When we got close enough, we hopped off 81 and headed down Rt. 11 south for a while.

As I lay motionless in Azgard's back seat, I drew in the energy. Soon I was saturated, almost overflowing with mystic energy. Which was good considering how taxed my reserves were going to be all to soon.

The miles flew by. We started out fairly tense but the further we got without trouble, the more relaxed we became. That in itself could be dangerous. It was important to remain alert.

We decided to sleep in shifts and drive straight through. Driving that way should take us 2 days. Of course that's without any trouble on the way. We found that as long as at least two of the guys remained awake there wasn't any problem with REM disorientation. With six other drivers, I opted out. I would turn my attention to acting as "look out."

I lay back down and "pulled a Strange." I know that sounds bad. I've got to find better ways of saying it. Personally I blame my mentor's other student. A real wise ass named J. Arthur Bradley, who preferred to be called Artie. I mean, really, a magus named Artie?

Anyway, old Artie was always one for cheesy names, particularly if he could make it sound obscene in some way. With Astral Projection, for instance, it was always, "pulled a Strange" after the comic book character, Dr. Strange or he'd say, "dumped the meat", or, one of my favorites "getting the full-body bris"

Be that as it may, I left my body and hovered over the cars, keeping a watch on the surrounding countryside. Given that Marguerite could see me without effort, I remembered to get "dressed." The all white outfit was beginning to grow on me.

At one point near the West Virginia/Kentucky border, I floated back to the suburban to let Marguerite know what was up. I found her staring out the window at an old house beside the highway. Given how intent she looked I glanced at it myself. I wish I hadn't. A particularly brutal domestic scene played itself out. We were moving pretty fast but I was able to see a man with a baseball bat swing hard and fast at a very young woman's head. They were clearly ghosts.

"Oh my God," I said to Marguerite, "do you have to witness such things often?'"

She shrugged noncommittally and kept looking out the window.

"Is there anything we can do?" I asked

She took a deep breath then matter-of-factly said "Not from a moving car. Besides unless they come to you there's usually nothing you can do. "

"Still, I feel bad for that woman having to go through that over and over."

Marguerite turned to me and smiled. "Oh, don't worry about that. He's the only Ghost."

I gave her that "whatcha talking 'bout, Margie' look (which by the way, she says is not nearly as cute I must think it is)

"You probably can't tell, given your avoidance of spirits," she said with only a hint of condescension. "But she's just an echo. Whatever other issues she might have had, that young woman didn't stick around to repeat that little atrocity ad infinitum, ad nauseum. Violent deaths may result in ghosts but not always. In this case, he's the one who can't move on. He has to manufacture her image for his little psychodrama. Hopefully people will avoid that house. I wouldn't want him to get the opportunity to reenact his little atrocity with living puppets."

"Oh and I did notice you were projecting at me again," a wry smile crossed her face. "Thanks for wearing pants this time."

The rest of the trip was uneventful. I spent a great deal of it out of my body. This meant my sights were running full blast so I got to find out some fascinating things about our country. For example, I learned that there are a hell of a lot of ghosts in Kansas, that Montana has a serious faerie population. (For some reason, I hadn't expected that.) and that Denver, Colorado has a destiny that hangs over it like an anvil. What kind of Destiny? Lets just say that "heads" it's paradise. All in all the trip was uneventful and therefore rather pleasant by comparison. As we got nearer our destination my control over things kept, ahem, slip slidin' away.

Chapter Three

WE HAD CROSSED INTO northeast Oregon. Stopping briefly near La grande, I sent out a mental call to the local Magi in residence. (Yes, I know the singular is magus but I've never warmed up to that word.) Her name was Alexandra Cominad. She was part of The Magi Concordance. The Magi Concordance is the group I answer to formally.

The Concordance has divided itself into regional districts, also called concordances with a small "C." This is a loose agreement of Magi in a given region. We agree to behave by certain rules and assist one another.

This is also a way for the Concordance to keep an eye on itself. (Rogue magi, what an ugly thought.) She was most assuredly not a part of the "Disreputable Urban Magicians" clique with which I am otherwise associated.

I was in astral mode when the response came floating in hours later. We had made it across Oregon and had already turned south to follow I-5. The delay in response may have been the local Magus running her own background check.

Alexandra Cominad is the Magi representative for the Pacific Northwest concordance. Most Concordance Magi operate alone, not counting an apprentice or two. Cominad worked with a small team. This included her apprenticed son. Though she was far from disreputable, she was fairly urban, even urbane. Her response was a semi-autonomous sending. A sending is a constructed apparition capable of relaying messages. More advanced ones could even answer a few simple questions. The best could even ask questions.

For example this one asked, "Gives, what the hell do you think you are doing?" (Perhaps her genteel reputation was overrated. Perhaps I just bring out the worst in people.) Still, Cominad had a very impressive sending. It's usually easy to identify the source of a sending, Most sendings look artificial in some way. Some look like mannequins. Some, like mine, are wispy and amorphous save for the face and hands, which are just shy of cartoonish. That might be just people at my skill level. For some Magi, the faces are such an afterthought that one can only tell who sent it by recognizing a particular mystic style.

Not Command's sending, however. Her sending was frightening in its detail. First, unlike my own sendings (or even my astral form) Hers were in full color. The hair was iron gray. It was knotted into a braid like in real life. The sending's eyes were a cold and steely blue. The face was far from cartoonish. Instead, it seemed etched. The body was in no way amorphous.

This was no generic representation but a fully formed model of herself. It was also clothed in intricate detail. She was dressed in an evening gown, like what a respectable, well off woman might wear out to the theater.

The dress, like her eyes, was a chilling shade of blue. The sending's clothes not only had details like buttons but the fabric had folds and the folds had shadows.

Either she had a lot of time to sit around and perfect her sendings or she was just that good. For a moment all I could do was stare. If the Sight didn't allow you to distinguish a living mind from a constructed emulation, I would have thought that she had come in person.

My dumb stares did not impress the sending any more than it would have the real woman

"Well, Mr. Gives? Why is the first that I hear of your visit is a little mental echo saying 'oh by the way I have an errand in your neck of the woods, hope you don't mind'?

"Now, if your errand was picking up a research tome or a meditation aid, or perhaps, to visit your former, fellow apprentice, that tone would be acceptable."

"Oh, Arthur's been reassigned here?"

"Don't change the subject. I'm waiting. Just what is this errand?'

"Ah, we're here to pick up the brother of the young girl in our group."

"Expecting trouble, are we?"

"Some. Why do you ask?"

"Because you've brought a clairvoyant and a previously unknown anthropomorphic hive mind with you. A hive mind, it seems, that you helped create."

"Oh. Yeah. About that. I can explain."

"Yes, you'll have too. Pull over at the next rest stop and I'll meet you as soon as I can physically get there".

The next rest stop turned out to be just to the north of Salem, Oregon, the state capitol. We had only about an hour's driving left in our journey. Stopping here seemed pointless. I wasn't about to argue the point with Cominad, however.

We had been driving almost 50 hours straight through and it was noticeable. We were all tired, a bit irritable, and had an odor to match our dispositions.

I did my best to clean up in the rest stop washroom before Cominad got there. Although I didn't answer to Cominad directly, she had a lot more respect and rank among the other magi than I did. She oversaw four other magi in the Pacific Northwest. She had charges in Seattle, Portland, and two in Eugene, Oregon. Eugene may be smaller than the other two but a lot of mystics (and mystic wannabes) are attracted to the area. Someone inexperienced can get out of their depth pretty quickly and end up needing a helping hand.

It was still the wee hours when Cominad showed up. A dark red SUV pulled into the space beside my car.

A young man of about twenty got out of the driver's side and opened the passenger side door. Cominad got out. Save for the change of clothes, she looked exactly as her sending had depicted her, a sign of a very forceful will.

I was suddenly trying to find the best way to suck up, lest she swat me like a fly.

I needn't have worried. Cominad in person was friendly and easygoing. She had the kind of ease born of supreme self-confidence.

She introduced herself as Alexandra and the young man as her son, Sasha. The interrogation I expected didn't happen. At least, she didn't start there. She chatted pleasantly with Marguerite and the Guys. She talked to Pandora in a more serious, concerned tone. Her tone reminded me of a doctor saying, "That's interesting. How long have you had this pain?"

Eventually she had Marguerite, Pandora, and the Guys go with Sasha to our prearranged accommodations.

She beckoned to me to get into my car. On the passenger side. I got in. She sat down in the driver's seat and introduced herself to my car.

"Azgard, I'm Alexandra, I've heard a lot about you from Arthur. If you don't mind, I'd like to drive you." With that she held out her hand for the keys. I gave them to her and she started Azgard right up.

"Nice," I said, "It must like you."

Cominad smiled and nodded noncommittally. I decided to push ahead with the conversation.

"So, You seem to be well informed about our situation."

The smile faded. Her mien became unquestionably serious "I'm not as informed as I'd like to be. Did my sending convey how deeply troubled I am by how uninformed?"

I spoke honestly, "No, it gave me the sense that you were annoyed by the situation." "And what sense do you get know."

"That of grave concern. Your Sending, if you'll pardon my analogy, sounded like a mother whose kid got detention. Now you seem more like someone whose kid got themselves hospitalized."

"I'd say that is an fairly accurate description of events. When I sent to you I was annoyed. I had only a little bit of information. When I got your "call" I checked in with *my* resident clairvoyant. All he could tell me was that you were coming in with a psychic of your own and, this is the part that made me take notice, "a newborn hive mind." I thought perhaps one of the Fay hive minds or a SSAS."

What's a SSAS? Okay bear with me. A SSAS is a Spontaneously Self-Aware Swarm. It's just a fancy way of saying that a group of some kind achieves sentience not as individuals but as group.

I'm told it happens most often with bees. It's been happing for years. The first recorded case I know of was sometime in the late 1500's. A bee hive in Great Britain became self aware and was able to make contact with a local coven of witches. Most likely there were cases happening long before that. It may be no one bothered to write them down or even knew about them.

That raises a few questions. Why don't these hives make themselves known and, for the more paranoid, why haven't they taken over?

First, communication is often difficult. Only trained mystics, like myself, and natural talents, like Marguerite, have much chance of "hearing" them. That's also assuming the swarm has anything to say to us.

This leads to the second point. They are still just bees (or ants or moths or whatever) and they are just more concerned with the collection of pollen for the production of honey etc, etc. than in talking to us.

They really often don't care what we are up to, as long it doesn't interfere with them. As for taking over the world, they have. As far as they are concerned they control as much of the planet as they need. Ironically each such hive mind has tendency to be a bit individualistic. They are few and far between and don't much care much about what's going on past their little neck of the woods. So, in that, they're pretty much like humans.

Now back to my dressing down.

"I simply figured you had enlisted the aid of the Fay or of a swarm to help you look for this friend. Then, I happened to catch the news and saw your lovely face on it. I dug a little deeper and discovered that your hive mind was anthropomorphic."

"How did you . . ."

"I have my sources, don't try to change the subject. Care to explain how that happened to the nice young men?"

I told her in brief what had happened. She listened carefully and thoughtfully. And then after I was finished, she was quiet for a time and then,

"Arthur was right, you are the luckiest bastard in the world. You screw up and create a puissant ally."

I simply shrugged and tried to look apologetic. I have a love/hate relationship with my "strange luck." It's a by-product of being Magi. Many of us have these little "side-effects." Some are fairly normal (well, normal for magi) like attracting fairy spirits, or causing electricity to flow oddly. I had kidded my friend, Arthur, about being Snow White's kid, in the way the woodland creatures flocked to him.

He said he preferred to think of himself as a modern St. Francis.

"But you're so into martial arts," I would say.

"That's the modern part," he would tell me.

Cominad changed the subject slightly. "So what's really going on? This isn't a simple 'here to pick up a friend.'"

It's never wise to lie to magi. So I told her essentially what I've told you so far, leaving out the late wife angle.

"So how are you going to find the brother?"

I told her we had pictures of Stephan and Koenig. We also had a basic description of the Jekyll from Pandora. I also mentioned that the odd server hits that were all generated within a 40 mile radius of the small town of Albany, Oregon, mostly coming from public or college library's. We figured that it really came down to old- fashioned legwork.

She harrumphed at that. "How much real detective work have you done?"

I had to admit to very little, actual detective work.

"Besides," she continued, "you've missed a few things that might help. I'll try to hook you up with a police sketch artist who can make something useful of the girl's description," she paused, "There's also a question that you have failed to ask yourself. Do you even know what it is?"

I told her that after driving nearly nonstop across the country, I wasn't even sure of my own home zip code anymore.

"Okay, this is a freebie, ask yourself, 'what does Koenig gain by taking the brother?' It's not leverage against his sister. She tried to have her killed if I recall your story correctly. What's so special about the boy?"

She had a good point and one that deserved some real thought. If we could figure out why Stephan was taken it might provide some more leads.

A few thoughts came seeping back into my mind: Stephan and the strange gifts he had "acquired" during his disappearance at age 11, The way Koenig, who was more mystically inclined than most Hydes, latched on to him.

I began to wonder if they weren't much more to Stephan than I had considered. After sharing these thoughts with Cominad, much of her stern demeanor dissipated. We spent the next little while driving to the motel in a nice, pleasant discussion about the use of various music to aid ones will-working.

"I can't believe you use pop music, or more to the point I can't believe you use it effectively."

I shrugged. "It works for me. What can I say?"

Cominad didn't comment but her expression showed that something was bothering her. Whatever it was, she didn't say. Instead she changed the topic to subtly bragging about her son, Sasha.

"He's really making strides with his work in the forests. He's been studying forestry at university. He's always had affinity for the woodlands."

I suspected this meant he had the gift of speaking with plant-life like Artie did with animals. By the time that Cominad and I reached the motel to meet the rest of the team, I realized Sasha and Artie working together would be unstoppable in the wild.

We joined back up with the rest of the group back at the motel.

We had chosen a dive of a place called the Marco Polo. It was in the small city of Albany that was our "target" town. The motel name had appealed to me and it seemed like it would be a real low profile sort of place.

It wasn't. Not nearly enough.

Chapter Four

COMINAD PARKED AZGARD AND we got out. The Marco Polo was a cheep two-story motel. Each room had an outside access. The second floor rooms lay along a lengthy balcony.

We headed up the outdoor stairway. As we got closer to the rooms, it didn't take enhanced senses to hear an odd buzzing coming from one of our rooms. Spinning the "Wheel" I came up with vision. Leaking out from behind the door was the telltale greenish glow of fairy light. Cominad and I looked at each other. We said nothing but we both knew that buzzing probably meant flitlings and lots of them. That almost always meant trouble.

Flitlings are the archetypal fairy of pop culture. They resemble tiny people with cute butterfly or dragonfly wings. On their own, they're not so bad[14]

In large numbers they're exceedingly dangerous. Make no mistake, These little buggers are not Tinkerbell[15]

Cominad didn't hesitate. She charged into the room. I followed her closely. Inside the room we found the Guys and Sasha, Cominad's son. All of the guys were unconscious. They all looked like they had passed out suddenly. Hector was collapsed next to the bed. Ramón was slumped across the cheap-ass air conditioning unit. Ty lay by the little in-room sink. A small plastic cup was still in his hand. James was sitting in the bathroom doorway. His bag of toiletries and towel were scattered on the floor next to him.

Only Sasha remained standing. Flitlings buzzed around him so fast I couldn't tell how many there were.

---

[14]   Just never make a deal with one, but that goes for all the Fay

[15]   Come to think of it Tinkerbell wasn't really all that nice either was she?

I could see him clearly, even if his attackers were blurred. Trickles of blood oozed from a hundred, tiny wounds. His clothing was in ribbons. It was "plastered" to him, soaked from this multitude of superficial injuries. For whatever reason, the Flitlings were playing with him. If they were simply trying to kill him, he'd have been dead long ago.

When Cominad and I entered the room, the buzzing pitch of the flitling swarm changed. It rose a couple of octaves and grew louder. You wouldn't have to be Magi to know that they had grown angrier.

There was an explosion of sweet fragrance in my face. I could feel my consciousness slipping away.

Cominad had moved past me to get to her son. She had taken a greater hit. She was already slumping to the floor.

I fought unconsciousness for as long as I could. I stayed awake for a heroic 1 1/2 seconds after I was dosed with the "pixie" dust. The Sight seared those one and a half seconds into my memory. This is what I saw;

The buzzing in the room got more intense. I could see the wounds appearing on Sasha were happening more frequently and were getting deeper.

Then something happened that I hadn't expected at all. The buzzing ceased. I could now see some of the horde surrounding Sasha. Each one was decked out like a miniature warrior. No two were alike in style. One was a Roman soldier. Another was a Spartan hero. There were soldiers from the U.S. Revolutionary, Civil and Korean wars. An Aztec warrior and Sioux brave brandished weapons shoulder to shoulder with one of Cromwell's Roundheads and a French musketeer. There were more but I didn't get clear images of them.

The miniature brigade massed around him, hovering silently. They formed three circles. Two circles crossed diagonally forming X's in front and in back of him. The other circle ringed him horizontally at waist level, crossing the "x".

Without any visible signal the all charged Sasha. Most were lunging or firing their minuscule weapons towards his heart. A few assaulted his head I heard a terrible rending. It was not quite the sound of flesh tearing but all too nauseatingly similar. I saw these tiny fairies tear some sort of light from Sasha's head, give it a twist, and then shove it back in between his eyes. I could fight the dust no longer. I fell into a surprisingly pleasant sleep.

Chapter Five

I AWOKE LYING ON THE bed next to Ramón. He was still unconscious. Of every one hit by the dust, he was hit the hardest. He had been closest to the door when the Flitlings came through it.

Pandora and Marguerite were tending to us. There wasn't much they could do except wait for us to wake up. They had heard a commotion from the next room and rushed right over. What they heard was me and Cominad charging into the room. Before that, they had been unaware of any trouble.

They had initially feared the worst when they saw the bodies strewn about the room. My buzz saw snoring had reassured them that we lived.

They had tended to Sasha first, of course. He was visibly injured. They were torn between wanting to find help and avoiding more attention. When the rest of us only seemed to be sleeping they decided that secrecy was best. They did their best to render first aid then prayed that one of us magi would wake up and make it all better.

It was going to be a bit more complicated than that.

Once I was awake, I tried to get up to check on Sasha for myself. I tried and failed. I sat up and immediately swooned back down. Not quite unconscious but certainly not coherent.

After another few moments, I was able to sit up again. This Herculean effort was rewarded with success and waves of nausea you could surf on. Soon I was able to take a look around. Cominad was awake by then and talking on a cell phone. She sat next to her son, holding his hand. He was lying on one of the double beds. He appeared to be comatose rather than just sleeping. Next to Sasha lay Hector, who was awake but apparently hallucinating pleasantly. Ramón was next to me, still out like a light.

Ty was laying on a roll away cot that hadn't been in the room earlier. He was awake but it looked he was trying to ride out his own waves of nausea.

James was sitting up in the chair next to the desk. He was drinking water directly from a water pitcher. Before he finished, Pandora came over to him with another pitcher. When James was done they traded. James started drinking from the new pitcher. Pandora went back to the sink to refill the old one.

"He's downed sixteen of those already." This was Marguerite sitting down on the bed next to me. She looked as though she had been crying. All I could think was "I'm sorry."

"Alexandra woke up first. She was awake almost as soon as we got into the room. She's been tending to her son ever since."

"Her magic?"

"Failed to have any effect." Marguerite confirmed for me. "Since we weren't sure what to do for the rest of you, we put you on the beds and called the front desk for some roll away cots. James woke up about an hour ago with this maddening thirst. We asked Alexandra. She told us to keep him hydrated till the effect passes."

Marguerite was sitting close to me, close enough I wish I had time to appreciated it. Even though she was close, she hadn't looked me in the eye. Marguerite is anything but shy and retiring, even under stress, particularly under stress.

"What's the matter?" I asked. At first she wouldn't look at me. When she did I could tell she had been crying and was now trying to fight back more tears.

"I'm so sorry." she said. Her voice was soft, barely even a whisper, but the shame in it was almost deafening. This wasn't one of those "I feel your pain" sorrys. This was an "it's all my fault" kind of sorry.

It was one of those rare moments when I felt uncertain what to say. Whatever had happened wasn't her fault, I knew that. I wasn't sure how to tell her though. I feared just telling her it wasn't her fault would ring hollow. Minimizing what happened would just come across as patronizing. It would also be a lie; we really were in rough shape, especially poor Sasha.

So instead I just reached out to hug her. Marguerite responded by relaxing into my arms and rocking gently as she continued her confession. She no longer fought back the tears.

"What good am I? I should have sensed the attack. I sensed every move by the police back in Virginia. What went wrong here? Was I just not paying attention? Was I overconfident? Am I just a burden to the team?"

This last question she actually directed to me rather than the world in general.

The rocking motion had been hell on my fight against nausea. It prevented me from saying anything lest I vomit. I just hugged her tighter and shook my head. She sighed deeply then fell silent.

I just held her in that moment, silent and eloquent.

When I finally felt able to speak I said, "They were Fay. They don't usually show up on any human's radar unless they want to. When they want to run silent, it's already a lost battle." The things I had been tempted to say right way. But right away, nothing had been the right thing to say. Thanks to the nausea, for once, I said it.

Eventually The Guys and I began to recover from the ill effects of the flitling attack. The same cannot be said of Sasha. Despite Cominad's best attempts, she could not awaken her son. She was able to heal the physical wounds pretty easily. They had been superficial.

After few hours, Cominad admitted she wasn't up to the task. Unfortunately that meant it was something nobody within a thousand miles or more could help with. She was the senior magus for the Pacific Northwest Concordance. She was also one of the preeminent healers I had ever met. If she wasn't up to the task, I'd be hard pressed to say who was.

"There really is nothing I can do. Nothing to do." Cominad said. I asked her what she meant. Cominad said that what had happened to Sasha wasn't truly an injury. What the Flitlings had done is pulled out part of his mind and slipped it into a "slow-time" bubble. There wasn't anything to heal.

It was also a very strong and well- woven enchantment. Breaking it would also assault Sasha's mind and he'd have no defense against it. Even trying to counter the effect by speeding up the "slow-time" could have disastrous results.

"This is truly out of our hands for the moment." Cominad is a very strong woman but she was also a mother. There was no way not to be struck by the sorrow she was feeling.

I started grasping at straws. "What about those on other paths?"

While it might be fair to call any will-worker a Magus or Magi collectively, we do make a particular claim to that name. We are the inheritors of the mystic tradition that comes down from Persian Zoroastrianism into the modern day via Christianity. As I said before, we come from *those* Magi.

"There's a strong Wiccan presence in Eugene. They seem to have a greater affinity to things Fay than we do," I said.

"Unfortunately, that may actually be our problem. I studied the effect on him as I've tried to work the healing. I've come to a couple of conclusions.

One: You must be on the right track because this effect was meant for you.

Two: Whoever opposes you has some pretty strong pull with the fair folk to get them to do this,

Three: You *are* one of the luckiest bastards in the world. Look at this spell."

I turned my "Sight" toward the spell. I spun the wheel and it came up touch. If Cominad noticed my moment's hesitation as my "Sight" sorted itself out, she didn't comment.

I reached out and put my hand on Sasha's head. I could feel the normal flow of his body's rhythm was off somehow. Concentrating for just a moment I could tell that some of his mental energy was being stopped up. The damn little fairies had locked up his mind.

I pressed down harder on his forehead trying to extend my perception. The mind is rather fluid even for the most rigid thinkers. My hand felt like I was touching ice. Sasha's mind had been flash-frozen.

He was in there but at the rate his mind was ticking over, it would take him months to realize that he wasn't standing up anymore.

"That attack was meant for you. It was designed specifically for you. Had they hit you with this, you'd be in a permanent lock down. The spell would be using your own energies to sustain itself, Sasha's energy doesn't match the spell well enough. The spell will eventually degrade and fail."

She left out that its failure could be years away. This just made me feel that much guiltier and that much more motivated to undo it. Cominad also added this other small hope.

"Chalk it up to 'mysterious ways' but you just go handed a big lead. Your enemy has friends among the Fair Folk or connections to those who do. That ought to narrow down your search list. Plus your enemy had just made this very personal for me. A very, very bad mistake."

You know that adage about Mama Bears protecting their cubs? Well, give that bear tactical nukes and you might start to get the picture of what a Mama Mage can do.

Chapter Six

No ONE SLEPT THAT night until they were near collapse. Cominad kept herself going by will alone. (Granted that is her specialty so it isn't surprising) Even when she had admitted she could not undo the enchantment, she didn't rest.

She made contact with the four Magi under her supervision. In short order, they had all been sent on various errands. Some of which were simply freeing up Cominad to attend to her son. The rest were helping figure out our next step in tracking down Koenig's Jekyll and Stephan.

My one time fellow apprentice, Artie, came up from Eugene. I recalled Artie as jovial and quick witted. He was always willing to make a bad pun.

Now, he bore a certain gravitas. In fact, he was quite somber. That was normal enough given the circumstances.

When he saw me he gave a bright, warm smile. It quickly faded as he got right to business. "Okay, we're moving you to someplace private. I've got a place. It's just north of here. Get your stuff together. I'd like to you head out as soon as possible." He turned to Pandora, "Are you the one who saw the Jekyll form? Do you think you're up to talking to the sketch artist?"

Pandora nodded. She looked as shaken and worn down as any of the rest of us. Artie turned to Vanessa with whom he shared territory in Eugene. She was a woman about his age. Despite wearing matching dark suits that gave them a curious "federal agent" feel, standing together they were a study in contrasts.

At 6'4 and 180 pounds he was as tall and skinny as remembered him. She was considerably shorter than he was. In fact she might be described as petite. Her red hair was long and straight. Artie kept his head shaved down pretty close to the scalp. I'd had once seen a picture of him as a kid in Jeri-curls. He blamed his mother and told me never to speak of it again.

(Sorry, Art). Her skin, where it wasn't freckled was so pale that she could probably get a burn in moonlight. Artie's skin had such an even, dark brown tone that I wondered if he had ever had a zit in his life.

Watching them work, getting the eight of us ready to move, erased all those differences. They worked together almost as smoothly as the Guys.

It seemed that in no time at all, they had us moved and resting comfortably in a North Albany house. North Albany lies across the Willamette River from the rest of Albany. This meant that it was in a Benton county as opposed to Linn. Even so, it was still part of the city of Albany.

The house was a lot like the Vanderhorn home. It was large, well-furnished but with a feeling that there was something missing. I was too tired to wonder what it was.

Perhaps it just had too much room that had stood empty until we arrived. With a both a finished attic and basement there was room for all us.

Sasha had been installed in the master bedroom. A private nurse had been found somewhere who was attending to Sasha as best as one could. A cot had been put into the room for Cominad but she never used it.

Marguerite had chosen a room that had been once been a sewing room. "A room of relaxation and productivity," she said. She hoped the air would help calm her.

Pandora had a room, I'm sure. I just never saw her in it. She was the least directly traumatized by the flitling attack. She seemed to want to make up for that by running herself ragged. Whatever assistance Artie or Vanessa needed, she ran to do it, sometimes literally.

If neither of them had need of her, then Pandora was tending to the Guys as they recovered. I noticed that Ramón got a greater share of that attention. I might have said something but I had been hit by a deluge of weariness. There comes a time when the best that you can do is get some sleep. I lay down in my room to avail myself of some much needed slumber.

It was an odd room for sleeping. I felt like I had been transported back to my high school days. The room was covered with posters of rock bands and movies. Eerily enough, they were the same bands and movies I had once idolized. Either whoever decorated this room was a serious nostalgia buff or the room had been unchanged since 1986.

It gave me a sense of timelessness. No, it was more of a sense of time being unimportant. I fell asleep pondering this sense of temporal irrelevancy. I did something I had never done before. I unintentionally slipped out of my body. At first I didn't realize it. I simply floated above myself thinking I was having the dullest dream.

When I wondered what Artie was up to, I reflexively floated out to where he was. Artie flipped between the various news channels catching up on the current events. In particular, he paid attention to the news about yours truly.

Artie sat watching the giant screen TV in the living room. My face seemed extra unpleasant at those dimensions. The news, though, was almost encouraging. It seemed it was unknown whether or not I was the victim or the perpetrator of various crimes. Whether or not I was still alive was a mystery. I was considered missing, as was the body of my late wife.

Shelia's body had been found shortly after I reopened her head wounds. She got the full crime scene work over and was sent to be autopsied by the medical examiner. She put herself back together after that. She actually did what I only seemed to do and disappeared from the morgue drawer.

I began to wonder where she was. I was still not really aware that I was projecting. If I had I wouldn't have taken the risk.

Once again I reflexively zeroed in on someone. This time I zoomed in on Shelia. There was no sense of motion. I knew I was suddenly very far from where I lay sleeping. It had not yet dawned on me that I wasn't merely dreaming.

I was in New York City. I knew because in the Sight. All human communities, from tiny hamlets to thriving metropolises, have their own astral backdrops. There are few cities that can throw the best and worst of humanity at you simultaneously through the Sight. Knowing how to read a city can be quite handy.[16]

I floated well above a high rise apartment building. I drifted down into building. I found myself in a well appointed but soulless apartment. It was clearly a residence where no one lived.

I drifted from the pristine hallway into the immaculate kitchen. The kitchen was empty. It had not been used in quite sometime. I was about to drift further through the apartment when I heard voices. I stopped at the door from the kitchen to dining room. I could hear two people speaking. A quick peek through the door showed me they were not in the dining room.

---

[16]   CC #472 Get to know your city: A guide to understanding urban soulscapes

I slipped quietly through the door and sneaked up to the little balcony that was just beyond the dining room.

I could hear Sheila's voice. She was talking with someone. This someone's voice seemed impossibly old.

Centuries old. Beyond that the voice sound oddly accented. He (it) was rather displeased with Shelia. "Why do you not simply kill him?"

"I have my reasons."

The old voice rumbled its displeasure, "Your service to Koenig is less than exemplary. That reflects badly on me. You make my favor seem weak."

"I'm doing what is best for all of us."

"I don't think you really see the big picture here. That my good is your good not the other way around." The old voice deepened and turned even more monstrous than before. It became a sound that was as rife with menace as a thousand cobra hisses or a multitude of swords unsheathed.

"Perhaps spending a month putting yourself back together will help you to see that."

When he turned toward my wife, excuse me, my late wife, I reacted. I didn't think or plan. I simply reacted. Even though I had recently done violence to her myself, I couldn't just stand by.

I moved out onto the balcony and unleashed the greatest amount of telekinetic force I had to date. It caught the monster quite unaware. The blast was enough to lift the monster, a vampire it turned out, off his feet, over the railing and out over the street.

As I watched him fall the many stories to the street, I realized two things. The first was that I recognized the vampire. He was a fairly well known actor. Or at least he had been when I was younger. I was amazed at how well he had hidden the fact. After all we had seen him grow up from child star, hadn't we? Perhaps this ancient monster had replaced the real person somewhere along the way.

The second was that I wasn't merely dreaming. The shock of that sent me hurtling back to my body.

When I arrived back into my body, I sat up, giving out a cry so alarming that Artie jumped up and ran back to my room.

"Are you alright? What happened?"

I simply looked at him dumbly and said, "Did you know that (name withheld by legal department) is a vampire?"

"Really? That's hard to imagine. He's so tiny."

I knew there would be hell to pay eventually for my actions. A mere fall wouldn't do in a really old vampire, it would only piss him off. That was trouble for another day, however. There were more immediate benefits for which I was grateful. I had managed to find out that Sheila was a continent away. Perhaps more once she fled the scene.

Being where (NWLD) the Vampire could find her wasn't going to be a long-term survival strategy. At least not a successful one, so I doubted she'd be returning to Koenig.

That was a relief. Perhaps we could get somewhere without Koenig's number one wolfhound dogging our steps. The flitling attack was a painful reminder that this wasn't going to be easy, even without my late wife's interference

All that was going to have to wait. My little unintended astral jaunt had left me even more fatigued than before. This was due more to the TK explosion than the journey itself. After outing (NWLD) as a vampire to Artie I fell back into a normal sleep.

Chapter Seven

WHEN I AWOKE I felt absolutely refreshed. Whatever Vanessa and Artie had done had worked miracles. I wasn't the only one. All of us from the "Virginia contingent" were felling rejuvenated.

Particularly Pandora, I had never seen Pandora look better. The lead in her eyes had been softening slightly since her revolt against Koenig. Now it was almost entirely gone. When she spoke with Ramón, her eyes positively shone.

While the rest of us ate breakfast, Pandora worked with the sketch artist that Cominad's crew dug up. It wasn't long before we had something workable.

There had been no change in Sasha and very little in his mother. Cominad was still determined to bring this whole mess to a speedy close, if for no other reason than to get her son's mind out of its deep freeze.

After breakfast, Artie came up to me and said, "Hey look out the window. We've got a surprise for you."

Looking out, I was quite surprised. It was a 30-foot long motor coach. Essentially an apartment on wheels.

"That's going to be your new mobile command center."

I was speechless.

"Who arranged for that?" Ty asked.

"I did," the response came from Cominad. I picked it up last summer. We used it once and I've been looking for another use for it ever since." I suddenly felt like the poor relations come a'callin'.

"Won't it be a bit conspicuous?" I asked.

Cominad shook her head. "It's going to be a support vehicle."

Cominad turned to address me. "I'm worried about two things. There are two details of the attack that I can't make sense of yet. Now that you're a little more clear headed, I want you give it some thought"

My old mentor was the same way. Anything, everything was a teachable moment. "This a lesson, isn't it," I said.

She put her hands up in the universal sign of mock apology. "Oh, forgive me! I had forgotten you have learned all things."

Again, it reminded me so much of my old mentor. It was simultaneously comforting, sad, and really annoying. She had the same way of prodding. She had the same expectation of your best. You just knew she would never accept half measures.

She slipped into this teacher role as unconsciously as I slipped back into my student one. For a brief moment we could focus somewhere other than the horror of Sasha's condition. Ironically, it was by studying its cause.

I knew I'd never get anywhere arguing with her so I sat back down at the breakfast table. I replayed the attack of the previous night in my mind. I made a show of counting off the details as I examined them again.

Cominad sat next to me and gently mocked me as I did.

"The flitlings attacked the *Guys* room. Knocking them out and surrounding Sasha."

"Ooh very good, such concision. No pesky details there."

"Fine." I thought. I went back and laid out all the details I could recall, body placements, clothing etc.

"Ty was laying at a forty-five degree angle to the little washstand. His head pointed toward the sink.

There was a blob of mint crest toothpaste on his slate-gray t-shirt. . . ." A forensic specialist would have been able to reproduce the room based on my description. Well, They could have if Cominad hadn't stopped me halfway through.

"Yes, yes, stop showing off. Focus. What was really wrong with that picture."

Arguably you could say the tiny winged soldiers but, hey, we're magi and weird is our business.

"Okay, okay lets see the guys were by the a.c. the t.v., the bed, and sink. Sasha's in the middle of the room and gets hit with spell meant for me." Oh shit. I see what she meant

Sasha got hit by a spell meant for me. Not incidentally, as if I had ducked an assassin's bullet. It was as if the assassin simply shot the wrong guy.

A lot of questions were now apparent. How did they know where to hit us? How did they know how to tailor an enchantment to take me out permanently? How, with that kind of information, could they have mistaken Sasha for me?

I stared into space trying to find a reconstruction that could fit the facts.

Question one; How did the enchantment get tailored to me?

Possible answer number One: Shelia gave them the key. That didn't quite make sense. Given what she said to me our last night together, she needed me with my faculties working. I doubt that a state like Sasha's would qualify

Possible answer number two: Koenig and her people had compromised my apartment. I didn't think that they took anything that could be used against me but perhaps I was wrong. Neither answer felt convincing. Perhaps more could be gathered by answering . . .

Question Number Two; how did they find us at the Marco Polo

They must have a way of tracking us. Otherwise how could they have found the motel room? They aren't tracking me directly. If they were, they would have waited for me and not used the attack on Sasha. They don't know what I looked like, because, again, they wouldn't have hit Sasha.

My bet was that they were tracking Pandora. She had a family connection to her brother that could have been exploited.

It seems likely that the Flitlings were told to attack the Magus traveling with Pandora. That's fairly bad planning when it comes down to it. It assumes only one magus being present.

It was as if Koenig had planned the attack then outsourced the execution.

Then it hit me. That's exactly what happened. Koenig (or her minions) crafted the enchantment. She then turned it over for someone here to use. That begs the question "who?"

Koenig's east coast operation had a bit of mojo flying about but nothing like what she hit us with here.

Someone out here was a lot more magic savvy. We had just hopped, skipped and jumped from the frying pan into the fire.

Chapter Eight

I STOOD UP. WE HAD to get moving. Sitting still was only going to work against us.

"Okay, people lets get on the road. Koenig's people are able to track us somehow. I suspect they're exploiting Pandora's connection to Stephan. Just sitting here makes us easier targets"

"So that's why we have the mobile command unit." This was Ty speaking up

"Arthur tell them about their new ride," Cominad said.

Artie put on his best "salesman" voice, "Ladies, Gentleman and Milo please step this way so we may inspect a wondrous blending of technological and thaumaturgical techniques."

We all did. Once we were ready, Artie resumed his little speech. If possible his spiel got even smarmier.

"This, my friends, is the very latest in enchanted motor coaches. Along with all the expected accouterments of a top of the line, luxury recreational vehicle, there are a number of enchanted enhancements, Enchancements I like to call them.

"These Enchancements include a perpetual obscuration effect, a self-replenishing air and water supply, and, let's not forget, the ever-full tank o' gas," Artie made a grand gesture with his arms. He smiled with such sincerity he could have been running for office. He continued with pitch.

"Stepping inside you can see that no effort was spared to make the needed transmutations. Though certainly opulent, this extraordinary conveyance was still utterly mundane and of little use . . ."

I had to break in, "Enough with the sales pitch already."

"Fine," Artie dropped back to his normal voice. There was small note of disappointment in it.

He continued. "As you can see, this one of those serious R.V.s, essentially a one bedroom apartment on wheels. We've made a few additions and changes though"

"Like extra-dimensional spaces?" This was James's interjection

"Ah, no." I said.

"You didn't make it. How do you know?" this was Hector.

"Trust me," I said, "Now let Artie finish so we can get a plan under construction. Stephan and Koenig's Jekyll are out there somewhere"

This put everything into a more somber perspective. I felt a little guilty for wrecking the jovial mood. Artie finished showing us the RV and the changes. First they had replaced the TV/ DVD system with an actual computer. There was also a computer that came as part of the RV. It did a lot of things. It figured gas mileage. It had one of the nifty navigation programs. All sorts of stuff like that.

This computer had other uses. Though not actually magical itself, the new computer stored thousands of pages of theory and history on the mystical arts, both from within our own tradition and from others. There was a quick reference list of alchemical correspondences and a surprisingly comprehensive list of angelic names. (That's something I prefer not to work with) There were also umpteen translations of the Bible, the Quran, the Bagda Veda, along with numerous commentaries for each. There was also a database of pop culture references.

Those are just the features I understood. After looking it over, Hector assured me that like everything else on board it was state of the art. (Which means that in the time it took to record this little "memoir" and have it see print, you could buy the whole thing used on E- bay for about 30 bucks)

The living/dining room area was an office now. The table functioned more as a desk than for eating.

The bedroom had the most changes. It had been converted into a working space. No, it wasn't a second office. This was a will-working space. It had been outfitted to Cominad's preferences.

The bed and other furniture had been removed. In their place a meditation mat covered the floor. It had a Seal of Solomon woven into the design. Its outer circle was ringed with angelic names in both Hebrew and Greek script. The design itself was golden on a deep blue field, the angelic names picked out in white.

Various tapestries of similar design hung on the walls. There were two Icons that hung along with the tapestries. One was, unsurprisingly,

The Epiphany. That's when the Magi show up in the nativity story bearing their gold, frankincense and myrrh. The Roman Catholic and Orthodox churches celebrate it on January 6th. Most North American Protestants barely notice it.

An "Epiphany" is also what we modern magi call that moment when one pierces the final mystery that allows the will to blossom. Sort of like a mystical birthday.

The other was the Annunciation. That's when Gabriel came to tell Mary she's going to have a baby. I wonder what significance it held for her. Perhaps it was simply she was a mother and could identify. Somehow I felt that was too simple an explanation.

There was shelf for an incense burner and some candles. The shelf had been made to keep the burning bits as stable as possible while this apartment, excuse me; this sanctum on wheels was in motion.

There was also a handy bookshelf. It held a few important books, the Hebrew Scriptures, a Greek New Testament. There was also The Zohar and a few works in ancient Persian dating back to before our spiritual ancestors traveled from the east led by a star.

There was also an Mp3 player in the room with those amazing little speakers that can really fill a room with sound, especially a small room like this.

If I was going to use it, I needed to add to her collection. It seems all she had where Gregorian chants and classical music.

Not that I dislike her choices, but there is music that calls more clearly to my soul.

There wasn't much that I needed to do to claim this spot as mine. I can't tell you what a tremendous gift it was for Cominad to allow me have it.

The rest of the gang got to work with logistics organizing. After setting some basic parameters for our strategy, I got to work on claiming the "workspace" as my own. I pulled a bunch of CDs plus one book from my car.

Cominad stopped me on my way back into the RV.

"Out of curiosity, may I see what you're adding?"

I thought about telling her it was too personal. This would have been an acceptable answer. It would have been a bit dishonest. It wasn't so much that I felt a need to preserve a personal boundary, I was simply afraid she'd disapprove of my choices.

She looked over what I had brought. It was hard to read her expression. The classic rock CDs she seemed to shrug off. Certainly not her choice but she didn't seem to question them as meditative foci.

It was the Weird AL and Muppet CDs that got her attention. She frowned at these but still chose not to comment. My dog-eared copy of *The Cat in the Hat* made her stop and give a cold, calculating look.

"Something wrong?" I asked

"No, not really I just find you're choices a bit unusual."

"Yeah, but I've got to go with what works right?"

"I suppose so."

She just gave me a long, hard look as if trying to puzzle out the true nature of my soul.

"I think you should be able to handle this. I'm setting my team back to work on our agenda. I'm going to keep on with Sasha. If your work uncovers anything contact me A.S.A.P."

Considering that she could have blamed me for the state Sasha was in, I was amazed at her magnanimity.

I finished putting my stuff in the RV. In what felt like no time at all, we, the Virginia contingent, were back on the road headed out. Essentially we were going in circles. For once this was intentional.

Chapter Nine

WE WERE PLAYING A hunch. We figured that Koenig's forces were making a connection to Pandora through Stephan. We decided to keep her under the RV's obscurement effect as much possible. It shouldn't hurt to keep her moving either.

We had a fairly simple, if unequal, breakdown of jobs. I would check out the occult landscape. James acted as my assistant. Ty and Ramon would do the more mundane legwork. Marguerite drove the RV while she waited for flashes of psychic insight.

Hector and Pandora shared the biggest job. It was what we called "the board." They worked to coordinate all the information we gathered. Whatever Marguerite gleaned from the ether would be combined with the information the two other teams brought in. They also used our on-board satellite web connection to search for even more information.

That was the plan anyway. Plans always end up needing a lot of tinkering along the way. At least mine do.

I needed to do some centering exercises before I was ready to hit the road. Rather than sit idle, the guys took copies of the Pandora's Jekyll sketch and some actual photos of Koenig to show around.

James drove over to Oregon State University in Azgard. It was in the pleasant little town of Corvallis. It's about 15-20 minutes from where we had been staying. Ty and Ramón headed to Eugene and The University of Oregon in the suburban.

Hector had been monitoring the news for things that concerned us. One thing came up.

"Hey boss," Hector yelled to me, interrupting my meditation. "I got big news."

I turned down the Muppet Movie soundtrack and yelled back, "It had better be good."

"Trust me, Jefe, this is good."

I got up and wandered out to look at the computer screen. Hector sat beside it just beaming.

"See, Mr. gives, I think Koenig's arrest is a big thing." It was, of course.

"Also check this out. They picked up Merton and bunch of other thugs she was using. This is good news, right?"

"I don't think it's bad. I also don't think Koenig will be out of action very long. How old is this? She may be free already."

"It looks like this was updated yesterday sometime. You really think she'll beat the rap?"

"No, I just don't think they'll be able to hold her very long. I doubt her flunkies will be more than inconvenienced. Still it may work to our advantage. Perhaps it means that Stephan is not so well guarded right now."

I felt a greater urgency pressing on me. I also felt a greater hope. We needed to make the most of this opportunity. I figured that Koenig would try to go to ground as soon as she was out of custody. If she did, that might make our task even harder.

"Let's see if we can't dive through this window of opportunity. Marguerite be ready to move on the first word from either James or Ty and Ramón."

I turned my mind back to my meditation. I allowed myself to float into the music as I contemplated the Divine. I'm sure that in the film version of this they'll change the tune to something more traditionally spiritual like a hymn or a Gregorian chant or Enya. They've got nothing on Manah Manah.

I was waist deep in the joy of just being. Let me tell you it's been hard to come by that lately. I felt ready to tackle the problem of finding Koenig and her Jekyll.

For the second time in as many days, I left my body without intending it. Perhaps it's something in the Oregon air. I rose up out the moving RV and floated with it for just a moment. Then my surroundings blurred as if I was moving at high speeds. I had no sense of motion however. Which is probably a good thing. The g-force acceleration would have been fatal to a flesh body.

When the world stopped rushing at me. I was a fair distance from the RV. The first impression I had of my new surroundings was *"up."* Everything I saw just kept directing my eyes toward the heavens. The trees almost seemed in motion as they jutted skyward. The mountains themselves looked as sharp as needles. I had trouble craning my head back far enough to see their peeks. For those who know the western mountain ranges, this is no surprise to you. I had been told that the mountains out here were higher but the reality still wowed me that first time. I had grown up back east where our mountains are smaller, older, and, as I like to point out to those living on the pacific ring o' fire, geologically stable.

My second, almost simultaneous, thought was *"green."* Let me rephrase that *"***Green***"*. No, no I mean **GREEN**. I hope I'm making myself clear. The trees were green. It wasn't just their leaves or needles that were green but the rich vibrant moss that had covered most of the trunks and branches. Even the blue sky above only emphasized the earthly green.

I thought that it might just seem this way because I was viewing the world through the Sight. When I "manifested" and saw the world through my ordinary senses, the world stayed just as green and tall. The only difference was that I could tell that I was in a campground.

I looked down at my represented form. To my surprise, I didn't look like a ghostly version of myself. My skin and my hair were still ghastly white but the rest of my image had picked up the theme of my surroundings. I was dressed entirely in shades of green. I was also stretched tall and thin like the image in a fun house mirror.

I wondered what had drawn me here. I looked around. It was early Friday afternoon by this point and already the campground was filling up with weekend campers. I wandered about trying to find out more.

A sign declared I was at Cascadia campground. I still didn't know exactly where I was. All I could tell right away was that my body was northwest of me about 40 miles and in motion. I wandered away from the main areas of the campsite. I figured whatever I was looking for would be off the commonly traveled paths. I was at the far end of the camping loop when I noticed an odd formation in one of the Campsites. There were three large tents. They looked as though they were intended to hide the central area of the campsite.

I went over to investigate. Inside the campsite, hidden by the tents, was a most unusual campfire ring. The ring wasn't a simple metal or stone circle like the other campsites. This site had a large outer ring and two inner ones.

The outer ring was made of numerous small, flat, smooth stones and was about four feet across. The next ring in was metal and had a silvery appearance. It looked to be about 2 1/2 feet across. The third, central, circle was fairly small only a foot in diameter. It was made out of a glazed ceramic. Each of the rings had five different ideograms carved into them. The ideograms looked like the could be Japanese or Chinese, perhaps even a mixture.

Five stones of the outer ring had been chiseled. The character stones were placed evenly around the circle.

The silvery ring looked as though the characters where struck into the metal, almost as if it were a large oddly shaped coin. The ceramic ring was exquisite. Each character both inset and intricately glazed

I looked about and made sure that i wasn't seen. I let my senses shift back to the astral. I faded out as my "eyes" readjusted.

It was clear that there had been some mystical use for these rings. I was getting an after image of three sets of flames. each ring had a fire going. Each fire was a different color, yellow outside, green within the second circle, a deep blue in the center.

With the Sight running, something else jumped out at me. The tents themselves showed no signs of human habitation. Their function was to conceal not to shelter. That was something I should have guessed. Each of the tents were examples of multi-room family tents.

I turned my attention back to the fire rings. After a moment of concentration, I noticed small filaments of energy extending outward from the fire. They all led the same direction. They stopped only a few feet beyond the furthest out of the tents.

There had been magical activity here. I could not tell what it was. It was so different from what I did, I just had no basis for comparison.

I dropped back to ordinary senses. Looking at the ground I could tell only a few things. One was that a car had been driven in and out a number of times. The tents not only hid the odd campfire rings but this parking spot as well.

I didn't have to wait long for answers. I was still checking things out when the air suddenly grew cold. There was a familiar swirl of blue light springing out of the air, about the height of my head.

In a moment, the air tore itself open. Out of it poured a short, slender woman wearing ragged, athletic clothes and a pair of sports glasses with the lenses badly spider-webbed with cracks. This woman was disoriented, bruised and the spitting image of the sketches made of Koenig's Jekyll.

Chapter Ten

THE WOMAN WAS EVEN smaller in stature than I expected. Pandora had said she was short and slight. I still expected her to come up past my chest. I am, after all, on the short side myself.

The Jekyll picked herself off the ground. She stood motionless for a moment, trying to steady her balance. Her balance failed and she toppled over.

On instinct, I rushed over to catch her. Being insubstantial, I'll leave you to guess how successful that was. If you've ever heard a person collapse to the ground you know how ugly a sound that is.

She lay face down in the dirt of the campsite. I could hear her whimpering. It was a heart-breaking sound. I needed to tell the team what I had found. I was loath to leave her even for the instant that it would take to get back to my body and tell someone.

I faded back out so that I could check the Jekyll out with the Sight. I winced at what I saw. She was in bad shape. She was badly dehydrated and exhausted. She had a number of deep tissue bruises. It looked like she had been beaten up from the inside. Given her nature I couldn't rule that out.

She needed medical attention. I have to admit, I should be better at some things. Will-working in my astral form for instance. It's an effort to interact with the physical world, let alone alter it significantly.

I wouldn't be able to work any healing until I was back in a meat body

Maybe she could tell me something that could help her. I returned to manifesting. When I tried to speak to her she didn't seem to recognize my presence.

I heard her mumbling. She tried to crawl somewhere. The words I could make out were something like "back pup." She was crawling toward one of the tents. She clearly didn't notice I was there, even though I had manifested and talked to her face to face.

She was feeling her way to one of the tents. I peeked into the tent and saw a backpack next to an unused sleeping bag.

"Do you want you're back pack?" I asked her. This time she responded to my voice.

"Who. . . . Phone . . .help," was all she managed to say.

Of course, it was a beautiful solution to both of my problems. I used a tiny bit of energy to "TK" the backpack open and get out her phone. I quickly dialed Marguerite's cell number. I heard a voice answer and once I was sure I had gotten a person not voice mail, I shouted (read whispered) "Cascadia State Park." Next I dialed 911 and gave them as much I could.

"911 emergency dispatch." came the voice

"I'm at the Cascadia campground site #12, I've found a woman who looks badly injured."

"Sir, speak up and repeat that, please."

I tried again. I was shouting hard enough that if I were enfleshed I'd loose my voice for a week.

Although I was lungless, the effort left me "out of breath." I could only hope that that second time was good enough.

I used what little energy I had left to assist the Jekyll. It seemed she might be slipping into shock. In my intangible state, I would be hard pressed to stop even that. Things looked grim for our Jekyll.

It was only a few moments later that I heard footsteps running toward the campsite. I faded out. It was the volunteer camp hosts. My guess was that 911 Dispatch called them to render any possible first-aid. They were an older couple. I found out later one was a retired doctor. At the very least they could keep the Jekyll from dying of shock.

I heard a car driving up and sirens in the distance. The car pulled around back to where the hosts and the Jekyll were. Thinking this might be a good lead, I hid myself in one the tents and risked a peek on the material side of life.

The car was the one I had seen all too briefly at the Park and Ride back in Virginia. That shouldn't surprise me. What surprised me was that I recognized the man who got out of the car. He was the man who was with Koenig back in my apartment. The same man I had seen the ghost swallow whole. I've got to say, I really didn't expect that at all. I made a mental note of the car's license plate. I faded out again just in case he looked into the tents.

Watching from an astral perspective, I couldn't make out the words he was saying to the Jekyll, but deep and sincere concern came through. He ran over to her and began talking to her in just the way you'd expect of someone who cared very deeply.

He held her and stroked her hair. He spoke to her in a low, soft voice. Though not sobbing, tears still rolled down across his cheeks. Those tears glowed with their own inner light. He had very deep feelings for Koenig or, at least, for her Jekyll. I got the impression that he not only loved her but was in love with her. Her lover? Her husband?

An ambulance and a police cruiser arrived together. Each group of professionals began tending to their work. The paramedics soon had the Jekyll loaded up and on her way to a hospital While the police spoke to the associate and the two caretakers. Koenig's associate insisted on riding in the ambulance. Which I guessed meant he was family or at least close enough. There seemed to be a growing likelihood that one of Koenig's men may also be the Jekyll's husband. If so, I really needed to talk to that guy.

As I watched them go, I was struck again by the host of unanswered questions that this had just raised.

Who was this guy? What was his relationship to Koenig in either form? How were they doing that teleport thing? I was so jealous.

They had left the car behind. I only hoped my team could get here in time to do something with it.

The police officer was pissed about the car. This confused me a bit until I realized that he might consider it contamination of a crime scene. I figure that officer wasn't going to be happy about a lot of things, like who made the 911 call and the odd forensics that teleportation would leave.

Sadly, if they decided that what happened here was a crime, it would go unsolved. After all, who would explain it to them? Besides, they'd either never believe the truth or even admit that they had considered it.

A forensics team showed up before my team did. I could tell my team was getting closer. My body didn't feel quite so far away any more. While the forensics squad did their bit, a small crowd gathered to watch from behind the police lines.

The forensics team was doing a fairly thorough job. I wondered what they would make of the fire rings or the unused tents.

More police from the nearby town and few state troopers came by. There seemed to be a fair amount interest in this case.

Given the strong presence of law enforcement, I decided perhaps it wasn't the best time for the team to come waltzing in. I probably had our best lead with the license plate anyway. I headed back to my body.

Chapter Eleven

I FOLLOWED THE INSTINCTIVE "GRAVITY" that one's body has for the soul. I pondered the new developments. Why was the Jekyll looking so beat up? What happened to Koenig's flunky after disappearing down the ghost's throat? What was his relationship to Koenig and her Jekyll? I was flying on automatic.

I was so engrossed in my thoughts, I failed to notice something important. I had noticed, for instance, that my body was in motion toward me. I was allowing myself to drift toward it. They must have gotten my message about Cascadia. What I had failed to notice was that they had put my body in Azgard. One of the guys was driving it down to me.

Yes, my car, the one that can block astral motion. That first time I was going slowly and I was inside.

I think you can see where I'm going with this.

Though it's hard to compare astral movement with physical movement, I was probably wafting at a good thirty miles an hour. My car was doing better than sixty. Had it been a purely physical collision at a relative 90+ miles per hour someone else would be telling this story. Fortunately my astral body doesn't have any organs to scramble. Still, the impact was less than pleasant.

I took a moment to chastise myself for sloppy thinking. Then I looked into the window to see who was driving. It was James. My body was strapped into the passenger seat next to him. Now, I like James, so don't get me wrong when I say I was disappointed to see him. He is the most excitable of the guys. I was just a wee bit worried how he might react if I suddenly manifested while he was driving.

I could just see him instinctively swerving and causing quite a mess. Granted he's not a bad driver. I still didn't want to test his skill needlessly

As absurd as it might sound the quickest way back to my body was to leave it behind. I reoriented my thoughts on the RV. Well, not the RV itself but on people in the RV.

I got a fairly clear reading on Marguerite. Once again I found myself blurring through the "ether" then I was standing before Marguerite. She looked up at me a bit startled.

I was less abrupt with her this time than when I was on the phone. This time I gave two whole sentences. "Tell Hector to have James open the passenger window and come back. Also try to run license this plate number, Oregon YSG-263"

I flickered back to James and Azgard. My message must have gotten through. I got there as he pulled a u- turn. James parked on the shoulder of the road heading back the way he had come. He actually got out and looked around then walked over to the passenger side. He had left the driver's door open so by the time he was undoing the seat belt I was back inside myself.

"Thanks," I said, "I can get it from here.

"Thank God. Do you know how hard you are to lug around?"

It wasn't long before we had rejoined the rest of the team. The guys had a lead of their own in addition to the one I had. Unfortunately, It seemed to contradict mine.

James had shown around the sketches of the Jekyll. At one of the libraries, he got an identification. The name he was given was that of Marianna Tamblor. She was a local resident in the university town of Corvallis, Oregon (Go O.S.U. Beavers)

Hector, with the aid of the all the nifty computer stuff, was able to access information about the car. The car belonged to Arnold and Wendi Scott both residents of another nearby university town, Eugene Oregon (Go U of O Ducks)

We were just formulating our plan when Pandora had a brainstorm. She suggested that we look at the actual driver's License records not just the vehicle registration. Once again Hector came through.

We were in for another slight turn in the case. The picture of Wendi Scott wasn't that of the Jekyll but that of our fair MS. Hyde, Koenig herself. I don't know why I hadn't expected Koenig to have an identity out here. I let myself get locked into assuming a greater separation of lives.

It also began to explain Arnold's presence in both lives. Maybe he helped Koenig keep secrets from herself. Maybe he helped her orchestrate the incredible level of deception necessary to keep things running.

Once again we sat down to take stock of our situation. We had to reformulate our plan

We pulled our little caravan off the road at an exit somewhere between Salem and Eugene. The truck stop there was Pioneer Village or Villa, something like that. We ate in the obligatory, little restaurant. Pandora joined us for dinner inside the restaurant. I figured that short amount of time wasn't that much of a risk. I was, of course, wrong.

I was actually feeling upbeat. We had found a significant amount of information. We knew Koenig's alias.

We knew the name (or one of the names) that the Jekyll went by. It wasn't much but it was a good start. With Mariana hospitalized, we couldn't get much out of her right away.

My action to stabilize her had healed enough internal bleeding for her to survive. She was still hurt enough that she required a significant hospital stay.

It would be hard to interview her there, especially if we wanted to avoid the police. However, if we were subtle enough, we could probably get closer to Arnold.

I gave out the assignments.

"Ty, you and James switch over to checking out more on the Scotts. I want you to observe Arnold particularly. See what he's up to. I want Marguerite to do what she can to keep tabs on Marianna in the hospital. Pandora, You and Hector see what you can find out about Koenig's life as Mariana here in Oregon. Ramón and I are going to go back up to the campsite and keep poking around." We finished eating and then split up again. Ty and James would take the suburban. Pandora and Hector had Azgard. Marguerite was to catch a ride with the Azgard crew. Ramón and I were taking the RV. I figured that it'd look less conspicuous at a campsite.

It was a plan. It might have even been a good one. Too bad it was all for shit.

Ramón And I walked out to the parking lot to get the RV.

"You do know that a couple of guys on their own with a RV is going to seem a tad gay." Ramón said to me as we walked. I was about to give a snide answer in response when I noticed a loud buzzing. It sounded like bees only a fair bit louder. If it hadn't been for the earlier attack, I might have imagined a swarm of hummingbirds coming our way.

I grabbed onto Ramón's arm in order to include him in my quick shielding effect. "Look out, Fairies," I cried!

"Exactly," Ramón said, misunderstanding me.

He must have seen them over my shoulder right after that because he went white as a sheet.

Chapter Twelve

I TURNED AROUND TO SEE what he was seeing. When I did, I felt nostalgic for the previous fairy attack. This time it wasn't tiny winged "soldiers of history" that came for us. In comparison that assault seemed almost chummy.

There are more kinds of fairy creatures than get the usual press. Some say the Fay are formed from humanity's dreams and nightmares. You can find just about anything imaginable in one Fay realm or another. I'd hate to encounter whatever nightmare birthed these things.

This attack looked like a school of winged lampreys. As they got closer I could see them clearly. Every inch of the beasties that wasn't a buzzing bee-like wing was a vicious, cruel-toothed mouth. Just looking at them made me feel sick to my stomach. Those little monstrosities were moving fast. My shielding effect was not going to buy us a lot of time. I figured my best course of action was to projectile vomit.

If this doesn't seem like the most reasonable action, I must remind you a few things. About 20, eight-inch long tubes of squirming flesh were attacking us. Yes, I know how phallic that sounds. Also, let me point out that all those tiny, drooling, razor-lined mouths gave the flying lampreys the appearance of being covered in running sores.

I think nausea is a perfectly reasonable response.

"Use what's inside you," my mentor taught me. "It's like method acting. Drawing from within makes your intent more truthful." Of course he didn't mean it quite so physically.

I had been surprised by the suddenness of the attack. I didn't have much time to plan. I just reacted.

Thankfully, I had been saving up as much energy as I could ever since we started our journey west. I had a fairly good base to throw some Mojo around.

Unfortunately, I had stuffed myself at dinner. The excess food in my gut grounded me out mystically. I was going to have trouble extending that power beyond my physical body

When I turned and truly saw the horror careening towards us, I felt my bile rise to my throat. My stomach churned. I think I may have started vomiting before I realized that this was my saving grace (so to speak.)

In that split second I had one of those small "e" epiphanies. By the grace of God, a plan popped fully formed into my head.

With the energy I had stored up, I wove three linked effects. The first was to strengthen my own systems. I needed to withstand the other two effects. The second was to increase the mass of the mishmash of my digesting food. The last was to increase the power of my own stomach acid. That's when I surrender to my nausea.

Skipping ahead might be advisable for those of tender constitution.

The combined result of all this was that the first wave of little beasties was hit by a cone of highly corrosive, wet cement-like glop. My will-work and their innate magic resisted each other and both disappeared in a small, foul-smelling conflagration. I believe this took down a third of them.

We were lucky. The remaining lampreys were smart. At least smart enough to veer out of reach of another blast. If they hadn't, I'm sure they would have finished both Ramon and me.

This gave me enough time to actually think of another form of attack. I was empty and I didn't think dry heaving at them would be quite as successful. It was also enough time for Ramón to summon in his "brothers." They rushed to our aid the quickest way possible. Just as the time they faced Merton and Shelia, the guys focused all their minds on controlling one body.

Ramón began to blur into action. He struck nasty little death-lampreys out the air. It took an intense amount of bravery to even touch those things. I could see he was cut from his first blow. By the time he had cleared another six Nasties out the air. His shirt was torn up to the elbows on both arms. He was bleeding pretty badly from a multitude of small but deep cuts. The side of the RV and the ground near him looked like it had been finger painted by a particularly disturbed child. It had splotches of bright red human blood from Ramón mingled with the dark maroon of flying lamprey guts.

I hadn't quite depleted my stash of energy but it wasn't enough to throw into another attack. Instead I went the next best route I reach forward and made a cross in the air behind Ramón. I lent him all the energy I could. His skin toughened to resist further damage. The bleeding from his wounds began to slow.

Ramón had reduced the number of attackers down to three when things got strange, a relative term at best here. Pandora came rushing around the front of RV. The lampreys turned from Ramón and zoomed over to her.

As they descended on her, she shrieked, covered her head, and shouted. I struggled to pull in enough energy to do something. It was like trying to gasp for air underwater.

Pandora didn't need my help however. The lamprey things zoomed over to her, but that's all they did. Once they got to her, they just hovered. I swear that they looked like they were just waiting for instructions

Once Pandora recovered enough from seeing these things rush her, she shooed them away by vigorously waving her hand.

And they went.

That's when the bell went off in my head

"I think I know why they wanted Stephan," I said picking up a dead fairy lamprey by the wing

"Why?" Pandora asked

"Because I think these babies are his"

Chapter Thirteen

"W**HAT THE HELL DO** you mean those things are his?" That was Pandora. Our plans had changed. We were gathered inside the RV, having what could only be called a rational discussion in the most ironic sense. I had really touched a nerve with Pandora, though exactly which one still needed to be cleared up.

"I think both the things that attacked us tonight and at the motel answer to him. That's why they didn't hurt you. Remember how I thought that Koenig's crew was using you as a locater. Dinner was the first time you had been out of an occlusion effect since we got the RV. I think that that yon little beasties are being sent after the Magi closest to you in an effort to get me." I gestured outside where James was working to clean up the foul things. He was the only one of us who could stomach dealing with them. (He said he had been inured to such horrors by Scottish cuisine),

"How on earth could he control those things? Besides, why would he hurt you? He doesn't know you."

"No, he doesn't, but Koenig's man does and he has contact with the Jekyll. Close contact from the look of it."

"Maybe, but that doesn't explain how he's bossing the little monsters around."

The next part took a bit of arguing back and forth so I'll do my best to condense it. I reminded Pandora of all the little oddities that Stephan had experienced growing up. The disappearances, the odd but very valuable little trinkets that every one assumed were shoplifted.

I was sure he was one of the few humans that somehow hold a fascination for the Fay. It happens sometimes. There are plenty of theories why. Some almost make sense. Only the Fair folk could tell you the truth. They could but they wont. They tend to deny it happens or at the very least not talk about it.

"Still, Stephan is the gentlest soul I know. I can't imagine why he would turn so deadly trying to attack you.

At his point Ty interjected, "Hey, look outside."

We did. Thankfully James had finished cleaning up the lamprey mess and come inside.

Outside, a deep fog had rolled in out of nowhere. I didn't need supernatural senses to tell me this wasn't a turn for the better. The fog was so thick the *Pioneer Villa* truck stop had completely disappeared from view. The fog itself seemed to glow with its own diffuse light.

"We may need to discuss this later," I said. I took the ensuing silence as agreement.

Shapes began to emerge from the fog. At first they were only silhouettes in the mist. They looked like men on horseback. Their proportions were wrong. They were too tall, too thin. They were stretched so far that they should have collapsed under their own weight. The shapes crossed each other, circling the RV.

Staring into the fog I noticed something that gave me pause. The implications encouraged me on one hand and frightened me on the other.

Azgard was visible in the fog just a few yards away. It was roughly in the place where I remembered parking it. I was comforted by its presence.

The scary part was that I shouldn't have been able to see Azgard from the RV, even without the fog. It had been parked on the far side of the suburban. I had the distinct impression that it had, once again, loyally followed me. If it had followed me, where had we gone?

The shadow puppet horsemen kept circling in the fog. They stayed out just far enough to keep me wondering if there was any substance behind those shadows. This went on for what felt like an hour. The clock on the RV's stove said only about ten minutes had passed.

One of the shadows began to approach the RV. The odd elongation diminished and more of its detail began to emerge. Soon the figure had resolved itself. It was still a tall, thin person on horseback, just no longer impossibly tall or thin.

The "horse" was a steel gray, clockwork contraption. It counterfeited the living movement of a real horse all too well. Even watching the gears spin, the horse seemed more mammal than machine.

The person riding the clockwork horse wore a suit of armor but no helmet. Long, reddish blond hair flowed down around a face of stunning beauty. Looking back on it, I'm not sure how else to describe it. I recall no detail, not the curve of the smile or shape of the eyes. Unearthly beauty and a loss of detail are common in interactions with Fairy beings. Gazing into that "face" I had the feeling I was looking at a mannequin. An exquisitely crafted one, mind you, but something empty, false, and hollow

I suspected that there was more than a little enchantment to make me think the face was so beautiful.

Some say the Fay are built from human imagination, that when we look at them, we are seeing an idea rather than a thing. It may be the rider wore the idea of beauty, rather than being beautiful.

It got off the horse and strode over to the side of the RV. It stopped just in front of the main side door.

Through the windows, I could see it much more clearly. It was decidedly lacking in secondary sexual characteristics. Even in the armor, one could tell it lacked breasts or womanly hips. It also completely lacked a beard or the broader shoulders to make it seem more masculine. The armor that it wore was the only thing to have any real character to it. It was not made simply of bits of interlocking metal, as I had first thought, but of coins.

The coins were from all around the world. I saw US silver dollars and Euros. I counted British Pounds, Pesetas, a Chinese Pang Lian, Drachmas, Rubles, and Denarii. There were modern coins and ancient coins. A Spanish Doubloon rested next to a US golden eagle. At the time, the armor was only a mild curiosity. Now, I'd bet there were thirty pieces of silver worked into the armor somewhere. The figure spoke in a loud, melodious voice.

"I've come to negotiate the release of the girl."

Chapter Fourteen

"I'M GOING OUT THERE," I said. If I had expected any arguments, I would have been disappointed. No one questioned that I should go. What surprised me was that the Guys seemed to be arguing among themselves. It was hard to tell since it mostly consisted of pointed looks and the occasional hand gesture. It was like watching mimes argue. Disconcertingly like watching mimes argue.

In the end, perhaps 15 seconds later, James spoke up and said, "I'm coming with you."

I had noticed that the guys took to the new weirdness in their lives like ducks to water, as the cliché goes. I also had seen over and over how brave (or foolhardy) they are. So I wasn't surprised that they thought one of them should come with me. I was certain, however, that they didn't know how dangerous just talking to the Fay could be.

I began to tell James this when he held up a little booklet. It was one of my little correspondence course offerings *Negotiating with Fairies: Ten Tips on How to Get Out Alive and Relatively Intact*

"I had a lot time to poke around you're apartment waiting for you to wake up and question your ex . . . ah . . . Late wife."

"Right, so you do know how bad this could go," I said.

"You're going to need all the help you can get."

"No offense, but how you can help?"

"I was going to go in for pre-law when I was done with 'taking a year off to find myself'"

"Was?"

"I was taking a year to find *myself*. Now I've got to find these bozos too."

We laughed at that harder than we should have. Tense situations can do that to you. It was also just what the doctor ordered.

So James and I went outside feeling more relaxed and encouraged than we had any real right to be. Okay here's a freebie. The following is in essence ***Negotiating with Fairies: Ten Tips on How to Get Out Alive and Relatively Intact***

1) ***Don't.*** Simple as that. Don't. Don't trust the Fair Folk any farther than you can spit the Moon

2) **Don't go looking for them.** If they know you want something you start at a disadvantage.

3) **Define your terms.** After all, what does "in a timely manner" mean to an immortal?

4) **Always work in you native language.** Remember, dead clever word plays can leave you just that.

5) **Sweat the small stuff.** Sure, any reasonable being would, let us say, infer from your contract that the air in your quarters should be A: generally breathable, *and* B: not on fire. This may not have crossed a fairy's mind. It may have also thought these points unimportant, as you didn't bother mentioning them.

6) **Don't be greedy.** Just like a "real world" deal, if it seems to good to be true, it probably is. Like any other con artist, they'll be counting on your greed. What may seem small to you, a name, a memory, the color of your eyes, can be a very big deal. If a fairy really wants something of yours, you're better off keeping it.

7) **Don't be "clever"** Sure you're smart, you're ingenious. You can outwit the Devil, the IRS, and Bugs Bunny. Being clever just may mean you'll outsmart yourself. The Fair Folk just *love* irony

8) **Be straightforward.** The fair folk assume, from eons of experience, that they'll get you on either your greed, "cleverness" or dishonesty. Keep the negotiation as simple and direct as possible.

9) **Don't get distracted.** Beauty and grandeur are simple enough tricks for the Fay. Don't let them sweep aside your good sense with a little razzle-dazzle, no mater what fantasy they seem to step out of.

10) **Don't trade away hypotheticals,** sure, you don't have a first-born child right now . . ..

11) [17]**It's like smoking.** It seems cool at first; it's very addictive and can kill you and people close to you. The best tip yet, just don't start.

I hope I've made myself clear.

As James and I stepped down from the RV, the fog began to dissipate. I spun the Wheel of Sight and came up with a jackpot. All my senses were on high. I knew I wasn't astral projecting. That meant we were in some sort of Spirit realm, possibly Faerie itself. However, I thought that was unlikely. It was one thing for the fair folk to be involved in mortal doings; it was another to invite us home. I would have guessed some sort of halfway realm or a dreamlet.

The first thing that struck me was the scent of the air. It smelled wild. More accurately, it smelled untamed. Looking about I could see rows and rows of trees. The trees were lined up so that they formed lanes. There was no underbrush between the trees, just deep green, thick, short grass. Each line of trees was orderly and well maintained. The grass looked fastidiously maintained. It looked more like a park rather than a wild place.

The untamed scent and the manicured appearance struck two very different notes. The combination created, not a discordant feeling, but a breathtaking harmony.

Every so often there were clear pools of water between the trees. I was very reassured to see Azgard some distance away, half hidden in another lane. It might be a bit of a sprint to get to him but at least "he" was there.

James was looking around quite astounded. "I think I've read about this place."

At first, I thought that was impossible then James remembered where he had read about a place like this. "This was in one of those books about that lion and all those English kids." I didn't know specifically what he meant. There was a lot of pop culture I missed out on as kid. Still, I understood what he meant. We were somewhere that should only have existed in a book.

I wondered if this place existed before the book or as a result. (That can happen. When enough human imagination pours into an idea, it becomes real somewhere. Or so the theory goes.)

The fairy that was standing in front of us was of the kind that many call elves. He was of the tall, wan, ethereal kind not the cookie bakers. Some

---

[17]   I know that's eleven tips but think of it like a Baker's Dozen.

others call them the Sidhe. That's pronounced "she." There's joke in there about gender confusion among elven kind but I'm not going to make it.

Honestly, the Fay are creatures that will always resist our classifications. So elf is as good a name as any other.

Two others joined this elf. It pleased me to see that, though they strove to hide it, something was making them nervous as well.

The new one on the left had no armor. It appeared to be dressed in streams of water. The water cascaded down its body creating a long, formless gown. The gown had strategically placed rapids so that its' gender wasn't evident, if indeed it had one.

The one on the right was clearly female. Though she wore a suit of full plate armor, there was no denying her femininity. She carried her helmet under one arm, revealing her stunning eyes and fiercely beautiful face. Her armor appeared to be made entirely of ice. These two outfits confirmed for me that we were in a spirit realm. If we were somewhere with more rigid physical laws, like home, a lot more magic would be needed to keep the gown and armor intact. With my sights going, I could see that wasn't happening.

Coin-boy, for lack of a better name, spoke up, "Magus Gives, would you be so kind as to conjure us a suitable environment for our discussions. I'd do it myself but I wouldn't want you to misjudge my actions and fear them to be an attack."

"No, no," I said, "Go right ahead."

"Oh I insist. I wouldn't want to be accused of broaching protocol." The bastard had me. I didn't know if it was a breech or not. It would be bad form to admit it. Damn fairy manners. I was already one down and we hadn't even sat down yet.

"How gracious," I conceded. If he could hear the sarcasm in my voice, he ignored it. Coin-boy had just put me in a dangerous position. He must know how intoxicating will-working could be on a spiritual plane. For those of us used to the physical world, it can lead to a dangerous euphoria.

Imagine having your inhibitions blown away coupled with the ability to make almost any whim real. I had only risked magical drunkenness once before, and that was under my mentor's supervision. Still will-working in a spirit realm is a rare opportunity. He knew I couldn't pass it up easily.

I reached out and pictured a table in my mind. I hummed a bit to help me focus. For some reason, "Lets All Get Up and Dance to a Tune" by the Beatles came to mind. A large, high table with vast chairs around it formed in my imagination. As I started to draw in the energy to make the mental form solid, I had such a rush that I nearly lost my senses. I started to giggle to myself. God help me, I was spell stoned already. I even knew that it was coming. If I didn't do something quickly, there would trouble. I needed a way to control the euphoria. A sudden inspiration came to me.

First, I finished making the table. It was an oval table eight feet high, twelve feet from end to end and about eight feet across. I put a tablecloth on it that swept down to the grass. By now I was rippling with the pleasure of such easy creation.

So I did the only thing that I could think of to bring me down. I translocated Azgard and hid him under the table. The strain of it would have killed me back home. In that strange wood, it just hurt like hell. That sobered me up fast. The basic energies of this place began to seep back into me. This eased the pain.

I did my best to smile in a particularly goofy manner. Not really a stretch under the circumstances but my mind was clear, or at least as clear as it could be.

Once the table had been fully formed and the chairs set around it, James and I crawled up into our seats. The elf trio just casually hopped into theirs.

"So you want to negotiate for the girl's release."

"Yes, Magus Gives, we do. We are prepared to come to quite a generous agreement"

"I don't even know who you are. Let alone why you're interested in the girl."

Coin boy smiled. It was charming and the whole place seemed to light up as he did so.

"You may call me Numis. My associate here is Cascadia." He indicated the one on his right in the gown of water. I recognized the name of the campground where I had seen Koenig's Jekyll. I wondered if her name was a coincidence. I doubted it.

He gave a casual wave over to the ice-armored woman. "She merely acts as my bodyguard, so you needn't be concerned with her."

I shrugged. James took my lead and tried to look as nonchalant as possible. I gave Numis my best serious face.

"And you wish me to release the girl to you?"

"No indeed. We just would like her freed." Numis's smile was colder than his bodyguard's armor.

"What makes you think she is with us of anything other than her own free will?"

Numis smiled. Cascadia fielded this one. "Though you have quite a reputation, Master Gives do not think we are easily fooled."

I was actually startled by this her statement. I ended up just blurting out, "Reputation?"

"Are you not the same Magus Gives who bested the malignant djinn, Sarathan?"

"I'd call it a draw. Mostly I was lucky," I said. I wonder how she knew about that. It had only happened a little while ago. I hadn't told anyone. Still, the Fay have resources I couldn't fathom.

"You were lucky that Sarathan is an arrogant fool," Cascadia continued. "However, we are neither arrogant nor foolish. We simply bargain on behalf of her kin who wish her freed."

"Again, I ask you, why do you think that she is held against her will?"

If it seems I was being unnecessarily obtuse about the whole thing, perhaps I was. I didn't want to give away too much of our real position. Had I been dealing with any human agency, I would have at once simply said that Pandora was not a prisoner. I would have asked where they got the erroneous information. With Fay creatures, the less revealed the better.

You see, here's the thing. They said that they only wanted her freed and that they represented Pandora's kin. Presumably this is Stephan himself. After all, we know it's not her parents.

However this absolutely truthful statement could also be absolutely misleading. Lying with the truth is a staple of politics everywhere. And nothing is more political than the courts of Fairy.

"Come now," Cascadia said, "you keep her locked up at almost all times. She invariably travels with one or more of your enforcers. We know that you have contact with the woman calling herself Koenig and that your wife also works for Koenig.

"Is it not then an obvious conclusion that you are here to reacquire Master Stephan for your employer, Ms Koenig?"

"Ah I see. However if I work for Koenig, as you say, then why negotiate with me?"

Cascadia responded, "We know that you are a . . ."

Here Numis interjected with, "Freelancer."

"Yes. You are an independent force, a power unto yourself. The Magi are kings are they not?"

I tried a disarming smile. I'm sure I looked like a grimacing monkey compared to similar smiles from the fair folk, "perhaps in a sense, but I am merely a vassal of a greater monarch."

"And that is not Ms Koenig?"

"Oh, no, not by a long shot."

"Excellent, Young Stephan has been asking us for assistance in freeing his sister. His youthful instinct was to try and take her by force. Which he has attempted to do twice"

Numis interjected again, "He has some small sway with the lesser beings of the fairy kind."

Cascadia winced. The wince itself almost invisible but there none the less. Still she continued, "Both those attempts have failed and we were able to prevail upon him to attempt a diplomatic solution."

"Well, that's just admirable of you," I said.

"Just what did you think I would want in return for the young woman?" To his credit, if James had any worry about the direction the talks were going he gave no indication. In fact he seemed so contented and complacent I beginning to worry.

Numis spoke up, "Oh, we have many things we might trade for her freedom. Simplest of all is money.

We can give you copious amounts. And yes, real money, large and lasting sums from the real world. If some of it that money has outlived the government that minted it, then it has only appreciated in value, I assure you."

"Honestly," I said, "My problems are not going to be fixed with money. I don't think I could even begin the task of negotiating until I've done something to bring my friend, Sasha, out from under his enchantment."

Numis waved its hand and I could see the power emanate from it. A simple twist of the wrist and flick of the fingers and that energy sailed away from Numis' hand and into one of the nearby pools of water. I had no doubt that this would indeed be a help to Sasha. It was bit early for obvious tricks.

"Consider this an act of Good Faith. Your friend shall recover presently."

"Why, thank you. That was most generous. I do think we can negotiate after all or we could if I happened to be holding anyone prisoner."

"You still claim that you are not?"

"That's right."

"So the young lady whom you have secreted in a magical vehicle and is never allowed out except for brief periods and is always under guard is not a prisoner."

"Yes, that would be true. She is not a prisoner."

"Indeed."

"Now if you'll excuse me I really have some pressing business concerning the sorting out of my identity and legal status." I paused to see if Numis would offer any help along those lines as well.

"Ah yes, though we could indeed help you to 'sort all that out' I think we have shown enough of our good faith."

Well, it was worth a try.

"Still, it would be dishonest of me to negotiate something that is not mine."

"So you still maintain that she is not your captive?" Numis said

"Indeed, I'll even assert that you know that as well as I do."

"Come now, why would we feign ignorance?"

"I'd say it's so that you can keep her brother in the dark about his real circumstances."

Only because I was using all of my heightened senses could I pick up a shift in the discussion. No one has a poker face like one of the Fay. I had just hit home with that statement. It had put them off their edge. That was not something I wanted just at the moment. If Numis and Cascadia thought I was too clever, my job would get a whole lot harder.

"I find that statement to rather insulting." said Numis

"As do I," Cascadia's demeanor shifted subtly. There was more menace in it than before.

"If, as you say, the young woman is not you prisoner than perhaps she could come out here and discuss this with us for herself."

"Oh she could but I'd prefer she didn't."

"And why is that?"

Now here's where it gets tricky.

Only a total fool would knowingly insult on the Sidhe. It's bad for your health and mental well-being. Yet, I needed them to think I was foolish. Their responses would tell me a great deal of information. Besides, I needed to bring this negotiation to a screaming halt. I didn't know enough about what was going on to pull anything *really* tricky. I'd be a fool to try to outwit Numis right now. I was convinced that Numis was the key to this affair. Call it a hunch.

"Because, I don't trust you," I said.

Numis' eyes flashed for a second, but he retained his calm. Cascadia glared at me. The Icy Warrior drew her sword from the scabbard across her back.

Cascadia spoke through gritted teeth, "You would dare to suggest that we, that *we* would break ancient protocols. That *we* would not honor the implicit safeguards of this negotiation?"

Now I was going to push it. Just a little. "Yeah, howdy," I said.

The bodyguard abruptly loomed at me from across the table. How does one loom across a table you ask? First, You gain about a story in height and then . . . you get the picture.

She spoke for the first time since she appeared. "If you do not apologize, I will ask for an honor duel."

Now this would be a bad thing. I doubted I could beat the Icy warrior in any kind of fight. Hell, a game of tiddlywinks could prove fatal. I had pushed them far enough for the moment. I knew what I needed to know.

Though the Fay generally can speak any tongue known to our world, they do have languages of their own. It is said that no human can speak them. This is true enough. I couldn't converse in any of the fairy languages. I can, however, apologize in two of them. The two phrases I know both translate to "I offer my most humble apologies to you and your family and/or house/lineage/ and/or totality of creation." It would be truthful enough to say I learned the phrases phonetically. I don't know what any of the actually sounds mean. It takes most of my concentration and a bit of magic just to reproduce them. Like Chinese, the languages are tonal. Unlike Chinese, they require harmonizing with yourself.

If I get it wrong I could, instead of apologizing say almost anything. This includes informing Numis that his laundry is ready or asking him if I may marry his sister's game warden.

I launched into my apology. It must have come off well. It had the intended effect. The icy warrior looked mollified and she put away her sword. Cascadia relaxed.

Numis? Well Numis looked pissed. This is exactly what I was hoping for. "Why?" You ask. Numis' anger tells me that he is not playing things even remotely straightforward. For some reason, Numis's anger seemed to cement his gender in the masculine.

Numis had been hoping to maneuverer me into a corner trying to "prove" to Cascadia what I had already told her. I'd be at disadvantage there. I still didn't know what he was up to but I was a step closer.

All it cost was focusing Numis's rage on me.

Fortunately, it's bad form to kill someone for making an apology, even for a people as mercurial as the Fay. I felt certain Numis was going to try to do something to screw me over, probably sooner than later.

"Well then, we accept you apology." Numis said. "Since it appears we are at an impasse, let us all go our separate ways. Is that acceptable to you?"

"I believe it is." I jostled James out of whatever little daydream he had gone into and asked him.

"I'm sticking with you." he said

"Fair enough." agreed Numis. He waved his hand and suddenly they were gone.

"Well, that was weird," said James, "lets go." we turned around to head back into the RV and saw that it was gone.

"Hey, ah, boss . . ." James said, the worry in his voice was as sharp as obsidian, "I can't hear the rest of the guys any more."

Chapter Fifteen

IT WAS HARD TO say exactly what the silence in James's head meant. Without further information it could be good or very bad. "Hopefully it just means that they are back home." I made a mental note. We may have discovered one limitation on the link between the Guys.

"Separating us like that is an old fairy trick," I told James, "take something someone says and use the most harmful meaning of the phrase. In this case I stupidly agreed that we should all go our separate ways. So we did. I think that the RV went as a unit because of the enchantments on it. You're still with me because that's what you said you wanted. Numis wants to appear as though he was just trying to do what we asked."

"Do you really think that's true?"

"Well, maybe, perhaps he just wanted a witness to my humiliation."

"I meant about the RV."

"Oh, yes. Now, let's see about getting out of here."

"You know a spell to get us home?" James asked. He waggled his fingers in a mock mystical gesture. I hesitated a moment. I didn't know one. I did have a plan, however.

"Actually this inter-dimensional stuff has never been my strong suit. Don't worry; we have an ace up our sleeve." I climbed down off of the big chair. Azgard, I was confident, could do the job. After all it had followed us here from the physical world under its own power. Presumably it could find the way home.

I focused my mind on dismissing the whole table set. There's enough of a showman in me that I wanted to do a dramatic reveal of the hidden Azgard. So with an unnecessary flourish of my hands and a bow, I grabbed the edge of the over-sized table cloth and threw it up into the air. I dissolved the discussion table and chairs to reveal an empty space.

"Boss, am I missing something here or are you?"

When I finished cursing and stomping, I realized that James was laughing. He was laughing and running over to examine the pool of water closest to us.

"I think I can find our way home," he said. "I've figured out where this place reminds me of."

I joined him and examined the pool trying to divine what he was looking for. "Go on. So where are we?" He stopped and took a deep breath as if he thought I might laugh at his idea.

"Have ever read any C. S. Lewis?"

"Sure, *The Screwtape Letters, Surprised by Joy, Mere Christianity . . .*"

"No, no, the Narnia stuff."

Now this is a bit embarrassing. I haven't read any of that stuff. No Narnia, No Tolkien, None of any of the other classic fantasy series that a lot of guys my age had read in high school or college. My parents had been rather strict when I was younger and had forbid any thing that even had a whiff of "the occult."

The closest I got was sneaking Dr Strange comics in with my Spideys and Teen Titans. In college, I was kept busy trying to keep up with my studies. (That's my story and I'm sticking to it.)

After I had my Epiphany, fiction about magic didn't seem all that important. I've never gotten around to reading much of it.

James told me that in one of the Narnia books, the characters go to somewhere called the Wood between Worlds. In this wood the various pools of water led to different worlds. Lewis's description was more of a wild wood rather than the park we found ourselves. It was still close enough to warrant investigating.

"So, what are you looking for?" I asked James

"Well, the kids in the book marked the pool by cutting up the sod near it."

"And you expect to find that?"

"Well, we're there aren't we?"

"Maybe . . . It is possible Lewis was describing a real place but I doubt it."

"You doubt it? *You* doubt it? Look around. If we aren't there where are we?"

"Putting aside whether or not Lewis was describing a real place, he may still have been describing fictional events."

"Okay, that point I'll concede. Still, perhaps there's enough truth in it to helps us. Besides what else are we going to do?"

"I suppose," I said, "but it seems so unnecessary."

"That's another thing about the Lewis account. The sense of timelessness . . . Maybe you don't feel it so much, but I'm worried that if I don't stay focused, I'll drift off into permanent inaction."

Now that he had mentioned it I did feel a certain lack of urgency that belied our stranded status. Now I was scared (sort of) and leapt (sort of) into action

"Good point, so we, uh, are looking for a divot, are we?"

I couldn't tell you how long we spent looking for that divot. As we looked, James and I chatted a bit more about the nature of the place we were. He told me story of the two children in *The Magician's Nephew*. They were essentially used as lab rats by a selfish Magician. The Magician had given them magic rings he didn't really understand.

"So we'd need these rings to get back out here?" I asked

"I don't know. You're the Magician here."

We didn't come to any real conclusions. Only that either Lewis had more real info than any one had realized or he was so influential that this place formed on the strength of his readers hopes and dreams. Not a groundbreaking conversation to be sure but it kept us occupied and alert. It was enough so that when rescue came we could take advantage of it.

Rescue came as I expected it, from Azgard, just from an unexpected direction.

We were looking at the edge of a pool trying to determine if a slight variation in the "lawn" might be the grown over remnants of the cutting in Lewis's book.

We were so intent on this, Azgard surprised us when it came splashing up out of the pool and onto the grass next to us.

Chapter Sixteen

WITH A SIGH OF relief and a supernaturally augmented sense of calm, we climbed into Azgard, shut the doors and drove it back down into the pool. It may have been the light but I think that Azgard's normal yellow turned a distinct green as we plunged down beneath the water.

The journey back beggars description. I find it difficult to describe what I remember. The memory isn't fuzzy or indistinct just contradictory. It is more like three memories layered upon each other.

The first is the simplest. Imagine a country road on a cloudy, moonless night, the kind of night where it seems that your headlights don't just illuminate the road before you but actually create it. Now wrap that image around an endlessly extending spiral.

The second layer of the memory was that of hurtling through a starfield occasionally dotted by a planet or moon until finally careening toward our own mother earth

The last layer was being submerged in a deep blue, almost purple liquid. There was no sensation of movement or even of time passing.

Now throw all those together in such a way that they make absolutely rational sense. It is only in retrospect that any of it seems at all odd

I wish James could confirm some of this for me but he can't. As soon as we hit the water, he was able to reestablish contact with the rest of the guys and he was needed. He slipped into the trance state that meant the main part of his consciousness was now "non-local."

While I was having a trip that Timothy Leary would have envied, James and the rest of the Guys were attending to a very tense situation.

There was a back up plan for when the Fairy delegation "failed." As soon as the RV was back in our world, exactly where it had been before the fog had closed around it, the rest of the gang noticed our absence.

Needless to say, this worried them greatly. They didn't know if James and I were still alive or not. They feared the worst. The Guys were the most concerned because they had lost contact with James. To their credit they didn't panic, they just made a beeline back to the Albany house. They didn't even take time to grab the suburban.

When they got to the house, it was dark and empty. There was little evidence that anyone had been there at all.

Ramón had been sent in to check out the house. They feared the worst again. The almost instant ambush back at the motel had also taught them caution. They formulated as much of a plan as they could. Considering that lack of information they did as best they could.

Ty was on top of the RV wishing he had night-vision goggles. Hector stayed inside with Marguerite ready to relay any psychic early warnings she might get.

Pandora also remained behind in the RV. She was trying to blank out her thoughts, reasoning that it might make her less noticeable to whoever was looking for her. Not being trained in meditation, She had chosen to blank her thoughts by watching *Full House* reruns on satellite TV.

As Ramón made his way through the house, he was hindered by the lack of power inside. He carried with him one of the billy-club sized Mag Lights. It was bright enough but it could only light up in one direction at a time. Ty's chances of catching sight of anyone through the windows before Ramón walked in on them were slim at best.

In the end, all these precautions were unnecessary. Ramón found the fuse-box and restored power to the house. It was just a case of flipping the main power switch back on. Cominad had also left a note there.

It read, in part, "I'm glad that at least one of you was smart enough to find this note."

The rest of the note was an exercise in brevity, "Sasha awake. Vacating premises. Shut down power when you leave"

Turning off the power was apparently part of their operating procedure for this safe house.

An hour and a half after they had returned from the Woods without us, the team was comfortably back in the house.

There were two sets of exceptions, James and myself obviously, also Pandora and Ramón. Pandora had refused to leave the RV. Ramón chose to sit with her.

They were discussing if they should try to retrieve the suburban. Ty was laying out an unnecessarily elaborate plan to regain the suburban when the coven arrived.

They arrived in two Vehicles, a Jeep liberty and a Toyota Avalon. They pulled into the semicircular drive way between the house and the RV.

From inside the RV, Ramón saw them enter. He said it looked like a scene from a movie, one where government agents show up to take charge. That is, if all the government agents looked like an extended family from the suburbs.

There were only about nine people in the Coven, six women, three men. They ranged in ages from 15-50.

They were dressed as you might expect a suburban family to dress if it were going out bowling or to the mall. Most were in jeans and t-shirts. A few were in what might pass for business casual. None them were obviously armed or armored, unlike our friend, Officer Merton

I'm sure in the movie someone would dress the coven in robes or some other "mystic" looking crap.

Admittedly, one of the men had an ornately carved wooden staff. However, he was leaning on it more like a cane than a weapon.

They were a fairly knowledgeable and powerful little group, relatively speaking. They weren't as strong as the Wiccan counterpart to the Magi Concordance but they knew a thing or two that could be trouble.

Unfortunately, they were the good guys. That's not to say we weren't the good guys. It's just that they weren't the bad guys either. They just had limited information, perhaps as limited as our own.

A woman about forty with short strawberry-blond hair moved to the front of the group. She was of medium height. Her clothes were loose fitting and flowing. Their wild colors almost glowed, even in the gloom of the night. She broke that mold of looking simply suburban. She seemed to be their leader, at least that's what their body language indicated, according to Hector.

She had a grim look on her face. The other eight people stood behind her and joined hands, forming a semi-circle behind her. The older man with the staff was at one far end to her left. At the far right stood the youngest, the girl who looked fifteen. She pulled out a twisted metal rod from her purse. From its description, it sounded like a copper wand with a crystal. The line started chanting something. (I wasn't there so I can't really give much more detail than that. I may not have been able to anyway)

The line behind the leader closed into a circle. As they did so, they deftly passed both staff and wand to the leader.

She took one in each hand and while the chanting behind her grew, she addressed the people in the house.

"I am a daughter of the Waxing Moon, a wise woman of the old ways made new. I am a sorceress, a seer, a medium, a *witch*."

She gave that last word a greater emphasis.

"I, and those behind me, have come to free your hostage. Send her out. Send her out so we may resolve this peacefully."

A long moment passed. Nothing happened aside from the chanting.

The wind rose sharply and the Daughter of the Waxing Moon had to speak up to be heard.

"Hunters? Are you listening? Let the girl go free and we will leave you in peace."

The wind picked up some more. It was beginning to actually roar.

It got so loud that the witch leader now had to shout over it.

"This is your last warning." light gleamed from the tips of the wand and staff. "Release her now!"

No one in the house knew exactly what to do. Since Pandora wasn't a prisoner, they couldn't release her.

They also didn't really expect that they would get time to explain. All the time the chanting was going on, Marguerite and the guys were trying to come up with a plan to defuse the situation. Pandora was all for just marching out and explaining things.

In the end, Pandora got her way by bursting out of the RV and walking right up to the leader. Which took the coven a bit by surprise since the RV was behind them.

Had I been there perhaps I could have helped in some way. But I wasn't and we'll all have to live with that. Pandora walked up to the leader, as I said. She had to shout to be heard over the wind.

"Look Miss Witchy, I'm not their prisoner. I'm their employer."

This is when Pandora jumped to her own dangerous conclusion. "Now give me back my brother."

The part that caused the trouble was that Pandora punctuated her demand by pulling out a .22 pistol. It was a tiny, little thing, delicate even. She cocked the hammer and pressed the small muzzle against the forehead of the D.o.t.W.M.

Things got ugly.

The chanting circle broke open, forming back into a line. their hands were still joined. But now their attention (and their will) was focused on Pandora. D.o.t.W.M. was at a loss for a response.

She had come expecting to deal with witch hunters and rescuing a captive, young woman. Instead that young woman was holding a gun to her forehead. She reacted instinctively and to her credit relatively without violence. She brought the staff and wand to bear down on Pandora and called up a restraining effect. I could tell that much from the astral traces

Unfortunately Pandora didn't know enough about magic.

Pandora reacted instinctively. She fired the gun.

Picture it from Pandora's point of view. She was standing there outnumbered. The person she relied upon as her magic expert was missing, maybe dead. Her "enemies" had just whistled up a windstorm. Now their leader was pointing a wand and a staff at her, both of which were glowing in a most alarming way.

All she knew was, that in the middle of this sudden windstorm, someone was throwing a spell at her. The last big spell she had seen was the one that laid Sasha out.

Sadly both women were successful. Pandora was indeed immobilized inside a crimson shell of force. Not, however, before she was able to put a bullet into The Daughter of The Waxing Moon's temporal lobe. Daughter of The Waxing Moon must have tried to duck during the whole process for Pandora to have missed the frontal lobe.

It was at this moment that James and I returned to our own plane of existence. Ramón was then able to use the heightened abilities of hosting all the Guys. He rushed out of the RV, grabbed up Pandora, Crackling energy shell and all, and carried her into he RV.

Some of the line of chanters had moved to render assistance to their leader. Another few ran toward the house. The rest made the mistake of trying to stop Ramón from protecting Pandora. I was glad not to be there to see his response.

If you picture the brutal, nearly fatal assault that Guys received the first time I met them then you can just change the names and the faces. This time the Guys via Ramón were dishing out the mayhem,

By the time Ramón reached the RV with Pandora, there was one broken jaw, two shattered patellae, and a compound fractured arm among the witches.

Needless to say we weren't winning any friends, merely influencing people. It made a bad situation a hell of lot worse.

Ramón had that RV rolling faster than I ever could have imagined. He and Pandora were flying down that hill headed Lord knows where.

Azgard, Hector's body and I were finally making it back to a semblance of reality I felt comfortable driving in. Coincidentally or providentially our return was about 5 miles off from where we had left. We came popping up out of a body of water. Somewhere called Freeway Lakes.

As I piloted Azgard up onto the dry land, James "awoke." He filled me in on what I had just missed. Our new position put us just minutes away from the whole fiasco. I drove there as fast as Azgard could go.

Considering it had just been underwater, it was quite impressive to even be moving.

Chapter Seventeen

$\mathbf{D}$RIVING BACK TO THE house seemed eternal while it was happening. I only hoped that I could do some good.

As we zipped through town we were stopped by a crossing freight train. I swore. I didn't know the town well enough to detour around it. Every minute might mean that someone died.

I was so frustrated. I could astrally project there in an instant. But to really work healing I needed to be there in the flesh. I really envied Koenig's little blue swirly teleport gates.

If I did project, the only good that I could do was get a message to Marguerite. That's assuming that none of Coven could interfere with my astral form. If they could then I might be able to talk to one of them directly. But then what would I say? What could I say? "Sorry we shot your leader?" Wouldn't help much, would it?

Still, maybe talking to Marguerite might accomplish something. I turned to James and told him to catch the wheel. I slid out of my body and through the open driver's side window. I flew right over to Marguerite. Once again, I made sure to get "dressed."

I appeared before her. "Fill me in," I asked her. I was hoping that she could tell me more than I had learned from James.

She just sighed. "Didn't you see what's going on out there as you came in?"

"Um, no I kind of rushed over. I didn't see anything on the way."

"Milo, you've got to get your head back in this game. Things are really going badly. We're trapped in this house. Ramón and Pandora ran off without a plan. And there's a well-meaning but misguided woman out there with a bullet in her head."

I peeked out side the window. The leader of the coven was indeed down. It looked like Pandora's bullet entered the side of her head instead of directly into her forehead.

Oddly enough, that cheered me up. Healing can be tricky (look what happened to the guys) Brain injuries are even tougher repair. However, Temporal lobes are easier than frontal lobes. How much easier? If she got healing in the next few minutes, she had a shot at full recovery. If the bullet had gone in her frontal lobe, I might be able to prevent death but there would have been lasting damage.

This was all moot. Without a body, I wasn't healing anyone. I looked at Marguerite. It was nice to have a medium that could see me in my astral form. Even if all I could do was communicate with her. If only all I had to do was speak through her. I was little more than a ghost. I felt as impotent as one. More so, considering what my apartment ghost was capable of. Then it hit me. As limiting as being disembodied can be, there were those who could help. People like Marguerite. She could help me just like Whoopi did for Swayze at the end of Ghost.

"Marguerite, I have an idea," I said, "But I'm going to need to, ah, that is . . ." I stopped I didn't know how to phrase the next part with out it sounding like a cheap come on.

"You need to use my body, don't you?"

It was the truth. As a medium, she could allow me to enter her (mind on my work, mind on my work) without violating her own personal sanctity. I could have asked anybody I suppose but only Marguerite had the experience needed to make an informed choice.

At that moment, I didn't have any distracting hormones to make what I was about to do sound dirty. It is only now, in retrospect, that telling you, "I slid effortlessly into Marguerite," makes me feel like a cad.

Having done so, I wondered how I never noticed how much pain Marguerite had. She was only forty-five but she had a serious case of arthritis. I had never heard her complain. I made a point of asking her how she withstood it. I couldn't ask her right then because, unlike the Guys whose minds are linked, our minds remained distinct. To communicate we would have to trade control of the vocal chords and listen to each other.

I walked past Ty and Hector. They had been wondering what was going when Marguerite started talking to herself. James had told them what I had just done and they had worked it out for themselves. The further proof of this was when Ty gave me encouragement by saying, "Go get 'em boss man." as we walked out the front door.

Just outside the door. There was a crimson, physical barrier like the one that had been placed on Pandora. Obviously it couldn't stop my astral form or I would have crashed against it on my way in. It stopped me now that I wore flesh.

I addressed the chanting coven, "Look, we are not witch hunters. I'm a healer. I can help your leader." I didn't expect them to trust me but I had to try.

"Look, She's already been shot in the head so what would be the point in hurting her further? You don't have to trust me further than that. You can put your barrier spell around me and your person while I work."

"You're lying. The crimson enclosure would block you from drawing in enough energy." This was coming from the older guy who had originally been holding the staff.

"We have a very limited window. Please let me help before this whole misunderstanding gets any worse."

Fortunately their concern for their fallen leader was greater than their fear. I moved over to Daughter of the Waxing Moon. The crimson enclosure reshaped around me/Marguerite.

I got straight to work pulling in the healing energies from the universe around us

If you're wondering why the witches didn't just use their own healing abilities, it's because the injury was beyond their ability to heal. At the risk of sounding like I'm bragging, this coven just wasn't in the same league that I was (and remember I'm not even in the same league as Cominad. How I wished she were there) I know this because had they been stronger in their tradition, they would have recognized the difference between Magi and Witch-Hunters. This coven had probably seen (or been shown) some of the Christian trappings I or Cominad's team carried. Artie, for instance, always carried a rosary.

While the witch hunters claim to work for the same boss, and I suppose it's unfair for me to judge them, I have my doubts. I mean when do they heal the sick, care for the poor. Feed the hungry etc, etc etc.

That aside, to the untrained eye, we can look an awful lot alike. The coven's confusion is quite understandable.

Another indication of their inexperience was that they would have known that their shielding bubble only blocks physical access to the necessary energies. Which means a purely flesh bound person would be cut off from them. However Marguerite and I together made an exception.

Healing is best done physical body to physical body which is why I couldn't just swoop down and do it astrally as a sign of good will.

Now, because they didn't trust us, they wanted to keep us separated by this physical barrier that would protect them from attack.

The irony suddenly struck me; it was only because I was here in my astral form skin riding Marguerite that the healing could even be attempted.

"Mysterious ways, " they say.

"One right tricky bastard," says me.

I positioned Marguerite and myself so that she made contact with Daughter of the Waxing Moon. While I straddled the barrier, I kept just enough of my soul-self inside Marguerite to maintain the connection. Drawing in the needed energy, I channeled it through my astral form into Marguerite. She then passed it on to Pandora's unfortunate victim. Marguerite had her hand over the wound, hiding it from normal view.

From my perspective, I could see the wound closing. The tissues of the brain and skull grew back, expelling the bullet until it popped up into Marguerite's hand. If this is ever a movie, they'll probably jazz this all up with special effects and CGI. In real life, all you would have seen was one middle aged woman touching the forehead of another.

The Daughter of the Waxing Moon jumped up and knocked out Marguerite with some kind of sleeper hold as soon as she awoke. This just shows how deep human mistrust can go.

I was tempted to manifest to confront her. I was uncertain what the chanting crew might do if something else unexpected occurred. The Daughter of the Waxing Moon lay the unconscious Marguerite down on the ground. That kind of knock-out doesn't last long at all and she was already coming around.

The coven leader looked cautiously around and poked hesitantly at the crimson shield. When she did the field flared for an instant then dropped. Most of the rest of her coven swarmed over her, making sure she was okay. There were a few that had been seriously hurt by Ramón's rampage to get Pandora out of there, if you'll recall.

During this time, one or two members ran over to Marguerite and began tending to her. As soon as she was conscious enough to show she wasn't permanently damaged, the coven tried to get her to heal their other injured members.

By this time, James in Azgard finally arrived. It seemed like a good time to rejoin my body. I was getting the hang the high sped blur technique so I tried it to get back inside myself. I'm sure it would have worked too, if James hadn't rolled up the driver's side window again.

Chapter Eighteen

WHEN JAMES OPENED THE door a split second later, I could do what I had intended, just not all cool and graceful.

As soon as I made my entrance the coven tensed back up. I walked directly over to the injured members.With Marguerite's reassurance, I was allowed to begin healing.

The Daughter of the Waxing Moon came over to me as I worked. She was carrying a small bag that she had recovered from the Toyota Avalon.

"Are you Gives?"

"Yes"

"Why are you helping?"

"Well, first, because these people have been hurt. Secondly, it was my team who hurt them. That was wrong and it shouldn't have happened"

"Yes, but hurting witches is what hunters do, isn't it?"

I don't know if it was residual confusion from being shot in the head or just the assault on her expectations but The Daughter of the Waxing Moon seemed to be having trouble grasping that we were not hunters. So I told her again.

"We aren't witch hunters."

"But you're Christian aren't you?"

"I am," I said, "Marguerite might be. You'll have to ask the guys, though I'm fairly certain at least Ramón is Roman Catholic."

James was right next to us and piped up, "My dad wants me to Presbyterian and my mom wants me to be Buddhist."

"So what does that make you?" asked the Daughter of the Waxing Moon.

"Taoist." James said.

Ty called out the front door at this point. "The only Taoism he knows comes from *The Tao of Pooh*."

"There you go," I said, "by the way, what's your name? You seem to know mine."

She blinked for a second, perhaps hesitant to give me her name. Now you'll have noticed that I asked for her name not her Name, but that distinction can be hard hear.

"Call me Krista," she said after another second or two. When she did, she relaxed. Perhaps it was the relief of deciding whether to trust us or not.

"But if you're not hunters why do you have the girl?"

"We're trying to help her rescue her brother."

Nothing works quite like the truth. Even if not believed at first, it has the advantage of staying power.

"So when she said that you worked for her, she really wasn't covering for you in some Stockholm Syndrome sort of way?"

"Nope, she asked for the help and her parents pay the bills."

By this time every one was healed up and I was bone tired. The guys had managed to reestablish meaningful contact with Ramón. He was finally bringing Pandora and the RV back. The shell around Pandora had dropped. She was now overwhelmed with guilt. I wanted to talk to her but it would have to wait until she got back with Ramón. We still needed to clear up our standing with the coven

"Now, I'd like to ask why you thought we were hunters?"

Krista looked at me as if she was about to say something that I might think was crazy. I suspected that meant she was going to tell the truth as well.

"There's a Lady of the Sidhe that lives nearby. She and her woman-at-arms came to us. They warned us that you had a young witch prisoner. We were also told that you were either going to force her conversion or execute her tonight."

She pulled a scroll from out of the bag she was carrying. On it were a number of highly realistic looking sketches and a map. The sketches were of our group, individually and together, some with names below. Only my name was accurate. The others were listed by fictitious names and real titles and ranks among one of the witch hunting societies.

It was one that still operated. It was started during the inquisition and later disavowed by the Vatican. I guess they just never got the memo.

"That would be Cascadia and the Wintry Warrior, right?"

"Yes, you know them?"

"We've just met. Those two and their compatriot Numis."

"Who's Numis?" she asked

"Numis, he was with Cascadia and the Woman in the Ice armor."

"I know them . . . but Numis?"

"He looked elven, like Cascadia, but dressed in armor that looked like it was made from coins."

"Coins?" Krista asked

"New coins, old coins, even some ancient coins all put together, looked a bit like scale mail actually."

Krista just shook her head. "Our coven is very Fay focused. I can tell you of every major fairy from Newport to Bend. I don't know anyone or anything like that."

She didn't have to tell me that the fair folk are slow to change. If she was right, then that means either a newcomer has moved in (unlikely) or we were dealing with a different type of creature.

For those of you unfamiliar with the lovely state of Oregon, Newport to Bend is a significantly sized area that includes the coast, two mountain ranges, thousands and thousand of acres of forest and the great obsidian lava fields and their associated volcanoes.

As worried as I was, I took the time to tell The Daughter of the Waxing Moon that I was impressed.

"That's quite some accomplishment. How did you discover so much."

The Daughter of the Waxing Moon shrugged. Hard work, diligent observation of the proper manners and inheriting a body of knowledge from nine generations of my mothers."

"Nine generations?"

"Yeah, I am the Heir of a long Celtic tradition and a long Native American one. The irony is that because of the way the intermarriages worked, I don't qualify as belonging to any tribe."

"Wow, nine generations," I said, "I'm surprised that you didn't have more powerful healing."

"I blame my own mother. She was big on the history, light on the technique. I have had to rebuild a lot of the practical magic myself. At least mom gave me the best Fay contacts to help me get that done.

"I think you may have just become our new go to guy, um, gal, um person. Whatever. If you're willing, we really need to talk."

A few minutes later we had reconvened inside the house. Pandora and Ramón were just about to return.

We sat around the same conference table we had used when we first got there. Our intention was to compare notes. We hoped to find out what was really going on.

Needless to say, not all of the Krista's coven could fit around it. Most of them sat in the living room. James and Hector played hosts offering the Coven members drinks and snacks. The coven was accepting hesitantly, still having trouble trusting that we were not here to hurt them. This was a harder sell considering the injuries that Pandora and the Guys dealt out.

Marguerite, Ty and I sat around the one side of the large table while three of the coven sat across from us. These three were Krista, Albert, who was the older man with the staff and Jessica, the young girl who wielded the wand.

We sat there making relatively small talk waiting for Pandora to arrive.

Jessica said something about us making up two trinities. "Except that we have your "father" for "Father, Son and Holy ghost." And "You have our . . ."

Krista cut her off before she could finish, "That's enough. Let's focus on our situation."

Marguerite couldn't keep herself from laughing, "It's alright, Krista, being called the Crone of Maiden, Matron, Crone doesn't bother me. I recall that at fifteen, forty-five seemed decrepit to me too."

Jessica immediately blushed a deep scarlet. Any further talk along this line was interrupted by Pandora's arrival. Pandora was accompanied by Ramón. He was doing his best to look like a fearsome bodyguard. Considering how he mowed through some of these folks, it wasn't a big stretch.

In fact, some of those who had experienced that wrath first hand looked away as his gaze swept the room. The physical wounds might have been healed but it's going to take a while to for everything to be forgiven.

Pandora sat down at the table. She looked coldly at Krista and pulled out a picture of her brother. She showed it to Krista then had her pass it around her coven. None of them recognized him.

"Sorry," Krista said, "but we don't know him. I wish there were a way for us to help you. Perhaps if we knew your story it could helps us sort things out."

Pandora looked at me. Her glance told me that she would rather have me relate the story than do it herself.

So I told them our story starting from when Staci and Stephan ran away. I kept the detail to a minimum trying to get through it all fairly quickly. As I talked, Pandora passed around the pictures we had of Arnold,

Koenig and her Jekyll, Mariana Tamblor. They weren't great pictures, just what we had downloaded form the Oregon DMV.

One of the coven, a woman about thirty, exclaimed aloud when she saw the Driver's license picture of Koenig. It was just the photo. We had clipped all the other driver's information away.

"Oh my God! That's Wendi! Krista you remember Wendi. She's Arnold Scott's ex-wife." I think my team was surprised to hear the phrase ex-wife. We all leaned in a little closer.

"You remember. She would come into the bookshop with Arnold sometimes. They'd always being sniping at each other. The last time I saw them in the store together, they actually got into a fight. I was about to ask them to leave when she stormed out."

Krista also seemed surprised. She studied the picture for a moment. She wore an expression of frustrated uncertainty. "So you actually think that this woman could be your wannabe crime lord?"

"Yes, we do. In fact, we know that she is. There is a lot more to here than meets the eye. What surprised me is that you refer to her as Arnold's ex."

The thirtyish woman introduced her self as Maxine Stuart. She had more to say about the happy couple. "Yeah, about four years ago he starts coming into the book store with a different woman and they're all lovey-dovey. He said that Wendi was gone and that this new woman was his wife . . . Yeah, that's her picture there," She indicated the picture we had of Koenig's Jekyll.

Maxine continued, "Anyway, this new woman starts coming in with Arnold. He's always looking for alchemical and hermetic writings. His new wife can't help but buy anything that has to do with Fairies."

"So, I take it this was an occult bookstore."

"Well, I carry more than that but I like to keep my new age section stocked with works of actual value. After all, I should know, shouldn't I?"

Maxine touched my arm lightly as she said this and gave a low chuckle. I found myself chuckling along and looking deeply into her eyes. She was a tall, thin woman. She had short, very straight, fine back hair and dark eyes. I found myself beginning to stare at her face. There was something intriguing about it. She was attractive, yet not so pretty as to become bland.

You may be wondering "can't this guy keep focused on his work? Is this really the best time to be noticing some woman? Does this have anything to do with the story of Pandora and Stephan?"

The short answers to those questions are "No," "of course not", and "Very much yes" We just wouldn't know that last answer for a while yet.

There were wheels within wheels churning up the ground before us. I just hadn't recognized all of them yet. My opponents knew things about me that I didn't know myself. Some of it had to do with my personal history right after my Epiphany.

I've mentioned that I had just begun to awaken to my abilities when my wife died. I was trying to figure out things on my own before my mentor found me. During that time my wife was murdered, rose from the dead and tried to kill me.

I was completely overwhelmed. I couldn't think rationally. I made a desperate instinctive leap to somewhere. A somewhere I couldn't get back from. In trying to get away from my ravening wife, I took myself right out of this world. I ended up in one of the Fay realms without any clue how to get back. I spent a considerable amount of time lost there.

I couldn't tell you how much time had past while I was there but it felt like years. I checked the dates on my return, about six months had passed.

My memories of that time are fuzzy. What I do remember is that physical beauty is cheap in Fairee. I'd say it's not even skin deep. What with all the spells and glamours that the Fay can effect, every one was excruciatingly beautiful.

Except, of course, for me. All that imitation beauty left me with a craving for the real, the genuine, the human. My studies, my work and, sadly, my general disposition have kept me from really finding the answer to that craving.

So that is why, though some may say that Maxine's nose was a bit too sharp or a wee bit pronounced, I found myself looking deeply into her eyes. I gazed into them in a manner that was unquestionably out of place for the gravity of the situation.

This wasn't an accident. Why someone would orchestrate our "chance" meeting was hidden to me at the time. I say hidden. But it wasn't really. It would have been obvious to me if I had been paying attention. I was just too caught up to look.

Chapter Nineteen

BACK TO THE ISSUE at hand, I didn't want to just blurt out that the ex-wife and the new woman were really the same person. Explaining that could sidetrack the whole conversation. I wanted to find out more about their common denominator.

"So what kind of guy was this Arnold?" I asked.

Maxine answered with a shrug, "He always seemed like a pretty good guy. Kind of quiet. Kept to the background. He had an interest in Alchemy.

I remember one argument that he and his first wife had. This is shortly before we saw him start coming in with Mary Anne, wait that's not right, Marietta something like that."

"Marianna," Pandora supplied.

"Yeah, I guess so." Maxine barely turned to face Pandora when she spoke to her. Instead, she tilted her head and gave a quick flick of her eyes. Then her intense gaze returned to me.

As she spoke, the look behind her eyes began to shift, "Anyway, so Arnold and Wendi argued over how he would apply his alchemy. He kept telling her that the purpose of Alchemy wasn't the changing of lead into gold but the transformation of the spirit from impurity to purity.

"Gold would more useful," Wendi said at the time. It was shortly after that Marianna started coming into the store with Arnold. I remember because she literally bought a copy of every book on fairies I had.

"But you know Marianna already, don't you?" Maxine asked us. "At least, you have her picture," she pointed to the drawing we had. At this point Krista took charge of the discussion again.

"It looks like you're investigating Arnold and his ex-wife and his current wife. Do you really think that any one of them could be holding this young woman's brother against his will?"

"Not any longer," I said.

"Well that's good I suppose." Krista said. "You can start looking for his actual kidnappers."

"Oh, I've found them. Or at least I now know who they are."

There was a sudden rise in tension. That was not unexpected. After all, I was being very dramatic,even Melodramatic, one might say.

"Arnold and Wendi Scott are responsible for the kidnapping and/or exploitation of Stephan, Pandora and quite a host of other people."

"But you just said . . ." began Krista.

I cut her off. I know. I was rude, sorry.

"Arnold is responsible for helping create the situation where Wendi under the name of Gretchen Koenig made a slave of Stephan. Currently, I think Stephan is living quite happily with Arnold Scott and the woman calling herself Marianna Tamblor."

This time, there was some confused silence. I pushed on.

"Of course, I won't be able to prove anything until I can actually find Arnold."

Marguerite spoke up. "Arnold is the key? I thought that Koenig's Jekyll was the key."

That statement required more of an explanation for the Coven. I had summed up the story so far in a very simplistic manner. All I had told them was that a woman named Koenig had enslaved Stephan and Pandora, among others. That she had a supernatural minion. (I omitted that this minion was my late wife.) That Koenig was traveling across the country using some sort of Magic. Magic which I suspected was alchemical in nature.

To be honest, I didn't know that much about alchemy. I was just basing my theories on the "lab" the Guys had found.

I had told just them how we had tracked down a connection to this area when the pictures had gotten to Maxine and she recognized our three good friends. Okay, they're just two . . .well maybe one and two halves. What I had left out was the whole Jekyll and Hyde routine.

Now, I had to explain the really funky stuff.

"Wendi Scott and Gretchen Koenig are the same person."

I had hoped for a startled gasp. I didn't get it. The coven members were surprised but all I got was a puzzled silence. Wendi Scott using an alias wasn't all that hard to swallow. At least it wasn't compared to telling them that Wendi Scott and Marianna Tamblor are the same person. That was much more of a chore.

It's odd what people will believe. For instance, this coven knew about the Fay realms and interacted with them. They accepted rather readily the healing of grievous wounds just by a laying on of hands.

The news of a real-life Jekyll and Hyde was met with a combination of disbelief, uncertainty and/or derision. There was disbelief on the faces of each of the coven members, except Maxine for some reason. She seemed to be preoccupied by something. After a moment, she spoke.

"I mentioned the disagreement that Arnold and Wendi had that last time in the store. Well, that wasn't the last time I saw them before they split. About a month before they split up, some guy comes into the store trying to sell some rare books. He was hoping either I'd buy them or connect him with someone who might. What he showed me were some pretty good finds. I decided to buy them and put them in my E-bay store.

"Except one book that is. It was an old handwritten manuscript. It looked positively medieval. The other books were good but not in the same league. As I flipped through it, it looked like a handwritten work on alchemy. At least, that's what the drawings looked like. The text was in two languages, Latin, which I never really studied, and what I'm sure was Arabic.

"I asked the man to confirm that this was an alchemy book. He said that's what he was told by the seller. He even spun a story about how there was a formula in this book, that had inspired Robert Louis Stevenson.

"I only thought of it because we were talking about Jekyll and Hyde."

I jumped in, "let me guess, you arranged for Mr. Scott to buy the book." She confirmed this with a quick nod. "Is there anything that you can tell me about this guy who sold the books?" I asked.

Maxine took a deep breath and looked apologetic. "I've been going over it in my mind and I can't recall much about him. When I try to focus on my memories of him, they get misty and vague. I couldn't tell you his height, weight or hair color. I can't recall any of the things I've trained myself to notice.

She made a little aside to me. She spoke in a low tone almost as if she were sharing a secret with me. "My store was robbed once. Ever since then I've tried to train myself to notice things. To really see things, like a real detective should. As she spoke I just nodded, my own gaze never leaving hers. There was a moment of silence then Marguerite cleared her throat reminding us that there were other people in this conversation.

"Anyway, the only things I can remember are his stupid tie-tack and cuff links. I mean, who wears cuff links any more? Oh, and he carried a pocket-watch. Besides being dressed for the wrong century, theses things had one other thing in common. They all matched. Sort of."

I nodded my encouragement for her to go on. I had one of those the prickling sensations that something important was about to said. Or maybe it was just my growing interest in her.

"Well, they were all coins, but not the same kind of coin. The pocket watch had a Liberty Dollar from the forties worked into it. His cuff links were Pesos, I think, and the tie tack was definitely a Loonie."

"Loonie?" I repeated.

"A Canadian Dollar Coin." Ty answered

I smiled; in fact I think I laughed. "Maxine, I could kiss you!" It was a statement that, as soon as I said it, caused some blushing. "You managed to remember the most important thing."

I turned to my crew, "Okay gang, let's get ready to roll. The sooner we find this Arnold Scott. The sooner we can get our answers. And I think now, due to Krista's group, in particular Maxine, we have a big piece of the puzzle."

"You do?" asked Krista.

"Yes, and we have Cascadia to thank for sending you to us. I wonder if she knew."

"I can ask her," Krista said.

"Really?" was my most urbane response. I don't know why that surprised me. I guess I just tend to imagine Human/Fairy relationships going one direction in favor of the Fay.

"That's great. If you're willing, find out exactly what she knows about Numis. It would really help. I think he and the guy that passed an alchemy book onto Arnold are the same . . . Entity. The one that I met in the company of Cascadia."

It suddenly occurred to me that those questions might have a price. "That is, if it won't be cost you too much."

Krista smiled sharply. "Remember, she sent us out to rescue a woman who needed no rescuing. Plus, she said you'd be a 'handful of witch hunters that would be easily handled.' I've felt the kind of power you wield personally. I can also see the unique nature of your teammates. Things could have gone badly. They actually did go badly, very badly. I have some important questions of my own for Cascadia."

We parted company with a plan to make future contact. Krista and Marguerite made those contact arrangements. It seemed as though we had gained some allies.

We had moved from people getting shot to cooperating rather quickly. Getting shot is the kind of thing that usually takes a lot of time to get over. To be honest, the miraculous healing helped. No, seriously, you've already seen what kind of bonds a healing can create when not properly done. Even when done right, they tend to make the recipient fairly well disposed toward the healer.

They had just seen what we could both harm and heal. Perhaps Krista just wanted to stay on our good side.

That troubles me a little. It makes me feel like a bully. I hate bullies. Of course, what's that they say about hating most what we don't like in ourselves?

Chapter Twenty

I WANTED TO TALK TO Arnold away from his wife in either of her forms. I wanted to find him and find him alone. The first part proved easy enough. The second part, well that was more difficult

Sadly, we saw no sign of Stephan. We found the "Scotts" right where the driver's info said we could. It was a nice, little neighborhood in Eugene, Oregon. Out of respect for their neighbors, I won't give a more specific address. They lived in a pleasant looking house built a little less than a decade before.

It was nice enough to look at. It also looked like every other house on the street. The houses weren't exactly the same but they were all variations on a theme. They fit together a little too well for my taste.

On the way down to Eugene, we recovered the suburban and I'm glad we did. Surveillance with an RV is difficult. The RV's cloaking effect might have worked well enough on the neighbors, but I didn't want to underestimate our opponents' abilities. Underestimating them has been a serious flaw in my thinking so far. It was time I learned from that mistake.

Case in point, when we found the house, I went out-of-body to give it a good looking over. The good news was that it was immediately clear we had the right place. The bad news was that the house was warded twelve ways from next Sunday.

If I had tried entering the house with my new speedy blur technique, I could have done some real damage to myself by hitting wards that strong. Who ever had inscribed the wards knew more about warding than I did. I tried to call Cominad for some help. I never got past her voice mail.

So we did surveillance the old fashioned way. That is to say without high tech or high magic. OK, maybe a little bit of tech and a wee bit of mojo.

The suburban was quite easy to cloak. It fit into the neighborhood naturally. It was just another SUV. If it was bit older than most, that only helped to make it that much more forgettable.

So from our semi-cloaked, aging vehicle, we settled down to the tedious job of staking out. We took turns watching the house.

As for gear, we didn't have much. The highest tech we had was a digital camera with a telephoto lens to make any voyeur proud.

What did we see? Not what I expected. This wasn't just any mundane stake out. This was a magical investigation. It should be rife with Mystery (notice the capital "M"), cosmic forces and perhaps even destiny at play just below the surface. So what did we see?

Nothing, we saw nothing. Nothing worth seeing anyway.

It just wasn't what I expected. I'm not sure I could explain what I expected to see. Perhaps we'd see some serious spellwork, perhaps secretive, or furtive comings and goings at the house. There was none of that, absolutely nothing. Aside from the stout wards on the building, there was nothing going on.

Well, nothing that was inconsistent with a man trying to nurse his injured wife back to health. Seeing Tamblor at the house threw us at first. We had expected her to still be in the hospital. A quick phone call later confirmed that Arnold had Marianna discharged from the hospital.

I had imagined we would catch a glimpse of Koenig now and then. She never showed. We could see Marianna passing by the windows of the house. Most of the time, she was upstairs. She would look out from the bedroom window from time to time.

Usually, she only got out of bed for quick trips to the bathroom. At least we assumed it was the bathroom. It was small room just off the master bedroom. It had one small window. That window always had the shade pulled down. All we could see was a light coming on behind that shade when someone stepped in there. She generally didn't stay longer than a few minutes. Except in the morning when she'd go in for about half an hour. Arnold's trips to this room also followed this pattern. If it wasn't a bathroom, it was a long way to go for a ruse.

Arnold would also make appearances in the kitchen and the living room windows.

All in all, it was very a frustrating stake out.

The first day, all we saw was Arnold taking care of Wendi in her Marianna form. He went downstairs and made breakfast. He took some up to his wife. While she ate, he worked at his computer.

With the telephoto lens, we could see that he was doing simple things. He pulled up a spreadsheet managing the household budget. Later, he began writing something he had titled *Modern Alchemy*. Ramón, who was watching at the timed, called me over to take a look.

The angle was pretty good for seeing inside. As to what he was writing, well, there were no secrets of the universe there. It was just a theoretical discussion of how one might engage the modern periodic table of elements in an alchemical way.

At lunch, we had a repeat of the same, downstairs to prepare food, back up to eat with Marianna, and work on the computer. It was ditto at dinnertime and then eventually lights out.

The next day went exactly the same. There were a few minor variances like no toast for breakfast this time.

Arnold spent half an hour longer playing minesweeper. I began to suspect that there was a "program" being run. Either that or they were in one serious rut. I looked at the different pictures stored in the digital camera's memory. Other than the time stamps there was serious quality of sameness. There were only minor variations in Arnold's movements at the computer or in the kitchen.

But it was Marianna that really gave it away. Granted there are only so many ways one can get up from a sick bed and go into the bathroom, but the sheer precision should have tipped us off by itself.

I was certain they were running a preset illusion of some kind. "But what kind?" I asked myself. With the wards up, I couldn't tell. If we were actually seeing inside, then the people we saw could be simulacra.[18]

If so, then the house was most likely empty, other than the simulacra. We would need to look for Arnold and Wendi, in either form, somewhere else.

It could be that the windows were enchanted to show certain scenes like a projection on a screen. If that was true, then they could be in there while

---

[18]   That's the plural of simulacrum, an artificial being made to resemble a specific person usually. For more about them see CC#369 *Golems, Homunculi and More; a guide to making new friends.*

their real actions were hidden from us. They could also be somewhere else entirely. Still, this was our best lead, so we were stuck with it.

We spent the next day trying to scheme ways of entering the house. The wards were quite advanced, stout and vicious. Not the kind of thing one learns from a correspondence course.[19]

Astral entry was out of the question. At least, it was for me. Perhaps Cominad could have managed it but she wasn't there and I was. I didn't know at the time why I hadn't heard back from her. She had a great reason but that doesn't come into the story just yet.

Breaking in physically didn't seem like a great option either. We have had enough trouble with the police so far. That and some of the wards looked like they could pack a wallop to a physical breach as well as an astral one.

I discussed options with the team. I laid out our basic problem for them. That we weren't getting in without someone inside letting us in.

Pandora suggested a way that I hadn't given much thought "We could knock," she said.

---

[19]   Although *Basic Wards and Barriers* CC #252 is still available

Chapter Twenty-One

I WAS TRYING NOT TO shoot Pandora's idea down too fast but ...

"I don't want to tip our hand if we haven't already. Marianna might not recognize any of us but I'm sure Arnold or Gretchen would. We don't know whom, or in what form, they might answer the door.

Pandora was undeterred. "Well, if we can't knock, let's gets someone else to do it"

"Who?" I asked.

Pandora smiled. She gave me a look that was both innocent and a tad bit condescending.

"The U.S. Postal Service might do it, if we ask nicely enough."

"Brilliant," I said.

Her plan was simple enough. We would send the Scotts a certified letter requiring a signature. Even if that didn't get them to open the door, we may learn something by observing through the windows. After a quick round of hammering out the few details, we agreed to go ahead with this plan. Two of the guys were dispatched to send the letter. It was still early enough in the day that it would arrive the next morning. We kept watch on the house. The pattern kept repeating. I was more and more convinced that no one was home. In the mean time, I called the contact number that Krista had left us and got Maxine's bookstore. Krista wasn't available at the moment and Maxine didn't have any big news.

"Krista contacted Cascadia. They're in talks. Seems like there's relationship re-evaluation going on." She spoke with a certain subtle, frustrated air. I didn't want to force my own prejudices about the Fair Folk onto her, so I bit my tongue.

That left Maxine and I to talk on the phone while we each waited for something to happen. We just talked about simple things, nothing earth shattering. It was only the semi-small talk of getting to know each other. If it weren't for the circumstances, I would liken us to two teenagers chatting for hours about nothing between dates.

There was a little bit of real information communicated. I told her the simplified version of how I ended up one of the Magi.

She told me how she got involved with this coven and her own mystic journey.

"Well, when I was a little girl. I had this really weird dream. In my dream I had found this magical charm. A bracelet I think. It belonged to a queen of some magic realm. Gods, this is embarrassing, but you must remember, I was seven or eight . . . Maybe nine at the oldest.

"Anyway, I returned this magic bracelet to the queen and she gave me three wishes."

"Soooo, what did you wish for?" Yes, I did sound exactly like a teen-age boy. It was that kind of moment.

I swear I heard her blush on the other end of the phone. It was hard to believe this was a conversation between two thirty-somethings.

"Well, I wished I had a place where I could keep all the books I wanted and no one would bother me about them. I mean, my mother was always telling me I had too many books for a room of my size."

"Always a bibliophile, then?"

"Absolutely, my second wish was for first editions of all my favorite books."

"At seven?"

"Yep. What can I say? I was a girl who knew her own mind even then."

"Cute, nerdy, but cute."

She gave me a brief light hearted, "Hey, now" when I said that.

"Still, none of that is *that* embarrassing," I said.

"Okay," she took a deep breath, "Lord and Lady, I can't believe I'm telling you this. I wished I could have a fairy tale of my own. One where a magic prince would whisk me away to his kingdom."

"Ah, I see. That's not very feminist of you."

"Hey, I was seven, I bet you were just as goofy at seven. What was your deepest wish at that age."

"Let me think. I had given up on being a superhero at five, so I guess, I wanted to be an astronaut."

"See. You should have stuck with superhero. It's closer."

We laughed at that, perhaps half sardonically. "What about you? You got your first wish. What with the bookstore and all."

She said "yeah" in really wistful tone. "So I guess, I just have to work a little harder and I'll get my second wish. All I need is some Lewis Carroll and the E. Nesbitt books." We chatted for little while longer. And then, like teenagers, we took far too long to say good-bye.

Chapter Twenty-Two

AT ONE O'CLOCK THE next afternoon, I was thrown for a loop. It didn't directly relate to our surveillance. Cominad appeared in astral form aboard the RV. Her astral form looked haggard and beaten up.

Unlike Marguerite, I don't see the astral naturally. This means I must have my sights on or be astral myself. When Cominad showed up, I wasn't able to see her. Marguerite had to tell me that Cominad had made an appearance. Since my "wheel of Sight" is rather unpredictable, possibly letting me see her but not hear her, I just jumped out of body myself. She started speaking as soon as she knew I could hear her.

"I'm sorry I haven't been able to make contact with you lately. Whatever you did to wake up Sasha, I appreciate it. I honestly do . . ."

"What went wrong?" Alexandra Cominad has a reputation among the magi. She didn't mince words or shy from painful truths. So when she starts a conversation with an apology and a "yes, but..." I know things are bad. Maybe real bad.

"There was damage done to his mind. He hasn't lost the basics of his abilities but he no longer seems to have any impulse control."

I don't need to tell you how bad that could be. No wonder Cominad astral form looked so worn down. It would probably take her and most of her team to keep up with him. It's probably taken this long to get him pinned down.

"We've got him in a containment circle. And he's now under medical sedation. I've got my team trying to figure out our next step."

"Is every one okay? I mean . . . did he hurt anyone?" I asked.

Cominad looked sadder for a moment, if that was possible. "He didn't hurt any people. We managed to keep him contained for most of the time, but . . ." It was obviously hard for her to talk about this. I held my tongue trying not to interrupt her by finishing her sentence. That would only make it harder.

"Something set him off and he did a fair amount of damage up in the forest." I recalled hearing of Sasha's love of the forests. He had pursued forestry as a career before his epiphany. Even afterward he had put his talents to work preserving the woodlands of the Pacific Northwest.

"When he regains himself, this will just break his heart," she said.

Then she turned to and transfixed me with a rather frightening gaze. "Have you found who's responsible?"

"Maybe. I know we are closer. We're staking out the house of Mrs. Jekyll and her husband. Also, there's a lead that's pointing to a spirit calling itself Numis. It passed itself off as an elf to me earlier. I've had information since that suggests it isn't one."

Cominad's astral form shuddered. "I know Numis," she said, "It's an aspect of Mammon."

This wasn't great news. But it wasn't the worst either. Mammon is one of the big spirits. It's the spirit of greed or I should say it's *The* Spirit of Greed. I'm not sure how to describe the existence of an aspect. In some ways Numis would be an agent of Greed. It's not entirely unlike someone being an agent of an organization like the FBI, if the FBI were really only one person spread out over many locations.

"I've got to get back to Sasha," Cominad told me. "Keep me posted, You've still got to root out Numis's mortal agents to foil its plans. I want to be there when you push through your end game."

"She was gone before I could reassure her that she'd have her chance. I wanted to see her face those responsible for her son's injuries.

It was good that she went when she did. Ramón and Hector, who were doing physical surveillance, could see the mail truck heading down the street toward the house. Ty and James brought Azgard up to the side of the RV. I hopped out of the RV and slid into the back of Azgard.

Ah, show time. Now this should get us somewhere. At least, we wouldn't just be waiting anymore.

If we saw no change in the behavior of Arnold and Marianna when the postal carrier rang the doorbell, that'd tell us one thing. If one of them actually answered the door, that would tell us another thing. At the very least, it would confirm that someone or something was physically present in the house.

I was convinced that we were just watching the equivalent of back screen projection. I felt certain there was nothing there but an empty house. That really bugged me. I'd hate to be wasting my time.

The mail truck pulled up to the corner. The mailboxes for that block were subdivided from a single, four- foot high metal box. It made life easier for the postal carrier, I suppose.

After dispensing the regular mail, the driver got out and headed toward the house itself.

This was go time. We had Ramon cruise the suburban past the door. Hector used the camera with the telephoto lens to capture images after the postman rang the doorbell.

The postman rang the bell.

He waited.

We waited, watching him watch the door. I sat with Ty and James in Azgard. He rang again. Ty paid James five dollars. I gave them a questioning look.

"I just bet Ty that the post-man would ring twice," James said.

I was about to ask for further explanation when the door opened. It was one of those fortuitous moments. Hector and Ramón were passing at just the right angle to the door so that they got a clear shot of who answered. As the information spread through their link Ty and James jumped as if electrocuted

"Son of a bitch," said Ty next to me, "That's Merton"

Chapter Twenty-Three

I ROCKETED OUT OF MY body. Zooming past the slightly open door, I could see that it was indeed Merton. A twinge of guilt hit me when I saw that he had a broken leg and fractured arm. I'm guessing that this was from when I landed on him with more than necessary force.

More importantly, I saw that the wards had been built in an unexpected way. The wards actually clung directly to the structure of the house. When the door was opened the ward moved with it. The ward no longer protected the house.

I suppose there were a number of reasons that one might do that. Ignorance was one reason. Making sure there was an escape hatch was another.

Most of my wards are one way. They only block movement one direction. Otherwise you could end up trapped if weren't careful.

That's when another reason hit me, just after I had rushed into the house. You could also build a ward like that to trap something.

I had a sinking feeling in the pit of my imaginary stomach. This feeling was confirmed an instant later when Merton slammed the door in the face of the Postman and said, "Gotcha."

I've got to admit, Merton had played it just right. He had carefully kept his attention off of me. That kind of thing can show up to the sights. Until he slammed the door shut, I couldn't tell that he knew I was there. That takes discipline. Since I knew he was aware of me, I risked manifesting to get a look at the physical picture.

I could see the casts on his arm and legs only because I knew to look for them. They were small and were of the same matte black hue as the rest of his clothing. I couldn't tell what kind of material they were made from but it sure wasn't the old plaster casts I remembered.

He was wearing a more streamlined version of the goggles I had first seen him wearing back in the Coroner's office. These could have passed for a big pair of sunglasses.

He grinned up at me.

"Oh, you make it too easy, " he said.

Then he did that little trick where he produced a silenced handgun out of thin air. Okay, it wasn't really out of thin air. It just seemed that way. He aimed the handgun at me with the easy grace of a skilled marksman.

Honestly, I was speechless. After all, what did I have to fear from a gun in my astral form? I had the feeling that one of us was missing the point.

Merton drew a very satisfied breath. I felt more certain that the one missing something was me.

He fired the gun. The impact of the bullet drove me through the interior wall separating the entry foyer from the living room. It seems that there were wards only on the exterior walls of the house. The bullet lodged in the wall as I passed through it. Without its force to propel me, I was able to slow myself before I shot through the entire living room. This saved me from careening into the next set of wards.

Being shot was a bit unnerving. I had never actually been shot before. I've been kicked, punched, stabbed, slashed, bludgeoned, bitten and sprayed with acid but never actually shot. Certainly a physical object has never struck me while I was in spirit form before. That was one for the books.

I didn't have time to puzzle out the odd interaction of spirit and physics that had just occurred. I didn't have time that is, if I didn't want it to happen again.

Merton swept into the living room. His causal competence was now layered with a smug satisfaction.

He fired at me again, double tapping this time. There was the muffled pop of the silenced weapon. Which I guess explains why the first bullet didn't go all the way through the wall with me. Ty tells me silencers slow down bullets. It's just enough to stop the sonic boom but leave them plenty fast enough to kill.

I needn't you tell this wasn't a normal situation. In the flesh, I would have just been shot. I would have been grievously wounded, if not dead.

You may have heard somewhere, "The spirit is willing but the flesh is weak."

Well, the spirit is also a great deal swifter than the flesh.

I did a half twist in the air as the bullets flew past my shoulder into the brickwork of the fireplace behind me.

I imagined that I would get more useful information if I let myself slide back out of manifestation into simple astral form.

"That won't help you. I can still see you," Merton said.

I was rather surprised to hear him speaking intelligibly. Normally I shouldn't be able to make out his words just the emotions and intentions behind them. I knew of only three things that I could hear clearly on the astral plane, spirits, mediums like Marguerite, or another person projecting as I was.

Merton was none of those things. I didn't really have much time to ponder what was happening as he was firing at me again. I tried to soar out the room as quickly as I dared. I didn't want to blur out again and slam into the wards. That could knock me out for . . . well I don't know. I've never gone unconscious while astral. I assumed I'd drift back to my body. What would happen when the wards blocked my way? There were too many unknowns for my comfort. And that's coming from some who thrives on ambiguity and mystery.

Because of this caution, Merton tagged me in the leg with one of his shots. I went spinning. I slammed into the wall next to the front door. Making a full "body" contact with the ward. It was like hitting an electric fence. These wards were more than just barriers. They had an offensive component. I sprung back off of it, shaken and slowed.

Merton was able to shoot me three more times, driving me back into the pain-field of the house ward. This turned out to be one of those blessings in disguise. It gave me the information I needed to turn this situation around.

Once I recovered enough to try to pry myself off the wall again, I noticed that the bullets that had driven me into the wall this past time had fallen to the floor. I had wondered how he had enchanted the bullets to strike me. It must be something fairly minor since the most they had done was push me around. They didn't do the kind of damage that a bullet would do to a physical body. The kind of mojo needed to pull off injuring an astral form was big league stuff. Numis might have been able to provide it, but I doubted he wanted to hand spirit-shredders to someone like Koenig or her thugs like Merton.

Enchanted ammo has only a limited effect anyway. If spirits could be killed, someone would have murdered Numis and his kind ages ago. The best that you can hope for from spirit shredding is incapacitation for a while. Had these been those kind of bullets, I would have probably been put into a coma for who knows how long. It may have been long enough that'd I'd die from old age.

These seemed more like the enchantment that allows a spirit to use a physical object without manifesting first. But that usually takes a spirit to infuse some of it essence into the object. That just didn't seem likely for a bunch of one-use objects like bullets.

Then it hit me (no pun intended.) There were tiny little wards on each of the bullets. Talk about a bullet with your name on it.

Merton was shooting me with tiny wards. That's a clever idea. Sadly it's also a little lacking in magical theory.

Sure, I can't pass through a ward in astral form and putting one on a bullet makes a tiny, very fast ward capable of "touching" me. But while I can't cross a ward, neither can it pass through me. I had just been allowing the push of the bullet to send me flying. I had just assumed it could.

Okay it can, but only so long as I'm not resisting.

This instant of realization gave me just enough umpf to finally pull myself off the wall for a second time. I slumped to the floor in front of the door. I knelt on the floor as Merton walked up to me. Now this was as much exhaustion as it was clever ploy. I honestly couldn't move much more than if I had been physically electrocuted.

Merton stood before me. His smugness was so unbearable, I manifested again. Then I wouldn't have to see it so clearly. He put the muzzle of the gun up "against" my forehead. Then he slid the barrel into my forehead about an inch.

"Let's see what they do from the inside."

"Bad plan," I told him. "It could be injurious to you. I recommend you surrender."

He laughed and pulled the trigger on a single shot. A bright golden light shot out the back of my head.

"What the hell," Merton exclaimed.

I had put my will into resisting the ward of that first bullet. Now the question of Physics versus Will was in my favor. I stopped the ward and with it the bullet. I didn't allow it to push me. The kinetic energy of the shot was turned into light. I was glad of that, otherwise it would have been just like hitting an obstruction in the barrel. I didn't want the gun to blow up in Merton's hand despite the "instant karma" appeal of it.

However, there was now a bullet stopped just inside the barrel. I felt obligated to warn him again.

"Stop! Don't fire again. There's a bullet stuck in your barrel."

I'm sure Merton had intended to punctuate his cry of "bullshit" with a gunshot. He got as far as "Bullsh-" when the gun shattered in his hand.

When the second bullet hit the first it pushed both outwards. They both dropped out the air as they hit me more golden light bursting out at the points of "impact"

There was still enough force redirected to rupture the barrel and burn Merton's hand. I hoped Koenig had good insurance benefits.

Merton was one hell of tough guy though. I'm sure that he was already in pain from the fractures in his arm and leg. Now he had even more pain from the injuries to his right hand. He still wasn't giving up. He slumped briefly to the floor and struggled to get up. While he did so, he pulled a combat knife from a sheath on his hip. The knife was clearly marked with the distinctive glyphs and symbols of a mystic ward.

Sadly, his perseverance was not illuminated by a great deal of intelligence. I had recovered enough that I could stand now. Before I had needed all my strength to resist the warded bullet's push. I couldn't do that and move. If I had tried to move without resisting he'd have driven me back into the "electrified" ward for another excruciating turn. I wasn't sure how many rounds of that I could go before the ward worked just like a spirit shredder.

I had recovered a bit, so this was another story. Merton did some kind of roll/lunge attack at me. Even hobbled by broken limbs and burned flesh, He was blindingly fast. He lashed out with the knife in his left hand.

Had I been in the flesh, he would have gutted me like a fish. As I said, he was blindingly fast. Fast, that is, for someone carrying around all that meat.

I grabbed the blade of the knife. I gave it a small twist and it popped out of his hand into mine. It wasn't really difficult. I was using my best strength against his. My will versus his brawn in what was essentially a spiritual battle. It was no contest, really.

His basic problem was that, while the wards allowed the objects to "interact" with my spiritual form, they didn't give them any destructive power. All the bullets could do was push me around (if I let them.) This combat knife, which would have done horrible things to me had I been in my body, was barely a club. It was like being attacked with a whiffle-ball bat.

Still, I had to admire Merton's tenacity. Broken arm, broken leg, serious burns on his gun hand and his back up weapon had just been taken away from him. Did he give up? Did he retreat? Did he even relent in his onslaught for an instant?

No, of course not. A reconsideration of his actions would have been far more rational than he was at the moment.

It was probably the pain, from old wounds and new, that really fed his fury. He had a driving anger that wouldn't be satisfied with anything less than my death or his.

I tossed away his ward-inscribed knife. While I did that, he rolled away from me and back into the living room. It was almost fun watching Merton fight. Nothing deterred him. He moved smoothly from one tactic to another.

I followed Merton into the living room. He pulled a duffel bag out from behind the sofa. With the ease of an experienced professional, he pulled out his next attack, hand grenades.

He had to be kidding. No, I could see them with a warding design on them plain as day. I was astounded. This was the worst idea yet. Someone must have set him up to fail. No one who had enough ward-making skill to inscribe such an irregular surface could possibly think that this would work.[20]

He tossed the first one at me.

I caught it. It exploded. The first thing the blast did was destroy the ward that was so intricately worked into its' surface. So there was nothing to even push against my astral form. All the energy and bits of shrapnel remained comfortably on the physical plane.

Merton, of course, was well clear of the blast and already sending in a second grenade. I just stepped away and let the blast sail through me. I felt something was odd. The feeling that Merton was being set up to fail was growing.

I've said some contradictory things about Merton. I've called him foolish and I've also said that he was very professional. I owe him something of an apology. It wasn't that he was stupid. It was that he was in denial.

He was the kind of guy who believed that there was a tactical solution for any problem. He had also always believed only in his senses. It was quite remarkable that he could work for Koenig at all. Everything he had known before told him that what he was doing should work because what I was doing wasn't really possible.

---

[20]   I couldn't have done it. Anything more convoluted that a flat plane or a sphere and I'm out of my league.

So there he was trying to kill me, using weapons that have no real chance to succeed. If I had a mind to, I could turn his weapons against him. I was half tempted to bat his next grenade back at him. That, however, would be too much of a failure to show compassion to my enemies.

I wished I knew how to stop him before he really did himself some serious damage. Also, I couldn't really get on with investigating the house while he had me trapped in here, dodging his inconvenient attacks. I wasn't even going to be able to grab the computer and run.

"Ah man!" I thought. Sometimes, I wish I could see the forest out there among all those trees a little sooner.

He had me running circles and not investigating the house. What's more, I was trapped inside the house and who knows what was going on outside. He may have been set up to fail but there was a purpose to it.

I suddenly needed a way to end this quickly. The only ways that immediately jumped to mind were rather drastic and injurious to Merton. Despite what way too much of Christendom says, I think the boss meant it when he said, "love your enemies." I'm fairly certain that includes not killing them.

I made a point of catching Merton's next grenade in my teeth and holding it there while it exploded. Of course, Merton wasn't looking at the time. He was busy being a one-man assault squad. Here's where the movie would convey more than this humble writing. Merton was throwing grenades in a fairly enclosed space.

Most of the downstairs was trashed by now. The interior walls were a mess. I wonder what the neighbors must think.

Presumably, the police would be coming out soon. After all, it's hard to ignore explosions like this. If I knew my team, they were just outside trying to get in. It'd take quite an effort to knock down the wards on this place. They were both physical and spiritual. You'd need something big to knock through them. Both to have the power to break through and to withstand the painful assault "wired" into the wards. Also, that "something big" would have to have both a physical and spiritual component. A tank couldn't do it. Nor could even a powerful Ghost or Fay Lord. You'd need something living that was mammoth. Actually, a mammoth would be ideal or even an elephant.

Sadly, I was in short supply inside the house and outside . . . Well, I don't think I'd given the team enough of a crash course in Theurgy/Thaumaturgy to know to do that.

So, ironically, while the most of the downstairs was being reduced to splinters, the big picture window in the living room was just fine, having been seriously reinforced by ritual warding.

Merton was running out of weapons. He had exhausted his grenades. I now needed to deal with shotgun slugs. Those things had enough kick to them that I needed to either dodge them or resist them. Either way I couldn't go about my task.

I think Merton was aware now that we were in something of a stalemate. The police were going to be coming soon, if they weren't already here. Once they were here, I wasn't going to be able to get the computer information. If I were able to open the doors to let in Hector then the police would be streaming in as well. There just weren't enough excuses in the world to talk our way out that mess.

Merton must have also known that, while he couldn't kill me, I wouldn't kill him. All he needed to do was wait me out to succeed. (What explanation he'd give to the cops, I couldn't even imagine.)

I was running out of time. As much as I oppose putting God in a box, I thought this was a great time for a little Deus ex-Machina.

Ask and it shall be given. While my team didn't have a mammoth or an elephant, they did have Azgard. As noted before, Azgard does have some fairly unusual properties. Azgard's arrival through the picture window sent both Merton and myself diving for cover. The driver's side door flung open. Hector charged through the debris field that was the downstairs. He moved with the liquid grace that I had come to expect from the Guys combining their awarenesses. I guessed that they sent hector because he was our resident computer guy.

Merton only took an instant to decide his next move. He knew that the situation had just changed, and not in his favor. He swung the shotgun toward Hector's back and fired. This time I did use my blur move. I put myself in front of the slug. I put all my will into resisting its momentum. The resultant flash of light looked like a magnesium flare. By the time the light subsided Hector was up the stairs.

Merton was clutching his face. Apparently the spirit-sight goggles didn't have much in the way of flare compensation.

I flew upstairs to check on Hector. He had hurriedly disconnected the computer tower. There were a few cords that still dangled from it. He held it under one arm like an over-sized football. When he took off running, he even looked a little like he were sprinting for a touch down. He would have looked more so if the "end zone" weren't down a flight of stairs in a war zone. I followed.

Merton made a dive for Hector just as he cleared the little hallway that lead to the living room. Merton's attack was swift and efficient. It would have been quite brutal had it connected.

Hector's right arm flung up and sent the computer flying forward over Merton's head. Hector's left arm went down, leading the rest of the body into a cartwheel past Merton's lunge. At the far end of the cartwheel, Hector was upright again. He caught the computer and continued his run. Hector dived out through the shattered picture window. The RV pulled up. Marguerite flung open the side door from within. Hector threw himself up the little stairs and inside. Marguerite forcefully pulled the door, slamming it shut

I was able to catch a glimpse of Pandora and other guys inside. When I manifested I could hear sirens in the distance getting closer.

"Now would be a good time to get out of here," I thought.

It was unlikely that the police would have anything that could cause me trouble, but hey why take chances. I wasn't really sure where my body was. Now that there was a way out I felt certain that I could just blur back to it. That felt wrong, however.

I felt like I was abandoning Azgard. I know that time and again Azgard has shown that it could take care of itself. Still, I couldn't just walk away, because time and time again Azgard was there for me.

It looked like Merton was getting his bearings back. I had a sudden fear that he would try to take out his frustration on Azgard. I acted on instinct. I slid behind the wheel just as if I wore my flesh.

Then engine was still running. I reached out for the steering wheel and felt pressure under my hand. That same quality that had prevented me from simply exiting Azgard in my astral form was now allowing me to touch it without the benefit of skin or bone.

I stomped on the gas and threw the car into reverse.

Chapter Twenty-Four

I SWUNG OUT INTO THE street and straightened out. Police cars were arriving en mass. I saw a small opening between two cruisers. I gunned the engine, shifted, and shot forward trying to maneuver into the gap before it was blocked entirely.

Normally Azgard goes unnoticed by the police. More accurately, he slips past their speed detection equipment, radar, lasers, what have you. They all just fail to focus on Azgard.

There is only so far one can stretch that sort of inconspicuousness. Rocketing out of a shattered house and through a forming police barricade is not the best way to stay "out of sight, out of mind."

The only "out of mind" here was the police estimation of my psyche.

To be honest, I don't know where I picked up the first two police cruisers. Perhaps they were the two I shot past to escape the house environs. Perhaps they were two others that saw me fleeing the scene.

The rest seemed to latch on like a vehicular conga line. Growing at the next two intersections, it gave me visions of the first *Blues Brothers* movie. I made last second turns at each intersection. I was running on instinct alone.

The police, however, where running on training and expertise, quite a plus in their favor. They only chase from behind for so long. Very quickly they had set up a roadblock.

A more rational part of my mind said I should just stop and let them puzzle out the empty car for themselves. Azgard had once extricated itself from an impound lot back in Virginia, why not here in Oregon?

My gut (or what would have been my gut if I had currently had one) told me that abandoning Azgard would be wrong on a moral as well as practical level.

So, I played chicken with the police blockade. When you're astral, time is very subjective. I rushed at that line of cars for what felt like hours. I knew, just knew, I couldn't win this. The laws of physics were against me.

Or I should say against Azgard. After all at the time, physics didn't really apply to me. Neither did biology.

For example, flight and intangibility aside, I had a virtually instantaneous reaction time. There was no synapse lag between thought and action. Being astral was a mixed blessing though. If I had been in my body trying to do this, I would have wrecked into the side of building on one of my first hairpin turns. I just wouldn't have had the reflexes.

However, if I had my body, I could have channeled energy to cloak us, or possibly made us carry enough mass to plow through the blockade.

If only Azgard could fly like my astral form.

Hell, it was a thought. Azgard did slip between worlds and always find me somehow.

So, the instant before the instant before we would have hit one of the blockading police cruisers, I pulled up on Azgard's steering wheel and willed it into the air.

It was a jump worthy of Jake and Elwood at their finest. No ramp, no bump, no hydraulic push, it was just a clear, unmerited elevation that cleared the tops of the cruisers. Mostly. At least the damages were confined to having to replace all those pretty blue lights.[21]

As much as I had hoped for true flight, that sadly wasn't going to happen. On the far side of the cars, we returned to earth. The fun was only beginning.

Azgard landed with a bone-jarring thud. (presumably) We went into a skid as we tried to make the next turn out of the blockaded intersection. Some physics did apply after all. We were able to keep that slide under a modicum of control. Police cruisers were on our trail again rather quickly.

We made it onto the "belt line" that runs between Springfield and Eugene. By this point, they were pulling out all the stops. I could hear helicopters over head. I think at least one of them was a news chopper. I wondered if the chase was being televised. The police have a number of tactics they can use in chases. They had tried a roadblock. Next they tried to use spike strips. Azgard had a sense for them somehow. Every now and

---

[21] The Concordance required a sizable, anonymous contribution on my part later

then the car gave a little leap into the air. This kept us going until we reached the overpass that junctioned with I-5. I had never seen so many unhappy, uniformed people with guns outside of an epic war movie. Knowing that they were all unhappy with me was somewhat less than comforting.

I know I had tried this trick before but up we went. This time how ever instead of just jumping over the cars (and trucks and people and . . .) We headed over the side of the bridge. We flew farther than we should have, but we were still going to come down hard. Not only hard, but into traffic. We were going to land in the middle of northbound I-5, facing northeast.

I looked down and wondered how much this was going to hurt Azgard.. I felt guilty that being astral I would escape harm.

And that's when the epiphany hit me. Azgard was not much different than the warded ammo that Merton had been firing at me. It was a physical entity that could interact with my astral form.

As Azgard fell, I slipped out the open window and flew beneath the car. Then I let Azgard hit me. I resisted the movement just as I had the bullets. Of course, Azgard was moving slower but with a lot more mass. Just as the case with the bullets, this wasn't about forces and physics but of the force of will. My will. And if you recall, that's what I do best.

The resultant Photonic discharge would have been literally blinding to anyone close by. Fortunately, there wasn't anyone close enough. Azgard's body blocked most of the light.

I had stopped Azgard's fall. This left me hanging a few feet off the ground, holding a car over my head. I'm sure it looked darn cool. Unfortunately, my will was spent. Azgard slowly lowered to the ground, pinning me underneath. I had the sudden sensation of being unable to breathe. While this is normally troubling, it was especially alarming since I didn't know where my lungs were at the moment.

As you can imagine, I was in a fairly bad predicament. Let's take this moment to focus attention on events elsewhere.

Chapter Twenty-Five

Wᴴᴀᴛ ꜰᴏʟʟᴏᴡꜱ ɪꜱ ᴀ distillation of what was related to me by the other six members of my team. As expected, they each had a slightly different take on events. This is my best reconstruction.

Pandora drove the RV away from the Scott's house. She drove like a professional. Our resident clairvoyant, Marguerite, aided her in navigation. Her powers were working overtime that night. It's what allowed them to avoid the police. Admittedly, I was also keeping Eugene's finest more than occupied.

The team made their way back to the highway. They headed north towards the Albany house. James monitored the Police scanner. With it, they were able to track the movements of Azgard pretty easily.

James set up our second stolen (ahem, liberated) computer there in the RV. They had left the suburban behind. Following a sudden insight of Marguerite's they pulled off I-5, switched drivers, then headed on their way to Springfield's Gateway mall. It was Ramón who relieved Pandora at the wheel. Ty and James began to formulate strategies for recovering Azgard and myself, if it should prove needed.

Pandora later said it was one of those times when she felt particularly useless. After Ramón took over driving duties, she felt all she could do was hold my body's hand and talk to me. She said I reminded her of a coma paitient.

I was lucky. If she hadn't been watching over me, things might have ended there for me.

"Hey, Marguerite," Pandora said with surprising calm, "Milo just stopped breathing. And I'm not getting a pulse either."

Pandora didn't know CPR but Marguerite did. So did TY. I suppose by extension that meant all the guys did. I'm so glad Pandora wasn't driving.

No offense to Ramón but I don't think he would have been as attentive to me as Pandora was. She was just what I needed.

I also learned an important lesson that day. When I leave the flesh behind, it seems I leave behind a residual will to live. It's what keeps my body going. I had expended all of my will power while outside my body. This meant there was none of that residual will to live keeping my body on task. That's why I stopped breathing. My heart was also shutting down.

Marguerite and Ty put me down on the floor of the RV and began to get to work. Even as Ramón kept driving, Marguerite and Ty kept working on me keeping my body alive. They got to gateway mall about the same time that the police were making a very cautious approach toward Azgard.

The police surrounded Azgard. They did the whole explosives check. They started first with a remote controlled robot. Admittedly, I don't really know what they started with, but that was the first part I noticed. It slipped up next to, then under the car. I suppose it must have had some kind of chemical detectors on it. I was not manifested, so all I could tell was that something mechanical was passing near, and through, me.

Shortly after that, in objective time, subjectively it seemed like years, I sensed the presence of people near Azgard. They had an intent, intense energy about them. It was the bomb squad guys taking their next step. I sensed fear kept at bay by dedication

Can't say I blame them for their uncertainty. That flash of light was not going to conform to much, if anything, in their experience. For all they knew they were all going to die in the next moment, despite whatever it was that their little robot could tell them. I think that rates pretty high on the brave-o-meter. If you ever get the chance, buy one of those guys a drink for me.

Of course, at the time, I was a bit more concerned about myself. As soon as I started to die and the CPR started, I felt myself being tugged back to my body. I was, as mentioned, pinned beneath the inert weight of Azgard. So, in addition to feeling that couldn't breath, I was trapped.

It was a bit like being buried alive, I suppose. If it is, then remind me not to let that happen again. I was nearly going crazy. The last time some tried to do CPR on my empty body, I shot right back to it. This time, I couldn't get out past my car. I felt like I was being pulled. No, that's not quite right. It was more like I was falling. Except that I would have to be falling in two different directions simultaneously. While I'm as fond of novel experiences as the next guy, that was one sensation you could keep.

The people around Azgard dispersed. In my fearful state, one thought penetrated. It made everything even worse. "Don't bomb squads detonate suspicious packages?"

That was a fairly terrible moment. I would hate myself if I had "rescued" Azgard from Merton only to be exploded by the bomb Squad.

Suddenly Azgard lurched. It was being pulled up on to a one of those flatbed tow-trucks. I didn't actually see any of this. First, I was pinned underneath a car in astral form. Even if I had been manifested to see the physical world, all I would have seen was the underside of my car. The second reason was that as soon as Azgard was lifted enough to let me out, I snapped back to my body.

Chapter Twenty-Six

In A More Ideal world, I would have awoken to Marguerite pressing her lips into mine, giving me the "kiss of life." Better yet, it would have been Maxine. Instead, it was Ty. Which isn't to say Ty is unattractive but his manly charms are wasted on me.

"Where are we?" I asked with my first unaided breath. Or at least that's what I tried to say. What came out was a strangled cough. I was hit with the physical side of my exhaustion. My words were weak, barely even a mumble. It was good enough to let Marguerite and Ty know I was back but that was all.

I lapsed back into unconsciousness. So again, I have to relate to you a reconstruction rather than memory. Now that my breathing and heartbeat were self-sustained once again, the team turned it attention to our next move.

James was convinced that we should do everything we could to get Azgard back. Perhaps he felt that turn about was fair play. After all, he and I would still be trapped in the Wood between Worlds if not for Azgard.

The rest of the guys were generally of similar opinion, surprise, surprise. Yet they couldn't agree what the best course of action. Should they try and wake me? This was James's idea. Perhaps they should try to steal Azgard back. This was Ramón's.

Ty thought, given what they knew, of Azgard's capabilities, that they should give it a chance to free itself.

Marguerite was more concerned with why her Little Psychic Newsflashes had directed her to bring the team to the mall.

Pandora was the surprise. "Just have Faith," she said. "Milo has a plan. Well actually given how he works, I'm sure it's more of a flow chart. But the first thing he'd do is make sure everyone was all right. And is everyone alright?"

Quick glances my direction reassured most of the team that I was resting comfortably. After everyone else had nodded a basic assent, Pandora continued.

"James, you've been listening to the scanner, what's their plan for Azgard."

"Sounds like it's been cleared for explosives so they're dragging Azgard off to the forensics garage."

"Well, that gives us a little time, I think. But more importantly, how is Milo? Is this another stunt he'll sleep off or does he need serious medical attention?" Pandora looked around at the team.

This question stopped them cold. They hadn't considered that I might actually be that bad off. I take that as a vote of confidence rather than indifference.

"Should we take him to a hospital?" Pandora asked.

"Can we?" responded James, "A description of him went out on the police band during the chase."

"How'd they get a description if he was astral?" asked Pandora.

"Merton. Remember he's seen us before."

That brought up another fear. Merton had also met the guys. A moment later that fear was confirmed as they heard basic descriptions of Ty and Ramón come over the scanner.

This was also the same moment they found out why they had been directed to this particular mall at this time.

There was knock on the RV door. Pandora peeked out the window. It was Krista and Maxine.

"Thank Astarte we found you. I've been able to pin down Cascadia. She's willing to talk to us about what's going on but only for another half an hour."

This presented a problem, of course, because it looked like it was going to be a long, long time before I woke up again.

Krista really did a great job of setting up the meeting. Not just in getting Cascadia to consent to the meeting. She also got Cascadia to meet on Krista's terms.

Cascadia was a "landed" fairy, which, as in medieval human society, meant that she was the equivalent of nobility. Of course human nobles just own the land. They are not aspects of it.

So, had I been awake, I would have been surprised that Cascadia had consented to giving an audience. I would have been flabbergasted to hear that it was outside her own domain. I would have passed out again when I found that she was going to meet our team in the food court of the Springfield Gateway mall.

Pandora and Ramón elected to remain with me in the RV. Maxine also decided to stay by my side. Something I wish I could have been grateful for at the time. Ramón sat in the driver seat with the engine going. He watched the mall entrance. I'm not sure how fast a getaway you can make in an RV, but that was the plan if things went bad inside

Marguerite went with James and Hector. Krista led the way.

The food court was just inside the mall's southeast entrance, just next to the buck-fifty movie theater.

As they entered, they could tell that Cascadia was already there.

How? Well for one, the food court bore more than a passing resemblance to a medieval noble court.

This resemblance wasn't obvious, but it was clear to any one who knew what to look for.

All activity, whether consciously or unconsciously, revolved around the center most table of the dining area. All the foot traffic flowed to give it the greatest accommodation. The tables immediately next to it were empty. The tables that were next to those were entirely filled. The people in them went about their business as usual for the most part. A body language expert could have told you that they were all acutely aware and protective of someone sitting at the center-most table.

That someone was, of course, Cascadia. I wasn't there, but I doubt that all those people were her actual entourage. Last time I saw her, she had only one other with her other than Numis.

She struck me as a fairy that traveled light. All these people where probably just those attracted by Cascadia's presence. Most of whom would probably have trouble explaining their actions to themselves, let alone any one else. So, if you were there that day and you wondered why you lingered so long in the food court, now you know.

Krista led Marguerite and the two Guys over to the table. James had met Cascadia and the Icy warrior before. Meeting them in this more mundane setting was a bit of a let down. While they were still amazingly beautiful women, the two Fay were clearly slumming it. Their wardrobes barely sparkled at all. Cascadia was dressed in a Women's business suit. The suit combined forest green and a brown that made one think automatically of bark. The Icy warrior wore a running suit in a light blue that would have been described as "frost" by anyone more fashion conscious than me.

Marguerite, Hector, and James sat down at the table with Cascadia and the Icy Warrior. Ty had run down around the outside of the mall until he came to the anchor store that capped off the near end of the mall. He was working his way back around to the food court from the other side.

There wasn't a specific purpose to this. They just thought it would be good to have someone nearby but not easily observable. As he made his way, a well-dressed woman joined him. She had steely, blue eyes and iron gray hair braided to the back.

Krista introduced Marguerite as she sat down.

"Lady Cascadia, I present the Medium Marguerite Winston, Mister James Hong, and Mister Hector Rodriguez. They assist the Magus."

"Greetings," Cascadia smiled brightly, "One of these is already known to me. Indeed, I am surprised to see him here. I was surprised to find that his master had made it back from "the wood" so quickly, let alone manage to bring another home as well."

If James rankled at being referred to in such a subordinate way, he never showed it to Cascadia.

"Our little cadre has a number of unexpected resources," James said.

"Oh, such a daring tone," The icy warrior said, "The Magus has chosen his champion well. You've got a great deal of courage. I think I might enjoy testing your mettle."

For some reason, James's eyes glazed over at the comment and Hector slapped him on the side of his head.

"We have little time for pleasantries, Lady Cascadia, we thank you for meeting with us. We have a number of questions concerning the entity known as Numis." Marguerite always had a way of cutting to the point.

Cascadia smiled. Her smile made the room seem dim in comparison. James said that he had a sudden impulse to build a shrine to her. Not too surprising, it's just another reason why negotiating with the Fay is so dangerous.

"What can I tell you about Numis? Spiritual entities are hard to pin down. Even for each other. He is greed and all avarice. Other than that he is pleasant enough. Do you not remember, James?"

James blushed to have been singled out by Cascadia. Later, He described as, "like being a kid called on by the pretty, young teacher and not knowing the answer. Now magnify that a hundred fold."

Marguerite interrupted before James could stammer out a non-answer, "We aren't looking to understand his deeper nature. Frankly, I don't care why you were working with him. We are just trying to locate him. We think it'll help get Pandora's brother back."

"How sad. Because those understandings would have helped immensely in your approach to Numis, if not actually finding Stephan."

James finally managed to speak up. As for what he had to say, I'll let you judge for yourself.

"Pardon our rashness, Lady Cascadia. You know how time weighs upon us, we who are mortal."

Cascadia and the Icy warrior both smiled at this. They did so in that patronizing way that adults have when a child unknowingly does something of which they approve.

Hector continued, "Any enlightenment you could provide for us, we would treasure beyond words."

Cascadia spoke, her words a gentle, soothing melody (or that's how they sounded at the time.) "I wish I could be of more help to you. Numis is more my companion's associate than mine. She asked that I accompany them to the conference in "The Wood.""

"Why did you send Krista's coven after us then?" Marguerite asked.

The icy warrior spoke up. "You are most foolish. Once again you have things turned about. But more I will not discuss with you. You have not earned it. You master has. By dodging the mind lock spell with which I armed my servants, he has earned the right to contest with me for those answers."

"We can speak for him." James said, "you called us his champions before, didn't you?"

"No, little man, I called you, the four of you, his champion. Which means I would gladly let you fight in his place but not to speak for him. We could fight if you wished but I would still only give my answers to him."

It's not often that puissant Fay warriors make major blunders. The Icy Warrior just had. She had identified herself as the source of the spell that had laid Sasha low. She did it where Hector and James could hear her. Which means Ramón and Ty heard it through the link. Ty relayed it to the well-dressed woman with steely, blue eyes and the Iron gray, braided hair.

And she, Cominad, knew what that confession meant.

I wish I had been there to see it.

Cominad strode over to the table. She calmly, patiently, almost deferentially listened to Cascadia actually answer one of Marguerite's questions.

"I set The Daughter of the Waxing Moon upon you because Stephan had requested my assistance. In truth, he told me that a pack of witch hunters had forced his sister to come looking for him. That they intended to take him back into servitude. I believe Numis had advised him to ask."

Krista spoke up. "You were unaware that Stephan is currently living with the alter ego of his captor?"

"Yes *I* was." The slight point of emphasis was lost on no one at that table.

"Numis was aware I take it? How about you?" Marguerite directed the second question to the Icy Warrior.

"I discuss nothing save with the Magus should he or his *champion*, best me." She spoke with grimmest smile that the guys could recall seeing. She had also fixed Hector with the fiercest, most compelling gaze. Hector says he suddenly understood why moths fly willingly into the flames. The Guys tell me he still gets shivers remembering it.

Marguerite started into another question but was interrupted by Cascadia.

"Child, is someone ill? Why do you gather such an excess of healing energies?" This last comment was directed at Cominad.

"I am Alexandra Cominad of the Magi Concordance. I am the senior Magus of this district. I call you to account for the harm you did to Alexander Cominad, my son." although it was Cascadia that had spoken to her, Cominad addressed the Icy Warrior. Cascadia looked as though she were about to speak again. The Icy warrior held up a hand. She spoke instead.

"Go away, little woman. His injury was incidental. I know the strictures of your kind. Do not make me use them against you."

"I do not fear you, Sister Winter. You know less and less with each day."

"Then let what happens be on your head." The icy warrior waved a hand and a frost settled on the people and the tables that sat in attendance of Cascadia's makeshift "court". The people rose up and turned toward Cominad. As one, they came at her. They moved with a languid, liquid grace. Despite that grace, they still had same inexorable quality of a train that has begun to derail.

"How will you keep to your vow? How can you keep them from harm?" The laughing mockery that was in the warrior's voice was so clear that I almost heard it even unconscious, out in the parking lot.

Cominad just smiled and took off her shoes. She was more than ready to fight.

Just a note: while many of those who share our faith have embraced the Augustinian Just War Theory, The Magi Concordance has not. To be sure, there is a wide range of opinion among magi, but in general, we agree it is not our place to inflict lasting injury or death upon any human being. Christendom may have found ways around the *love your neighbor* instruction to justify deadly violence. The Magi have not.

That being said, Cominad has a much more martial stance than I do.

The first of the Icy warrior's enthralled minions to reach Cominad was met with a roundhouse kick that broke his jaw. The next went down with a blow that audibly cracked her breastbone.

Hector jumped over to Krista and swooped her up over his shoulder and made a charge for the doors.

James had turned to do the same for Marguerite but she had already cleared the closing mob. He had to move fast to avoid being caught in the crush of the chilly minions.

These minions were paying attention only to Cominad. Once James was past them, he became someone else's problem.

By the time the Guys and Marguerite had cleared the area, there were five forms unmoving on the floor. Fourteen others surrounded Cominad on three sides. Cominad had reached the table at which the two Fairies sat.

Cascadia simply observed her with an amused expression. The Icy Warrior became visibly annoyed. She stood, reached into the jacket of her track suit and produced two small, translucent daggers. The icy blades of the daggers were twisted wickedly.

The Icy Warrior reached forward and tore her daggers through Cominad. Her attack was rewarded with an arterial spray that purpled the blue of her tracksuit. The Icy Warrior chuckled, crossed her arms, and waited for Cominad to slump.

Cominad struck her in the face hard enough to cave in the fairy's physical shell. A red slush oozed from where her nose had been. Frozen incisors clattered to the floor and began melting.

Cominad's own hand had been pulped by the attack. She stood there for an instant. Her broken fingers mended and the skin began to knit back together over the bones. With the blood that still dripped from her index finger, Cominad drew a sigil on the forehead of the Icy Warrior just above the gaping wound that was already icing over.

The Icy Warrior, ahem, froze. The minions that she had forced into servitude seemed to awake. They broke off their attacks. Confused, they wandered back to their seats. The five on the floor stirred. Soon, they rose and they too returned to what they had been doing before. It was as if the whole thing had not happened. They did not seem to see a gray haired woman dragging a damaged manikin out of the building.

My team, in case you are wondering, was long gone. As soon as things started going bad, Ramón rushed the RV over to pick up the team as they fled out the mall entrance. By the time Cominad had dragged the Icy warrior out of the mall, the RV was already out of the parking lot.

For those who are wondering, "How the hell did Cominad do that?" would you let me get away with saying it's a trade secret? Didn't think so.

Okay, in essence, it's very simple. Cominad flooded herself with healing energy. In fact, one could say she supersaturated herself with it. I first heard of Supersaturation in high school chemistry. A normal solution is a liquid that has something dissolved in it. Normally, a certain amount of liquid can only have so much dissolved into it. A supersaturated solution has been forced to hold more. One of the interesting properties of this supersaturated solution is it capacity to be seeded.

For instance, let's say that you have a supersaturated solution of "random element x" and a piece of "random element x" crystal. Well, you can take that itty, bitty tiny piece of crystal and drop it into the liquid solution and presto the whole solution crystallizes.

So Cominad, being supersaturated with healing energies, was just waiting for something to heal. It would happen automatically. For instance, if she breaks her hand by throwing one hell of punch, the energy flows and bada boom bada bing the hand is healed.

When she annihilates someone else's jaw with that blow, lo and behold, that jaw will heal almost as fast as it shatters. Now, it'll still hurt like hell and that someone is most likely going to pass out from the pain. But hey, no lasting harm, no foul right?[22]

---

[22]   Okay, I'm not convinced this is a valid loophole concerning the use of violence but it is rather effective

It's also nice for fighting beings that are only wearing a physical shell rather than a real body, like the Icy Warrior. The healing energy doesn't help them one bit.

When The Icy warrior went down, she had to depend on her own magic to fix her shell. Magic Cominad jammed up with a quick sigil. The Fair Folk may have vast power, cunning and immortality on their side. But there are reasons why the earth belongs to us, humans. People like Cominad are part of that.

Chapter Twenty-Seven

The RV HAD MADE it almost four blocks before Cascadia caught up to it. Cascadia was standing at a bus stop and waved Ramón down. Ramón stopped and let her on the RV, just as if he had been driving the cross-town bus. It's just one of those things. Fairies have that effect on people. If Cascadia had meant us harm, it might have been a different story. I think that something of The RV's protections would have kicked in had she meant us harm. At least, I like to think so. It helps me sleep at night.

The first thing Cascadia did surprised every one aboard. She apologized.

"I regret wholeheartedly my participation in this affair. I was given certain assurances by Numis, none of which seems to have held true."

Cascadia paused as if expecting some sort of response. All she got was stunned silence from the team and Krista and Maxine.

I, on the other hand, snorted in my sleep. I suspect that it was just an ill-timed snore. Cascadia thought otherwise. Her eyes flashed momentarily with anger. Something I'm glad I was not awake to see. Then she realized I was unconscious.

"Sleep is no excuse for you to mock me, Magus." She waved a hand at me and I awoke.

Actually, that's not exactly true. What she did was give me a dream sending. There was no way that I could awake at my level of exhaustion. It took a quite a bit of magic to bring me from semi-comatose to where I could actually dream.

The funky part is that her dream sending was as direct a representation of the real world as could be managed. I was now dreaming what was really going on. Almost. Let's just say there were some problems with the real world/dream-time interface.

The human body has a defense mechanism during sleep that keeps us from trying to act our dreams physically. Cascadia turned mine off. So that when I dreamed that I sat up and walked around in the RV, I actually sat up and walked around in the RV.

Ordinary sleep walking occurs outside of REM dream sleep. They presumably don't have fairies messing with their heads. Presumably. Perhaps that should be looked into . . . Every one, including myself, now thought I was awake.

Cascadia continued her apology, "Numis asked me to allow Ms. Scott to access the Fay realms through my domain. He said it would result in an increase in my holdings, so I agreed. Then he said she needed help protecting a young boy who had fallen prey to panderers.

"Normally I would have left mortal business to mortals but he said that he would personally add another 5% to my holdings if I simply met the boy. Of course, once I had met Master Stephan, I couldn't refuse."

Pandora was actually brave enough to interrupt with a question, "You mean that literally, don't you? He's got some power over you doesn't he?"

"I'm not going to discuss that. Now as I was saying, first this, then that, and finally he says, "'There are some witch hunters coming for the boy with his sister. Have some of your pets deal with it.'"

Krista and Maxine where appalled to be described as pets. The pain showed on their faces.

"Don't be upset with me for his words, Daughter of The Waxing Moon, He can't conceive that I might hold friendship with your coven." Krista seemed a little mollified by that.

"I did not and do not want trouble with the Magi. Especially now that I have met their local representative. I hadn't realized that she had gotten so ferocious."

I spoke out of my dream, "Well, someone did mess with her baby."

"Yes, I think that this will be the last time that the wintry one will underestimate the power of the 'merely mortal' bond of motherhood"

For some reason that struck me as really, really funny. I'm hoping it was just that I was still applying dream logic to the real world. I noticed that every one was staring at me as I laughed. I did a quick check to make sure I was dressed.

"All joviality aside, I wish to make amends for my participation in Numis's scheme. I don't really know much that could help you. Worse I can not intervene while Stephan is still convinced that you are his enemies."

Pandora spoke up again. "Why *is* that? What makes Stephan so important to you?"

"You do not know?" asked Cascadia. Cascadia hesitated. She didn't want to admit to the truth of her predicament, to us or to herself. She seemed very human in that moment.

Eventually she did speak, "Your brother is one of those rare mortals who have some inexplicable essence that overwhelms us and, for lack of a better word, entrances us."

"You really *are* saying that Stephan has some power over you."

Cascadia looked annoyed. "Yes, child, that is what I'm saying. Now, I can give you this information." She turned to Marguerite and placed a hand over her forehead for a second. "Here, this is the place that you can find the ones you seek."

Then she was gone. If it seemed abrupt to the others in the RV, it seemed completely natural to me.

"Well, Margie?" I asked. "What have you got?"

Marguerite got up from where she was sitting in the forward passenger seat. She walked over to the table.

She asked Hector to get her a sheet of paper and a pencil. After he had done so, she began to sketch out a rough picture of what she could see in her mind's eye.

"I have a picture in mind. It's a house set back from the road into the woods."

I dreamed that I walked over to look at the picture. In reality I walked over but I didn't see the same picture as everyone else. With Cascadia no longer present the strength of her waking dream had slipped a little. What Marguerite drew and what I saw where not exactly related. I saw a house in woods all right but what I saw belonged in a book about bears and a young blond trespasser. At the time, this didn't seem at all incongruous to me.

"Does anybody recognize this place?" I asked. None of us did. (Well, I recognized it. I just didn't know the Three Bears' address)

Hector had an idea. "Maybe there's a lead in the computer we liberated from the house tonight."

"Get on that, I'm going to go out for while." I walked into the back room and lay down on the meditation/prayer mat. I closed my eyes and projected out of my body. Or so I thought, instead I just continued dreaming.

Marguerite was so focused on getting the details right on her sketch that she didn't notice that I remained with my body.

Ramón never stopped driving during the whole time Cascadia was with us. He had driven in what was essentially a huge circle. We were still within several blocks of the Gateway mall. There was still a huge police presence around us and around the I-5 exits. He was hoping that the obscurement effect on the RV would help deflect attention from us. He cruised around and around, waiting to get back up on the highway. Suddenly, he called back with some good news.

"Azgard's coming up behind us."

This was news I didn't get to hear zoned out in the meditation room. Had I really been projecting, I would have undoubtedly noticed Azgard's proximity. Instead I was busy "flying" over Eugene, Oregon. For reasons known only to my subconscious, Eugene in my dreams had about as much resemblance to the real Eugene as the nations of E.P.C.O.T. center have to the real world.

So while I wandered around my own personal Eugene trying to find Azgard (and thinking Eugene should have more rides), the focus of my immediate concern was taking care of itself.

Ramón pulled the RV into a Macdonald's parking lot. The parking lot was too small to adequately handle the RVs presence. That wasn't something that deterred Ramón.

Azgard pulled up next to the RV. My friend Artie got out of the driver side. As he walked up toward the RV door, a group of three police cars blazed past on the road. It looked as though they were headed toward the Gateway Mall.

Artie knocked on the door and was quickly let inside.

"I think your fearless leader would like to have these back," he said holding up a set of car keys. "Where is he by the way?"

Marguerite told him I was back in the meditation room, "Either sleeping or projecting, one of the two."

"Well, tell him that I got his car back. It wasn't easy. I won't go into detail but I 'm going to have to work my butt off making sure nobody looses their job with the city.

"Now I have a question for you. Have you seen *my* boss?"

Marguerite relayed to him what they had seen, which didn't include the very end of the battle.

Artie gave a "hmph" and then said, "Sounds like I need to check on that. Have Milo send me a message when he gets back. Cominad was going to get an update from your crew before she gave out our next assignments. I'm sure she'll be in touch once she's finished with Ms. Frosty there."

Artie stepped out of the RV and headed back over to Azgard. Hector followed him out.

"Artie?"

"Yes, Hector?" He pulled a partially disassembled bicycle from Azgard's back seat. Then he closed Azgard's doors and made sure they were locked. He reattached the bike's front wheel. He pulled a bike helmet from his back pack.

"Are you just going to leave Azgard like that?"

"What do you mean? Can't one of you drive it until your boss gets back from his float about?"

"Sure. But won't the police be looking for it?"

"As long as you don't draw attention to yourself, no one will notice a thing."

"You're sure?"

"Oh yeah, I nearly had to ram the RV to get Ramón to pull over."

"Really, I hadn't noticed."

"Exactly. All those police rushing up and down the road are looking for this car. They drive right past it most of the time. If Milo hadn't driven out of a house right in front of the police, we wouldn't have this problem. I always said he was too flashy."

With that, Artie said good night and hopped on his bike. He shot off in the same direction as another set of screaming squad cards.

Hector walked over to Azgard and got in. After an instant of consultation with the other guys, he headed out of the parking lot and down the road the opposite direction of I-5, away from the bulk of the police activity. He turned on Azgard's stereo. An old country remake of "Take Me Home, Country Roads" was playing. Hector didn't know how important that was going to be to us.

Chapter Twenty-Eight

Bᴀᴄᴋ ɪɴ ᴛʜᴇ ʀᴠ, James had taken over the computer duties. He was going through the files, hoping to find something of importance. So far the files fell into two categories, The Encrypted and The Mundane. There were also a bunch of files with extension names he didn't recognize.

Most of the data were just the everyday standard things one expects to find on a PC. There was the household budget. There was quite a collection of photos and music. All the pictures seemed to be fairly ordinary. None seemed to hold any clue as to the location of the house Cascadia showed to Marguerite.

There were also games, including snood. All in all, everything recognizable was very run of the mill. The closest thing that James could find to anything unusual was a tarot deck program.

After a while of not finding anything Marguerite asked James to let her have a crack at it.

"What do you know about computers that Hector doesn't?"

"Nothing. But maybe I can use my abilities to help us ferret out something that may not be obvious."

"What the hell," James said, "worth a shot."

Marguerite sat down and closed her eyes. She held one hand over the keyboard and the other over the mouse. She let herself slide into a trance. Her hands began navigating automatically. In a moment, a song was pumping through the RV's sound system.

The song was "Take Me Home, Country Roads." It was not the one by John Denver but a variation by the Statler Brothers. Their song makes a few changes. This one makes it explicit that they are referring to western Virginia.

For example, they change "West Virginia" to "Old Virginia" and Shenandoah River to "Shenandoah valley."

What made this song important was how much that song meant to me personally. As I heard the song being played on the RV sound system it drew me closer to reality. Not all the way, but I was interacting with real people again.

It had been quite a while since I last heard that song. The last time was right before Shelia's very old car tape player ate the very old mix tape containing it. The song had just ended when it was eaten. At the time it didn't matter much because Sheila and I were pulling up to our honeymoon cabin at the time.

Hearing that song again really took me back. I was still dreaming in that pseudo-wakefulness that Cascadia had placed upon me.

I rose up and walked back out to the RV's living room/dining room. I was singing along with the music.

Instead of Marguerite I saw Shelia sitting there at the computer. She looked just like she did during the drive up to our honeymoon cottage at the edge of the Shenandoah National Forest.

And because it felt like I hadn't seen her for so, so long, I walked up and kissed her.

I don't know if it was because she was in a trance like state herself, or perhaps she was just humoring me, but Marguerite didn't push away from the kiss. Instead she returned it. Not vigorously but still pleasant.

I was in a dream state so I honestly can't tell you how long it lasted but it was long enough for Maxine to clear her throat.

I turned over to look at her and said, "Just a minute Shelia, I'm kissing Shelia. Say, how long before we get to the cottage?" again this all made sense to me in the dream.

Marguerite "awoke" and put her hand up to the side of my face and then along the temple. "Yep, it's official," she said, "he's still asleep."

"You mean like sleep walking?" asked Ty.

Marguerite shrugged. "That would explain why he's calling two of us by his late wife's name."

I noticed that the Maxine-Shelia looked like Sheila as she was on our recent night in Harrisonburg. She was holding the picture that Marguerite had drawn. This time I didn't see it as the three bears' house but as the honeymoon cottage. This makes it the most accurate perception I was having at the time.

"Hey, is that the cottage brochure?" I asked. Maxine, who is very bright, caught on immediately and played along.

"Yes, but it looks like the directions were misprinted. Do you remember them?"

"No, but I bet the other Shelia could look up the website. Blue Ridge Honeymoons.com or Org or whatever."

With that, I tried to kiss Marguerite again. This time she politely rebuffed me saying that she had to look up the website. I was undeterred. I simply walked over to the other Sheila and began kissing her. Maxine seemed somewhat amenable to this course of action. Perhaps she was just humoring me as well. Given what I recall of her enthusiasm, I like to think not. A clearing of a throat also cut this kiss short. This time it was Krista. "Do you really think that's a good idea?" she was directing it toward Maxine but I responded.

"Look, Janet," I perceived Krista as Sheila's stepmother, my former mother-in-law, "we're married now."

Krista, somewhat unsure what to say next, simply blurted out, "that's not what I meant."

"I see. You mean I should kiss the living Shelia, not this one," I said and stepped back over to Marguerite

The implications of that statement were covered over by Marguerite's outcry.

"Eureka, I've got the address. Now all we have to do is get all the way back to Virginia."

"Oh, that'll take too long," I said and swept Marguerite up from in front of the computer and carried her bride-over-the-threshold style towards the meditation & prayer room.

Fortunately, Krista knew a spell that could render me back into normal unconsciousness before I could try to further my intentions. Even more fortunately she had taught it to Maxine, who used it.

Chapter Twenty-Nine

I SLID BACK INTO UNCONSCIOUSNESS. I didn't get to hear Ty suddenly speak up.

"Hector says that Azgard's stereo has been playing that same song. He also says the steering is fighting him a little."

"Tell him to go with it," that was Marguerite. "It may be Azgard knows something."

She turned to address Krista and Maxine. "Perhaps we should drop you off somewhere. If I'm right, I think Azgard may be able to find us a quick route back."

"I'd appreciate that," said Krista. "It's been quite a wild ride for me. A number of my assumptions have been challenged over the last few days."

Pandora asked her, "Like what?"

"Well, I guess the biggest one was 'That nice, young, blond girl won't really pull the trigger.'"

Pandora tried to give an innocent, little "oops" face. I gather it doesn't work so well when trying to shrug off assault with a deadly weapon. Pandora quickly added how honestly sorry she was.

Krista was magnanimous. "Under the circumstances, I understand why you shot me, that's another big surprise. That I'm neither dead nor brain damaged helps to mitigate some of my anger."

She paused for a moment. Then she spoke up again

Really, I've learned a lot in the last few days. One of my assumptions was that if anyone would shoot me, it would be Milo. I'm also quite surprised to find out that his organization allows women to be members at all, let alone hold positions of authority."

Marguerite chimed in, "Can you imagine Cominad taking orders from anybody?"

"But she must have from somebody," this was Maxine, "she wasn't always a senior Magus, was she?"

"No, I guess not."

Krista, Marguerite, and Maxine continued to talk. Pandora went and sat in the forward passenger seat while Ramón drove. James and Ty were looking at something on the computer. Presumably they (and the other two) conversed silently.

What they discussed was evident when they presented their plan. I should say plans. Even though they were in many ways a unified mind they still had their differences. TY and James favored a bold, decisive and decidedly violent approach to retrieving Stephan from the cabin should he prove to be there. They wanted to have as much surprise on our side as possible. They wanted to offset any surprises Koenig may have. Even favoring this "go get 'em" attitude, the Guys were still bright enough to plan for reconnaissance.

"We want to get this right. We'll only get one chance," said Ty.

They had gotten floor plans and 3-d rendered topographical maps of the area of cabin. (Gotta love the Internet) If they could have gotten a live feed rather than goggle earth they'd have gotten it. I have no doubt that they would have succeeded with no or little damage to our team.

It would, however, put a real hurting on Koenig and her crew, possibly even killing some of them.

Hector knew I wouldn't like the guy's plan as it was. The other guys did too but Hector shared more of my outlook on violence. When Hector tried to explain it, Ty argued as follows,

"Yes, The boss wouldn't like handling things this way. But lets face it, he can do things we can not. We can't parade unnoticed through a room. We can't knock bullets out of the air. We sure as hell can't stop someone else's spell by unweaving it. If we want to stop someone saying a spell, we have to silence them and silence them with all haste. That may take drastic action on our part. We may need to counter their power with preemption. If Mr. Gives isn't right by the time action is needed, we'll have to do this our way."

"When the boss wakes up-," Hector said.

"If the boss wakes up," There was an uncomfortable lag before Ty added, "in time."

The discussion stalled there. Hector didn't have an alternate plan to propose. So there really wasn't anywhere else to go.

Marguerite pointed out that any plan was tentative until we were actually back in Virginia to implement it.

A lot could change crossing the country. Indeed it would.

Krista was dropped off at her house on the way. She gave Pandora a long hug before stepping out of the RV. She wished us well and said a quick "blessed be" to Maxine. Maxine had opted to remain with the team.

"Are you sure you know what you're doing?" Krista had asked Maxine. Maxine gave a little shake of her head and an apologetic smile.

"No, but my gut tells me to go this way."

Marguerite later said that, at first, she had a bad feeling about Maxine. It wasn't anything she could put a finger on. This bad feeling was also in direct contradiction to the sense Marguerite got from the Maxine herself.

Maxine seemed so genuinely eager to help that Marguerite couldn't help but grow to like her. That didn't mean she was ready to trust her completely.

"Still, sometimes, it's like getting a chill standing in the sunshine. The closer I looked at her, the nicer she seemed. But out of the corner of my eye there was something a little off."

At the moment, there were more immediate concerns. I still hadn't re-awoken and they needed to get back across the country quickly. Their only plan, so far, was to see where Azgard was leading them.

PART III

Chapter One

R AMÓN PULLED THE RV into the entrance of the Cascadia campground. He wound along the road until he came to the site where the Marianna came through from the east coast. The three tents were still there. I'm sure that broke campground rules. Hector and Azgard were parked next to the rings.

Ramón, Ty and, James got out of RV and began to walk around the edge of the campsite. The women joined Hector at the rings.

"They remind me of something from the book, the one Numis showed me," Maxine said. "The one that Arnold Scott bought from him."

"I bet this opens a gateway. I wonder how it works. Any ideas?" Hector asked.

Maxine took a deep breath, "Magic basically works through willpower. All the bells and whistles are just to help guide the will."

"You mean they're unnecessary?" asked Pandora.

"I wouldn't say that exactly. sure, maybe, some people can do it without the tools but it'd be like . . ."

"Trying to hit a home-run without a bat," Hector interrupted Maxine.

"I'd say it's more like trying to sew a stitch without a needle."

In the distance, James switched from pantomiming punching baseballs to sewing without a needle. This brought wry smiles to the team but not much else.

"So we need someone's will to awaken the rings," Marguerite said.

"Maybe, that or someone who can go through the motions to take advantage of any residual power," Maxine said.

"We could wake the boss up," Hector suggested.

Maxine walked a circle around the fire ring. "I don't know. I think Cascadia really messed him up somehow. Mistaking two different people for someone else . . ."

"You didn't seem to mind," Marguerite commented. Maxine didn't respond but she blushed subtly and looked back down at the rings

Pandora refocused the conversation, "Are there any clues to making this work?"

Marguerite closed her eyes and let her mind and senses wander, trying to get a picture of what transpired here. Maxine began a close examination of mystical traces. Pandora and the Guys began to look for more mundane clues.

Hector popped into the RV. They returned shortly with a camp map and brochure. Ty started to ask questions of Pandora. They were hoping something she remembered about Koenig would make more sense with our new information.

"Let's see. Koenig would show up every day for about two weeks. Then she'd be gone for a week or so."

Hector pointed out that there was a limit on how long someone could stay in the campground at a shot.

"Perhaps that explains Koenig's movements."

Marguerite guided the conversation to focusing on what could be pieced together.

"What else do we know?" she asked.

Hector spoke up, "It looks like the ritual she used involved fire. At least, fires were burned inside the rings." He thought for half a moment more, "Whatever ritual she used had to be quiet. It would still be during the campground's quiet hours. That is if she left here shortly before she arrived in Virginia. I doubt her trip was very long at all."

"She never looked like a person who had been up all night," Pandora said.

Ty traded places with Hector beside the fire ring. He stared at it intently.

"Maxine, do you notice that?" He pointed to some symbols along the inner ring of the metal circles.

"Yes, that's odd, everything else looks like western traditional alchemy, the little I know of it, but that looks like Chinese possibly Japanese."

"James says they're a mix. They're the five elements that Japanese alchemy recognizes. Wind, Earth, Water, Fire and Void but the characters are off. For instance that's the earth symbol favored in Chinese writing not Japanese."

Pandora was going through the items in the tents. "Hey, I found something," She called out. She brought out a small, clay teapot. It was marked by the Kanji for Water on one side, the Kanji for Earth on the other. It had a small, silk cloth attached to the spout by silken threads. The cloth was white with the symbol for Wind painted in blue dye on the fabric. On the bottom of the pot there was the symbol for Fire.

Ty looked at it. The rest of the guys came running in from their various lookout points. They stared at each other for just a second.

"I think we've got it," Ty said. "The ritual needed to be subtle right? Well, just how noticeable is making tea? It would be something ordinary. Up until that last instant, I bet it wouldn't look like much of anything."

"Make tea?" Marguerite said. "That simple? Something's missing here, I'm sure. What were the Japanese elements again?"

"Wind, Fire, Water, Earth, and Void," James said.

"Void? How do we indicate void? Maxine, would you help us do some research. I'm sure we can find something on the web."

Maxine began to search through various books in the RV's "library on disc." Ty surfed a few sites Maxine recommended.

Outside, Marguerite was now talking with somebody official with the park. The RV was too long for these campsites. Marguerite was assuring the person that we weren't staying. In fact the RV was leaving right then.

Whether it was mere coincidence or providence depends on what you believe, but it was at this point that I woke up.

Perhaps it wasn't completely coincidence, (if at all). I was passed out on the prayer mat in the RV's back room. Next to me were the storage areas for both the music discs and the digital library. So as Maxine sorted through for titles that looked promising, she was kneeling on the floor beside my head, murmuring the titles of the books and music. I had had the RV long enough that I was ruining Cominad's careful filing system.

I woke to her sweet and gentle voice saying, *"Ethiopian Book of Enoch, Dare to be Stupid, Precepts of Solomon, Johnny Cash 16 Biggest Hits . . ."*

It was a gentle, pleasant awakening, one of far too few in my life. For an instant, I deliberately tried to repress the question of why I was waking up next to Maxine. Then I realized that there were not very good (or at least fun) reasons why she would be there.

"Hey, put in the Muppet Movie Soundtrack," I said.

Chapter Two

MAXINE GAVE A LITTLE jump. Apparently I had startled her. Before anything else could be said, Ramón and Pandora reentered the RV with the intention of pulling it out of the campground.

Ramón plopped himself into the driver's seat. Pandora came back to check on me. As soon as she saw Maxine and me in close-quarters on the floor, Pandora withdrew quickly. I think she may have been blushing but that would seem out of character. I'm sure I saw her smiling.

At this point, all I remembered was dreaming that I had kissed Shelia twice or possibly two Shelia's one time each. It left me feeling a bit off balance. I hadn't had dreams like that for quite some time.

I got up from the prayer mat. My muscles and joints protested this highly ambitious movement. Maxine also stood up.

"Now that you're awake, you can help us figure Wendi's little puzzle."

Ramón cut in before I could ask, "What puzzle?"

"Boss, hop out. I'm going to take the RV over to the day use area. The rest of us will keep in touch with you through Hector."

A moment or so later, Maxine, Pandora, and I were gathered around the fire ring with Hector and Marguerite. James was keeping an eye on the campsite from a small distance. Apparently, the Guys have gotten a wee bit paranoid since we started our little adventure.

The gang filled me in on the teapot puzzle. I agreed that it looked like there was some way that the opening was invoked by using the marked items. But it left two short, Fire and Void

I looked around at the rings first with my normal senses. I didn't see anything that the others hadn't already caught. I saw the three rings set within each other with my bodily eyes. I got a better sense of them physically than I had before. Something gets lost in the translation when you look at the physical world through astral eyes.

I walked around the fire ring. I poked my head into the tent. I walked back over to the fire ring and looked at it with as open a mind as possible. It was then that I saw that the ashes in the ring weren't just ashes. There were tiny, minuscule, almost microscopic bits, No, call them flakes, of glass. The flakes were a gray blue, almost blending in with the rest of the ash.

"Hector?"

"Yes, Boss? (I've really got to get them to call me something else)

"What color were the glass bottles you saw in the storage shed?"

"Um, gray with a blue liquid inside them.

It was nothing I could put my finger on, but seeing the campsite in the flesh had helped me to put together how Koenig (or Scott or whatever you want to call her) might have worked the effect. In fact, it lead me into a series of speculations. If I had had more time in the M.E's office before Merton showed up, I may have been able to wrap up this case almost immediately. Or at least saved us a cross country trip (by car, anyway.)

"Okay gang, let's gather up what we have." Marguerite gave a funny look and handed the teapot with the silk cloth to me.

"Go for it." She said and started to tidy up the campsite from its minor disarray. James came up to the campsite. He was pushing a wheelbarrow full of firewood.

"I thought you were keeping an eye on the Campsite?" I said.

"I am. I'm also talking to the park service volunteers and deflecting their interest from what's going on right here."

"Fair enough." I turned my attention back to opening the "door." I would have been more comfortable if I knew for certain what was going to be on the other side of that door.

I looked at the assembled items, the inscribed teapot, the dyed piece of silk and the fire ring. It had come together for me, almost.

I pointed to the ideogram for fire. "Hector, I'd like you to get a knife or something and carve this character into the firewood." I handed Pandora the teapot and she went off to a nearby pump to fill it with water.

Marguerite picked up the wire grill from next to the fire ring and fit it into the inner most ring. She gave it a slight twist and there was a distinct clicking sound followed by a faint chime.

Hector asked me, "Should I carve the character on the length of the wood or on the ends?" I shrugged.

"Do what feels right?" I hadn't meant it to sound like a question but it's just what came out. "Of course, I don't think we have a lot of time."

"Got it," he said. He went to making the fire figure in quick strokes of the knife. It looked a lot like the combat knife that Merton had.

"Where did you get that?" I asked.

"Oh this, Merton threw that at us when we charged up the stairs to get the computer."

"Really, I missed that." Honestly I had. Of course I was a bit busy at the time.

"Luckily, so did he."

Hector looked like he was going for the quantity over quality route with the carving. He saw me looking at his work.

"I figure it's a pretty simple figure and that'd be easier to make a whole bunch rather than a few very ornate ones."

Maxine joined the conversation. "Magic is seldom about what's easiest. At least not good magic."

"You're right," I said, "but it's also about intention and symbols. I think that what Hector is doing should suffice. The trick I'm trying to figure out is 'void.'" How will we represent void?"

Maxine asked, "How did they?"

"I think it was done with the bottles of blue liquid somehow. I'm not sure how to replicate it. Or even if I should."

"Ty's telling me that void was sometimes thought of as sky or heaven."

"How is that different than air?" Pandora asked.

Japanese conception of the elements was certainly not my strong suit. So I just shrugged. That was getting to be a habit that was annoying even me.

"If they were using "Sky" that could explain the bottles of blue liquid."

"Liquid Sky?" Marguerite said. "What a terrible movie." when none of us seemed to know what she was talking about she called us all "infants" and went back to cleaning up the campsite.

I turned my attention back to the problem of the "door." Whatever the blue liquid was, I doubted we'd be able to find any. The team and I gave a pretty thorough search for some about the campsite just in case providence was going to prove us wrong.

It didn't. I hoped that meant it was saving up the help for when we really needed it. I also remembered that in my vision of the fire between each of the rings burned a different color. Difference in heat could do that. So could adding different powders and such. Given that there was at least one alchemist in their midst, a basic understanding of chemistry was not unfeasible. Surely, one of them would know what to add to change the colors of the fire.

Our search had turned up nothing but the teapot and cloth. Whatever else they used must have been used up already. Replicating someone else's effect without their tools is rather difficult.

Hector piled his "Fire" carved wood inside the rings. He laid the wood so that it formed another ring between the outer stone ring and the middle silvery ring. The slivery ring was only two feet across. And the ceramic one was only about a foot across. Hector had to break up some of the smaller bits of wood and fill in with kindling in the very center. Then he did something that surprised me. Instead of trying to carve tiny Fire characters on the twigs and kindling he tried to arrange them so they left a shape the general outline of "fire"

That's when I had two tiny insights. The first was that we were making our own ritual. I needed to be less concerned about what Koenig had done and start doing what was going to work for us. They had a ritual for invoking these particular elements. That needn't be the only way.

The second was I knew how I was going to invoke "void." "Really", I said to myself, "There's nothing to it."

The team made groaning noises when I told them that.

Chapter Three

I HAD EVERYONE GATHER INSIDE the tents to provide cover. Maxine set the filled teapot down on the small, metal grill that capped the ceramic circle. She used a kitchen match to light the innermost ring. Pandora took a small twig, lit that from the inner ring and lit the kindling of the middle ring. Marguerite deftly lit a candle from a middle circle twig. Hector had sprayed the ring of wood with some *Magic Start* lighter fluid. ("Hey, it couldn't hurt" he said) Marguerite used the candle to touch off the final ring of wood.

While the fire was being lit, I was getting myself in the right headspace. I sat in Azgard with the engine running and the windows open, listening to some carefully chosen tunes. I was listening to an mp3 playlist I had entitled *Synchronicity Freeway.* I stole the name from a comic book by Neil Gaiman. If he didn't coin the term, I don't know who did. The playlist was one of my more eclectic collections.

Once the fire was good and going, the rest of the team plus Maxine crammed themselves into Azgard with me. Azgard comfortably seats five. We had eight. Ramón, the largest, and Pandora, the smallest, shared the front passenger seat. They didn't seem to mind.

The back seat was a tight fit with five people. Marguerite sat on Ty's lap. Maxine was very thin but tall. She sat on Hectors lap, turned so her back was to the door and her legs stretched over James in the middle and up onto Marguerite's lap. Everyone was resigned to the fact that personal space was going to a luxury on this trip. That is if we ever managed to get on the road.

I had made the presumption that the door opened on to a road of some kind. I was conscious that it was dangerous to presume too much. It was a good bet though, Koenig had arrive by vehicle before. It wasn't too unlikely that there was some sort of road.

I said a short prayer and then let myself drift into the music while staring at the fire-ring. The mp3 player was moving through its playlist the Police's *Synchronicity* was first (the first one not part II) followed by *Moving Right Along* from the Muppet movie.

Perhaps the fire was very hot or the teapot was good at conducting heat or I just underestimated how long it would take for the water to boil, but suddenly I could hear a faint whistle starting. I knew that I had to switch from passive focus to active mode. I skipped ahead in my playlist until I found the song I wanted. Bruce Cockburn's *Understanding Nothing*

The escaping steam lifted the silk cloth. It went up on its short tether like a mini-parachute. I reached out and sensed the air above the fire rings and teapot. It was warm and wet from the steam. There was also the subtle thrum of power slowly stirring to life. I began to shape the figure for "Void" in my mind. I imagined it hovering above the silk cloth. Then I started to empty the image. It seemed to take forever. I pushed the air away from image.

That really let me know how considerable air pressure really is. Moving air was simple enough. Keeping air from rushing in to fill the gap was difficult. A minute or two passed and I was sweating like I was standing in the fire. The song was winding down. My vision was blurred from strain and sweat was in my eyes. Finally, at last, I had emptied a small area in the shape of the Void character. I held for as long as I could. I struggled to put Azgard into gear (Azgard's an automatic, but struggling to put a car into drive just sounds so lame.) I gave one short "hold on" warning to the team and gunned the engine.

There was no open doorway yet. I had emptied the area of the Void figure of all matter. While that might have qualified as a vacuum under a scientific definition, it was still full in a mystical definition. That is, it was full of will. My will. Only when I let my will go would there be true void there. It would last only for the time it took for air to rush back in. I was hoping that split instant would be enough.

I stomped the gas. We shot off. Azgard even gave us a little leap upwards. I dropped my hold on the effect and there was a small pop of miniature thunder as air refilled the empty space. In the instant before the pop, we were rewarded by a swirl of blue light. The blue light formed a cylinder around the fire rings. We shot headlong into it. We emerged from a cylinder of reddish light in a verdant forest almost the twin of the park we left. Only the trappings of humanity were all gone.

Now don't get me wrong. There was evidence of civilization. It just wasn't a human one.

As we came out of the cylinder of red light, we shot past two mounted figures. There was a road of sorts. Where there weren't trees, there were areas of tall grass. Most of the grass was a beautiful, deep green. Some of the grass was almost the color of gold. All of it was about three to five feet high. Some had already gone to seed. The golden grass formed a rudimentary path.

Azgard landed firmly in the middle of this path. We didn't wait around but just headed down the "road" before us. It stretched up past the forest towards the river.

"Follow the yellow grass road?" I asked aloud. Before any of my team could answer, the two mounted figures had caught up to us.

"Gentle mortals, we have be instructed to guide you." The two mounted figures were dressed identically. They wore a strange blending of traditional Native American garb and Elizabethan finery. The one who spoke came up around the driver's side. The other flanked us on the passenger side.

Their mounts were horses. The horses' coats were so black, I swear light just fell in. Their hooves and eyes were the color of bone.

The mounted figures themselves were clearly not human. I can't say they were animal headed. At least, they were not similar to any animals I ever knew. Their eyes and foreheads were human enough in shape. It was just below that, that the structural differences came. The "nose" bridged out into an almost geometrically triangular snout. The lower jaw extended past this a tiny bit with tusks the curled back and around again. Their skin was covered in feathery scales.

Of course, the creepiest part was that, despite having that mouth, the one who spoke sounded almost exactly like a posh accented, strangled cat. After hearing it speak, I wanted to listen to nails on a chalkboard to relax.

"We are instructed to guide any who come through," it said.

"Sorry," I said, "but we aren't part of the tour." I gunned the engine a little more to speed up. According to the speedometer, I was doing about 70 now. Azgard was staying dead center of the golden path. The two "guides" were keeping up with us easily. We came to an area where the tall grass petered out. Instead, the ground was covered by creeping ivy. The golden path was still there. It was now yellow ivy.

The two guides started to crowd the car. The one on the right lifted a hand, drawing it back like it was going the throw something. There was a flicker of lightning and in its hand there was bolt of electricity. The bolt itself was held aloft like a spear. Gotta love the Fay realms. Where else can someone hold a bolt of lightning in their hand?

Chapter Four

I DID THE ONLY THING that popped into my head. I swerved. Azgard rammed the legs of the horse. An ordinary horse would have been gravely injured. This horse just dumped its rider on the roof of the car. The guide rolled off the far side of the car and landed on the golden ivy below.

I took a grim satisfaction in that. In our world, I'd never have tried that. I don't like to use violence on any one that might actually die. For example, even if I could pull off that stunt of Cominad's in the food court, I wouldn't. I'd feel bad causing that much harm to a person. Fay creatures are generally so much more resilient that I was more concerned with staying alive than protecting them. I mean, it's not like I was smacking them with cold iron. Iron is to fairies what silver is to werewolves. I don't know why iron burns them but it does. Maybe it's a magnetic thing.

We were clear to one side of us. I intended to make the most of that. That meant breaking one of the cardinal rules for humans in Fay. I thought I should tell the team.

"Gang, you know how in fairy stories there's one thing you should never do but everyone seems to end up doing anyway?"

There was a mixture of assent and confusion.

"Could you be more specific?" Maxine asked. "There are lots. Don't eat the food. Don't take gifts . . ."

"The one about not leaving the path."

"Isn't that really bad. Like fatally bad?" the question came from one of the Guys. I couldn't tell which one. I wasn't paying close attention. I was too busy taking advantage of the lack of Mounted Guide.

We rolled out over the green ivy. Where were we headed? Don't rightly know. After all, this was an unfamiliar realm. I didn't know how it connected to our world. I suspected that there was an exit at the point that corresponded with that "park & ride" near highway 81.

Of course, just driving there was impossible. We didn't actually know which way to go.

What about the path? Well, that path wasn't set down by me or anyone I know. I maybe cynical but I think that it probably just led to an even worse trap than one we were escaping.

The still mounted monstrosity followed after us. It came around the car on the driver's side. The horse pulled up even with me so that the rider could easily look down into the car. The rider reached into the folds of its Elizabethan-American outfit. It pulled out a vintage 1930's luger. At least that's what the Guys told me later. I just knew it was a gun pointed at my head.

Again, I followed my instinct. I slammed on the brakes and started to turn the car to the left. The first result of this was that the bullet missed. It missed Azgard entirely thankfully. The next result was that Azgard tore through the back legs of the horse. Never fear, the horse was fine. At least, from the amount of cursing it did, I doubt we had done any permanent damage. The rider was thrown.

Azgard was in a spin. The sudden maneuvers on a thick carpet of ivy didn't do much for the traction. We slid, spinning, down a fairly steep hill

Eventually we stopped spinning. I wondered, "Are we out of the woods?" The sound of angry voices drifted over us and my heart sank. I looked for the source of the shouting. It was the two monstrous riders atop the hill arguing with their mounts. The horses were, it seems, not allowing the riders to remount. Lighting flashed around them, punctuating a point that the thunder drowned out.

The team agreed that this was the time to try to slip away. So as simply as that, we did.

Chapter Five

WE DROVE A SHORT way. Farther down the hill was a stream. The banks of the stream were nice, compacted sand. I've seen worse surfaces for driving.

Where we came in looked like an untamed version of the Cascadia campground in Oregon. Where we were now was anybody's guess.

"We need to find our own path," I said, "I'm sure we can call one up. It's just a question of focusing on the right thing."

"Well, we know there's an exit at the Park and Ride," Pandora said, "How about that?"

I tried to get a clear picture of the place, to really focus my thoughts on it. Nothing. I tried to enlist the help of everyone else. Most of the Virginia crowd had at least seen it from the highway at some time in their life.

Still nothing. I guess the place just didn't have the resonance for us that it must somehow have for Koenig. Maxine came up with an idea. "How about we use some other Virginia location." It wasn't a bad plan. Some place with resonance that wouldn't be too obvious coming out.

"Why not head straight for the cabin?" Hector asked.

"Cabin?"

"Don't you remember? We discovered that Koenig had fled to this cabin where you and your wife had honeymooned."

"I thought that was just a dream. Um, if that wasn't a dream does that mean . . ."

The laughter of the entire team was less than welcome right then. Unwelcome to me that is, it seemed to do them a world of good.

Ty let me off the hook. "We know you were in a weird dream state. You'll have to teach me that one, so I can go around getting away with just walking up and kissing women."

The plural there didn't really sink in. As I said, in my dream, I perceived both Maxine and Marguerite as Sheila, albeit at two different points in her life/unlife. My dream logic told me it was really only one person.

"So, um, whom did I kiss?"

In the back seat, James threw a hand up to his chest and cried out in mock anguish. "Oh how callous, to pretend as if he doesn't recall."

"Ha ha. You know that I'm not going to be baited about kissing a guy. I'm way too secure for that."

"How about an underage girl?" Pandora asked, and though I hate to say it, coquettishly.

I must have looked dismayed because once again the gang laughed aloud, releasing even more of the tension they were feeling.

"Don't worry," Maxine said, "you only kissed two thirds of the the adult, human women in the RV."

Then the plural hit me.

"Two thirds?"

"Well, just Maxine and myself," Marguerite said.

"Darn." I said.

"Darn?" This came simultaneously from Maxine and Marguerite.

"Look at it from my point of view. I kiss two different, attractive women and I only remember kissing my ex-wife."

This time we all laughed and no one pointed out that, technically, Shelia was my late wife not my ex-wife.

Amidst this laughter, I noticed something important. As we laughed, a path was becoming more and more distinct in front of us. I didn't know where it led. But it might be somewhere important to go. Soon the path became obvious. After all, it's hard to ignore when you go from a bumpy, jarring ride to smooth, well maintained roads (just make the trip south on I-81 across the Mason-Dixon line and you'll know what I mean)

The new road beneath us was cobblestone, so it wasn't all that smooth. It was just so much better than off- roading in a Volvo that was over twenty years old. The road curved away from the riverbank toward a forest. The cobblestones themselves were, anticlimactically enough, ordinary cobblestones. No yellow brick, No scattering of precious stones, there wasn't even an unearthly shade of red, reminiscent of fire, blood or sunsets. I tell you, some realms just let you down.

We followed the new road towards the forest. It wasn't like the Cascadia area. There wasn't a conifer in sight. Instead, there were only deciduous trees. They looked like they were straight out of a children's picture book. The deep brown trunks rose up from the ground with an unshakable symmetry. Each trunk branched up into a perfect sphere of jewel green leaves. They grew with a more exacting geometry than the fractal formed trees of our world.

The road wound among and under them. As we entered the forest proper, a hush fell over us. I couldn't say why we all fell silent. It seemed perfectly natural at the time.

After a few moments, we came to an intersection. At this intersection, there was a building on each corner. One looked like a small barn. Another was built like an old west jailhouse. In fact, all the buildings had an old west feel to them. The last two buildings at first looked like houses. As we got closer only one still looked like a home. The other was now clearly a saloon.

This "settlement" seemed out of place. I realize that is both an understatement and a redundancy. Old west style buildings set in deep forest at the cross roads of cobblestone streets, it could hardly get much odder.

Until a woman stepped out of the home and tried to wave us down as we went past. For a second, I felt like I was a child looking at a Richard Scarey drawing. The person who stepped out the house was a cat-headed woman wearing a calico dress and a red shawl. Like the mounted rider earlier, there was a geometric aspect to her. She looked as if she had a cat's head modeled on an icosahedron. She had pretty, reddish brown fur and a smile that even more greatly recalled the open, friendly illustrations of Mr. Scarey.

She was "yoo-hooing" at us while she waved a large, red checked handkerchief. She was carrying a picnic basket. Azgard stopped for reasons that I've yet to fully fathom.

The cat-headed woman gave off a serious schoolmarm vibe as she came up to the driver's window. I wanted to drive off but Azgard either wouldn't or couldn't budge. Sometimes you just have to play these scenes out. I rolled down the window to speak with her.

"Hello there, sonny. I have this basket of morsels for your young lady back there," She nodded toward Maxine.

"I'm sorry. We don't have anything to trade for them, perhaps we should do this another time," I said. It's a bad plan to take gifts from Fairies, doubly bad to eat fairy food. The conventional wisdom is that you could get trapped in the fay realms if you eat their food.

"Oh, this little parcel was bought and paid for a long time ago. It is free and clear her property. No obligation attaches to it, unless you want to pay me storage for holding on to it a little longer."

Do you remember what I've said about negotiating with fairies? We took the basket. It seemed the least inadvisable action at the moment.

The cat-marm handed the picnic basket to me. I passed it back to Maxine. Azgard's engine roared back to life. I smiled sweetly at the cat-marm. She returned it pleasantly and waved.

I hope we didn't seem rude as we burned rubber on the cobblestones leaving.

Maxine looked inside the picnic basket. I was about to warn everyone not to eat any of the "morsels" when Maxine gave out a little happy squeal.

"Books, it's filled with books," she said.

"Do you have any idea what this is about?" I asked her.

She thought for a moment. "Oh my god. Look it's a first edition *Alice's Adventures Underground, Five Children and IT,* and the rest of the Nesbitt books, It's my second wish." There was a girlish enthusiasm that rang like a bell in her voice.

"Look out for the magic prince," I said to her

"Aren't you afraid he'll whisk me away?"

I could see her smiling at me in the rear view mirror. I may have even blushed for a second, then I said, looking into her eyes, (via the mirror) "Let him try," I said quietly, "let him try."

"Maybe he could give us directions." Marguerite said

I saw what she meant, as we drove, we had come out of the forest and back into a grassland. A sort of Technicolor prairie greeted us. Imagine if the *Wizard of Oz* was reversed and Kansas was rendered in that unrelenting palette.

The further we, went the more the path petered out. Soon, we were just sitting in the middle of an open field. Overhead was a crisp, cerulean sky. The wind had an almost musical quality.

I stopped Azgard. Without a path, just driving wouldn't get us anywhere. Literally, we could end up treading ground like a swimmer treads water. There was even a real possibility that we could drown in this prairie sea.

Chapter Six

I WONDERED HOW TO REESTABLISH a path. I polled the team for suggestions. Hector pointed out that we were laughing and a path formed. We decided to try it again. It proved difficult to laugh on cue.

Ty tried a joke. "So, God is walking along the fence between heaven and hell and sees the fence needs to be repaired. He calls the devil over and says to the devil. "You haven't done your part of upkeep to this fence. Now get on it". The devil refuses.

"'Fine," says God, 'Then expect to hear from my lawyer.'

"'Where are you going to find a lawyer?' the devil asks"

No one laughed, not even me and I thought the joke was funny. It goes back to the laughing on cue problem.

Hector tried to make us laugh with impersonations. He did some famous people like the President and Arnold Schwarzenegger. He also did a fairly funny rendition of yours truly having a discussion with Ty. He held up his hands and used them as improvised puppets. He was pretty good. But the situation's grimness held sway.

As you can imagine, nothing happened. I got out of the car and walked around it. The rest of gang joined me in stretching their legs. No one needed to be reminded not to wander off.

"I feel as though I'm missing something. Something important here." The rest of the team echoed my sentiments. We each felt that the answer hovered just out of reach.

I stretch out my hands and looked heavenward. "Anything. A sign. A hint. A bit of encouragement." Hector came up beside me and looked up.

"Do you really expect an answer?"

"Of course, there's always an answer. It's recognizing it, that's the tricky part. Hell, We may already have the answer and we're just too short sighted to notice."

"That doesn't seem fair."

"Maybe. But we all need to learn somehow"

Hector sighed. "Oh, the Lima bean answer."

I looked at him quizzically.

"That's just a variation of the 'cause it's good for you' non-answer parents give. Is that what faith is? Believing suck answers?"

"No," I said, "Faith is more believing that you can make a better answer."

Hector let that soak in a minute. Then he stepped in even closer to me, lowered his voice to a hush and said,

"Since were kind of stuck for the moment, can I ask you a personal question?"

I shrugged, I'd have really preferred to talk to Maxine a bit more but apparently Marguerite was regaling the other two women with her tales of her "misspent, psychic youth."

The other three guys were dutifully watching the horizon for potential threats. "What's your question?"

"Do you really not remember kissing Marguerite or Maxine?"

Again, I shrugged. "In my dream, they were both my late wife. One of her was from right before our honeymoon, the other from . . . later." I trailed off. If Hector suspected how much later, he didn't say anything. He also didn't prod any farther.

He chuckled, thinking about my dream inspired actions. "It was the funniest thing. The music started playing and you just popped up and started kissing people. It's not even that great a song."

"Hey, that song was our song, mine and Sheila's. It was what we listened to right before we got to the cabin. That is, if I wasn't dreaming a different song from what was playing."

"Your song is a Statler Broghers' remake of a John Denver song?" He chuckled again.

"Hey, it's a great song, not to mention geographically correct, unlike that other version."

"Oh yeah," he said and he began to sing it aloud.

"I didn't know you knew it."

He broke off from singing for a second. The song seemed to linger in the air. "James has perfect pitch and we all seem to have a really good memory now. I bet we could do it in four parts."

As if to prove the point, all four guys raised their voices in song. And that's when it happened. About the middle of the fourth bar, an unseen accompaniment joined them. It sounded simultaneously like a harp and a banjo. With that invisible instrument, another change occurred.

The green, green grass in front of Azgard turned to a deep violet. There was a violet swath of grass that led from in front of Azgard, up the hill, and over the other side.

"Quick, everyone to the car. Guys keep singing, everyone join in."

Chapter Seven

IT WASN'T EASY TRYING to sing as we crammed ourselves back into the car. That didn't stop the Guys. Their voices remained clear and smooth, as did the road before us. We started to make rapid progress. We weren't even finished the second chorus before the violet grass became indigo cobblestone. The path led off towards the mountains. Soon the path took on the form of a modern roadway. (Less the congestion, of course.)

We merged on to a larger thoroughfare. It could have been any where in the United States, if it weren't for the unnaturally vibrant colors of the scenery. The roadway itself lost some of its Violet hue. It began to look more like an ordinary highway with the entrances and exits one would expect from a limited access highway.

It lacked the normal road signs however. Instead, the roadway had wordless markers in a variety of colors with directional arrows.

Eventually, we found ourselves on what, at home, would have been an interstate. A city skyline appeared on the horizon. Other travelers shared the road with us. Most of them seemed to be geometric animal headed people in various cars and car-like conveyances. There was one exception. A man driving an antique Nash Rambler passed us. The driver looked human. He also looked like he could have stepped out of some fifties Noir film. He waved at us, smiled briefly then took an off-ramp marked with a deep jewel-toned emerald. I figure he was another magus with issues of his own to deal with. Though I wondered who he was, I was mostly relieved he was not part of Koenig's crew.

I navigated traffic while the rest of the team sang. Between the seven of them, they always kept up at least a four-part harmony. It may have been some aspect of the realm that aided them because Pandora said that she had never been able to carry a tune in her life before, let alone harmonize like that.

What ever it was, I was grateful. Once we were past the city, we finally left the Technicolor plains and headed back into a mountainous region. It wasn't very long after that that we made a turn south, assuming the sun's path ran east to west in this world. After that, the path markers led us from the main highway onto a smaller, secondary road that ran parallel to the highway. Small towns started to spring up along the side of the road. The towns were comprised of wispy, ghostlike structures. They were more like imprints in the air than anything actually there.

"I think were getting closer. I think those building are in our world."

"Oh, my god," Pandora exclaimed, "This is route 11."

"11?" Maxine asked.

Maxine asked.

"It's the old highway running north-south. It was a major thoroughfare before interstate 81 was built. It still runs parallel to 81 much of the way." Marguerite explained.

"It's also where the park-n-ride where I first saw Koenig's Jekyll disappear is located," Pandora pointed out.

We approached an intersection. A path marker with a very large arrow directed us to turn. Even before we made the turn, we saw an open, paved area that had an violet octagon on a post.

We pulled into the area. The guys stopped singing.

"I think this is the other side of the park-n-ride," I said. "I wonder why the path led here. I would have expected it to take us to the cabin."

"Perhaps it's because we all sang," Hector said, "The cabin only has meaning for you but the park-n-ride has connections to the all of us through the case. Plus," he added, "it might be the path of least resistance."

He had a point. I made a mental note to talk to Hector about his instinctive grasp of magical theory. But we had more immediate concerns. I addressed Azgard and gave his dashboard a little rub.

"Azgard, do your thing." The scene around us didn't so much fade as return to normal colors. Getting out the car, we could all feel that we were back. I don't know if I've ever been more grateful to look out onto the gentle green hills of Virginia.

"Hey, my cell's got signal again. It's even updated the time." James said.

"What time is it?" I actually dreaded the answer. I was more concerned about what day it was. Time being so fluid in the spirit realms.

"Well, we left at about 8: 15 AM Pacific time and it's now 11:18 Eastern and clearly morning not night. So, taking in account the date and adjusting for the time zone difference . . ." James smiled mischievously. "Our trip took us 3 minutes."

A thousand miles a minute, I hope Mister Ehst, my old Driver's Ed. teacher, never hears about that.

Chapter Eight

Our trip through Fairyland hadn't passed at the same subjective rate for all of us. I felt we had been there maybe an hour to and hour and a half. Marguerite felt it had been about a four-hour trip. The Guys said that for them, our journey passed very much like a dream. It seemed to take forever at the time but even now the details were fading.

Maxine said that it felt like ten minutes with fully half the time being in the forest where she received the books. Pandora said she couldn't remember anything between when we drove through the gate back in Oregon until just then.

"Well, one thing I can remember. We were telling jokes. I just don't recall any." She added, "I feel like I haven't eaten for days."

We were discussing the prospects of food when Pandora spotted something that was staring us in the face. Over at the edge of the park-n ride was a car. It was the car that she had seen that first day she followed Koenig.

I approached the car slowly. I spun the wheel of sight. Immediately I regretted it. If you recall, I tried to scry on this location before. My view was blocked by some kind of major blessing. I said it was strong enough that it might have blinded me up close. In my haste to check out the car, I forgot that. I was right. The blessing was blinding. My vision was flooded by an overwhelming beauty and wholeness.

I dropped to my knees. All else was lost to me, save for a sense of joy and wonder at just being. For an instant, I felt as if everything made sense and the world fit together in the most astounding way. The sky above shone with a blue that was unassailable in it's perfection. The trees surrounding the parking lot were the utter truth of every forest, ever.

It was like catching a glimpse of heaven. But you know what they say, it's a nice place to visit, but I wouldn't want to live there. Or I couldn't, not yet. There was work to be done.

I turned off my Sight as soon as I managed to pull myself together. I really need to find out why this place was so blessed. I couldn't tell that much about the details for much the same reason that looking directly at a light source often obscures it shape.

As interested as I am in that, I had to put it on the back burner. I walked up to the car. I hoped there weren't any wards or enchantments that I might trigger. The car itself was a modest one. One of those small Hondas, blue-gray in color. I opened the driver's door. No problems, thankfully.

I wondered why the car was here. I called over to the gang that I thought things were safe. Hector and Ty joined me

"What do think? Why is this still here?" I asked.

"Well, it was a few days before the cops started dismantling Koenig's operation. She probably commuted in from Oregon and then didn't make it back here," Ty said.

Hector added, "Remember, you said that her Jekyll form came through on her own. No car or anything like that."

This was true.

We searched the car. In the back seat was a small duffel bag with a set of casual clothes, jeans and some t-shirts. They looked to be sized for Marianna not Koenig.

Then in the glove box we hit pay dirt. Marianna kept a journal. It was journal of her trips into a fairy realm.

A quick skim showed that it was indeed the one we had just come through. Each entry was headed both by the date and a day number. The last entry was two days after we handed the server over to the police. It only took them two days to begin dismantling Koenig's empire. That explained why the car was still here. No one had come to move it. Koenig's flunkies were busy with problems of their own.

Given how I saw Marianna arrive in Oregon looking rather roughed up, I imagine she also had had a particularly bad time of it, possibly both as Koenig and as Marianna.

I took the notebooks over the rest of the team. It was Pandora who noticed something rather important. "Look here. This one's dated three weeks ago. That's the night before I realized that Stephan was actually gone." She pointed to an entry.

May 29 Day 1478:

I met Numis in the City of the Plains today. We met at Sapphire's for tea. He brought a friend with him. His name is Stephan. Apparently, he is the darling of the local Fair Folk. I certainly have never seen them flutter or hover over anyone quite like that before. Sapphire, herself, came out and attended to his order.

I don't know why exactly. He looks human enough, certainly not like any of the local populace.

Numis told me the boy's tale. It horrified me. The boy was imprisoned as some sort of sex worker. In the United States, no less. Numis said that the boy had found a way to contact the folks of this realm. For some reason, one of the crossing points is near where he was held captive.

The boy had seen one of the Fay following a foul woman he called Koenig, the leader of his captors, he called out to it. The fairy, surprised it could be seen, stopped and listened to the boy's story. This same fairy came back later and helped the boy escape. The fairy took him to Numis, who then brought him here.

Numis asked me for a favor. He wanted the boy, Stephan, to come and live with Arnold and me. Moved as I was by Stephan's plight, I wasn't sure I could help, or more accurately, that Wendi wouldn't muck it up somehow.

I asked Numis why the boy couldn't stay here. The Fay seemed to be rather enamored of him. He said that Fay realms were no place for a young boy. He needs a stable home in the real world. I couldn't say "no," could I? After all, from what they tell me, the people who held him are truly despicable. At least, they are operating only on the east coast. It seems unlikely that they could pursue him through this realm to the other side of the country. I agreed to take him. I even cut short my normal 8 hours of exploration.

Oh. My. God. Marianna really doesn't know. Stephan doesn't know. Poor Stephan. His "fairy savior" turned him over to the architect of his problems and he doesn't even know. His grand escape has just led to a different kind of exploitation. Numis and Koenig would not have missed the value of some who was living fairy nip. This could be quite tricky rescuing him. After all how do you rescue someone from his rescuers?

Chapter Nine

A QUICK SAMPLING OF THE rest of the entries revealed that Marianna was an explorer of sorts. She had traveled many places in the realm of the geometric animal heads. She had even been to the four building, old west town in the forest.

"Sapphire's" it seems was a teahouse. It was a favorite place for Marianna to go. I wish I could have read more of the journal. I was painfully interrupted. You see, the car hadn't been left accidentally. It had been left as bait.

The paved area of the park and ride erupted. Chunks of asphalt flew upward. The chunks didn't fly outward like they should from an explosion. Instead, they clung together like they were magnetized. The chunks formed a hulking, vaguely human shape about twice the height of a person.

There was a head-like mass with no facial features on top of a clump of a body. It had two rudimentary arms. The lower body was just a solid base extending up from the ground. To tell the truth, a kindergartner could have made a better person in play-dough.

Of course, most of them couldn't have made a play-dough person that could wallop me across the length of the Park 'n' Ride. I landed out in the middle of the road. While I was busy coughing up blood, the Asphalt Mass picked up Azgard and smashed it head on into the ground.

I'm not sure which hurt me worse at the time. The mass picked Azgard up again. It held Azgard like a club. The rest of the team scattered before it could play road-golf with them. The Asphalt Mass then stopped then spun around as if looking for something. It may have been. Soon it began to move directly toward Pandora.

Ramón scooped Pandora over his shoulder and began to run away from the mass. The other three Guys dropped where they were. Ramón was blurring into the distance. Of course, the blurring may have been just me and my concussion.

The Asphalt Mass followed after them. "Splashing" up the parking lot like a wader does water. None of the debris struck any of the team, thankfully.

Pandora had shifted her weight so that Ramón had the easiest time carrying her. They veered off the roadway into the woods beyond. It was an instinctive move to be sure. It was also the right one.

When the Asphalt Mass reached the far side of the road, it tried to follow into the natural soil. It teetered like a drunken linebacker and fell over. It lay still when it hit the ground. It was reduced to a massive mound of asphalt and dirt. There was even a bit of mud oozing from it, like blood from a wound.

Speaking of which, back at the Park 'n' Ride, I continued coughing up blood. My body was futilely trying to clear blood out of my punctured lung. Maxine and Marguerite knelt beside me. They were at a loss for what to do. I coughed again. The rib that was digging into my left lung, cut deeper. I looked around vaguely wondering if there were any bits of my gray matter lying about.

I was in bad shape. They say a boy scout is always prepared. Sadly, I'm no boy scout. I am, in my way, an opportunist. That is, I try to look for the opportunity in a crisis. After all, they say God moves in mysterious ways, I say God is one right tricky bastard. Luckily, He's a bastard who continues to believe that anything, anyone, any situation is redeemable.

Case in point. I was lying in a pool of my own vomited blood. My incredibly strong bones had met their master in the Asphalt Mass. I was broken beyond even my own natural and supernatural ability to repair. It was taking all my excess stored life-energy just to keep myself alive. I didn't have any left over to begin the healing process. If I didn't find an answer I would run dry and then I would die.

There was an effect that I knew that could save my life. It was developed in India to help those who had been grievously wounded by elephant trampling. The main component took days to make so the magi who developed the effect always made sure he had a completed one, just in case. Now, that guy could have been a boy scout. The effect requires a large human shaped shell of enchanted earth to encase the wounded person.

"How providential," I thought.

I forced myself to turn over and begin crawling over to the asphalt mass. I made it about a yard. I collapsed. I looked little more than bloody rags and hamburger. I had nothing more to give.

At first Maxine tried to help me. She couldn't budge me. That hidden extra mass I was so fond off was suddenly a liability. Then Maxine and Marguerite both helped to drag me over to the mass. This was only slightly less painful than crawling over myself. Any paramedics reading this knows how much extra damage was being done to me. With this extra damage, I wasn't going to make.

It was a classic loose/loose situation. If left alone, I'd die as my strength ran out. If they continued to drag me, the new wounds would kill me quicker.

I refused to admit defeat. My frustration turned to rage. I twitched my fist at the sky. (It was the best I could muster)

"I refuse this death," I spat out with some blood, "If you want this task seen through, you'd better pony up some help."

I tried to look at Marguerite and Maxine. Too much blood had run into my eyes and I couldn't see clearly. I thought I was looking at one of them when I felt a woman's arms reach down around me. She lifted me like I was a child. Carefully, gently, she carried me over to the mound of dirt, asphalt and clay. It looked more like a waiting grave than a source of hope. She set me down on top of the mass.

I had no time to loose. I started to work the effect even before I knew what angel had carried me. I began to repeat over and over *Chi L'allam Chestoh* in Hebrew then in English, "His steadfast love endures forever."

In my own blood, I wrote the Tetragramton, the four letter Hebrew abbreviation for The Name of God, on my own hijacked Golem[23]. On my forehead, I wrote "Ehud"(he that praises) then I collapsed on the mass and began to merge into it. Before the earth covered over my eyes, I caught an uncertain, blurry glimpse of curly, brown hair and golden eyes.

The irony was not lost on me, like I said, *"One right tricky bastard."*

Once the merger was complete, I could stand up. Much of the excess mass fell away. What was left was much shorter. The Asphalt Mass looked more human with me at its center. Over all, my new "armor" was about seven feet tall and proportioned like a professional wrestler.

---

[23]   I realize that technically it wasn't a Golem but it was close enough.

How does encasing myself in asphalt, dirt, and mud help me heal up? That's a good question. I was using the asphalt full body cast as a life support system. It wasn't just that it formed a protective shell. It's that it was mystically animated. That takes a lot of energy. Enough energy that some of it will bleed off. Essentially, I was living off the residual animation. This left me free to use my own life energy to heal myself.

Though it saved my life, merging with the mass left me quite limited in other ways. The only senses I had were the senses available to the mass. Whoever conjured it originally had given it only a rudimentary set of senses. My vision seemed to be entirely based on tracking prey. My hearing was muffled. I heard noise but details were lost.

I tried to look around for the person I could only assume was Shelia. I could tell that two people were there with me. I could feel their living energies. I felt the living trees nearby, as well as an insect or two in the air. There was also the muted "glow" of the three Guys as they spent their time *elsewhere*. I could also see the earth, rock and metal that were now strewn about the Park 'n' Ride.

What I couldn't see was Shelia. Nor could I sense where Azgard was. Where I expected to find a crumpled lump of metal there was nothing. I hoped that was a good sign somehow

I think Maxine might have been talking to me. It sounded like her voice and I could tell exactly where she was. I had no ability to discern what she was saying.

I tried to speak but my voice was made unintelligible by the layers of muck around me. I knelt down and tried writing in the leftover dirt at my feet. Even I couldn't read what I was trying to write.

Being encased in asphalt had it's own problems. I started back towards the park-n-ride lot. I tried to cut across the shoulder of the road and the small grassy strip. I stopped dead at the edge of the paving.

Now I knew why the Asphalt Golem fell. It ran up against the edge of its reality but had too much mass to stop. As far as it was concerned, it tripped over a low wall into nothingness. There was no more world for it. Had it been a truly aware being, I would have felt sorry for it.

"Amateurs," I thought. Annoyed at this minor inconvenience, I walked the extra few feet down the road to the proper lot entrance. As I walked I almost lost track of what I was doing. My mind wandered through a hundred subjects. Time seemed to flow in fits and starts. One step took forever, the next five done before I was done wondering why the first step took so long. I don't know if that was a result of being in the Asphalt Mass or from my massive injuries. My muted senses where a mixed blessing. I wasn't exactly sure what was happening but at least the pain wasn't overwhelming.

Even with my muted senses, I noticed just how badly the lot was torn up. I wondered whose tax burden just went up. Was it the whole state or just the locals? Was I registered to vote at my address? I wondered if I could get my old place back. I wondered when the last time they paved the roads around here.

As I pondered all that, a strange sensation came over me. I had the urge to squash my friends. Perhaps urge is too strong. It was more like a little voice in the back of my mind. Speaking not so much in words but in base impulses.

I looked over at my friends. The three remaining Guys had stood back up. They stood talking with Marguerite and Maxine. Ty noticed my interest and asked "Boss, is everything Okay?" Or so I was told later. At the time, it was just a nonsensical squeaking

I lifted my club-like hand experimentally. I felt the strength inherent in the form. Sure enough, I could probably squish the life right out him. But it just seemed pointless to do so. Why was I even thinking about it?

It occurred to me then that whoever had called up the Asphalt Mass was still trying to control it. They were still expecting to have a mindless automaton so the force of control was weak.

Though I was sure that in a contest of wills, I could cream whoever built this shoddy golem-wannabe, I am not one for unnecessary risks. I still needed at least an hour in the "suit" before I could even think staying alive on my own. So before I came close to pulping my dear good and loyal friends, I ran. I couldn't explain what I was trying to do. I just did it and prayed for the best.

I moved out of the lot and back onto the road. I tried to home in on the control signal but it was too diffuse. Whoever had set this up must not actually be keeping tabs on it directly. I opted to run down 11 south toward the 'Burg. Instinct I suppose. I wish it had been later evening so I would have not been so visible. Once the golem's maker had realized that I had hijacked it, he would be coming after me fairly quickly.

Over all, he caught on and caught up pretty fast. It was only about five minutes before Arnold Scott and one of Koenig's flunkies came roaring up beside me. Scott leaned out the passenger side window and held a talisman up towards me. He was using it to focus his will into a command to turn around.

I resisted the command by stopping in my tracks and pounding the ground. Scott was lucky I'm as committed to non-violence as I am. Otherwise, I might have channeled his command to different ends.

Scott redoubled his effort at control. I don't know if he realized I was inside the mass or thought I had merely taken it remotely.

With each of Scott's attempt to command the Mass, my fight to not destroy was becoming increasingly painful. This time I resisted by using the Mass's ability to merge with the ground.

I sunk my arms into the roadway then poured the rest of me in after them. I was able to keep track of the events topside through the Mass's rudimentary senses. I could tell basic shapes above me as long as they were on or right above the roadway.

Azgard suddenly reappeared. I knew it was Azgard. After all, it was a big hunk of metal that glowed with life. I could feel it hurtling down the road from at least a mile off.

It rammed Scott's car from behind. Hitting one of the rear wheels in a way that caused it to suddenly flip around and face the way it had come.

I wasn't sure who was driving Azgard. I couldn't sense anyone behind the wheel. One of the guys leaped out through one of Azgard's windows onto Scott's car. Then he flipped and did a feet first dive into Scott, driving him back into his car and following in after him. I know the Guys can only achieve that fluidity of movement through their four-way focus.

I couldn't see what was happening inside the cars. All I know was that a second or so later, Providence once again smiled on us. Scott's talisman came flying out the window. Later, the Guys said it was an accident really. They had just been trying to subdue Scott and the driver.

Didn't matter. Without the talisman, Scott could not control the Mass. With it, I could make the Mass do things Scott hadn't dreamed of yet.

Chapter Ten

AT THE TIME, THE sensation of flowing through the ground wasn't at all disturbing. When I recall it now, I come close to loosing my lunch.

I reached up through the ground and "grabbed" the talisman with the club that passed for my left hand. The talisman sank into the dirt of the club and reached my hand. As it did, my senses exploded. It was like looking at myself in a mirror with a mirror behind me. It took me a second to adjust for the feedback. Once I did, I was able to "see" a heck of lot better.

I oozed up from the ground. With the talisman in my hand, I was able to perceive myself well enough to trim the mass into a much more usable form. For example, I shaped workable fingers. I could also form eyes capable of distinguishing between one person and another.

I could now see just how crumpled Azgard's front end was. The Asphalt Mass had slammed it into the ground hard enough to shorten the car's length by more than a foot. I doubt an ordinary car could still be moving.

Both cars came to a stop around me. Ramón threw the driver of Scott's car out of the door in front of him. The driver was a man in his late twenties of lithe build and sinewy muscle. Ramón followed him, dragging Arnold Scott. Shelia rushed out from the driver's side of Azgard and made some sort of humming noise. Both the driver and Scott went glassy eyed. Though to give him credit, Scott resisted the effect longer. He lasted almost twice as long as the driver.

Shelia, and Ramón gathered around the two. Ramón began questioning them. I realized I still couldn't understand human speech even with the talisman.

"Where's Pandora?" I tried to ask. When I spoke I was just as incapable of being articulate as I was of understanding. No surprise there but I had to try.

I tried to write something in gravel of the shoulder but I couldn't remember how to form the letters I needed. The others were busy interrogating Scott and the driver. I didn't even bother showing them my worse-than- chicken-scratches.

Even holding the talisman, I didn't have a good sense of time. I suppose that rocks generally don't. The questioning continued. Scott and his flunky were answering whatever questions were put to them. The answers didn't seem to please the team

Suddenly Hector, James and Ty were there looking worried. Ramón had taken Azgard and gone back to the park and ride to fetch the others.

Hector ran over to me and made motions at me, trying in a futile attempt to communicate more than the obvious emotion.

He and the rest of the Guys piled back into Azgard and headed off. This left Marguerite, Maxine, Shelia, and me standing there with our captives.

Or so I thought. Maxine had already grabbed the keys from the ensorcelled driver and was heading around to the driver's side. Marguerite herded Scott and the driver into the back of the car. She got in the front passenger seat and did her best to close the door.

Even after a second reshaping, the Mass and I were too big to fit inside the car. I stood there stupidly, feeling useless. Maxine pulled the car around. The damage to the car from Azgard's hit was considerable but not crippling. Maxine barked at me, then sped away. I have no idea what she said but I decided I should follow as best I could. I turned to Shelia, whom I could only sense with my eyes. Actually that's not entirely true. There was a tiny, tiny glow there that flickered like a lighter low on butane. She didn't say anything to me. I couldn't say anything to her.

I just left her there as I leapt to follow after Maxine.

Chapter Eleven

THE SCENERY BLURRED AROUND me. I not only kept up with Maxine and Marguerite, I passed them and caught up to Azgard and the Guys. I may not have been able to leave the road, but in it's element, the mass was hard to beat. Looking back I'm just glad it was dumb enough to try to run across its boundaries.

Thinking about it, the Mass wasn't stupid, just mindless. Like a machine, it could only follow its programing. Scott was the stupid one. He tried to force the mass outside its natural boundaries. I mean you wouldn't send a fire elemental to retrieve a submarine, would you?[24]

Once again, we reach a part of the story that would look really cool in a movie. Two cars careening headlong into danger with an unearthly, if rather earthy, monster following close behind them.

The cars would cut through corners and fields to skirt the traffic. There wasn't that much traffic really, but you know Hollywood would add a jump here or there.

Ironically, I did the jumping. I found that though I couldn't step off a roadway, I could cut the corners off an intersection by jumping from one road to the other. As long as I could see the road I wanted to be on, I could move some serious distance.

I was able to get ahead of the cars whenever we came to a hill. I'd leap to the top of the hill and then down it about a half-mile. I don't think I should have been doing this in middle of the day. There were a few witnesses here

---

[24] If you don't know the answer to that, may I recommend *Elemental Operational Parameters or How to Avoid Drowning Yourself in a Fountain of Superheated Mud* CC # 641

and there. I think that may have resulted in some drug testing and/or urban legends.

Eventually, the cars reached a point where I could not go. Azgard and Maxine's purloined car turned up a private driveway. It was one of those long, country driveways that curled back into a wooded area. The woods partially hid a house from the road. I was alert enough not to assume that a driveway was the same as a road. So I gave it a test. Right at the end of the drive there was line that was at once thinner than a razor's edge and as thick as a world. I simply could not cross it.

I sat down and waited for something to happen. I didn't have to wait long. From out of the woods around the house, a mounted figure appeared. He was wearing the kind of full plate armor that you only see in storybooks. The armor gleamed in gold and platinum hues. The figure was astride a giant, golden boar. Whoever he was, he had a lance that gleamed like white-hot flame.

He carried it over one arm. In the other arm, he carried Pandora.

The boar leapt across the road, clearing it easily. When the Boar and Rider were mid-leap they came quite close to me. The Rider rammed his lance into the body of the Asphalt Mass, shouting, "This is for my sister!"

The lance struck me and exploded. It left a crater in the asphalt shell and sent me sprawling. The crater was not quite deep enough to reach me. It was still uncomfortably close

The boar landed in the field on the other side of the road. They didn't look back to see how I had fared after the attack. Thank heaven for little favors.

They rode off toward the woods on the far side of the field. The woods were only fifty yards from the road. they looked like they were getting farther and farther away until they vanished, miles into the distance. They, however, never made to the trees on the far side of the field.

It may seem hypocritical of me to say, but some days I just hate magic.

Chapter Twelve

M_Y SENSE OF TIME_ was distorted all to hell as I waited in my asphalt shell. I don't actually know how long I waited. It gave me a little time to piece events together. Shelia had shown up, obviously, and bailed my ass out of the fire. I still didn't know exactly why, so I was real tempted to look that gift horse in the mouth.

Never the less, once she had placed me atop the Asphalt Mass, she righted Azgard and driven it off to find Ramón and Pandora. Once she did, she must have stashed Pandora here in the woods near this house. Then she brought Ramón back to help bring down Scott and his accomplice.

Once Arnold Scott and his driver were stopped, the Guys must have realized in what a precarious situation they had left Pandora. They rushed off to get her. They were only a few seconds too late.

Eventually the team came out. They were carrying Ramón. Even my muffled hearing could tell he was moaning in pain. The team got into the cars again and pulled away.

I followed the two cars. When we stopped again, we were in the parking lot of a small tavern not to far from the Virginia/West Virginia border. Marguerite got out of the "borrowed." car. The rest of the team gathered around her. It certainly looked like she had taken charge of things.

Scott and the driver seemed to be out of Shelia's mind altering enchantment now. Their body language suggested that they were resigned to the situation.

Marguerite walked over to me and began talking. At first she sounded like an adult speaking in those old Charlie Brown specials. Then little by little a word or phrase would become intelligible.

Marguerite spoke, "Mwa-mwamwa, mwa mwa Get out of that . . .Mwa mwa . . ... and get back on traw mwa mwa. You big mwa mwa mwa.

320

And then, with only that much warning, the asphalt armor flaked off me. It crumbled, if not so much to dust, then to gravel. I had used up all the energy in the Asphalt Mass it seems. I was back to staying alive on my own. Fortunately, I had reached a point where that was only painful not impossible.

I took a breath, my chest hurt. I still had a broken rib but it wasn't puncturing a lung anymore.

"Glad to see your back, boss. Now maybe we can get back to work." This came from a very bruised looking Ramón. I'm taking it as a vote of confidence that they didn't seem worried about the extreme measures I had taken to stay alive.

Or maybe they just didn't know how close to death I was. Right then was not the time to tell them. Ramón was right. We had work to do.

I really wanted to talk to our "guests." No disrespect to the rest of the team but I think I knew more of the right questions to ask. I turned to go talk to Scott. He saw me look at him. Our eyes met for a split second. That resigned look disappeared. It was replaced by fear.

Seeing the fear come into his face made me uncomfortable. Actually watching his fear rise was grimly satisfying. It was my satisfaction that made me uncomfortable. For a second, I questioned if the fear in his eyes might not be justified.

Then I realized it was.

I didn't know how much power Scott actually wielded. He had made some impressive stuff. But it all seemed like he was working from a formulated approach.

My own will working is far more fluid. That gave me a real advantage. Yes, our search had been frustrating and difficult. When I looked at it from his point of view, it must have been terrifying.

No matter what he did, he could only slow us down. He had thrown everything he had at my team and myself and we still were there. If he believed what Numis had told Koenig in her Marianna form, he must be scared shitless. He looked as though he expected to die.

I still had trouble gathering much sympathy for him.

"Arnold Scott, it's long past time we actually talked."

He gave a wry smile; at least it was at first. The smile quickly soured into a grimace. After that he gave a little shrug. He wasn't smiling as much as he was baring his teeth.

It wasn't a snarl. It was Scott showing us what was written on his teeth. One didn't need to know ancient Greek to recognize that there was a spell detailed there. It looked painted on.

The driver spoke up at this time. "He can't talk. At least not about anything you'd ask."

"And you?" I asked.

"I don't know anything useful. Really that's why I'm here. I was just supposed to drive."

"Okay then you won't mind answering the things you do know about."

"Won't do you any good."

"So what's your name?"

"You think I'm stupid, I'm not giving you that."

"Why not?"

"You're a Magician, right? Scott here said that you could use that against me. He says you could do worse than ratting me out to the police.

I didn't think asking for his name would work. Still, it told me about how much this guy really knew about what was happening. He must have seen enough to trust Scott about the name thing

I wouldn't have used his own name against him. Using someone's name like that . . . that's just one of the most serious violations one person can inflict on another..

"Something to call you then. How about that?"

He hemmed and hawed a bit seeming to to try to think of something appropriate. It dawned on me he was stalling for time. Call me 'Reynard'." He said Reynard with a French accent.

Before he said any more, Maxine spoke up. "Hey, this tooth paint should just brush off.",

She addressed Scott directly, "What is this stuff 'Nudent?' How'd you get such fine application work done?"

Scott spoke; I was surprised at the calmness in his voice, "What can I say? I have a gift."

It hit me. All that fear that was there just a moment ago had vanished. Hell, he looked like he was even trying to contain his glee.

"So what gives, a moment ago I could see the fear in your eyes. Now you look like your trying not to jump for joy."

"Well that's because we've won."

"I see. How's that?"

"We got the girl. And any second now you'll be getting a visit from her brother's friends."

"Oh great." I thought, "more fairies. Team, back in Azgard. We've got inbound."

Scott actually snorted. "That won't help once the sister points them in the right direction. They'll be on you in short order."

"Really? Why would she do that?" I asked

"Stephan says she was always a bit vindictive. You can't imagine she won't want revenge after what you've done, do you?"

"Revenge? Against *us?*" I started laughing. Then it occurred to me that may not help the discussion. So I tried another tactic for a minute. The rest of the gang was already in Azgard. They were giving me that, "hey, are we going or not?" look.

"How much do you know about Koenig's operation." I asked him.

"Enough to know that your lot is responsible for some pretty unspeakable crimes."

I shook my head and didn't know whether to laugh or cry. I may have done a little of both. Scott noticed this.

"Don't laugh this off, Stephan has sworn to annihilate Koenig and all those connected to her."

Now that broke my heart, "I hope not, I really, truly, hope not."

I jumped in to Azgard and sped away. As soon as we made it around the curve of the road, I did a u-turn and threw up a quick cloak around Azgard. We pulled back into the tavern parking lot. We watched as Scott and Reynard plucked an extra key from a magnetic carrying case hidden under the car.

Scott seemed almost gleeful as they drove. He was talking animatedly. Reynard looked pensive and just nodded to whatever Scott was saying to him.

We followed. I started thinking about that first time I saw Arnold Scott, back when I thought he was just another flunky of Koenig's. He seemed so different in my apartment holding a knife on the ghost. That first time he was so grim and ruthless. He cut the throat of what seemed a young man rather coldly and efficiently.

The next time, he was so concerned for Koenig's Jekyll form, Marianna, it was touching.

Now, he seemed to be placing himself in the good guy category with no association with Koenig.

I replayed that first meeting again in my mind. It was the one that stands out as odd in retrospect. I saw him there again, his knife to the ghost's throat. His dark suit matching his grim visage as he stood placidly, more a tool of Koenig's will than a person. The only real personalizing effect was his tie clip. His tie-clip that looked like it was made from an old quarter.

In the words of the immortal Homer, "D'oh!"

That first meeting wasn't with Koenig and Scott. It was really Koenig and Numis. Numis is the one the Ghost swallowed. Whether or not that would have been fatal to the real Arnold Scott, it was only a minor inconvenience to Numis. It explains why he was so annoyed when we met again later.

It also meant that Arnold Scott was as taken in by Marianna's trip logs as she was. I could picture it.

Arnold and Wendi Scott were hold up with Stephan somewhere here in Virginia. It's where they fled after Arnold checked Marianna out of the hospital. Wendi either spends all her time as Marianna or hides her Koenig time from Stephan. She's certainly close enough to keep in contact with her various flunkies. She wouldn't have to hide from Arnold because he only knows her as Wendi. It wouldn't occur to him that his real enemy was right there all the time.

As it struck me that Arnold did not know that his wife's Hyde form had the Koenig alias, I suddenly felt the need to enlighten him.

Chapter Thirteen

"GUYS DO WE HAVE a picture of Wendi Scott as Koenig?"

"Even better." said Hector. "I've been carrying this print out.

It was a "wanted poster" of Scott as Koenig from the FBI's *Innocence Lost* national initiative.[25] At the top was red bar with white letters. It read:

WANTED BY THE FBI.

Underneath it was the crime:
CONSPIRACY TO TRANSPORT MINORS TO ENGAGE IN PROSTITUTION, FLIGHT FROM CUSTODY

Underneath that was:GRETCHEN KOENIG.

It was followed by a row of three pictures of Wendi Scott in her Mistress Hyde form. That was followed by a physical description and information on where she was last sighted. (Ironically, in police custody) There were several alias listed but I didn't recognize any of them. I kicked myself. If I had just checked up on what the police back east were doing, it might have given us more leads.

I'm not sure exactly where they got two of the pictures but one of them was clearly a mug shot. I presume that she must have gotten caught, albeit briefly, when her east coast operation was being rounded up. Turning over that first server looked like it was having ongoing results.

---

25   HTTP://www.fbi.gov/innolost/innolost.htm

I wondered what Arnold would make of it. I decided it was time to ask. I dropped the cloak around Azgard and pulled up even with Arnold and Reynard. Reynard smiled at us and feinted at sideswiping us.

Normally, I'm very protective of Azgard. That day I took a risk. I know what happens when '04 Camry meets an '83 Volvo. Lets just say steel beats fiberglass. Reynard didn't actually hit us but he did hit the gas hoping to outrun us.

He failed.

"Buddy, it's all you," I said softly to Azgard. Azgard launched its front end into the air maybe a yard or so, a minor wheelie if you could even call it it that. Azgard landed its front tires on the trunk and rear bumper of the Camry. It reminded me of old nature films of wolves catching rabbits. The trunk area crumpled, the rear axle broke and Reynard's car ground to an ugly stop, sparking all the way. Reynard and Arnold jumped out of the car. Each of them was now armed with a handgun.

"Did nobody search their car while I was busy playing mound man?" I asked.

Reynard held his with practiced calm. Arnold held his weapon like he was afraid he might really use it.

"Okay. Everyone stay here in the car. Act as though the guns frighten us," I said.

"No problem, boss," that was James. His tone revealed that he was making light of his actual fear.

We all held up our hands. Reynard motioned for me to get out of the car. I did so very slowly with my hands up in the air. Arnold seemed to relax a little. He might not have if he realized that my slowness was just a stall to gather more energy. I wanted to be ready to heal up any small wounds their handguns made. Small being relative to my recent injuries. I would have been in better shape had I been pincered between speeding cars.

"Okay, Arnold, may I call you 'Arnold'? Now that I have your attention, I want you to see this," without lowering my hands I TK'ed the wanted poster over to him.

Arnold's eyes grew wide because I was violating one of the rules of magic he knew. Well, "rule" is such a loaded word. I just did "magic" with no gestures, no incantations, nor any other magical trappings. Arnold was very much an external magic kind of guy. Most amateurs are. The gifted ones eventually graduate to internal will working. Once they realize the tools are aids to, rather than the source of, power. Even then it takes most of us a while to let go of those tools. Most of my fellow Magi and I still find it helpful to use tools.

Arnold was not even in the second class there. Ironically, he could shape a teleport much more powerful than my own but there were little things that still boggled his mind.

While he was shaken a bit by that small display, Scott didn't let it faze him for long. He aimed his gun more confidently at me. He held out this hand. Clearly expecting me to land the wanted poster in his hand. I did. He flicked a quick glance at Reynard. It was an unspoken, "Kill him if he blinks wrong," looks.

Arnold looked at the wanted poster. "What kind of Photoshop crap is this? Hell, you wouldn't even need Photoshop just a paint program."

"That's true. It would be easy to counterfeit a paper." I said. "But you could always look it up online for yourself. The web address is right there." This earned me a glare.

"So what's your purpose with this. You actually expect me to believe that Wendi in either form could do something like this?"

"I expect you to look for the truth. Now I'm only surmising a few things here, but I don't think the you really understand what you've done."

"What I've done?" his snort sounded like a distant gunshot. "I didn't drag a girl across the continent twice to convince her brother to go back into sexual slavery."

"No, you created the woman who enslaved her."

I may have struck a nerve with Arnold. His gun's muzzle was suddenly making an imprint on the skin just above the bridge of my nose. I must have blinked when he was moving.

I tried to remain calm. I reminded myself that I had lots of energy stored up, that I should heal from almost anything. Of course, a brain scramble is never something one shrugs off lightly. I swallowed hard which is remarkable considering how dry my mouth had just gone.

"Numis gave you the formula, didn't he?" I asked.

"Numis?"

"The guy with the coins for tie-clip and cuff links. The guy who sold you the book."

The gun wavered. His lip quivered. There was distinct quaver in his voice. "He showed me how to liberate my Marianna from inside Wendi."

"Yeah, you ran the whole Jekyll and Hyde bit backwards. Let me guess. Wendi was a bitch who made your life miserable . . ."

"And everyone else's around her."

"Right, So you used the formula that Numis gave you and let out Wendi's 'Good' side. Then what happened?"

Reynard was starting to look worried. He was starting to glance over from me to Arnold more often. Arnold answered my question. "Wendi went her own way on her time. Marianna stayed with me."

"How did that work?"

"Wendi was fine with it. She had worked out a life for herself elsewhere. Said I had been holding her back anyway. She was out and about roughly half the time." Arnold got a wistful expression on his face for a second.

"Seems like the split allowed each part to 'sleep' while the other was out and about. Marianna was with me evenings and was Wendi late at night. About one or so the switch would come. Basically Marianna would lie down, Wendi would get up and go out. Usually, she never said a word. Then Marianna would return about day break."

"What about Marianna's time in the Fay realm?"

"She'd go off to that after our breakfast together. She never talked about it that much. She said it was private. Besides, she didn't really remember it clearly. That's why she had all those notebooks."

As previously noted, most people have a tendency to remember time in the Fay realms poorly. So her notebooks were more than just the records a naturalist would keep when observing. They were a way for Marianna to know where she had been.

Except, of course, they were lies. At best, they were half-truths. The time differences between that realm and ours would make it possible for Marianna to spend some time there, then have a day as Koenig. With the time difference between the east and west coast, Koenig could head back home at 9:00 pm Eastern time and be right on time for dinner with Arnold as Marianna. What she did during the late night hours, I still don't know. Probably she was enjoying her ill-gotten gains in some leisurely way.

No one would be the wiser. I wondered just how much Marianna really remembered. After all, if what Pandora saw that first time trailing Koenig is accurate, then the switch comes right before the journey home. Of course, that may be the answer right there. A quick trip back through the other realm could scramble her memories.

"Arnold, I have bad news for you." He just glared at me ready to disbelieve anything that came out of my mouth.

"The truth is, that life of Wendi's, the one that you prefer not to know about? Is. This. One. Here." I jabbed my finger at the wanted poster to punctuate each word. "It's all true. She's been taking advantage of the fairy memory fog that affects Marianna to scam out extra time for herself."

He still didn't give an inch. There was no way he was going to believe me. I had an idea. "Have you ever met a man by the name of Merton?"

"Yes. He's a P.I. I hired him to watch the house in case you came by."

"Are you the one who armed him with the warded weaponry?"

"Yes, but that was supposed to a last resort only. In case he needed to defend himself."

That was relief. "Well now I don't feel so bad about what happened to your house. So tell me how you got in touch with him."

If the house reference meant anything to him he ignored it for a moment. "Well, the guy who sold me the book put me in touch with him. I had made some 'Items' for Merton." Arnold looked away. I think his conscience was catching up to him.

"Sold him some items. Let me guess, a pair of goggles to see spiritual objects (he nodded) and some small ampoules that let him step in and out of that faerie realm Mariana goes to?" another nod.

"Guess what." Again, I shoved the wanted poster at him. This time, I pointed to something I had only just noticed a moment before. Merton was listed as a know and wanted associate.

"That's not, that's not . . . possible."

"You used an alchemical technique to separate out the good aspects of you wife's personality into a body of her own. Then you built her a portal to never-never land where she plays at being a naturalist and you think it's impossible someone found a way to exploit that?"

"But that would mean . . ."

"It means you've been used by Wendi. We know her as Koenig. Merton is one of her flunkies. Probably this guy, Reynard, too. I'm guessing it's his job to keep an eye on you. It would be bad for you to see the inconsistencies." Arnold didn't even so much as give a glance at Reynard yet. Something else was bothering him. I had a guess what that was.

"It also means that Pandora is not going to help her brother send anything after us. She knows the truth. Stephan isn't the one who escaped. She is. I shudder to think how Stephan is going to take the news that his would be saviors are in fact his captors. I just hope you get the chance to explain you ignorance."

Arnold turned to Reynard. During this whole time, I think the only thing that kept Reynard from shooting me prematurely was that he didn't want to prove my point by acting like a thug.

Now the jig was up and he was going for broke. He pointed his handgun right at my forehead. I saw *that* look cross Reynard's eyes. I jumped to the side. I prayed that I had enough energy stored up to take the hit. Reynard just tracked with me and would have pegged me in the face easily, if Arnold hadn't slapped Reynard's gun hand downward. Reynard pulled the trigger and a short burst barked out the handgun. (James, just reminded me that it most likely a Beretta 93R. I'll take his word for it.)

As it was, I still got hit. The right side of my pelvis shattered. I crumpled sideways. The healing energy went right to work. (Not to brag but this is something I'm pretty good at. At least for myself. And I had a lot practice just that day even) My bones had reknit themselves by the time I was fully lying on my side.

I started to pull in more energy to respond to Reynard's attack. What I saw next convinced me I needed to look into this alchemy stuff more.

Reynard had turned his gun on Arnold. He let loose another burst. The bullets flew right into Arnold's chest. Arnold didn't even budge. His shirt was torn apart by the gunfire, revealing a Kevlar vest intricately patterned in florescent blue ink. The smashed slugs still clung to the fabric. They glowed with a faint, fading green light.

Arnold just gave Reynard a quizzical look. Reynard's eyes grew wide and he reoriented his aim upward towards Arnold's face.

I thought it was high time to return the favor Arnold had just done for me. However, I was still trying to stand up when Arnold just reached out and touched the gun. He tapped it with a ring on his right pinky finger.

The effect was instantaneous. Starting at the point of contact, a green fire swept over the gun. Before the line of green flame, everything was normal. Behind the line, the gun's metal became clear glass.

When Reynard pulled the trigger again, nothing happened. Reynard dropped that gun and started to reach behind him. This time I could be of service. Before Reynard could get a grip on his back up weapon, I slipped a "telekinetic hand" into his. It's just a small effect, almost a parlor trick really.

It was effective nonetheless. Feeling the grip I had on his hand, he turned and kicked backward trying to free himself. I had the advantage though. I wasn't there. I was still lying on the ground a few yards away.

Reynard wasn't foolish though. The failed kick didn't even unbalance him. He turned his momentum into a roll away from Arnold. Arnold was trying to grab Reynard with his ring hand. Reynard took off running. He must have not wanted to find out what Arnold's ring could do to his flesh.

I tell myself I should feel bad about enjoying what came next. I'm not that spiritually perfected. I still had a TK grip on Reynard. So just as he jumped to clear some of the collision debris, I yanked his arm backwards. I pulled back on Reynard's arm a lot harder than I had intended. I had wanted merely unbalance him in order to hinder his jump. Instead, he hit the ground with a dislocated his shoulder. Reynard groaned in pain and decided to stay down. I may need to work on some anger issues.

I turned my attention back to Arnold. "Arnold, now that your associate has tried to kill both of us over what I have to say, are you ready to listen?"

Arnold nodded. "I think I can give enough to check this out for myself. Stay here. I'm going to see if my laptop's survived the crash."

He went over to his car and climbed in the wreckage. After a moment he settled into the passenger seat. I saw a blue-white light reflecting on his face. Reynard was cursing and yelling at him that it was all a trick and yadda yadda blah.

Arnold leaned out of the car and fired his gun. The shot hit relatively close to where Reynard lay on the ground.

There was silence for a long time after that.

When Arnold finally got out of the car, he walked past Reynard with regarding him whatsoever.

When he reached me, I could see he was crying.

"It's so hard to believe. Wendi on her worst day never . . . never . . ."

"Would do something like that?" I asked.

He just nodded.

"She has now."

Arnold looked like he was going to be sick, "It's as though all the good in her was . . ."

"Removed," I finished for him. I said matter of factly. Even deadpanned it sounded like an accusation.

Arnold looked directly into my eyes. I saw no deceit there, only shame. Sudden remorse flickered in that shame. It was not simple guilt or impotent regret. It was good, honest penitence. It grew into the kind of anger that deserves to be called righteous, the kind that looks in the mirror first.

"What can I do?" he asked.

"That's simple. You help fix what you broke."

Chapter Fourteen

Lest you think that the rest of the team was idle during all that interchange, let me assure you, they were not. Once the gunfire portion of the evening was over, Maxine showed some of her skill. She made a quick incantation that left Reynard dazed and dazzled. Obviously, my description of her enchantment is a little vague. I wish I had been able to watch her work. I always find it interesting to see the methods other traditions use.[26]

Will-working is also a highly personal thing. For people, magic stems from deep within us. Perhaps more accurately, something at our core reaches out and interacts with the world at a very deep level. For each person it is a unique expression of their personality and spirit. Watching it can sometimes be an intimate, almost sensual, experience. If I had been able to watch her work with my sights going . . . I made a point to have a long, deep conversation with her later.

Once Arnold got out his car to talk to me, the Guys worked their collective butt off moving the wreckage of Arnold's car. Working as smoothly as only they can, they had it all the way off the road by the time Arnold was asking me what he could do.

When that was done, Hector and James took Azgard. They were headed back into the 'Burg. We needed another car with all these people. We also needed a base of operations. We assumed that none of our old places were safe anymore. Ty and Ramón stayed to make sure Reynard didn't give Maxine any trouble.

---

26 See *Jumping the Path: A Comparative Look at Will-Working Traditions* CC# 408

So, we had a short wait. Marguerite was trying to coax a vision into being. That's generally not the kind of thing you can force. She took a deep breath to clear her mind, to put herself in the right state to receive a vision. She tells me that's hard to do when people have been shooting at her friends. "So nothing?" I asked.

She gave me one of those "give me a break" looks, "Nothing specific. But I am noticing things. Unusual Things."

"Go on." I said tentatively, not very sure I wanted to hear.

"Haven't you noticed that there's nobody else on the roads? It's the middle of the afternoon now. There should be at least some traffic even out here in the boondocks."

Arnold spoke up, "That would be my doing. I wanted to avoid collateral damage."

"Very admirable, how are you doing it?" I was genuinely curious. After all he seems to have no end of nifty tricks.

He shrugged and said, "I'm surprised you don't know how I'm doing it. You seem to know more than I do."

"Maybe, but you done things I've never seen before." He swelled with pride to hear that, but just for an instant.

"Everything I do is just the redirection of energies in one form or another."

"Really?"

"Really, take a look at this." we walked over to the car. He directed my attention to the interior, pointing up to the ceiling. The cloth interior of the ceiling had been torn away. Radiating out from the dome light, there was an inscribed circle. It was quite the piece of work. Especially considering that he had to inscribe it reaching up while twisted around the seats of a relatively small car.

"What did you use for that?"

"Enochian and Greek," he said, matter-of-factly.

"I meant your medium."

He grinned sheepishly, "Oh, a sharpie to start with, then I used a soldering gun to burn it into the ceiling."

I was still too drained to want to spin the Sight Wheel. So I just asked. "So what exactly are you redirecting?"

"Guardian angels."

"Angels?" I gave him a look to show my lack of credulity. That was something that I wanted to talk to him about in depth. It's a bit of a misnomer to refer to guardian angels. People think a guardian should keep whomever they guard safe from harm. Guardian angels don't do that. They work more to help guide us into situations where we can grow as people. This sometimes puts us in more danger not less. So I had to wonder what exactly the angels were being told to do.

Arnold may have picked up on my suspicious glare. He hasten to continue his explanation.

"The circle glows astrally to get angelic attention. The Enochian is the instruction. A request really."

"A request to do what?"

"To steer their charges away from our vicinity."

"So it's a caution sign for guardian angels?"

"Essentially"

"This is all that in the book Numis sold you?"

"More, I couldn't begin to describe all the stuff in there. Formulas for redirecting all kinds of energy." he pulled open his bullet shredded shirt. Underneath it was the Kevlar body armor with a number of circles and inscriptions. "Mr. Grasp said this should strengthen the armor tenfold."

"More than that," I said. "Body armor may stop bullets but it doesn't negate the impact like what I saw early. I assume Mr. Grasp is the guy who sold you the book. The one with the coin themed jewelry."

Arnold nodded. "There's also a formula for turning surface tension into sexual tension."

"Excuse me?"

"It lets you turn any water based liquid into a Love potion. Just inscribe the transmutation circle on the bottom of the glass or the table, whatever."

It was one of those moments when I knew I had just heard something terribly important. The moment was interrupted by the return of James with a Lincoln town car.

Chapter Fifteen

"Okay, gang, pick a ride and follow me. Time to see the grand new digs," James said.

Maxine, Ty and I rode with Arnold in Azgard. Marguerite and Ramón and James rode in the Lincoln Town Car. Reynard was now subdued with a pair of hand cuffs that James had brought back with him. He rode in the back of the town car next to Ramón. I didn't ask where he got the handcuffs, nor the car. All the Guys are too young for rentals, and none where inclined to steal. If it were important, I'd find out about it.

Arnold and I continued talking shop while we drove. That was after Maxine reintroduced herself.

"So I take it that book has been 'helpful'." Arnold just looked stunned. "Ms. Stuart? You're working with these people? How did that happen?"

Maxine related the whole ugly story. Almost all, she did omit the erstwhile kissing portion.

The new information seemed to weigh heavily on Arnold. "God, I wish I never saw that book. Or that guy."

"I know what you mean. If I had known it was anything other than a sale from one collector to another . . ." Maxine let the sentence drift off.

"More importantly," I said, "What do we do next?"

"I need to know more." Arnold said. "Tell me what's been going on here and lets try to match up what I thought with what was really happening."

"Actually, why don't you start. Tell us what happened when you first got the book from Numis."

Arnold related in a halting, apologetic manner what he knew from his end of things. In a way, it was remarkably simple.

Wendi was a miserable person. She was unhappy and was very good at sharing that unhappiness. That was about all she was good at sharing. If she had one flaw, it was that she never could understand why she never had enough. There was never enough money, enough clothing, or enough toys. We aren't talking mere greed. It's possible Wendi was a bit of an acquisitions addict.

One day Arnold, who had always had a bent towards the Alchemical, made a joke about how she should find a philosopher's stone. The idea of an item that turns base metals into gold intrigued Wendi. She was a practical person however and didn't give it much thought. She only said. "If only I could turn you into gold then you'd be worth something." With that she was ready for the next topic.

Arnold, on the other hand, was struck by it. He had a vision of himself a golden statue, and then the vision changed. He saw Wendi as if cast in gold. Arnold was smart enough to know that purpose of Alchemy was the spiritual perfecting of one self. He knew that the lead-into-gold quest was more important as metaphor. The idea of transmuting Wendi infested his imagination. He became obsessed with finding anything to do with alchemy. Perhaps he could find a way to finally make Wendi happy.

Enter Numis. He comes in with a book o' secrets. It promised happiness to everyone. To Arnold, he promised a change that would allow Wendi to finally be happy.

To Wendi, Numis promised an opportunity to pursue her "needs" unfettered. That's all of the talk that Arnold overheard between Numis and Wendi. He was far too busy being dazzled by the book that Numis, the so called Mr. Grasp, had opened before him.

Well, after a little research and experimentation, bada bing bada boom, Arnold works the transformation on Wendi. Marianna is created.

She was just as sweet and loving and kind as Wendi could have been IF it weren't for her greed and fear. Numis explains that they have essentially released a Dr Jekyll from a Mrs. Hyde.

Arnold was a little concerned about what would happen if Wendi just disappeared.

"Oh, she'll have to spend at least half her time in her old form. But I have a plan for that. If it's amenable to you," Numis told Arnold and Wendi.

Numis claimed he had need of an assistant like Wendi and when she was "out and about" he'd like her to work for him.

"I should have questioned more. I see that now. But back then I didn't really want to. I had what I wanted plus all those formulas. It's been really nice. It seemed like I had everything . . ." Arnold drifted off into silent self recrimination.

Now wasn't the time to focus on that so I changed the subject.

"Arnold, I need to ask you this question. Have you ever been inside my apartment?"

"No," He looked puzzled by the question, "why do you ask?"

"Koenig, that is, Wendi, showed up there with someone wearing your face."

"Why would she do that?"

"She was trying to intimidate me."

"I meant use my face."

The only thing that sprang to mind was, "Patsy? Maybe she wanted you to take the fall for something? She tried to shoot me. I suspect if she had been successful, the false you could have been used as a decoy.

"That would have sent any investigation the wrong way. I can see it . . . Still, to use my face . . . This Koenig person Wendi became sure has some elaborate schemes. I just can't believe she shares a body with Marianna."

"Actually it's not surprising. All the good qualities that Marianna has used to be mixed in with her worse qualities."

Arnold gave me a sideways glance. "You aren't going to trot out the Star Trek bit when Kirk was split in a transporter accident. How his good half needed the bad half to function."

"Not at all, but the basic decency that kept the original Wendi from doing anything too criminal all went into Marianna."

Arnold didn't say anything to this. He just stared out the window. Maxine took this moment to interject.

"Something's troubling me," she said, "I knew both Wendi before and after the separation. Of course, I didn't know that Marianna was really Wendi, but the difference is more than just good and bad. Marianna is a sweet person. She's too sweet in fact. She must have come into the store quite a few times before I ever noticed her."

Arnold made a noise that sounded like an emphatic agreement.

Maxine continued, "She was almost a non-entity even while talking to her. I don't mean to sound harsh but she always struck as the kind of woman who would rather disappear than cause a ruckus, even to stand up for herself."

Maxine's voice carried a tone somewhere between pity and contempt.

"Whatever Wendi's bad points were she seems to have gotten all the nerve, all the strength in the split. Are you trying to tell me that those things are evil? That good women are weak?"

"No, but magic is formed out our thoughts and desires. Wendi was fairly abusive, wasn't she?"

Arnold nodded Silently, then added, "Wendi always prided herself on not taking crap from anybody, for standing up for herself, always knowing her rights."

"But not anybody else's. I should know." This was Maxine, "She was very outspoken when she felt slighted. Even if she hadn't been. Hell, I remember once she acted as if I was trying to cheat her when a book she ordered was late because a UPS shipment was misaddressed."

"Yeah, try living with that. I didn't want someone who was weak, just less strident."

Something about this made me curious. It sounded like Wendi was a real hot head. The Koenig I knew was very calm and collected, "how did Wendi behave after the separation? I mean was she so contentious?"

"No, Come to think of it. Wendi . . . or should I start calling her 'Gretchen' . . . seemed to stop caring about all the little things that used to drive her mad. Marianna felt strongly about a lot things but she was always too bashful to really pursue them. That is other than the whole Fay exploration thing. That was the exception, so much of the time she was really very timid."

"Must have been nice for you." Maxine's voice was chill enough I wanted to turn up the heater.

"Good women aren't weak but it sounds like Wendi thought so," I said.

"Boss, we're there." Ty said. This cut our discussion short. I had been driving on autopilot following the Lincoln. We had skirted around the edge of the burg. We came up into the relatively upscale developments west of town. You may have seen the kind of place. The houses are nice. Many are too big for their comparatively small plots of land. Even the smaller houses have that mark of quality construction that says, "I work too much."

These are places where the workaholic doctors, lawyers and business folk can comfortably avoid their families, knowing that they have provided them the best of homes in the best of neighborhoods.

The house we were pulling into sat on the corner of two forgettably named streets, something like Parkway and Green street. Seriously, I forget what they were called. Both doors of a two-car garage swung upward as we approached. I followed James's lead and parked inside it.

Hector hit the button to close the doors behind us as we climbed out of our various vehicles. We followed him through the connecting door from the garage to the main part of the house. We passed through the laundry room into the kitchen. I don't know why I was surprised when I saw Charles Vanderhorn sitting there. "So, I hear you've lost two instead of finding one."

Chapter Sixteen

"S**O, I HEAR YOU'VE** lost two instead of finding one." his tone was sad but lacked the accusation of the words themselves. I stammered a non-reply, flustered by my own shame. He motioned for me to sit down next to him at the kitchen table.

There was sadness in his voice when he spoke again. Sadness mixed with the barest flicker of hope. "Hector says you're not just someone with a nifty bag of tricks, that you have faith. Right now I'm feeling a little low on that. Can you tell me that there's a plan?"

"Do you mean do I have a plan or . . ."

"I'd like to know that there is a Plan with a capital P. First, I lose my kids and I was devastated. Yet it gave me the impetus to get sober. That led me to helping other kids since I couldn't help my own. I thought that made a kind of sense. Then Stacy came home alive. All my assumptions went out the window. It really made me think more about the nature of my higher power.

I don't know much about the bible but I know the story of Prodigal son. How the son just takes his inheritance while his father is still alive and leaves his family in the dust. How the Prodigal son's dad was still overjoyed to see the son come home, even though the son had basically shit on his dad..

I *know* I know exactly how that father felt. My dead kid was alive again! Everything else was nothing. Nothing else mattered. I was, well, you saw how I was that night you all came. Now they're both gone. Again. Can you tell that there is a Plan?

He just looked at me. His expression said it all. I didn't know what to tell him. I didn't know if my take on things would help him. I was fairly sure that it wasn't going to comfort him.

"Charles, I hope you can take this for what it's worth. Beyond wanting us to be good to each other, I don't know if there is a *Plan*." He looked at me confused and worried.

"But I also don't think we've been left on our own. Whenever I'm tempted to think that there is a capital P Plan, something happens like this that makes me think things just happen." Charles somehow deflated even more. "But whenever I'm tempted to think that it's all just a crap shoot, something else happens that tells me other wise."

"Must be nice."

"It has its moments."

Vanderhorn's cell phone rang. "It's a local number," he said.

"Hello," Charles answered. The speaker was turned way up on the phone. I could hear the faint hiss of an open connection.

"Hello, This is Charles Vanderhorn, can I help you."

The voice on the other end was unmistakable. It sounded like Pandora's only slightly deeper.

"Holy shit, it is dad!" the line went dead.

"Stephan! Stephan!" Vanderhorn yelled at his phone. Then seeing the pointlessness of that, Vanderhorn hit the button to automatically return the call. It went to a voice mail. The voice on the recording was Arnold's, "You've reached Arnold Scott, please leave a message and I will get back to you."

Arnold was there but had remained quiet until now. "I didn't record that." Charles took a look at Arnold for the first time.

"Are you the one responsible for this mess?" There was plenty of accusation in his tone this time.

Arnold didn't get to answer that. The front door and great deal of the surrounding wall crashed in. There was Stephan upon his majestic, golden, riding boar. This time he wasn't alone. A petite, dark haired woman outfitted in the same feux-medieval manner followed him into the house. She rode, and I still can't believe it when I say it, a giant rabbit, sidesaddle.

Stephan grabbed his dad and slung him across the boar's saddle. Without pausing, he turned and left through the hole he had come in.

Mariana (who else) "rescued" her husband. How she got so physically strong, I'm not sure. She lifted him one handed and tossed him on the bunny behind her. With her other hand she lobbed a barbed-tipped spear at me. Well, it flew in my general direction. Either she had terrible aim or she wanted to make it clear this was a warning shot.

Her spear landed nowhere near me. It bounced off the kitchen wall about 10 feet from me and clattered to the floor. I ran over and scooped it up.

The team, which had earlier spread through the house trying to decompress emotionally, rushed back in. By the time they had assembled, both riders were gone.

Carol Vanderhorn rushed into the kitchen with Marguerite. I said the only thing I could think of at the moment.

"Come on, let's get out of here before someone on a giant guinea pig kidnaps Carol."

Chapter Seventeen

THE GUYS IMMEDIATELY STARTED for the cars. Ty assisted Mrs. Vanderhorn. She was a bit dazed. Whether from the attack or the absurdity of the attackers, I could not say. Absurdity is a weapon often exploited by the Fay and their associates.

We split up again into the same cars as before. Mrs. Vanderhorn replacing Arnold in Azgard. There was one other alteration. We left Reynard. It was a split second decision. His, not ours. He still had his hands bound behind his back when he bolted out the hole in the front wall.

"Let him go," I said. "He's probably safer on his own without us. We're certainly safer without him."

"But what about leads to find Pandora?" Ramón asked.

I held the spear aloft. "We have this to point us the way."

We withdrew from the house. I led us to a place where I have always felt at home. We drove to a hill that overlooked the small (And I mean small) private university where I did my undergrad work. At the top of this hill were only a couple of buildings, the campus radio station and The Detwiler Center, a small building named for a former president of the college. It was used by the various student groups on campus when they needed meeting space. We parked next to the campus radio station and walked past it up to the crown of the hill.

The radio station had no windows and the other building seemed to be empty at the time, so we had a modicum of privacy.

"I need a moment to collect myself. I'll just pop into the 'D' Center to prepare," I said.

I used a small trick I had learned in my college days to get into the building. I couldn't believe they still hadn't fixed that one window latch.

After getting myself inside, I went to the main door and opened it for the others.

Marguerite and the Guys came in and found places to sit in the large open room that comprised most of the main floor. The room was ringed by large windows and the ceiling was vaulted so that room felt expansive with a strong upward flow. Maxine hung at the door for a moment then entered a little nervously.

"It kind of reminds me of a church," she said, not elaborating any further.

Ty spoke up, "Well, it is a Christian college, after all."

Maxine turned to me just before I headed to the lower floor,

"That must have made your parents happy."

I laughed, "Actually, they were appalled."

Maxine gave me a quizzical glance, "but you said the disapproved of any magic based stories, even fairy tales."

"Oh, that's because they were the kind of atheists who believe that all human misconduct comes from a belief in the supernatural. When I came here, they thought it was just youth rebellion."

Maxine started to ask me another question. I cut her off. "Excuse me, I need to get ready quickly. We have a limited window of opportunity."

Maxine nodded. "Is there a water fountain or a bathroom here?" she asked

"Yeah, follow me." I led her downstairs. It was where I was headed anyway. "There's the water fountain," I said pointing to it. It was in the small downstairs corridor between the two rest rooms and a small storage area.

"Thanks," she said, "I've got this killer headache." She reached into her purse and pulled out a small travel cup and couple of odd looking tablets. They were about the size of her thumbnail with something imprinted on them

"Home remedy," she said.

"Magic home remedy," I thought. Briefly, I wondered how effective it was.

I left her too it. I entered the men's room and used the basic facilities. After washing my hands, I stood before the mirror and stripped down to my underwear.[27] After our trip through fairy and being encased in a ton of asphalt, I needed a cleansing physically, mentally and spiritually.

---

[27]   Pray that in the movie, they cast someone who isn't too similar to me in physique.

Doing a cleansing as a sink bath made it harder to find the right frame of mind but I was getting there. The door banged open. It was Maxine. She stood in the doorway for a moment. Then she gave me a look that was almost predatory. She had had opened her blouse a few buttons to display her cleavage to good effect. She held up her little travel cup. It was filled with water.

"I thought you might be thirsty," she said.

My concentration was blown. "A little," I said. This was so not the time I wanted something to happen. There was also something about the way she was standing there offering me water that reminded me of that last night with Shelia. "Look, I really have to get this done," I said. or at least I think I said that. I couldn't hear myself over the roar of my protesting libido.

Maxine took a slow step into the rest room. It was big enough that I could take a few steps back from her. I honestly didn't want to but I had a job to do. Damn it.

I was about to call for Marguerite when she suddenly appeared. I could tell that Marguerite was pissed or something like it. She played it cool however.

"Hey, do you have any more of that headache remedy?" To know about that, Marguerite must have been listening on the stairs after we came down.

At first, Maxine seemed to ignore the question. Then she dragged her attention away from me and said, "Sure." She handed Marguerite her purse without looking at either one of them.

Maxine took a step closer to me. Marguerite took a step and interposed herself. She pulled the small bag of homemade tablets from the purse. Marguerite gave the pills a quick glance and asked Maxine, "Do your tablets usually have these marks on them?"

Maxine stopped and looked at the tablets. She was confused. "No," she said. I looked at them over Marguerite's shoulder. On one side was a small symbol that was similar in design to the one on Sheila's serving tray that night. The other side had a strange round mark like the tarot suite of pentacles with a diamond stuck in it. The suit of pentacles is also know as coins. I didn't like the implications here.

Marguerite physically turned Maxine back towards the door. "You and I have got to talk about this." With that, Margurite pushed Maxine back out through the door.

I got back to my cleansing. Rushed as it was, I think it helped. I redressed then went back up to rejoin the team. We headed out to the crest of the hill proper.

I caught Marguerite's eye and gave her a meaningful look and a quick glance at Maxine.

"I've got it covered," Marguerite mouthed at me. She gave a little swirl of her finger pointing me back to my own task.

We fell into the ritual fairly naturally. Given that it was improvised, I'm rather proud of the team for how well it worked out.

Marguerite helped keep Mrs. Vanderhorn calm. Her agitation was mostly from the surreal events of the evening. Witnessing our current actions didn't help her feel at ease. It must have looked a little strange.

To start the ritual, I finished off my half-assed, interrupted, cleansing bath. Reverently, I poured a bottle of water over my head. At the top of the hill I "swept" the area by walking an inward moving spiral. I did this to clear my mind as much to clear the area of extraneous energies.

The Guys came and stood next to me. They each put their right hand on one or the other of my shoulders. I held the spear aloft and prayed. I opened myself up and allowed the resonances in the spear to echo into me. Soon, a direction formed in my mind's eye. I let energy flow up from the earth into me and then out into the spear.

I heard a gasp. I opened my eyes. The gasp had come from Mrs. Vanderhorn. The spear had begun to glow red at the tip. The glow was too bright to be blood but was lurid nonetheless. The butt end of the haft glowed with a faint cerulean. I could hear Mrs. Vanderhorn murmuring to herself, trying to believe her eyes. She was still adjusting to another new reality into which she had been thrust.

The spear grew brighter as I poured intention and hope into it. After a minute or so more, it flared briefly and jerked in my hand. It clearly pointed in a specific direction. The glow slowly faded to visible sight.

I spun the Wheel of Sight. Jackpot! It came up visual, just what I wanted. I could see a thin but bright line of light streaming out from the spear and disappearing over the horizon in the direction the spear had jumped, the same was as the honeymoon cottage. It was a clear and easily discerned line. Darn.

"We need to get a move on now," I said. The guys started heading to the car.

Mrs. Vanderhorn asked why. "Are they in danger?" she wanted to know.

"It's possible. Though I don't think Stephan plans to hurt anybody. It's just that not only did my effect confirm their current location, someone sensitive to this kind of thing might pick it up. Plus, the longer they are with Koenig in either of her forms, the more likely that they'll be able she'll be able to bring them under her sway again. Then she could spirit them away without resistance.

"We'd have to start from scratch again and nobody wants that."

This information galvanized Mrs. Vanderhorn.

She made a beeline for the Lincoln. (It was her car after all.) I hesitated a moment trying to find the words to explain the danger we might be heading into. I needed to know if she had the resolve to face this.

"Mrs. Vanderhorn . . .," was as far as I got before she cut me off

"Don't try to talk me out this, " In my Sight she actually began to glow. "I am not going to stay behind and watch while *that* woman tries to steal my family from me *again!*" Her glow expanded and ignited like a flame to my astral sight. You didn't have to have special senses, however, to feel the ferocity of her passion.

"There is no place on, above, or below the earth that she can go that will keep me from getting my family back.

"If she tries to go into one of those fairytale worlds I've heard mentioned, I'll knock down whatever gate stands in my way. I'll knock it down with my bare hands and your head if I have to." That bright line of light I mentioned earlier was a nite-light by comparison now.

"If, when we finally catch up to her, she dares to stand between me and my family, I will wear her ovaries for earings." Her spirit shone so brightly that it was just shy of illuminating her physical form visibly. If it had, I bet she would have been visible from space.

If Mrs. V. could lend me the power of *that* conviction, Koenig's band would never know what hit them. "Now what is it you need to say?" she asked me.

"I think you should ride shotgun with me."

Chapter Eighteen

DESPITE WHAT I SAID, it was Hector who rode shotgun while Maxine drove. Mrs. Vanderhorn rode beside me in the back seat of Azgard. Marguerite and the rest of the guys followed in the Town Car. I discovered later that Marguerite had sent Hector along with us to keep an eye on Maxine. Marguerite and Maxine had some serious conversation while the Guys and I had worked the ritual. Later Marguerite would tell me she was of two minds.

Her immediate judgment was to make Maxine stay behind while we headed out to confront Koenig. Her psychic glimpses, however, kept telling her that Maxine was needed, not just in the group, but near me. Exactly why was not made clear. Got to hate those vague voices prophesying anything.

As we drove, I soaked up the energy radiating from Mrs. Vanderhorn. I say "radiating" for a reason. I wasn't drinking her energy like some sort of vampire. I was soaking up that energy like a sunbather catching some rays.

What's the difference? One way would make me an outright parasite, the other was just a tad opportunistic.

After all, she was sending out all that energy like a gift to the universe[28]

I was still running my Sight. Even as I soaked up the power, I kept an eye on where the spear's light trail was leading us. Maxine drove because I'm a terrible driver when I'm not primarily focused on the physical world.

It wasn't long before we had made the short trek from Harrisonburg up past the park 'n' ride. The light kept indicating north, even from there. I

---

[28]   Note: We all do this by the way. Keep that in mind

was relieved. I had been concerned that we needed to journey back into the Fay realms. We headed north on 11 for about another half an hour or so.

My sense of time was getting a bit muddled. I had soaked up so much energy from Mrs. Vanderhorn that I felt I had begun to glow a bit myself. Heady stuff, Mrs. V's conviction was.

I was especially glad to be full of that determination when we drove up into the woods near Luray, Virginia. Under other circumstances driving right up to my honeymoon cabin might have shaken me.

There were lights on in the cabin. There were also a dozen or more pinpoints of light glowing out from the foliage surrounding the cabin, visible only to the Sight. I hadn't expected the stares of dozens of hidden watchers. I savored my borrowed conviction. I was going to need it.

With the Sight going I cold see the patches of intention and attention surrounding the cabin. My Sight also told me that I was seeing the attention of human beings. This was another surprise. After all the Fairy help that they've had, I had doubted that Stephan or Koenig would call on mundane forces.

Perhaps they were Fay after all. Perhaps the welcoming party just had a really good mask of their own, deceiving my Senses. Maybe it was a mixture of Fay and humans.

I told Hector to have the others breakaway. They did, following the road further up into the woods.

"Are you sure about this, Mrs. V? I can sense that they got a lot of help up here trying to stay hidden. If you want us to get you to safety, this is the last chance."

"I'm in this all the way."

"Okay then. Maxine, Hector, Mrs. V, this could be where it all hits the fan. Stay pretty close to me. We're going to be taking some big risks. This will get tricky. Just exit on the same side of the car as I do. That'll make it easier for me."

We pulled into the parking area next to the cabin. None of the watchers moved. I opened my door and climbed out. Maxine did the same with Hector following her out the driver's side. Mrs. V. came out the door right behind me.

Once we were clear of Azgard by a few feet, the watchers made their move. Law Enforcement agents of several different branches swarmed us. There were agents of the FBI, State police, ATF, and whoever pretended to be in charge of Homeland security those days.

A couple of official looking vehicles zoomed in, out of nowhere it seemed, to block our egress. I looked up at the cabin. With my Sight, I could see Marianna peeking out through an upstairs window.

I would do the only thing I thought I could do. (Other than surrender) I would throw a veil.

That may sound simple but the difficulty has a lot to do with numbers and intensity. In Richmond, I was able to get people to ignore Marguerite, Hector and myself. That took a lot out me actually and that was hiding only from a few people who weren't all that interested in us.

Now, I was trying to totally mask our presence from a great number of very interested observers. It's a good thing that I had all that energy stored up.

"Hector, Maxine, when the time comes, do what you do best."

I don't want you to get the impression that the police were idle here. They had commanded us to lie on the ground and all that. We had complied. Four men in "FBI" emblazoned jackets were walking up to us slowly.

I waited until they were close enough to block a little of the view of their fellow officers. Not entirely of course, that wasn't going to happen. When the rest of the officers and agents had to look past their comrades in order to see us, that's when I threw the veil. I made sure to extend it far enough to include the four FBI agents.

And then we were gone. Needless to say, everything went to hell.

Chapter Nineteen

THE NEXT NEAREST OFFICERS charged in on us. As they did, I extended the veil to include them. Those who were within the veil could see us. They might as well; they were going to trip over us any way.

Hector shot up and went all matrix on those closest to him. The much more athletic Ramón would have done it better. I take that back. He would have just done it more forcefully. Ramón would have been a dazzling flurry of strikes and kicks. Hector was small and lithe. He was better at dodging around and letting the officers get tangled up in each other.

Maxine waved her right hand gently in the face of the two officers closest to her. A whispered incantation followed and she turned them into sleepwalkers, dropping their guard and their guns. She moved on the next two. And so on, and so on.

Mrs. Vanderhorn was picking up the fallen guns. It was clear she had great respect but no love for guns. Efficiently, but without haste, she extracted the magazines from the weapons and started to make piles. Guns went to her right, ammo to the left. She even remembered to remove chambered rounds. I gave here an admiring look. She shrugged.

"Didn't Charles tell you? We met as reservists."

For my part, I was getting a grinding headache from providing this cloak. If it weren't for the assistance of Mrs. V's iron conviction, I think I'd have passed out.

More agents and officers flowed into the area of my cloak. Just as quickly Hector and Maxine were taking them down in their own special ways. Mrs. Vanderhorn was down on the ground but not cowering. She was still collecting the firearms that were falling.

If I may continue the Matrix theme, she began to remind me of Trinity. If Trinity had been a mid-forties soccer mom in one of those trendy tracksuits.

A few shots did get fired. Thankfully none of the bullets connected. The sound alone was dangerous. The sound strained the veil, almost breaking it. "Almost" in this case was a very happy word. This part of the frackus only lasted for a few seconds. Then no more came in.

"Every one down," I said. I had a sense that a few of the more spooked officers where about to start just hosing the area with gunfire.

The four of us hit the ground, dragging any of the standing officers with us. A hail of bullets flew over our heads. I cringed imagining round after round hitting Azgard. I took a quick peek behind me. I was both relieved and disconcerted to find that Azgard was not there. I hoped it meant he was okay and not too angry with me.

I motioned for others to huddle with me and we made a crawl out of the original area. I kept the veil centered on me. It was a good thing we were crawling. I couldn't have managed much else. Even with the boost from Mrs. V, this was quite draining.

As we moved away, the fallen law men (and a few women) became visible again. A number of the agents and officers went to tend the fallen. The rest pulled together trying to cover each other backs. The Fay don't do that often. Their nigh immortality makes it unnecessary to worry about fallen comrades. No need to tend someone who will be up and fighting again in ten minutes time. This change in tactics gave us the opening we needed

We made it past the perimeter that the police had formed. Our situations had reversed. I could see all the officers in the middle and we were on the outside. I could see the concern that the officers had for their incapacitated comrades, confirming for me that they were all human.

"Maxine," I said. "I want to try something."

"It's about time," she said with a good-natured smirk. I let that slide lest my own mind wander.

"How many people can you hit with that sleep walking spell"

"Two at a time I can do it fairly quick though."

"I want you to try casting it over there." I indicated the area where the officers were now milling about, tending to those who were incapacitated in one way or another.

"On whom?"

"All of them. I think I can use the rest of Mrs. V's determination to help you kick it into overdrive."

"You can do that?"

"We can try."

I placed my right hand on Maxine's back, between the shoulder blades. I saw myself as a glowing ember. I pictured myself full of light. My light had a sunny yellow color. I looked into Maxine and found her light. It was deep in her core, burning fiercely. It had a deep indigo center edged with bright, cerulean blue. I let my light flow out of me into her. In my Sight, it seemed as though the light in her rushed to meet the light coming from me. A good sign that she trusted me and that this was going to work.

As more of my light mixed with her light, she also began to glow. My golden light mixed into the blue. Some might expect that our lights would turn green like paint colors would. It didn't. Nor did it result in a white light like it would if this were light from the visible spectrum.

Instead, it became one of those colors that only exist because Maxine and I were there to see it. Our minds were trying to give visual representation to a spiritual event. The result was that to our mystic senses, we glowed indigo gold.[29] It was just what the doctor ordered.

Maxine's spell flowed out from her. Carried by this new and powerful "light", it blanketed the law officers in front of the cabin. The ones not already on the ground slumped serenely into sleep. Maxine kept it flowing until it covered up to and around the cabin.

As the spell reached the cabin, it stopped like water encountering a rock in a stream. The light simply flowed around it.

Hector watched as the officers all dropped into slumber land. "You couldn't have started with that?"

"Ah, yes, if I had known they were all human."

"You can't tell with those funky senses."

I blushed. "I can. I just thought it was Fay running a really good mask."

"Way to outsmart yourself, boss."

---

[29] I would have said "indigold" but that's far too clever and, I think, trademarked, so shh.

Chapter Twenty

I DIDN'T COMMENT ON HIS painful observation. Instead, I just nodded my head toward the cabin. I saw the curtain flutter in the upstairs window were earlier I had seen Marianna. We headed toward the cabin. Stepping over the slumbering forms of the downed officers, I asked Maxine, "How long before they wake up?"

She smiled and shrugged. "They'll be out at least until sunrise," she frown slightly then, "Do you think all these people were on What's-her-name's payroll?"

"Unlikely. Mariana isn't wanted by the police, even if Gretchen is. So she can call the cops on us. I do believe we are wanted felons after all"

"Suspected terrorists," said Hector.

"In at least two state," I finished.

"You lead exceedingly complicated lives," Maxine said.

We had almost gotten to the door. Hector informed me that the rest of the team had worked their way back. They were on the far side of the cabin watching from cover of the woods. (I love those guys) I told Hector that they shouldn't rely on the woods for cover from any non-human opponents.

"We know," he said, "we *know*."

There was a flurry of motion on second floor of the cabin. Small ampoules of a sickly greenish liquid flew out of the windows. We all scrambled to avoid getting hit.

We weren't the targets though. The ground just around us was. Watching the ampoules hit and break apart was a dizzying, disorienting adventure.

Where each little bottle hit there was an "explosion" of ground. I don't mean the ground blew up. I mean that it expanded. Where there had been two yards between us and the cabin there was now ten. Behind us the distance that separated us from the fallen authorities quadrupled. Hector and Mrs. V were now uncomfortably far away.

The door in front of us expanded in a similar manner. It flew open and Stephan, on that damn boar, came charging out. He was making a beeline, not for me, but for his mother.

I ran towards Mrs. Vanderhorn to intercept. I shouted orders at Hector and Maxine.

"Subdue the Boar! Secure the house!" That may have been wildly optimistic given our situation but I was still feeling a little of the juice of Mrs. V's anger.

Speaking of which. I needn't have worried as much as I did. As Stephan approached his mother, she yelled to him.

"Stephan Michael Vanderhorn! You get off that disgusting pig right now!" Stephan pulled up the boar just short of his mother. He seemed uncertain.

"Mom! Quick jump up!"

"Stephan. Michael. Vanderhorn!" she repeated, "You come down off that filthy beast and talk to your mother."

He looked about. He saw me running towards him and his mother. The steely glint returned to his eyes.

He lifted the sword, leveling it at me. He seemed about to charge.

I had few options here. I could try to dodge his attack. I could counter it with some sort of offensive effect. I know a few kinetic detonations that would have been useful.

I admit it. I had a real temptation to go all action hero. (I could have. I'd have to cheat, of course, using magic to make up for a lack of martial prowess. But I *could have*) Sadly for my machismo, I have too much brain. I could see that making any sort of threatening move right then would only prolong the situation. So much for my adolescent hero fantasies, eh?

I threw my hands up in a "Whoa there" gesture and stopped running. I even started to back away. Stephan smiled and was about to spur his porcine mount in my direction. He had the look of a man cherishing victory. I think he was having a full on "movie star" rush of his own.

That rush was fairly short lived. Mrs. Vanderhorn had used the harness on the boar to pull herself up. She put her left hand firmly on Stephan's shield arm. Her right hand, she used to grab a hold of his ear and *twist*. I didn't think parents still used that kind of move.

"I said come down off this pig immediately, mister. And. I. Meant. It!" That kind of wrecked the mood for Stephan's personal movie moment. The effect was almost instantaneous. He didn't come down off the boar so much as it shrank beneath them.

For a second, he sounded like a normal fifteen-year-old boy. "But mom?" The last word was drawn out to make it at least two syllables. The horse-sized boar had become a more normal size. Which still means that it was a fair sized beast. Ask any pig farmer just how big a hog can get. This one could almost look in me in the eye. Still, that's better than towering over me.

While Stephan looked at his mom, trying to understand, the pig glowered at me. When Stephan obediently dismounted, the boar took the opportunity to charge me. I was far enough away that I could dodge out of its first pass. I hoped to roll to my feat and face it again. I wanted to be able to do something should it charge me again. Worse yet, it could charge Hector or Maxine, who were somewhere behind me.

The good news is that the pig did not go after either of them. The bad news is that this pig was not bound by any earthly physics. A normal boar that size would have had to take more time to change direction.

I hadn't even stood up fully before it hit me from behind. It gored into me with its tusks. The tusks pierced my flesh easily enough but they were stopped by the extra density of my bones (once again, I was grateful for that happy mistake)

Still, all this was quite painful. With the tusks still in me, I couldn't begin to heal myself. The boar was actually carrying me away. I craned my head. I could see Stephan and his mom arguing. I couldn't hear very clearly what they were saying but in my Sight, there was a light that seemed to be passing back and forth between them. I didn't need to hear to know that they were reconnecting. Given what everyone in the family has told me about the past, this may be the first honest conversation they've had.

"HEY, PIGGY LOOK," I shouted and pointed at the mother and child reunion.

"Don't try to trick me, human, besides I prefer to be called Oliver."

Chapter Twenty-One

I DIDN'T HAVE TIME TO argue with the pig. He threw me off his tusks. I landed at the edge of the newly "created" terrain. The terrain-in-a-bottle was one of Arnold effects. I had to admire his ingenuity. Or I would have, if I wasn't distracted by the buzzing of tiny wings.

The miniature squad from that first night in Oregon rose out of the bush next to me. They were armed with a spell. The network of energy lines traced back and forth between them, a glittering web of light visible to ordinary sight. There was a familiar feel to that net. It was the same spell that had done so much harm to Sasha. You may recall that spell had been tailored made for me.

I had to put a stop to this onslaught fast. I've avoided mentioning everything I've packed for this little rescue trip. This was, in part, to limit tedious lists. I packed all sorts of gear into my duster's over-sized pockets. Most of it didn't prove useful. I had, for example, a yo-yo, an airliner bottle of Southern Comfort, and some silver Christmas tinsel. See what I mean about lists

I didn't want to give the full list out of shame. Some of the items were mean, perhaps even a tad vicious. Case in point, as the fairy fighters flew towards me, I reached into my pocket and pulled out a small, white paper sack, the kind that normally holds candy. Tonight it held a fistful of iron filings. Iron can be quite harmful to the Fair Folk. For some, it is an irritant. For others, barest touch will burn like a white hot fire. All in all, iron is great deterrent to a fairy, if you don't mind it's undying enmity.

I scattered the iron filings into the fairy flight path. The result was predictable. Most of the fairies scrambled out of the way. Only one failed. One was all I needed. It was enough to disrupt the spell the squad carried.

Even though it was to save my life (or more accurately my mind), I felt bad for the one who took the brunt of the filings attack.

He was dressed like an 18th century Prussian mercenary. He fell, looking chewed up by 21st century ordinance. There were flashes of light and crackling sparks where the iron burned into him and then through him. He lay on the ground smoldering like charcoal.

There is no stench that compares with burned flitling. If you mix the smell of rotting roses with burning plastic fumes, that'd be a start. Now while taking a really good whiff, drive a screwdriver up into your sinuses. That may give you an idea.

"You bastard." This was from Oliver the Boar. He had run off to attend some other part of the fracas. When he noticed the screams and the smell he charged me. He didn't even take time to grow back to gargantuan size.

This time I was prepared. I "dug" deeply into the earth to draw my energy. I used it to fortify my physical body and give a boost to my strength.

This time, rooted as I was, when Oliver hit me, it was to my advantage. I grabbed Oliver by the tusks and pivoted around. Oliver launched into the air. His corpulent pigginess smacked another two or three flitlings out of the air.

The rest of the flitlings fired upon me with their miniature weapons. Just because an arrow or an M-16 round is tiny that doesn't make it harmless. True, those miniature assaults do need to use a healthy dose of magic to make up for their size but magic is what fairies do best. I wouldn't underestimate the damage they could do.

Like other so called Disreputable Urban Magi, my duster does more than keep the rain off. Mine stops most hostile enchantments. Against a normal projectile it wouldn't help much. Against the first volley of magic enhanced micro-ammo, it was sound. Tiny little bullets and arrows and a musket ball, all poofed out of existence as they collided with my jacket.

Then one of the flitlings did something unexpected. She grew in size. Other than size and gender, she looked like a traditional medieval knight. She shot up from six inches to almost four feet high. Her arrows were now about as long as an old school lawn dart. There's a reason lawn darts are outlawed most places. They can do significant, sometimes fatal injury.

Her first arrow pierced my duster and rammed into my left shoulder. My arm went numb down to the elbow.

She moved to notch another arrow. I didn't worry about that. The miniature Vietnam era U.S Marine had followed her lead and was now aiming a small but serviceable assault rifle at me.

These are the times it's good to have friends. Hector and Maxine had caught up to me. Hector barreled rather ungracefully into the marine. At three foot ten, the enlarged flitling couldn't put up the kind of resistance a real marine would have.

Maxine made a wave and chanted something that sounded Gaelic. The reaction of the "lady knight" was even more extreme than the sleepiness that had overcome the police officers. She turned, gave a sword salute then bowed to Maxine. She began to shoot at her comrades that still fluttered in the air.

Oliver righted himself and returned to his former, gigantic size. He tried to attack us but Maxine's new friend kept putting herself in the way.

Hector and the marine flitling were doing their part to bring the action movie quotient of the evening back up, though to be honest neither matched the action star looks. Hector's no Antonio Banderas. At least not with those glasses and buck teeth. From a distance, the overgrown flitling looked like a child in a Halloween costume.

Hector was able to hold the "marine" for the moment. They seemed fairly evenly matched. Hector had the advantages being part of the Guys gave him. The overgrown flitling, though hampered by his size, was not to be taken lightly. His hand-to-hand prowess would have done honor to the Corps.[30]

I don't know who would have eventually won that fight. Thankfully, we spared further violence. Stephan came running over, followed closely by his mother. He called out to the flitlings and the boar to stand down. As they did, so did we.

There was a blissfully awkward moment where, in the absence of violence, we were all at a loss for what to do next.

---

[30] Note: It should not be inferred, construed, or concluded that the United States Marine Corps has any association with Fairies. Even if they do, they're not supposed to talk about it.

Chapter Twenty-Two

THAT MOMENT PASSED QUICKLY enough.

I broke the silence. "Are you ready to talk to us now, Stephan?"

"Yes." he said.

"Then we need to, before all these law enforcement types wake up."

This statement caused him a moment of uncertainty. He looked to his mother who gave him a reassuring nod.

"Oliver," he said, "go and bring out Pandora and my father. Tell Ms. Tamblor's mount to head home."

The great boar trotted over to the cabin and went inside. It was an eye wrenching experience, seeing something that big go through a door that small. Magical beasties, got to love them.

There were gunshots from the cabin. The massive rabbit that Mariana had ridden broke down a front window and part of the wall surrounding it. It hopped out into the artificial no-man lands then up into the air. Suddenly, it just wasn't there anymore.

Even as fast as the rabbit moved, we had time to see that it wasn't carrying any one. Oliver came right behind the rabbit. He was bleeding. He was running even faster than he had before.

"Quick! Master Stephan! The Koenig is here," Oliver said.

And Koenig walked out of the cabin through the hole in the wall. She held Pandora in front of her, one arm around her throat and a handgun to Pandora's temple.

"Dismiss your servants," she told Stephan. He did so without hesitation.

Stephan turned his eyes to me. There was an accusation in them. "You brought her here," he whispered.

Behind her was Merton, talk about a bad penny. He brought out Mr. Vanderhorn and Arnold. He was covering them with a fearsome looking handgun of his own.

They herded us all fairly close together.

"Now, we're going somewhere I feel safe," Koenig said. Then she threw an ampule down on the ground. There was swirl of bluish light and a falling sensation.

We were in a large cinder block room. At the top of each of the walls was a small boarded-up area, presumably a window. This made me think we were surely in a basement

The room was well lit with overhead lights. There were various electronic devices around the room, cameras, microphones, computer equipment. At one end of the room were the stairs up. On the other end of the room, the business side of the cameras, were two studio sets.

One was a reproduction a young person's bedroom. A small single bed and a few posters on the fake wall behind it. It was generic enough to be either boy's or a girl's room but it definitely had the aura of youth.

We were standing in front the other one. It consisted of little more than a black board with a teacher's desk and few student desks in front that. There was something on the teacher's desk that puzzled me. There was a tray with a few glasses on it. The tray bore a design. It was the one that Shelia had carried, just like the one on the tablets Maxine had. This tray was about twice the size of Shelia's.

I still had my Sight running. I could now see the mystical impact of the tray. In an instant I understood. This was the design that that transformed surface tension to sexual tension that Arnold had mentioned. Making love potions from ordinary water must be a real boost when making porn movies with reluctant actors. One sip and Koenig has them feeling this is something they wanted. A whole glass and who knows what she could manipulate her victims into.

My anger at Koenig grew even fiercer. I hadn't thought that possible. That was before I knew she had a drug that could make her victims think everything was their idea.

Of course some of that anger was for personal reasons. I had thought Shelia used that masking effect so I wouldn't recoil from her undead nature. Shelia hadn't been hiding her undead nature from me, she was hiding the transformation tray. She showed me the ordinary water before it was transformed then set it on the tray once I stopped "looking." I was pissed because I fell for it. It was an anger fueled by shame and the fear that Shelia's machinations may not have been necessary.

I was also angry because of how they had manipulated Maxine. I bet those little tablets weren't nearly as powerful individually but if she had been taking them on a regular enough basis, it would turn a minor flirtation into something more serious, more distracting.

The idea that Koenig tried to use what I felt for Maxine against me got my ire really going. Unfortunately, thinking our connection might be fraudulent was like a blow to my solar plexus.

I took a deep breath. I tried not to be too eager to vent my anger on Koenig and Merton.

With all that was running through my mind, I almost failed to notice a painting hanging on one side of the blackboard. It was the one from my apartment of an eighteenth century seafarer. On one edge of the frame was a warding symbol. I wanted to ask how it ended up here. I had more pressing issues. I wasn't the only one who felt punched in the gut.

Stephan looked about to weep.

"Oh God, the studio," he said in a hoarse whisper. He sat down hard on the floor next to his mother and began to rock back and forth. His eyes had a far away look in them. He mouthed something I couldn't make out. Whatever it was, he repeated it over and over.

"It looks like the family was reunited after all, " Koenig said. "I doubt that will be much comfort. This is the most secure place I have. Since you've wrecked my business, it doesn't look like I'll be able to exploit Stephan's ability to attract either kind of fairy anymore, I might as well let Merton kill you. But I'm so loathe to come out of this without any profit.

"That's not going to be an option." I said through clenched teeth

"The profit? I know," She sighed. She looked wistful. "all good things . . ., I suppose. Numis said that if his his parents got him to it'd be over. My own fault I suppose. I let him "rescue" his father after all. Once he started talking to the boy. It was all down hill from there. Daddy started loosening my grip."

"Then mom finished it off," I said.

"And now Merton is going to finish off the lot of you. Who says there's no balance to life."

"No, Merton's not. I've done my best to restrain my young associates. But I doubt that I will be able to now."

"What the hell's that supposed to mean." That was Merton. I glanced over at Hector for a fraction of a second before I could stop myself. Merton noticed this easily enough. His gun was still pointed at me but he looked over at Hector."

"Oh really? He's not the fast one," Merton said.

He laughed for about six tenths of a second. When that time was up three important things had happened. Hector had disarmed Merton. We had been nearly deafened by the gunshot that Merton fired in the process and there was a bullet lodged in my left lung. I would have preferred the through and through, especially since any healing I did now was just going to scab around the bullet and make real healing harder.

Still, Hector had the gun and Merton did not. Yay, team. The victory was short lived. Hector had deprived him of one gun. Merton simply drew another from beneath his jacket.

"Great. Now it's a stand off," He said. "You think you can move fast enough to stop my next shot."

Koenig was utterly aggravated now. The cool demeanor she had been affecting was gone.

"God damn it! Numis never said you would be this much trouble. Merton just get us out of here," she looked at him expectantly. Merton, for his part, just kept eye contact with Hector. Merton's own weapon never wavered. It had moved from covering me to pointing directly back at Hector.

Everyone had the good sense to move back and be quiet. Everyone that is except Stephan and myself. Stephan was still just sitting on the floor. I was propping myself up with one arm on a student desk. My other other hand over the entry wound in my side. I coughed a little and some blood leaked out of my mouth. I'm glad my abilities are not entirely incantation dependent. I don't think abraca-gurgle would have much mystical heft.

I spat out a bit of blood, hoping I could speak clearly enough. "Wendi, it's over. You're done," I spat a little more blood for emphasis.

She scowled. Her face contorted with distaste.

"Don't call me Wendi! She's gone!" She became aware of her lack of composure. She calmed herself and began again, "Besides, you're bluffing. You have a bullet wound. Most of your accomplices are elsewhere. You have one man with a gun. You may have us out numbered. But this is my domain and I have everything I need."

She paused as if waiting for me to supply her the straight line. What the hell, I'll play. Time worked in my favor I thought. "What's that?" I asked

"I know how to get out of here. You see the stairs don't lead anywhere. The house that used to stand above us was torn down. It was quite the trick preserving the basement. The area is paved over. If it weren't for Arnold's exits-in-a-bottle. We could have never done it."

I didn't need to look to see the shame on Arnold's face. He wouldn't be the first person who facilitated evil because they were unwilling to ask the right questions.

Wendi walked over to stand next to Merton. "I hope you enjoy your starvation. Merton, now!" she commanded.

Still covering Hector, Merton reached into a pocket of his jacket and pulled a bottle of glowing blue liquid. He raised his hand to smash it on the floor next Koenig and himself.

If I was going to move fast enough to do something, I needed to dump my body. I didn't relish the idea. Injured as I was, leaving my body could be all the signal it needed to go into final shut down. The bottle left Merton's hand. I left my body.

"What good does that do?" you ask.

The liquid was magically active. It has a presence on the astral plane. At the speeds my spirit body can move, I can make a real attempt to catch it before it hits the ground.

The world dropped into slow motion as I exited my body. Merton had quite a powerful arm. by the time I could reach the bottle of liquid, I wasn't sure I could keep from breaking the bottle's seal. I would only be grabbing the liquid. My hand would still be intangible to the bottle and pass right through. Stopping the liquid and not the bottle could make the liquid push out the stopper. Either way we have magical liquid splashed around and *voila* they're gone.

Instead I hit the liquid so that it pushed the bottle towards Pandora and her family. As a natural reaction to the situation they had huddled around Stephan. I hoped at least to get them out of here.

The bottle spun as it tumbled through the air towards them. The stopper did indeed come undone. It splashed a fair sized area around the Vanderhorn family. The splash area was big enough to take Arnold and Maxine with them.

Hector was too quick for his own good. He had also dived for the bottle. Even with help from the other Guys, he was too slow. After all, he has to obey the laws of motion and gravity, etc, etc.

What he managed to do is tackle Merton. Merton got off a wild shot. Fortunately, no one was hit this time. I scrambled back to my body before something in my hypothalamus decided it was "Game Over." Hector and Merton replayed a previous scene. That is, Merton goes down swiftly to the onslaught of the Guys.

Must be embarrassing to a professional like himself. Hector had Merton in a wrestling hold. One arm pinned behind him, the other outstretched while Hector had him in a half-nelson hold.

Unfortunately for all the advantages the Guys had, Merton was still a professional and outweighed Hector by about half. Merton was able to get his legs back under himself and flipped about. There was a distinct cracking as Merton allowed his arm to take the force of the change. (Better than the neck, I suppose)

Merton spun free of Hector and reached into his jacket pocket again. Worried that it might be another weapon Hector moved with that blinding speed that I was growing to depend on. Hector grabbed Merton's hand with enough force to crush the bottle within it. Merton cried out as glass shards ground into his hand. That glowing blue liquid splashed out striking both Hector and Merton.

Then they were both gone.

Chapter Twenty-Three

"**S**O, IT'S JUST US now, I recommend you surrender. I've got this whole thing under control," I said to Koenig. I'm sure it would have sounded more convincing if I could stand upright.

"I guess I"ll have to do this myself," she said. It was mumbled to herself rather than to me. She walked towards me. It's funny what you'll notice in such circumstances. Pandora had described Koenig as a robust woman. She certainly impressed me as tall when I had met her previously. Now I noticed how imposing she was. Before she had been wearing women's business suits. Now she was dressed in what I can only call designer army surplus.

Her clothing followed a pragmatic military aesthetic. There was no way, however, that it could be mistaken for anything other than custom-made high-end clothing. Her clothes certainly flattered her figure even though they weren't constructed to enhance its visual appeal. Her outfit should marketed to the professionally violent as "comfortable clothes for uncomfortable business."

As she reached me, she knelt down. I had slid down behind the teacher's desk by this time. She pulled a combat knife from her belt.

"It looks like your having trouble with this wound. I was told you could heal up anything we threw at you. I guess that was an exaggeration. I knew Numis overestimated you."

She punctuated her point by driving the knife into my bullet wound. The bullet's entry wound was on the left side of my body. There was no exit wound. There should have been but my extra dense skeleton had enough stopping power to prevent an exit just not an entrance. I'm glad Merton wasn't using the hand cannon I saw earlier. I was doubly glad he hadn't shot me in the head.

The bullet had ricochet inside my chest, puncturing my left lung and clipping my heart. If not for my healing abilities, I would have been dead already. I was little better off than when I was injured by the asphalt mound. I had enough energy to stay even but not enough to force the bullet back out.

Koenig drove that knife into the entry wound, past my shattered ribs, into the softer tissues of my lung. I grabbed her hand at the wrist.

"Oh, you can't save yourself now. Your struggling is only opening the wound larger" I ignored her. That was easy. I was too busy working past the pain.

It takes two things to work the "wonders" that are my stock in trade; Faith and Will. I've never had any one thing test them both as much as trying to guide Koenig's hand so she would dig out the bullet. I managed to divert her knife to my ends. It was enough to carve out an exit between my rib cage and spine. her combat knife in so far that her fingers were as well.

The bullet plopped out onto the floor. I pushed Koenig's knife hand out of my chest. The wounds began closing from the inside out. I let my eyes glaze over and my head slump to the floor. There was nearly a gallon of my blood on the floor. Which is quite a trick, I know. Koenig dipped her finger in some of it and started drawing a circle on the floor next to me. I know a summoning circle when I see one. She made a quick and dirty job of it, but it would work.

As soon as she was done, she whispered one word. No chant or long intonation, just the single word, a name, "Numis."

The room grew cold. The light grew brighter but more brittle. Numis had entered the room.

"So, you call on me again to fix your mess. I am not inclined."

"But there he lies destroyed."

"No, even if he dies. He has not been destroyed. I said use his weakness against him. But you did nothing of the sort."

My blood made a wet, splurping noise as Koenig stomped her foot like a petulant child. "I sent his ex-wife after him."

"Late wife. A mistake! He stilled loved her."

"Exactly, he would be weak against her."

"Was he? How has it gone for you since you brought her on board," Numis gave a dismissive sniff.

"Besides, for his kind, love is power not weakness."

Koenig was not a shouter. She could make a whisper more threatening that a loaded weapon in your face. She used that tone on Numis next, "He.

Bedded. That. Monster. You said getting him laid could undo him. Who better than that abomination to make sure?"

"Anyone. If you had done it right, his shame would have undone him. You should have tricked him and the girl into drinking the transmuted water."

I realized that Numis was right. If the water did as promised and something happened between me and Pandora, it would have cut the legs right out from under me mystically speaking. The shame would have crippled my will. I don't know if I ever would have recovered.

Koenig still wasn't getting it, "What I managed was good enough. He was weakened. Look at him. He can not survive this."

The room suddenly grew much colder. There was chill in Numis voice that underscored his lack of flesh and blood.

"Slattern, even as you prattle, he is healing his wounds." There was a rustling as Koenig turned back to me. Through unfocused eyes, I saw her about to stab me again. I was in no condition to put of a real fight. On the other hand another stab wound would be more strain than I could handle.

Her thrust was lazy. She wasn't expecting resistance. It was fairly easy to grab her wrist. I twisted her wrist. Her combat knife clattered to to the floor, out of reach. She struggled against my grip. She punched me with her free hand. I was feeling generous so I tried to block it. Unfortunately, I was too slow.

Let me say again that Wendi as Koenig was robust. Lest you think I am being diplomatic for fat, fat, she was not. She was tall and well muscled. She was the kind of woman who could model for a statue of a Greek goddess. (Sure maybe not Aphrodite, but maybe Hera or Dianna.)

She also knew what she was doing in a fist fight. I was nowhere close to stopping her blow. I turned my head so that she wouldn't hit me squarely in the center of my face. Her free hand collided with the side of my face with a force that I would not have credited from a human being. But then she was free of many of the inhibitions that would have tempered the attack.

I heard bones cracking under the force of the the punch. Then a cry of rage and frustration.

I said I was being generous by trying to block. Those bones cracking where not on my side of the equation.

Still, it wasn't a painless event for me either. This new influx of pain was just what the doctor ordered to jump start an adrenal rush. My mind cleared, my senses sharpened, I was able to tell why this particular basement had been chosen. Earthly energies bubbled up here like a small spring. (It made the teleport bottles easier to use.) I was able to draw some in to bolster my own strength.

I reached out and managed to grab Koenig by the hair. I stood up, trying to force Koenig to the ground. She pivoted at the hips and tried to knee my groin. I pivoted as well, taking the kick on the outside of my thigh.

I had the superior center of gravity. She went down on her back. I knelt beside her so I could grip her arms.

Our eyes met. Her face was flushed with anger. Her disarrayed hair had a certain care-free look. Her chest heaved with deep breaths. Her shirt was plastered to her chest. This displayed her breasts more than adequately. The black fabric hid that blood had created the effect rather than water or sweat.

The visage of her rage so parodied impassioned intimacy that I found my anatomy reacting in ways that were not only inappropriate but also life-threating.

She leaned up bringing her face close to mine. I could feel the heat of her breath on my cheek. Her breath was sweet and spicy. Although my autonomic nervous system had kicked into overdrive, the look in her eyes told she would rather savage my face with her teeth than to . . .

"Go for the kiss," Numis whispered to her. "Even without the water, he's vulnerable. Koenig craned her head around to look for Numis. Instead of tearing into me or planting some forced kiss, she displayed her long, smooth neck. Its feminine lines drawing my eyes both upward to her face (which wasn't without a certain charm) and downward to her increasingly enticing body.

For an instant, she forgot to fight against me. Her throat was open to me like the willing victim in a vampire movie, her wrists held in my hands. She was neither truly fighting nor finally yielding. It created an image of both strength and surrender. I had thought my physiological reaction was inappropriate before. Now, I was almost giddy with a hormone surge like I hadn't had since high school.

"This is the time to take advantage of his weakness," Numis said. Koenig turned to look directly into my eyes. I felt like I was falling.

"Dear God, help me." I whispered. That prayer was, in a way, an intellectual exercise. In that moment, I knew what I wanted and I knew that what I wanted was wrong.

You may have noticed that even if I didn't act on it much, amorous intent isn't ever far from my mind.

Numis was right. It's my big weakness. The weakness he sought to exploit.

I understood why he wanted to throw Maxine's coven at us. He knew that they couldn't overcome us. He could have sent other warriors for that. He figured one (or more) of the coven's women could distract me for a while. The frightening part was right at that moment, I didn't care.

Here in the end, he had me by the balls and not quite so metaphorically speaking. My will, strong as it was, has this flaw you see, a chink in my armor. I was caught by the defect in my character. My weakness for women had come a-calling and found me home and waiting.

I bent my head forward to kiss Koenig on the neck, just below the jawline. Then I gave her a tiny nibble there as well. The moment became electric. Gretchen let out a small gasp. She turned her head to face me and kissed my mouth hard and demanding. I returned that kiss with vigor. And then it happened

Religious folks often say, "God works in mysterious ways." That, "our weakness is God's strength." That, "All things work together for good for those that love the Lord."

I've said it before. I'll say it again, "God is one right tricky bastard."

Numis was counting on my weakness for the touch of a woman. He had forgotten about Koenig's weaknesses.

Gretchen, it seems, suffered from a variation of Groucho Marx's axiom of club membership. He wouldn't join a club that would have him as a member. Koenig couldn't stand a person who would want her as lover. People better versed in psychology than I can parse out why.

All I know was that in the moment that I had lost. In the middle of that great, golden, electric kiss, she shoved me aside. She shoved hard enough that I struck the back of my head against the teacher's desk behind me. The sudden flash of pain swept the hormone rush from my system.

Koenig tried to stand. She did a fairly impressive kip up to her feet. It would have been more impressive had she not fallen again by slipping in my blood.

I now had my own feet back under me, both physically and figuratively. Quite honestly, I was tired, so very tired. I was tired of all the crap that's gone on since Koenig entered my life. That weariness lay on me like a coating of wet cement. I just wanted to give up but I didn't have the energy to surrender. I had nothing left but my despair. That and one tiny shred of determination not to let the darkness win.

My mentor used to say, "everything is a gift, if used in the right way." And that was my salvation. All I needed to do was share.

I looked at my ennui and exhaustion in my mind's eye. It was a vast, heavy net weighting me down. In my imagination, I pealed it around me. I sent will and energy into the net, giving it astral form. I flung it out before me.

Koenig had managed to get to her feet and was charging me again. She intended to tear off my head with her bare hands. Instead "the net" slapped her full in the face. I may have been the only one to see it, but anyone could see the effect.

Koenig just stopped. She looked at me, puzzled, as if she suddenly couldn't comprehend why she was bothering to fight me. She sat down. She grew very still and looked only at the floor.

She was the picture of defeat. Tears leaked from her eyes. They trickled down her face. There were no sobs or attempts to brush them away. She just sat there.

In a small, timorous voice she said, "Please, don't hide me inside her. I want to live."

Chapter Twenty-Four

I DIDN'T HAVE TIME TO respond. Numis coalesced out of the ether. The body he wore left no doubt about his rage. It was roughly humanoid. It glittered and shifted. To say it looked like a human shaped pile of coins would be to "Disneyfy" it.

What he looked like was an obscenely muscled semi-human beast with armor-like scales. Now replace the scales with coins and bits of gems then add the stench of rotted meat and you'll begin get the idea. The actual smell was "Calculated Indifference to Suffering" but rotted meat is fairly close.[31]

Numis growled at me and waved a claw at Koenig. There was blue, swirling light again and she was gone.

"Useless twat. The prospect of fifty years confinement and she goes all to pieces." That was all he said before he turned back toward me and slashed at me with a claw.

I jumped back but the desk was behind me. It prevented me from getting very far. I landed on top of it with my legs stretched out before me. Not what I had planned but it was good enough. Numis missed.

Numis lunged at me again. I put my feet into his chest and pushed. I sprang backwards over the desk to the floor.

Don't get me wrong, This was not a graceful, acrobatic maneuverer. The only grace was that it worked.

Numis's claws tore into the desk. Instead of pulling them free he used his prodigious strength to lift the desk and throw it behind him. That was a mistake.

---

[31]   for more info see CC# 539 *Physical manifestations of Abstract Ideas. Or How to spot* **Trouble** *by its' scent.*

Numis wasn't used to fighting in a meat body. He should have just hit me with desk. Maybe my healing could have taken it, maybe not. His throw bought me time, Time enough to draw a line. Don't forget, there was a lot of spilled blood here. Most of it, if not all, was mine. I used my shoe to draw a semicircle in the blood that reached around behind me on both sides to the wall. I sent a massive amount of hope and will into forming a barrier. There was no time for little embellishments like angelic names in ancient scripts to give it a nice mystic feel. It was only big enough for me to crouch in it. It also happened to contain the portrait of the young mariner.

It wasn't elegant only effective. Numis smashed his clawed fists into the ward. Blue-white sparks jumped where Numis ran his claws against it. Numis threw himself at the ward only to be knocked back. A shower of sparks lit the room. Twice more he charged but my ward held. Which was a bit of a mixed blessing. It kept Numis out but trapped me.

Numis considered his options for moment. He resumed a more human form, the one I had seen back in the *Wood between Worlds.* Numis pulled a chair from nowhere, sat down and pulled a cigarette from that same non-place. It was already lit when Numis began puffing on it.

"Look," he said, "we have an obvious stalemate here. At least in my directly getting to you. But don't forget, I win by default." Numis exhaled smoke and pointed with the cigarette to punctuate the point.

I didn't bother answering. It was time for the lets-make-a-deal portion of our program.

"If I just leave. You'll eventually starve down here. Even if you can dig your way out, I'll have gone, picked up Koenig, and shaken some sense into her. We'll just start over somewhere else."

"So, I might as well give up?" My tone was enough to convey that I was not convinced.

"Actually, I'm offering you an new position. It's simple, you're obviously much brighter and more powerful than my former agent. With you, I wouldn't need someone like Stephan to expand my holdings into the fay realm. Just think what I could offer."

"Not interested."

"Oh, I know that money itself doesn't appeal to you. You don't have that miserly instinct. But think of what that money could buy. You could be a man of leisure. A man of *pleasure.*" as he spoke he drew pictures in the smoke. They were almost pictures anyway. Somehow he made the smoke convey the image of a lush estate populated with beautiful women.

"So is that the Hugh Hefner package?" I asked.

"You could make Hef look like a monk."

I have to admit that was more enticing. But the air had been poisoned, so to speak. As tempting as I might find the offer, I couldn't accept it from Numis. Still, I was going to have to reflect on that particular weakness.

Oh well, more personal growth for me, provided I survived my refusal. "Sorry, I think I'll pass on a purchasing my harem from you."

"So, tell me what then can I do for you?"

"Two questions. I am still puzzled why you chose to look like Arnold Scott when you and Koenig came to my apartment."

Numis chuckled. It was not a happy sound.

"He'd be a convenient patsy if we needed one for your murder," Numis smiled as he said it.

Again cheer had nothing to do with it.

"And the second?"

"Why, Maxine?"

I could see the wheels spinning in Numis's mind. He wouldn't outright lie to me but he'd want to make it hurt as much as possible. "I set up all those little coven tramps, there's nothing particularly special about her." It bothered me to hear Maxine dismissed like that. But the implicit exoneration was wonderful, another failure by Numis to understand human psychology beyond greed, his weakness.

"Well, that's all I wanted to know. So, what you like to be bound into?" I asked Numis, my smile broadening. I hope it conveyed more cheer than I currently felt.

"Bound into? Oh, we're Solomon now, are we? Binding foul spirits into glass globes? Or would you prefer something more modern? Perhaps you would prefer a whiskey bottle? That's more your style, isn't it? Like the one on your desk," he said.

"A bottle can come in many forms. How about the desk or one of these cameras? Perhaps one of the light bulbs? Give the lamp a modern twist, eh?"

Numis started his cheerless laugh again. "You know that if you come out of there to try binding me, I'll just gut you."

"Really, then why'd you wait? No, The most you would have done earlier is skewered a leg or an arm, hoping to have pain cloud my judgment . . . that'd make your deal more appealing wouldn't it?"

Numis threw his hands up in the air.

"Fine, you caught me. I'm all about the deals. Looks like you 'win.' I'll just go and leave you all alone." Numis started to fade into a mist. "This really is your last chance."

"But I'm not alone," I said.

Numis stopped in mid fade, re-coalescing. It strode up to the edge of the ward and glowered at me.

"Not alone? All your friends are gone, stripped from you a few at a time. And here you stand cowering behind your flimsy ward and you have the audacity to tell me you aren't alone." It paused, thought for a moment.

"Oh, you mean your 'faith.'" Numis said the word like you or I might say "mildew", or "filth."

My smile began to have more of the cheer I was looking for. "Now, I've got you nervous."

"Hardly, I'm not one of the fallen angels who still cringe at the Maker's name. I'm one this world's spirits. What's more, in this place, I'm invited." Numis waved a hand indicating the studio. "Hell, they made a home for me here. A hearth, a shrine. You can't cast me out of *this* place with what's left of your faith."

I shrugged, "Maybe not, but I don't have to. Part of faith is knowing that the answers to our prayers are sometimes already built into the problem."

Numis smashed at the ward. It sparked again but held.

"How long did it take you to win free from my ghostly roommate?" I indicated the portrait over my shoulder, "Four days? A week?"

Numis shrieked then flung himself hard at the ward. No sparks this time. I could feel the strain inside my little safety prison. "I rent him in to tiny pieces, utter destruction. you won't see him again." I was surprised. Numis just outright lied to me.

"Destroy a human soul? You? That's a power reserved by One for One. No, you got free then had one of your minions seal up his earthly link and bring it to your little shrine here. Too bad it's such a sloppy seal."

"Wishful thinking. I swear if you don't join me. I'll rip your ward asunder and then eat you alive, like I did your spooky little friend." Numis shifted back into his monstrous form.

I felt obligated to show one last mercy. "Choose an object to be bound into. Something you know that can break . . . someday."

Numis stalked toward me again. He was gathering strength. This time, he was going to come through the ward regardless of my will.

"Okay, I can see this dance is over. You know you can't win me over and I've given you as many chances for mercy as I can. This time it's for keeps."

Numis gave up all pretense of humanity and howled. It was a void and hollow sound, like the bells of a child's funeral.

Numis lunged. His claws slashed the air, carving it out before him. There was no ward to meet him this time. Numis sailed on through the air on a direct path to slash my throat with his long, jagged claws.

I, for my part, was dropping to my knees. On my way down, I lashed my elbow back and smashed the seal on the Young Mariner's portrait. (I said it was a sloppy seal. Done in wax, actual wax. Bet they thought that was clever.)

As I dropped to my knees, I curled up (well, down, really) and dove forward to try to get out of the way of the two spirits as best I could.

Two spirits? Yes. I knew Numis was lying when he said he had destroyed the ghost of the Young Mariner.

I knew that the same way that you know no one has stolen sun during the night.[32]

The Young Mariner was flying out of his imprisonment in the painting just as Numis reached where I would have been been standing.

The ghost grappled with Numis. They stayed physical only for an instant more. Then they shifted over to their more natural spirit selves. I dropped out of my body so I could better observe the fight.

It was fairly one sided. Numis had been going nonstop since it won free after their last bout. The Young Mariner had nothing but time to rest.

Numis slashed at it with one of those wicked claws. The Mariner barely even noticed. He just dug his fingers into the mass of coins and gems that represented Numis's body even on the spiritual planes.

Then he took that fistful of coins and shoved it into his mouth.

And that was how Numis fell. A Spirit of Greed, of insatiable consumption, consumed. Bit by bit by bit until he was gone.

The Young Mariner floated down to me. "So that which you have said? It is true? You can bind it?"

"Yes. If you will allow it, I can bind Numis inside you."

"For how long?"

"For as long as you exist."

---

[32] Actually, that may not be the best comparison but it'll work for now.

The Young Mariner laughed. "Three hundred years after my death, my life finally makes sense." He continued laughing. "Go ahead, boy. This is too rich.

I said the prayers and invocations. Numis was locked inside the Young Mariner now.

"How do you feel?" I asked him.

"Grand, Grand indeed." He smiled like all the lights on Broadway. "All its power, 'tis mine now, isn't it?"

I nodded. My mind worried that I may have made a mistake. But my heart didn't.

"And you thought I was fun before," his eyes lit up like Vegas neon. If anything would have given me misgivings, it would have been that. It didn't.

"I should tell you my name. Then you may understand my mirth. My Christian name is Ethan, which means ' firm, enduring, strong-like."

"Go on."

"The rest will make sense to you with that. Now, let's do this back on your side of things"

I slipped back into my flesh and he became corporeal. He did it with a lot more at ease than I expected. He stuck out his hand for me to shake, "Good Day, friend, my name is Ethan Solomon Bottle."

Our laughter lit the room like sunrise.

More accurately it lit the room like a backhoe tearing open the far corner of the studio. Ethan ghosted out with a quick, "Don't forget my portrait, lad."

There was shouting down the opened hole. It was The Guys having come to my rescue. With even one of them having been down there, it wasn't much of a challenge for them to find it again. Indeed, even as events unfolded down here, the rest of the team had been arranging our rescue. The fact that we started reappearing a few at a time only emboldened the effort.

Through the opening, the Guys made a living chain of themselves to reach me. Ramón, the biggest was at the top anchoring them. Next down was Ty. Even in the early morning light he was wearing his sunglasses. His suit was also amazingly unrumpled. Next was James smiling like a man with funniest secret in the world. I somehow just knew that this human chain was his idea. He was taking such pleasure in its efficacy. At the end holding out his hand to me was Hector. An odd choice for the end perhaps given how slight his build was compared to mine. Yet Hector had more than enough strength of spirit to do the job. Working together the Guys hauled my exhausted, extra-large posterior out of that hole.

I sat down on the ground and tried to get my breath. I looked up to see Maxine and Marguerite silhouetted against the morning sun. A lovely sight made lovelier by relief at their safety.

Maxine played nurse to my wounds that had not yet healed. Marguerite assisted by handing her items from Azgard's first aid kit. I could see Marguerite chuckling to herself over Maxine's unneeded fussing. Clearly, however, she didn't want to deprive Maxine of the moment.

Azgard was not far behind them. The side windows were shattered. The front wind shield was spiderwebbed with cracks from bullet holes. There were other holes and dents all along the driver's side of Azgard. There was someone sitting in the passenger seat but I was too busy looking at the damage to notice whom.

"He's seen better days," Ty said. "But there's another one you owe him. We were fairly sure we could find this place becasue Hector had been down there with you but when we found Azgard sitting here, we knew we had hit paydirt."

I didn't say anything. I was kind of choked up at the moment. I wasn't sure how I was going to get the repairs done that Azgard needed. I wondered if there was anyone out there who healed machines. I took a deep breath and turned my attention to the others that had come.

Not too far off, I could see the Vanderhorn clan gathered around their car watching us. They were waiting for some "all clear" sign. When I finally felt well enough, I waved them over.

"Thank you for saving me. I hope you can forgive me for not doing a better job for you."

"Don't worry." Charles said, "I'll just deduct it from your payment."

We laughed at that, not because it was funny but as a form of release. Laughter really is the best medicine.

"Where the hell did you get the backhoe?" I asked.

"Oh, *She* got it for us." Ty said. He gave me a sly look over the top of his sunglasses. He pointed to the woman who was sitting in the passenger seat of Azgard. I really looked at who was sitting there this time.

My heart nearly seized when I saw it was Shelia.

Chapter Twenty-Five

I HOBBLED OVER TO MY car and got behind the wheel. Every one else kept back from Azgard. The team was giving us our privacy, mostly. They were far enough away that Shelia and I could speak privately. They were also watching the car intently.

The Guys were on guard, ready to spring to my defense. Marguerite watched like a concerned mother. The Vanderhorns were wary but uncertain what to do.

Maxine was the hardest to read as she watched. She looked indifferent to the conversation. Yet, I caught a glance that penetrated that mask. She looked away again before I could tell much more.

I did my best to put thoughts of her aside for the moment.

"So, Shelia, I suppose I should thank you. I guess this makes up for drugging me that night," my tone was not so subtly mocking.

"You can't shame me with sarcasm," Shelia said, "I doubt you can shame me for that night at all."

"It certainly backfired on Koenig from what Numis told me."

"I did it for my purposes, not hers," Shelia said. It was the best way to thwart her desire to destroy you while still following her orders."

"I still don't understand why you kept helping me."

"I told you. I need you," Her tone was earnest. It frightened me.

"Well, not so long ago you needed to eat my heart. What changed?"

"It's what didn't change. Honestly, don't you know what I am?"

It was silent for a moment until I realized her question was genuine.

"No. I don't. Why don't you tell me?"

"I'm not sure I can. You won't believe me unless you work it out for yourself."

"Fine, I'll have a go."

"We already did."

I didn't laugh. Instead I just glared, "You have all the earmarkings of a typical ghoul. You are clearly undead. No breath, no heartbeat. Your body regenerates injuries and you have increased strength and reflexes. You hunger for human flesh. You also have a voice to memorize your prey. You have a slight aversion to sunlight but nothing like a vampires. So I'd say you were a ghoul except for the gibbering madness that infects them."

"Do you know why Ghouls go crazy?" she asked.

"There are theories."

"I'll tell you this much. A human personality is like a fire that lights the mind. As that fires ebbs and goes out, a kind of madness sets in. When the last embers die out, the final madness is irreversible. A human wouldn't survive the process. Because of their supernatural nature, ghouls do, but not as well as as vampires. They actually retain more of their original personality for some reason. "

"Okay," I said, "go on."

She sighed unnecessarily just to show her frustration. "Weren't you taught that humans always give life to what they love?"

"Not in so many words, but yes, I learned that."

"Well, how much more true is that of Magi?"

Something clicked in my head. "So, you *are* a ghoul?"

"Yes." She almost seemed to hold her breath in anticipation.

"But you're saved from madness because there's a bit of *her* left."

"Yes."

"Because I still have feelings for Shelia?"

"Not just feelings. Own up to it. You still love her."

"That's enough to sustain her?"

"A spark of her anyway. Puts me quite a quandary."

"I can imagine," I said derisively.

She scoffed at me, "No, you don't. That new girl's a bigger threat to me than any I've faced yet." She nodded indicating Maxine.

Anger blazed in my heart. Here was the thing that represented my own worst loss threatening something good even before it began. I steeled myself, readying my will for battle.

Shelia must have sensed it. She threw up her hands in a surrender. "That's my quandary. As long as you love what's left of her, her spark stays "alive" and I stay sane. Eliminating what's-her-name could be the last straw for you and poof your affection for your Shelia evaporates and so does my sanity. Let things progress and you may forget about your precious Shelia and then where would we be?"

I tried not to let it sway me. I gathered in more will to act.

"It's your dilemma too. Destroying me destroys the last spark of your Shelia."

That pulled me up short. I looked her deep in the eyes. I risked turning on my Sight. I got an olfactory blast. I fought back the urge to vomit from the stench that was "Shelia the Ghoul." Then, almost like a flower emerging from sewage, I caught a whiff, a gentle, familiar aroma. It was Shelia's scent, a combination of her favorite perfume and the way she smelled just after coming in from the sun. I felt my eyes water for a new reason. Remembered loss is an incredibly sharp blade.

"I think I should go now." She put a piece of paper in my hand and gently folded my fingers around it. With that, she left. The rest of the team, taking my cue, did nothing to stop her.

I looked at the paper in my hand. All that was there was an address and the date 7/14, our anniversary.

Chapter Twenty-Six

THE REST IS JUST wrap up. I now have a nice comfy office from which to to tell you all this. Ethan's portrait now hangs over my desk here, rather than at home. I had thought my new friendship with Ethan would stop the furniture shifting in my apartment. When it didn't, I moved the portrait to my office. I didn't really expect to use it much any way. I pretty much conceded that fight when I tripped over my office desk walking out of my bedroom one morning. So clearly, Ethan has only expanded his prank domain. The rest of the team has come through our ordeals much to the good thankfully.

Stacy (though she'll always be Pandora to me) and the rest of the Vanderhorns relocated to the 'burg.

They are trying to make it work as a family. It's hard no doubt, but having had a taste of the alternative, they keep plugging away at it.

Stephan is learning how to not exploit the "poor, little Fairies." Personally I think... well never mind what I think about the "poor, little Fairies."

The Elder Vanderhorns continue their work with their missing child/ runaway help website. If they are getting any unearthly help from Stephan's friends, they are keeping awfully mum about it.

Marguerite wouldn't go back to simple fortune telling. She persuaded Mr. Vanderhorn to keep our little investigation firm open. Her name is on the door and the P.I. License. The Guys operate under her license.

Hector runs the tech department. Okay, he is the tech department. Ty works well as Marguerite's second in command. He also tends to be the face of the organization. He's very good at meeting with clients or people who need to be interviewed for a case. Ramón still plays the part of the muscle when needed. But it's his almost indefatigable energy that makes him excellent at leg work. James works quietly in the background. I get the feeling that whenever there's a particularly clever plan, that plan first hatched in James' head. Pandora is part of the firm, much to Ramon's contentment.

I don't mention myself as a part of this since I am still legally dead. I have an office but no title and technically no pay. It'll take a while for that to get sorted out, if it ever does. It's better than facing terrorism charges, however. Don't think that I'm not grateful for that.

Koenig didn't face the civil authorities. She faced the Magi council. I misspoke when I had said that she'd be hidden inside her Jekyll. I was wrong for two reasons. First, in one respect, she was the Jekyll. That is, she was the original from whom "the other" was spawned. What made this uncommon was that her good aspect was removed rather than the more common "bad side purge."

The second was that I was kind of lying. They don't imprison one personality inside the other. They just reintegrate the Jekyll and the Hyde within the original body. I had assumed that would be Koenig's other form. I had simply overstated what I thought would happen.

Does the Concordance have the right to do this? To decide that someone who wanted to be two people should be one again? Maybe, maybe not, but they did it.

However, once back together, Wendi Scott decided it would be best if she spent some real time studying that fay realm. The Concordance was okay with this. Officially, they called it a banishment. The Concordance is so old fashioned. Arnold Scott went back to the Pacific Northwest. He faced no criminal charges. What D.A. was going to charge him with making dangerous magic potions. The Magi Concordance had Cominad give him a stern lecture. Then they offered him training if he wanted it. (They know talent when the see it) He said he'd think about it.

For now, he's trying to figure out how to replicate those fantastic formulas so that they can work without drawing on Numis's power. I hope he can figure it out. It'll make commuting back and forth to see Maxine that much easier. I mean our lives are mostly on different coasts right now and there is no reason to change that . . . yet. Especially since I don't want Shelia to get too worried.

That isn't to say I don't get to see her at all. Part of my new duties is to make sure that the cross-country path Koenig used is patrolled at both ends of the line. I split this chore with Cominad's branch. So, there are times I "have" to cut through to meet with them. Poor me.

Azgard even seems to enjoy these little trips. Vanderhorn paid for Azgard's repairs to a guy who didn't ask questions. I wonder where he found him.

Cominad herself often watches this path. The Concordance asked her to release Sister Winter before it became more of an interplane incident. If Cominad felt a little cheated of her vengeance, she was wise enough to let it go. Or so she says. I have noticed the fair folk step a little lighter around her neck of the woods since then.

In the long term, Sasha recovered almost fully, though he still seems a little haunted at times.

Merton did face criminal charges for his part in the prostitution ring. Prison is an ugly place for former police officers. It's even uglier for child pornographers. The less said the better, but I doubt many will miss him.

As for my own legal status. As I mentioned, I'm still officially dead. Yet, I'm gainfully employed for the first time since I learned the world wasn't what it seemed.

The local cops think I'm the victim of identity theft by some unknown terrorist(s), The Feds are trying to track down the truth. So the closer I stay to home, the better off I am. (other than a little, very quiet, bi-coastal dating)

I don't know where Shelia is. Furthermore, I don't want to know. The address folded up in my wallet doesn't mean anything.

Note:
Due to circumstances beyond our control
the correspondence courses mentioned in this
recounting cannot be made available at this time.
We apologize for the inconvenience